Text Book Of

MANAGERIAL ECONOMICS

For

BBA Semester - II

As Per New Syllabus

Mrs. Kiran Jotwani
M.A. (Economics), B.Ed.

NIRALI PRAKASHAN
ADVANCEMENT OF KNOWLEDGE

N3754

Managerial Economics **ISBN 978-93-5164-979-3**

First Edition : January 2016

© : Author

Published By :

NIRALI PRAKASHAN

Abhyudaya Pragati, 1312, Shivaji Nagar,
Off J.M. Road, PUNE – 411005
Tel - (020) 25512336/37/39, Fax - (020) 25511379
Email : niralipune@pragationline.com

☞ **DISTRIBUTION CENTRES**

PUNE

Nirali Prakashan : 119, Budhwar Peth, Jogeshwari Mandir Lane, Pune 411002, Maharashtra
Tel : (020) 2445 2044, 66022708, Fax : (020) 2445 1538
Email : bookorder@pragationline.com, niralilocal@pragationline.com

Nirali Prakashan : S. No. 28/27, Dhyari, Near Pari Company, Pune 411041
Tel : (020) 24690204 Fax : (020) 24690316
Email : dhyari@pragationline.com, bookorder@pragationline.com

MUMBAI

Nirali Prakashan : 385, S.V.P. Road, Rasdhara Co-op. Hsg. Society Ltd.,
Girgaum, Mumbai 400004, Maharashtra
Tel : (022) 2385 6339 / 2386 9976, Fax : (022) 2386 9976
Email : niralimumbai@pragationline.com

☞ **DISTRIBUTION BRANCHES**

JALGAON

Nirali Prakashan : 34, V. V. Golani Market, Navi Peth, Jalgaon 425001,
Maharashtra, Tel : (0257) 222 0395, Mob : 94234 91860

KOLHAPUR

Nirali Prakashan : New Mahadvar Road, Kedar Plaza, 1st Floor Opp. IDBI Bank
Kolhapur 416 012, Maharashtra. Mob : 9850046155

NAGPUR

Pratibha Book Distributors : Above Maratha Mandir, Shop No. 3, First Floor,
Rani Jhanshi Square, Sitabuldi, Nagpur 440012, Maharashtra
Tel : (0712) 254 7129

DELHI

Nirali Prakashan : 4593/21, Basement, Aggarwal Lane 15, Ansari Road, Daryaganj
Near Times of India Building, New Delhi 110002
Mob : 08505972553

BENGALURU

Pragati Book House : House No. 1, Sanjeevappa Lane, Avenue Road Cross,
Opp. Rice Church, Bengaluru – 560002.
Tel : (080) 64513344, 64513355,Mob : 9880582331, 9845021552
Email:bharatsavla@yahoo.com

CHENNAI

Pragati Books : 9/1, Montieth Road, Behind Taas Mahal, Egmore,
Chennai 600008 Tamil Nadu, Tel : (044) 6518 3535,
Mob : 94440 01782 / 98450 21552 / 98805 82331,
Email : bharatsavla@yahoo.com

niralipune@pragationline.com | www.pragationline.com

Also find us on f www.facebook.com/niralibooks

Preface ...

It is a matter of joy to present this book of Managerial Economics. It is an attempt to apply economic analysis in the formulation of business policies. The language, methods, and the various techniques of economic analysis have been presented in a simple and lucid manner. An effort has been made to enhance clarity through suitable tables, figures (diagrams) and towards the end an overview of case studies is presented.

I sincerely thank Shri. Dineshbhai Furia and Shri. Jignesh Furia, the publishers, for the confidence reposed in me and giving me this opportunity to reach out to the students of commerce and management studies.

I am grateful to the Dean, Faculty of Commerce, University of Pune Dr. S. Jadhavar, Dr. G. M. Dumbre, Chairman of Board of Studies (BBA) and the Chairman of the Board of Studies (Business Economics), Dr. S. R. Nikam and my colleagues for their valuable suggestions.

Nirali Prakashan along with its enthusiastic team comprising Mrs. Supriya Singh, Mr. Nirmal Kumar, Mr. Malik Shaikh, and Mrs. Anjali Muley, have made significant contribution towards guiding the book for publication.

While best efforts have been put in towards the writing of this book, suggestions and feedback from readers are most welcome at niralipune@pragationline.com.

Mrs. Kiran Jotwani

Syllabus ...

1. Introduction to Managerial Economics   **4 Lectures**
     1.1   Meaning, Nature and Scope of Managerial Economics
     1.2   Subject Matter of Managerial Economics
     1.3   Essentials of Microeconomics and Macroeconomics for Business Decision Making

2. Demand Forecasting   **6 Lectures**
     2.1   Usefulness of Demand Forecasting
     2.2   Methods of Demand Forecasting
         (A)   Expert Opinion
         (B)   Survey Techniques
         (C)   Trends in Economic Data
         (D)   Linear Trend Analysis
     2.3   Reliability of Demand Forecasting

3. Production Function and Cost Function   **12 Lectures**
     3.1   Law of Variable Proportion
     3.2   Laws of Return to Scale
     3.3   Isoquants (or) Equal Product Curves
     3.4   Short Run and Long Run Cost Concepts and Cost Curves
     3.5   'L' Shape Cost Curve

4. Pricing Policies   **8 Lectures**
     4.1   Cost-Plus Pricing (Hall and Hitch Approach)
     4.2   Pricing of Multiple Products
     4.3   Transfer Pricing
     4.4   Going Rate Pricing
     4.5   Peak Load Pricing

5. National Income Determination and Changes in It   **6 Lectures**
     5.1   The Determination of Equilibrium level of National Income
     5.2   Under Employment and Full Employment Of National Income
     5.3   Effects of Government Expenditure and Net Export on the Equilibrium
     5.4   Concept of Investment Multiplier, Process of Income Multiplication and its Limitations

6. Macroeconomic Problems and Macroeconomic Policies   **12 Lectures**

Macroeconomic Problems
     6.1   Problems of Inflation and Stagflation
     6.2   Problems of Growth: Benefits and Cost of Growth
     6.3   Balance Of Payment: Causes and Effects of Disequilibrium of Balance of Payment

Macroeconomic Policies: Monetary Policy and Fiscal Policy
     6.4   Goals of Macroeconomic Policy
     6.5   Tools of Monetary Policy
     6.6   Expansionary Monetary Policy to Cure Recession (or) Depression
     6.7   Tight Monetary Policy to Control Inflation
     6.8   Fiscal Policy to Cure Recession
     6.9   Fiscal Policy to Control Inflation

✱✱✱

Contents ...

***

Chapter 1 ...

Introduction to Managerial Economics

Contents ...

Learning Objectives ...

➢ To equip the students with sound knowledge of managerial economics.

➢ To provide an understanding of the scope and subject matter of managerial economics.

➢ To understand the essentials of micro and macroeconomics for business decision-making

1.1 Managerial Economics

1.1.1 Introduction

The success or failure of a business is dependent upon the decisions taken by managers. Increasing complexity in the business world has brought forth greater challenges for managers. Rapid changes in technology, greater focus on innovation in products as well as processes that command influence over marketing and sales techniques have contributed to the increasing complexity in the business environment. This complex environment is coupled with a global market where input and product prices fluctuate and remain volatile. These factors increase the difficulty in evaluating precisely and determining the outcome of a business decision. In such a situation there arises a pressing need for sound economic analysis prior to making decisions. Managerial economics is a discipline that is designed to facilitate a solid foundation of economic understanding for business managers and enable them to make informed and analysed managerial decisions, which are in keeping with the changing and complex business environment.

The discipline of managerial economics deals with aspects of economics and tools of analysis, which are employed by business enterprises for decision-making. Business and industrial enterprises have to undertake varied decisions that involve managerial issues and decisions. Decision-making can be delineated as a process where a particular course of action is chosen from a number of alternatives. This needs an unclouded perception of the technical and environmental conditions, which are integral to decision-making. The decision-maker must possess a thorough knowledge of aspects of economic theory and its tools of analysis. For example, statistical methods are pivotal in estimating current and future demand for products. Further, decision-making theory and game theory, which recognise the conditions of uncertainty and imperfect knowledge under which business managers operate, have contributed to systematic methods of assessing investment opportunities. Almost any business decision can be analysed with managerial economics techniques.

Thus, managerial economics includes decision-making and thus it will be quite helpful if we identify and understand some of the basic concepts underlying the subject. The various decision problems are based heavily on these concepts, methods and models.

In management studies, the terms 'Business Economics' and 'Managerial Economics' are often synonyms. However, both the terms involve 'economics' as a basic discipline useful for certain functional areas of business management.

Managerial economics is essentially applied economics in the field of business management. It relates to all economic aspects of managerial decision-making. Managerial economics is the integration of economic principles with business management practices. A course in managerial economics, thus, provides an understanding of the framework and economic tools needed by managers or businessmen as an aid to a better business decision-making.

1.1.2 Meaning and Definitions of Managerial Economics

Managerial economics is concerned with the application of economic theory and methods of decision sciences to analyse decision-making problems faced by business firms. Thus, managerial economics is both conceptual and practical. The first important problem faced by a business firm is the choice of a product to be produced or the service to be provided. The second important problem is to take the decision about price and output of the product so as to maximise profits or to attain some desired goal.

Managerial economics draws heavily on the decision sciences for the techniques used for decision-making. The techniques of decision sciences used especially for business decision-making are optimisation techniques, methods of statistical estimation, game theory of decision sciences. These techniques help managers in achieving firm's objectives. Thus, "managerial economics refers to the application of economic theory and methods of decision sciences to arrive at the optimal solution to the various decision-making problems faced by managers of business firms".

- Managerial economics has both descriptive and prescriptive roles.

- It not only explains how various economic forces affect the working of a firm but also predicts the consequences of the decisions made by the firm. This is its descriptive role.

- Managerial economics prescribes the rules for the improvement of decision-making by the firms or managers so that they can achieve their objectives efficiently. This is its prescriptive role.

- Managerial economics deals with not only private firms but also public enterprises. This is because managers of all types of organisations face similar problems.

According to **McNair** and **Merriam**, *"Managerial economics consists of the use of economic models of thought to analyse business situations".*

Managerial economics can be defined as, *"the discipline which deals with the application of economic theory to business management".*

In words of **Spencer** and **Siegelman**, managerial economics is, *"the integration of economic theory with business practice for the purpose of facilitating decision-making and forward planning by management".*

According to **Mansfield**, *"Managerial economics is concerned with application of economic concepts and economic analysis to the problems of formulating rational managerial decision".*

1.1.3 Nature/Characteristics of Managerial Economics

The characteristics of managerial economics sums up the nature of managerial economics –

1. Managerial economics is **micro in character**, as managerial economics does not deal with the entire economy as a unit of study. It studies the problems and principles of an individual business firm or an individual industry. It aids the management in forecasting and evaluating the trends of the market.

2. Managerial economics is **pragmatic (practical) in nature**. It tries to solve complications ignored in economic theory to face the overall situation in which decisions are made. Managerial economics considers the particular environment of decision-making. In pure micro-economic theory, analysis is performed, based on certain exceptions, which are far from reality. However, in managerial economics, managerial issues are resolved daily and difficult issues of economic theory are kept at bay.

3. Managerial economics largely uses those **economic concepts and principles** which are known as 'theory of the firm' or 'economics of the firm'. Thus, its scope is narrower than that of pure economic theory.

4. Managerial economics belongs to **normative economics**. It is concerned with varied corrective measures that a management undertakes under various circumstances. That is, managerial economics involves value judgements. It deals with goal determination, goal development and achievement of these goals. Future planning, policy-making, decision-making and optimal utilisation of available resources, come under the banner of managerial economics. It tells how best to achieve these aims in particular situations. It not only describes the goals of an organisation but also prescribes the means of achieving these goals.

5. Managerial economics also incorporates certain aspects of **macroeconomic theory**. These are essential to comprehending the circumstances and environments that

envelop the working conditions of an individual firm or an industry. The knowledge of macroeconomic issues such as business cycles, taxation policies, industrial policy of the government, price and distribution policies, wage policies and anti-monopoly policies, etc. is an integral part to successful functioning of a business.

6. Managerial economics **aims at supporting the management** in taking corrective decisions and charting plans and policies for future.

7. Nowadays, managers and entrepreneurs make it their business to have a good working knowledge of managerial economics.

8. Thus, we summarise the salient features of managerial economics.

9. It is a **science as well as art** facilitating better managerial discipline. Scientific methods have been credited as the optimal path to achieving one's goals. Managerial economics is also called a scientific art because it helps management in the best and efficient utilisation of scarce economic resources. It assists the management in singling out the most feasible alternative. Managerial economics facilitates result-oriented decisions under conditions of uncertainty. It is concerned with the firm's behaviour in optimal allocation of resources. Thus it provides tools to help in identifying the best course among the competitive activities in any productive sector.

1.1.4 Scope and Subject Matter of Managerial Economics

The following topics may be said to generally fall in the scope of managerial economics.

1. **Demand Analysis and Forecasting:** A major part of managerial decision-making depends on accurate estimates of demand. Demand analysis includes demand determinants and demand forecasting. Before production schedule can be prepared and resources employed, forecast of future sales is essential. Demand analysis is essential for business planning and occupies a strategic place in managerial economics.

   According to Spencer and Siegelman, "A business firm is an economic organisation which transforms productive sources into goods that are to be sold in a market, and, demand analysis is undertaken to forecast demand, which is a fundamental component in managerial decision-making". Demand forecasting is of importance because an estimate of future sales is a primer for preparing production schedules and employing productive resources. Demand analysis helps the management in identifying factors that influence the demand for the products of a firm. Thus, demand analysis and forecasting is of prime importance to business planning.

   Demand theory relates to the study of consumer behaviour. It deals with questions such as what incites a consumer to buy a particular product, at what price he or she purchase the product, why do consumers stop consuming a commodity and so on. It seeks to determine the effect of the income, habit and consumer's taste on the demand of a commodity.

2. **Supply Analysis:** Important aspects of supply analysis are supply schedule, supply function, law of supply and elasticity of supply and factors influencing supply are subject matter of managerial economics.

3. **Cost Analysis:** Production and cost analysis is central for the unhampered functioning of the production process and for project planning. Achieving a certain profit it requires the production of a certain amount of goods. To obtain such production levels, some costs have to be incurred. At this point, the management is faced with the task of determining an optimal level of production where the average cost of production would be minimal. Production theory facilitates in determining the size of firm and production level. It explains the relationship between average and marginal costs and production. Production theory also deals with other issues such as conditions leading to increase or decrease in costs, changes in total production when one factor of production is varied and others are kept constant, substitution of one factor with another while keeping all increased at the same time and methods of achieving optimum production.

Cost analysis includes cost concepts and classification, cost output relationships, economies and diseconomies of scale and cost control and cost reduction. The factors causing variations in costs must be recognised and management is to arrive at cost estimates which are significant for planning purposes. Discovering economic costs and being able to measure them are necessary steps for more effective profit planning, cost control and sound pricing practices.

4. **Pricing Decisions:** Theory of exchange is popularly known as 'price theory'. The success of a business firm largely depends on how far the pricing decisions taken by the firm are correct. Pricing decisions involve price determination in various market firms, pricing methods, differential pricing, product-line pricing and price forecasting. Price determination under different types of market conditions comes under the scope of this theory. It helps in determining the level to which an advertisement can be used to boost market sales of a firm. Pricing is an important area in managerial economics. The accuracy of pricing decisions is vital in shaping the success of an enterprise.

5. **Profit Management:** Business firms are generally organised for the purpose of profit-making and in the long run profits provide the chief measure of success. The element of uncertainty existing in estimating profits is because of variations in costs and revenues which in turn, are caused by factors both internal and external to the

firm. If future was predicted with perfection, profit analysis would have been a very easy task. However, with uncertain conditions, expectations are not realised and hence profit planning and its measurement constitute a difficult area of managerial economics. Profit management involves the use of most efficient technique for predicting the future. The probability of risks should be minimised as far as possible.

6. **Capital Management:** The most complex area for any business manager is that relating to the firm's capital investments. Capital management implies planning and control of capital expenditure. Capital management covers cost of capital, rate of return and selection of projects, etc. Thus, the theory of capital and investment deals with following issues such as – selection of a viable investment project, efficient allocation of capital, assessment of the efficiency of capital, and minimising the possibility of under-capitalisation or over-capitalisation. Capital is the building block of a business. Like other factors of production, it is also scarce and expensive. It should be allocated in the most efficient manner.

7. **Issues:** Managerial economics encompasses some aspects of macroeconomics. These relate to social and political environment in which a business and industrial firm has to operate. This is governed by the following factors like the type of economic system of the country, business cycles, industrial policy of the country, trade and fiscal policy of the country, taxation policy of the country, price and labour policy, political system of the country, etc. The management of a firm cannot exercise control over these factors. Therefore, it should fashion the plans, policies and programmes of the firm according to these factors in order to offset their adverse effects on the firm. In recent years, techniques such as linear programming, inventory models, game theory, etc. are a part of managerial economics to integrate managerial economics and operation research.

1.1.5 Role of Economics in Managerial Decision-making

The contribution of economics towards the performance of managerial duties and responsibilities is of prime importance. The contribution and importance of economics to the managerial profession is like to the contribution of biology to the medical profession. It has been observed that managers equipped with a working knowledge of economics surpass their otherwise equally equipped peers, who lack knowledge of economics. Managers are responsible for achieving the objective of the firm to the maximum possible extent with the limited resources placed at their disposal. In the event of resources being unlimited, like air or sunshine, the problem of resource management would not have arisen. But the fact is that resources like finance, labour and material are limited and hence it is the responsibility of the management to optimise the use of these resources.

Though economics is defined in various ways it is essentially the study of logic, tools and techniques, to make optimum use of the available resources to achieve the given ends. Economics affords analytical tools and techniques that managers require to accomplish the goals of the firm that they manage. As such a working knowledge of economics is not only a necessity as a formal degree but is indispensable for managers. Uncertainty and risk arise chiefly due to volatile market forces, changing business environment, emerging competitors with highly competitive products, government policy, etc. Appropriate business decisions and formulation of a business strategy in conformity with the objectives of the firm holds great importance. Further pertinent business decisions require an unambiguous understanding of the technical and environmental conditions which business decisions are taken. Application of economic theories to explain and analyse technical conditions and business environment, contributes greatly to the rational decision-making process. Keeping in view the increasing complexity of business environment, the economic theory as a tool of analysis and its contribution to the process of decision-making has been widely recognised.

According to Baumol, the three main contributions of economic theory to business economics are –

1. The practice of building analytical models, which assist in recognising the structure of managerial problems and eliminating minor details, which might obstruct decision-making has been derived from economic theory. Analytical models help the management in retaining focus on core issues.

2. Economic theory comprises of 'a set of analytical methods' which may not be applied directly to specific business problems but they do enhance the analytical capabilities of the business analyst.

3. Economic theories offer an unequivocal perspective on the various concepts used in business analysis, which enables the manager to swing over from conceptual pitfalls.

Role of Managerial Economists

In the knowledge-based economy and business, those who have expertise in managerial economics are referred to as managerial economists.

A managerial economist is an economic adviser to a firm or businessman. The business economist, by virtue of his expertise, helps the businessman or the manager in arriving at correct decisions in the nature of the product to be produced, the quantity of it to be produced, its quality, cost, price, diversification of business, renewal of worn-out equipment and machinery, modernisation etc.

A managerial economist in a business firm may carry on a wide range of duties, such as –

- Demand estimation and forecasting;
- Analysis of the market survey to determine the nature and extent of competition;
- Advising on pricing, investment, capital budgeting policies, etc.;

- Assisting the business planning process of the firm;

- Directing economic research activity;

- Briefing the management on current domestic and global economic issues and emerging challenges.

The business economist has to keep an eye on the fast changing technological developments, because the decision taken will be within the framework of such developments. The business economist has to keep pace with modern times as innovation of new products may adversely affect the business of the firm.

A business economist should work in harmony with the policymakers, because he identifies constraints and alternatives in decision-making. He should help the management in identifying long and short-run objectives and in reconciling the conflicting ones.

In modern business, particularly, big firms, employment of a business economist has become inevitable. However, the role of business economists depends on the type or nature of the business of the firm. For example, in a financial firm, it is to provide guidelines for investment, marketing and speculative activities.

To conclude, a managerial economist is a thinker, a friend and a philosopher to the businessman. He should be both conceptual and a practical one.

1.1.6 Importance of Managerial Economics

In order to achieve the objective of earning maximum proceeds, a managerial executive has to take recourse in decision-making which involves selecting a specified course of action from a number of alternatives. A sound decision requires fair knowledge of the aspects of economic theory and the tools of economic analysis, which are directly involved in the process of decision-making. Since managerial economics is concerned with such aspects and tools of analysis, it is important to the decision-making process.

Spencer and Siegelman have described the importance of managerial economics in a business and industrial enterprise as follows –

1. **Amalgamates traditional theoretical concepts to the actual business behaviour and conditions:** Managerial economics accommodates tools, techniques, models and theories of traditional economics with actual business practices and with the environment in which a firm has to operate. According to Edwin Mansfield, "Managerial economics attempts to bridge the gap between purely analytical problems that scheme many economic theories and the problems of policies that management must face".

2. **Estimates economic relationships:** Managerial economics estimates economic relationships between different business factors such as income, elasticity of demand, cost, profit analysis, etc.

3. **It assists in understanding significant external forces:** A manager has to identify all the important factors that influence any firm in a positive or negative way. These factors can broadly be divided into two groups – external forces and internal forces. Managerial economic plays an important role by assisting management in understanding these factors.

   - **External Factors:** A firm cannot exercise any control over these forces. The plans, policies and programmes of the firm should be formulated in the light of these factors. Certain important external factors that interrupt on the decision-making process of a firm are economic system of a country, business cycles, fluctuations in national income and national production, industrial policy of the government, trade and fiscal policy of the government, taxation policy, licensing policy, trends in foreign trade of the country, general industrial relation in the country and so on.

   - **Internal Factors:** These factors are under the control of a firm. These factors are associated with business operation. Knowledge of these factors aids the management in making sound business decisions.

4. **Basis of business policies:** Managerial economics is the foundation principle of business policies. Business policies are prepared based on studies and findings of managerial economics, which cautions the management against potential turmoil in national as well as international economy.

5. **Predicting relevant economic quantities:** Managerial economics assists the management in predicting various economic quantities such as cost, profit, demand, capital, production, prices, etc. As a business manager has to function in an environment of uncertainty, it is necessary to anticipate the future working environment in terms of the said quantities.

Thus, managerial economics is helpful to the management in its decision-making.

1.1.7 Techniques of Managerial Economics

The wide variety of economic concepts, tools and techniques in the decision-making process can be grouped as follows –

1. **The theory of the firm:** It explains how businesses make a variety of decisions. A firm can be considered an amalgamation of people, physical and financial resources and a variety of information. Firms exist because they perform useful functions in society of production and distribution of goods and services. If economic activities of society can be simply put into a two-sector model of production and consumption, then firms are considered the most basic economic entity on the production-side, while consumers are on the consumption side. The

basic economic model of a business enterprise (idealised version of real-world firm) is called the theory of the firm.

2. **The theory of consumer behaviour:** It describes the consumer's decision-making process. The role of consumers in an economy is of vital importance since spending by the consumers is on goods and services produced by firms. It is desirous to know the ultimate objective of a consumer. While it is assumed that firms attempt at maximising profits, similarly there is an assumption that consumers attempt at maximising their utility or satisfaction. It is true that more goods and services provide greater utility to a consumer; however, like firms, consumers are subject to limitations, such as their disposable income. A consumer's choice to consume is described by economists within a theoretical framework usually termed as the theory of demand.

3. **The theory of market structure and pricing:** It describes the structure and characteristics of different market forms under which business firms operate. A firm's profit maximising output decisions take into account the market structure under which they are to operate. The market structures are – perfect competition, monopolistic competition, oligopoly, monopoly, etc.

All the above theories are analysed with the help of a vast and varied quantitative tools and techniques.

1.1.8 Applications of Managerial Economics

Tools of managerial economics can be used to achieve virtually all the objectives of a business organisation in the most efficient manner. Any typical decision-making process may involve one or more of the following issues.

1. Decisions regarding the price of a product and the quantity of the good to be produced.

2. Decisions pertaining to the medium of advertising and the intensity of the advertising campaign.

3. Decisions to be made regarding employment and training.

4. Choice of production technique to be employed in the production of a given product.

5. Decision pertaining to expansion of business, investments and the mode of financing the investment.

6. Decisions to be taken regarding the level of inventory to be maintained.

7. To choose the product for production or a part of product to be produced or outsource or purchase from another manufacturer.

An important point to be understood is that application of techniques or tools for managerial decision-making is not restricted to the profit-seeking business organisations because they are equally applied to the problems of non-profit organisations. For example, a non-profit hospital makes use of these tools to optimise the use of its resources. A hospital does strive to provide its patients the best medical care possible given its limited staff, space, equipment and other resources. In addition, the government agencies, cooperatives, museums can also exploit the techniques of managerial decision-making to achieve their set goals in the most efficient manner. Further, managerial economics via its tools aids in making optimal decisions, that is, it describes the predictable economic consequences of a managerial decision. For example, managerial economics can explain the impact and effect of imposing automobile import quotas on the availability of domestic cars, prices charged for automobiles and the extent of competition in the auto industry. However, managerial economics does not address whether imposing automobile import quotas is a good government policy or not. Thus, it passes no judgement on the tools of managerial economics.

1.1.9 Managerial Economics and Tools of Decision Science

The major categories of the tools drawn on economic concepts for managerial decision-making are optimisation, statistical estimation, forecasting, numerical analysis and game theory.

1. **Optimisation:** Given alternative courses of action the manager attempts to produce the most optimal decision, consistent with stated managerial objectives. Optimisation techniques are probably the most crucial to managerial decision-making. An optimisation problem can be stated as maximising an objective, subject to specified constraints. For example, in the profit maximisation, the profit maximising condition requires that the firm selects the production level at which marginal revenue equals marginal cost. The techniques of optimisation employed depend on the problem that a manager is trying to solve.

2. **Statistical Estimation:** A number of statistical techniques are used to estimate economic variables that interest a manager. In some cases, statistical estimation techniques employed are simple, while in other cases they are much more complex and advanced. For example, a firm may wish to know demand function of its product, that is, the relationship between the demand for its product and the factors that influence it. The estimates of costs and demand are usually based on data supplied by the firm. The statistical estimation technique employed is called regression analysis and is used to bring about a mathematical model showing how a set of variables are related. This mathematical relationship can also be used to generate forecasts. For example, a statistician has data on sales of Indian-made

automobiles in India for the last 25 years. He has also determined that the sale of automobiles is related to the disposable income of individuals. Further, the time series data (for last 25 years) on disposable income is available to the statistician. Assume that the relationship between the time series on sales of Indian-made automobiles and the disposable income of consumers is actually linear and hence can be represented by a straight line. A rigorous mathematical technique is used to locate the straight line that most accurately represents the relationship between the time series on auto sales and disposable income.

3. **Forecasting:** It is a method to predict many future aspects of a business. For example, a retail firm that has been in business for two decades may be interested in forecasting the likely sales volume for the coming year in the face of competition. A forecasting technique, for example, can provide projection based on the experience of the firm during the last 20 years; that is, under this forecasting technique the future forecast is based on the past data. The term 'forecasting' may appear technical, but planning for the future is a critical aspect of managing any organisation. The long-term success of any firm has close relationship with the ability of the management to foresee its future and develop appropriate strategies to deal with the likely future scenarios. Intuition, good judgement and knowledge of economic conditions enable the manager to 'feel' and anticipate the likelihood in the future. Forecasting methods can help predict many future aspects of a business operation.

1.2 Microeconomics

1.2.1 Meaning and Definitions

Economic theory or economic analysis is an important part of the subject Economics, the other two being descriptive economics and applied economics. Economic theory or economic analysis gives a simplified explanation of the way in which an economic system works and the important features of such a system. Economic theory deals with an economic problem. An economic problem arises when a decision-making individual, society or a planning agency confronts a problem of choice, that is, a problem of using scarce means for satisfying the unending human wants. There are two main branches of economic theory – *microeconomic theory* and *macroeconomic theory*.

The term 'micro' is derived from the Greek word *'mikros'* which means 'small', that is, individual. In fact, 'micro' means a millionth part. Hence microeconomics deals with an analysis of the behaviour of individual economic units, be it consumers or producers in the entire economy. In the words of Prof. Kenneth E. Boulding, "Microeconomics is the study of particular firms, particular households, individual prices, wages, incomes, individual industries, particular commodities".

Microeconomics looks at an economic system in terms of its innumerable **decision-making units** such as consuming units (for example, individual consumers and households); producing units (for example, firms); individual factors of production (for example, labourers, and landowners) and individual industries (for example, cotton textile, iron and steel). In the analysis of price, demand, income and employment, microeconomics studies them with respect to a particular product, or of a particular factor of production, or that of an individual, firm or industry.

In the circular flow of economic activity in the community, microeconomics studies the flow of economic resources or factors of production from the resource owners to business firms and the flow of goods and services from the business firms to households. It studies the composition of such flows and how the prices of goods and services in the flow are determined.

The scientific study of a subject consists of the establishment of causal relationships between phenomena. To establish such a relationship, facts have to be analysed. We have to break up a 'whole' into parts. The constituent parts have to be linked up to form a sequence of events. The process of breaking up and providing the needed links is called analysis.

There are various kinds of analysis. A 'whole' can be broken up into big parts or into small parts. For example, the entire economy can be broken up into large components, such as the consuming section and the producing section. A relationship between them can then be established. Alternately, an economy can be broken up into small parts such as individual consumers and individual producers and then an attempt can be made to establish a link between them. When we break up an economy into small parts for purpose of analysis, we are said to adopt the micro technique and the resulting theory is called microeconomics. Similarly, when we break up an economy into big parts for purpose of analysis, the technique is macro technique and the theory resulting from such a study is called macroeconomics.

1. **Watson** says, "Microeconomics is the theory of the small, of the behaviour of the consumers, producers and markets".

2. In the words of **Shapiro**, "Microeconomics deals with small parts of the economy".

3. According to **Leftwitch**, "Microeconomics is concerned with the economic activities of economic units as consumers, resource owners and business firms".

1.2.2 Nature of Microeconomics

1. Microeconomics relates to individual decision-making units such as a consumer, a firm or an owner of the factors of production. Microeconomic theory explains how an individual optimises the use of available resources for the attainment of his objective. Microeconomics explains how a consumer would maximise his

satisfaction within the given income constraint, or how a firm would maximise its level of output (or profit) within the given resources at its disposal. Similarly, microeconomics explains the behaviour of an individual resource owner whose general objective would be to attain maximum income for the land, labour or capital placed under his command.

2. Microeconomic theory analyses the behaviour of a single economic unit, a consumer, a firm or a resource owner. The implicit assumption in microeconomic analysis is that all consumers, all firms and all resource owners behave identically. In other words, it studies the behaviour of a representative consumer, a representative firm or a representative resource owner.

3. Microeconomic theory is also known as price theory, as it is primarily concerned with the flow of goods and services from business firms to households, the flow of productive services from households to business firms, the composition of these flows and the pricing of goods and productive services. Prices of productive services serve as a guide in the allocation of productive resources (resources or factors) among a set of goods to be produced. Conversely, prices of goods help in determining the level of output in respect of each commodity and the level of satisfaction to be attained by every consumer in the society. For example, if the price of a good, X, is raised while that of Y remains unchanged, more resources that are productive will flow into the production of X and the output of X will increase in relation to Y. In the same way, it may be argued that if wage rate falls while the rate of interest remains unchanged, more units of labour will be used in the production of different goods and services.

4. Finally microeconomic theory or price theory is also a theory of demand and/or supply in respect of goods and productive services. It explains how an individual consumer or a firm attains equilibrium if the product and factor prices are determined exogenously by the aggregate demand and supply in the product and the input markets.

1.2.3 Scope of Microeconomics

Microeconomics is concerned with the following topics –

1. Commodity Pricing

Prices of individual commodities are made due to market forces of demand and supply. Therefore, microeconomics makes demand analysis (individual consumer behaviour) and supply analysis (individual producer behaviour).

2. Factor Pricing

Factors involved in production process such as Land, Labour, Capital and Entrepreneur get rewards in the form of rent, wages, interest and profit and therefore microeconomics deals with such rewards, that is, factor prices. Therefore, microeconomics is also called as 'price theory' or 'value theory'.

3. Welfare Theory

Microeconomics deals in maximising social welfare, with usage of fewer resources. It provides answers for 'what to produce?', 'when to produce?', 'how to produce?' and 'for whom it is to be produced?' In short, microeconomics guides for utilising scarce resources of economy to maximise public welfare.

1.2.4 Importance of Microeconomics

Microeconomics occupies a very important place in the study of economic theory. It has both theoretical and practical importance.

From the theoretical point of view, the contribution of microeconomics is as follows –

1. **Working of a Free Enterprise Economy:** Microeconomics explains the functioning of a free enterprise economy. It tells us how millions of consumers and firms operate independently of each other, but at the same time are able to ensure the smooth functioning of the economic system.

2. **Allocation of Resources:** Microeconomics explains how millions of consumers and producers in an economy take decisions about the allocation of productive resources among various goods and services.

3. **Price Mechanism:** Microeconomics explains how through the price/market mechanism, goods and services produced in the community are distributed.

4. **Price Determination:** Microeconomics explains how prices of various products and those of factors of production (productive services) are determined in the product market and factor market respectively.

5. **Market Structure:** Microeconomics provides a framework to study different kinds of market structures like perfect competition, monopoly, oligopoly, etc.

6. **Rules of Economic Efficiency:** An important branch of microeconomics – welfare economics   helps in defining and analysing the rules of economic efficiency. It explains how factors of production can be used efficiently to get the maximum output with the given amount of resources. It also indicates how a consumer can maximise his satisfaction by equating the ratios of marginal utilities to the prices of different goods that he buys.

    Thus, it explains the conditions of efficiency in both production and consumption and deviation from the optimum.

7. **Positive and Normative Role:** The role of microeconomics is both positive and normative. It not only tells us how the economy operates but also how it should be operated to promote general welfare. It helps in the construction of simplified models of economic behaviour and explains how far the actual situations deviate from the ideal situations.

From the **practical** point of view, the contribution of microeconomics is as follows.

1. **Policy Formulation:** Microeconomics is useful in the formulation and evaluation of economic policies designed to promote efficiency in production and welfare of the masses.

2. **Public Finance:** Microeconomics is useful in the study of public finance. It explains the incidence and burden of different taxes (direct and indirect taxes) on different classes of people and analyses its effect on the allocation of resources, economic welfare etc. It is useful in explaining the effects of public expenditure, public borrowing etc. Thus, it helps the Finance Minister in the formulation of tax policies.

3. **International Trade:** Microeconomics is useful in explaining the reasons for trade among different countries, gains from international trade, causes for disequilibrium in the balance of payments, effects of devaluation, factors determining exchange rate of currencies, etc.

4. **Usefulness to Business:** In recent decades, many concepts and tools of microeconomics have been extensively used by businessmen in the decision-making process. A new branch of economics known as Business Economics or Managerial Economics has contributed significantly to this process. Through demand forecasting, cost analysis and analysis of different market structures, managerial economics has simplified and improvised decision-making in business.

5. **Theory of Linear Programming:** The development of the theory of Linear Programming in microeconomics has provided a powerful and new analytical tool to analyse business problems. It helps in finding actual numerical solutions to business problems calling for optimum choice.

The significance of microeconomics can be summarised in the words of A. P. Lerner "Microeconomic theory facilitates the understanding of what would be a hopelessly complicated confusion of billions of facts by constructing simplified models of behaviour ...." They thus help not only to *describe* the actual economic situation but to *suggest policies* that would most successfully and most efficiently bring about desired results and to predict the outcomes of such policies and other events".

[A. P. Lerner – "Microeconomic Theory", in Brown, Neuberger, and Palmatier, Perspectives in Economics, 1968, Pg. 29]

1.2.5 Limitations of Microeconomics

Microeconomic analysis suffers from the following limitations.

1. Microeconomics deals with individual factors of production, individual producers, consumers, etc. Micro approach is not only inadequate but may lead to altogether

misleading conclusions. In economics, what is true of the parts is not necessarily true of the whole. The problem of the aggregate is quite different and far more complicated than merely a summation or multiplication of the individual parts of the whole. For example, saving is a private virtue but a public vice. Similarly a wage-cut may enable an individual entrepreneur to increase employment of workers but a general wage-cut would lead to decline in income, fall in aggregate demand and fall in employment. An *individual* farmer who is fortunate enough to realise a bumper crop is likely to find that his resulting income is larger than usual. This is a correct generalisation. But it does not apply to farmers as a group for the simple reason that to the individual farmer, crop prices will not be influenced (reduced) by his bumper crop, because each farmer is producing a negligible fraction of the total farm output. However, to farmers as a group, prices vary inversely with total output (this assumes there is no Government price fixing). Thus, as all farmers realise bumper crops, the total supply of farm products rises, thereby depressing prices. 'If price declines overbalance the unusually large output, farm incomes *fall*.'

2. In microeconomics, production and consumption are treated as two independent activities. Hence, the effect of changes in production on consumption or the effect of changes in consumption on production is not taken into account.

3. Microeconomics is static in nature because it takes into account market demand and supply and analyses them. It does not consider or take into account changes in quantities demanded or supplied.

4. Microeconomics neglects many interrelations in economic activities. For example –

    (a) In microeconomics we accept that Y > Exp (Y = income; Exp = expenditure) for individual persons, that is, some persons spend less than what they earn, while some others spend more than what they earn. Nevertheless, for the economy as a whole, aggregate Y = aggregate Exp, because one man's income is another person's expenditure.

    (b) Similarly an individual can invest more or less of what he has saved. But at the economy's level,

    Aggregate S = Aggregate I (S = Savings, I = Investment) during a period.

    This is because –

    Y = C + S

    Y = C + I

    S = I

(Y stands for income paid to the factors of production; C stands for consumer's expenditure on commodities and services; S stands for savings or income not consumed and I stands for investment or capital expenditures on real assets.)

(c) Similarly, a single firm can increase employment by drawing labour force from other firms. Therefore employment may rise or fall. But if we assume full employment (as in microeconomic theory) in the economy, employment, cannot rise.

5. Microeconomics theory is based on certain assumptions that are necessary for theoretical model building. However, these are unrealistic assumptions. For example, the condition of 'ceteris paribus' (other things remaining the same) or the assumption of full employment or perfect competition. In this respect, Keynes says that "to assume full employment is to assume our difficulties away."

6. Microeconomic theories are based on the principles of *marginalism*. Marginal changes refer to the addition of a single unit. Thus, we have concepts like marginal utility, marginal revenue, marginal cost etc. It refers to a very small change in the total. The theories explain equilibrium conditions in terms of margin, such as consumer equating marginal utility with price to attain maximum satisfaction or a producer equating marginal cost with marginal revenue for maximisation of profits. However, in practice it is difficult to realise this marginal approach.

1.3 Macroeconomics

1.3.1 Introduction

Macroeconomics is that branch of economic analysis that studies the behaviour of aggregates, that is, of all the units combined together.

The term 'macro' was first used in economics by Ragnar Frisch in 1933. Before Keynes, other modern contributors to the development of macroeconomic analysis were Walras, Wicksell and Fisher.

Economists like Marshall, Pigou, Robertson and Hawtrey have developed a theory of money and general prices.

However, the credit of blossoming *macroeconomics* goes to **John Maynard Keynes**. His famous work, 'General Theory of Income, Output and Employment' (1936) gave a strong impetus to the growth and development of modern macroeconomics.

1.3.2 Definitions of Macroeconomics

In recent years, increasing attention has been given to the study and analysis of the economic system as a whole. This is macroeconomic approach to economics.

1.   According to **R. G. D. Allen**, macroeconomics refers to *"the study of relations between broad economic aggregates"*.

2.   **Prof. Ackley** defines macroeconomics as *"it deals with economic affairs in the large, it concerns with the overall dimensions of economic life. It looks at the total size, shape and functioning of the entire economic experience, rather than working of articulation or dimensions of the individual parts. It studies the character of the forest, independently of the trees which compose it"*.

3.   In the words of **Prof. K. E. Boulding**, *"Macroeconomics deals not with individual quantities as such, but with aggregates of these quantities; not with individual incomes but with the national income; not with individual prices but with the price level; not with individual outputs, but with the national output"*.

It, thus, deals not with one firm but all the firms in an economy; not with one industry, but the entire industrial structure of an economy.

Macroeconomics may be, thus, defined as "that branch of economic analysis which studies the behaviour of not just one particular unit, but of all the units combined together".

To sum up the interpretations of the various definitions –

- Macroeconomics is a study in 'aggregates' and hence it is often referred to as 'aggregative economics'.

- Thus, it is the study of the economic system as a whole. It studies the overall conditions of an economy, such as, total consumption, total production, total savings, total investments, national income, national output, general price level, etc.

- It is aggregative economics which examines the interrelations among the various aggregates, their determination and causes of fluctuations in them.

- Macro analysis conceives of equilibrium between demand and supply in the economy as a whole.

Since macroeconomics deals with aggregates, it is known as 'the theory of income and employment or income analysis'.

> *Macroeconomics deals with great 'averages' and 'aggregates' of the system and not with particular units in it. It is study of macro-quantities and macro-variables.*

1.3.3 Nature of Macroeconomics

Macroeconomics studies the aggregates of the entire economy and as such the nature of macroeconomics can be understood with the help of the following aspects.

1. Determination of National Income and Employment

- Macroeconomics deals with aggregate demand and aggregate supply that determines the equilibrium level of income and employment in the economy.

- The level of aggregate demand determines the level of income and employment.

- Macroeconomics also deals with the problem of unemployment due to lack of aggregate demand.

2. Determination of General Price Level

- Macroeconomics studies the general level of price in an economy.

- It studies the economic fluctuations and business cycles, that is, it studies the problem of inflation and deflation.

3. Economic Growth and Development

- Macroeconomics deals with economic growth and development.

- It studies various factors that contribute to economic growth and development.

4. Distribution of Factors of Production

- Macroeconomics deals with various factors of production and their relative share in the total production or total national income.

5. Aggregative Approach

- Macroeconomics is 'aggregative' in its methodological approach. Macroeconomics has been developed to describe the typical nature of aggregate economic behaviour.

- It studies the overall 'averages' and 'aggregates' of the system.

6. Economic Variables

- Macroeconomics is concerned with the behaviour of macro-variables and macro-quantities such as aggregate demand, general price level, aggregate supply, total consumption, total expenditure, etc.

- Macroeconomics concentrates on variables such as the aggregate volume to output of an economy, total employment and total investment.

7. Income Theory

- Macroeconomics is referred as 'income theory' in economics. The reason is that when there is a change in aggregate demand or any other aggregate variable, it is linked with the level of income.

- In macro analysis, income and not prices, is the link between demand and supply.

8. Assumptions

- Macroeconomics is a more realistic approach as the theories explained in it are based on fewer assumptions. In this approach, there is no unrealistic assumption of full employment in the economy.

- It studies the determinants of full employment and attempts as to how the fullest possible employment can be attained.

Traditional economic analysis was largely confined to the study of individual aspects of economic behaviour. The results of such analysis were averaged out and generalised by the traditional economists to explain the aggregate nature of the system as a whole. However, modern economists realised the folly of extending generalisations of individual behaviour on the aggregate character of the system.

> *The nature of macroeconomics was well realised, that what is true of the 'part' may not be true for the 'whole'.*

After all, the problem of aggregates is not merely adding or multiplying the propositions of individual parts to the whole of an economy.

1.3.4 Scope of Macroeconomics

The Keynesian economists had developed macroeconomics to a great extent by the '60s. Its scope of study is vast and includes the following.

1. It deals with the theory of income, output and employment with its two constituents: (a) the theory of consumption function; and (b) the theory of investment function.

2. The theory of business cycles, that is, economic fluctuations, is too a part of the theory of income, output and employment.

3. Theory of prices – theories of inflation, deflation and stagflation.

4. Theory of economic growth dealing with the long-run growth of income, output and employment as applied to developed and under-developed countries.

5. Macro theory of distribution that deals with the relative shares of wages and profits in the total national income.

1.3.5 Importance/Utility of Macroeconomics

Macroeconomics is of great theoretical and practical significance.

1. To Understand the Working of an Economy

- The study of macroeconomics is crucial for understanding the working of the economy.

- The main economic problems of country are related to the behaviour of total income, total output, employment and the general price level in the economy.

- These variables are statistically measurable, thereby facilitating the possibilities of analysing the effects on the functioning of the economy.

- For example, the general price level gives us an idea as to whether the economy is facing inflation or recession.

2. To Understand the Behaviour of Individual Units

- The study of macroeconomics is indispensable even for the purpose of building and developing macroeconomics.

- For example, the law of DMU could not have been formulated unless the experience of masses of individuals had been collected and taken into consideration.

- Thus, no microeconomic law can be formulated without a pre-study of aggregates bearing on it.

3. To Evaluate National Income

- The study of macroeconomics is very important for evaluating the overall performance of the economy in terms of national income.

- With the help of national income data the level of economic activity can be forecast, that is, it helps in understanding the distribution of income among different groups of people in the economy.

4. To Deal with Challenging Problems

- The utility of macroeconomics has greatly increased in recent years as it deals with most of the controversial and challenging issues, namely those of unemployment, inflation, taxation, deficit financing, planning and economic development.

- No economist can overlook the study of such problems of the modern economic world. For example, general unemployment is caused by deficiency of effective demand. In order to eradicate it, effective demand should be raised by increasing total investment, total productivity, total income and consumption.

- Thus, macroeconomics has special significance in studying the causes, effects and antidotes of general unemployment.

5. To Evaluate Economic Growth

- The economics of growth is also a study in macroeconomics. It is on the basis of macroeconomics that the resources and capabilities of an economy are evaluated.

- Plans for the overall increase in national income, productivity, employment are framed and executed so as to raise the level of fiscal development of the economy as a whole.

6. To Formulate Policies for Business Cycles

- Macroeconomics has afforded immense help to the government in formulating and implementing appropriate economic policies.

- With the knowledge of macroeconomics, the governments are now in a better position to control the business cycles – inflation or deflation.

- Thus, macroeconomics assists governments to achieve uninterrupted economic growth and full employment with the help of suitable economic policies.

- It can be well said that macroeconomic tools lie at the base of all the present day plans of economic policies and at the base of economic development of underdeveloped countries.

- Macroeconomics has made valuable contributions in the field of social accounting.

7. To Study Monetary Problems

- Frequent changes in the value of money, inflation or deflation, affect the economy adversely.

- They can be counteracted by adopting monetary, fiscal and direct control measures for the economy as a whole.

8. To Formulate and Execute Successfully Governmental Economic Policies

- Now, government intervenes actively in economic affairs, and in doing so, governments do not deal with individuals but with masses.

- According to Prof. Boulding, modern governments are concerned more with the aggregates and averages – general price level, general level of production, and the general volume of trade – than with individual variables.

- Hence, it is essential to have accurate and reliable statistics of the 'aggregate variables' as the prerequisite for the formulation of sound government policies.

- The main precision of these governments rests in the regulation and control of over population, general prices, general volume of commerce, general productivity, etc.

- It is here that we can understand how essential the study of macroeconomics is for successful execution of governmental economic policies.

9. To Understand Accurately the Behaviour Patterns of Aggregate Variables

- It is true that it is difficult to understand the behaviour pattern of the 'aggregates' simply by generalising from the character and behaviour of the individual units.

- With the help of a simple analogy Prof. Boulding has driven home the point aptly, that is, individual variables and aggregate variables differ. He points out that the forest, though an aggregation of trees, does not exhibit the characteristics and behaviour of individual trees. It would be a misleading attempt if we generalise the behaviour pattern of the forest by studying the behaviour pattern of individual trees, as there is a clear difference between an individual tree and the forest as a whole.

    (i) An individual tree germinates, grows and decays; while a forest goes on forever with the same structure and composition.

(ii) An individual tree may not burn so easily, but forests are often subject to fires.

(iii) An individual tree cannot affect the climate of the surroundings in which it grows, but a forest can and does influence the climate.

- In short, the aggregate and its individual components are entirely two different things. If this truth is grasped, then the necessity and justification of macroeconomics becomes self-evident.

Importance of macroeconomics is so that we do not make a mistake in understanding the subject and suffer from certain 'paradoxes'.

1.3.6 Limitations of Macroeconomics

Macroeconomics can be functional and useful in its applications when certain inherent limitations that it suffers from are taken care of.

1. Excessive Generalisations

- In macroeconomics, the greatest danger is that, it deals with excessive generalisation from individual experience to the system as a whole. That is, in macroeconomics analysis the "fallacy of composition" is involved. The aggregate economic behaviour is the sum total of the economy of individual activities.

- But, what is true of an individual component may not be true of an aggregate.

- For example, there is nothing alarming when an individual withdraws his deposits from a bank, but if everybody tries to withdraw their deposits at the same time, the bank would surely collapse and the banking system will be affected adversely.

- Thus, care should be taken that too much generalisation from individual experience must be ignored.

- Another example, savings are a private virtue but a public vice. If total savings in the economy increases, they may initiate a depression unless they are invested.

2. Excessive Use of 'Aggregates'

- The second danger of macroeconomics is the danger of excessive thinking in terms of 'aggregates' which are heterogeneous in nature.

- When we take into account aggregates which are heterogeneous in character, the results can be misleading. As Prof. Bolding points out

    (i) 6 apples + 5 apples = 11 apples (it is a meaningful aggregate).

    (ii) 6 apples + 5 oranges = 11 fruits (this too is a fairly meaningful aggregate).

    (iii) 6 apples + 5 skyscrapers =? (This is surely a meaningless aggregate).

    It is (iii) type of aggregate that should be avoided.

- Macroeconomics would lose its utility if we were to resort meaningless aggregate.

- Thus, the main defect in macro analysis is that it regards the aggregates as homogenous without caring about their internal composition and structure.

3. In Policy-making

- In indiscriminate and uncritical use of macroeconomics in analysing the complexities of the real world can frequently be misleading.

- The study of aggregates may lead us to the conclusions that no change is needed in any government or economic policy.

- For example, if agricultural prices decline by 50%, while the general price level shows no change. The two types of price changes would neutralise each other. If guided by macro analysis alone, then no modified policy is needed in the economy. But, if considered independently the decline in prices of agricultural goods, it would call for the government to adopt a policy to support the farmers.

- It implies that measures aimed at controlling general prices cannot be applied with much advantage for controlling prices of individual products.

- Thus, relying on aggregate results alone may be misleading.

4. Impact on 'Individual' Differs

- An aggregate tendency may not influence all the sectors of the economy in the same manner.

- For example, a general rise in prices may not affect all the sections of the community in the same manner. Some may be influenced adversely and some favourably.

- Another example, the national income of a country is the total of all individual income. A rise in national income does not mean that individual income has risen. The increase in national income might be the result of the increase in the incomes of a few rich people in the nation, having little significance from the point of view of the community.

- Thus, the aggregate variables which form the economic system may not be of much significance.

5. Difficulties in Measurement – Statistical and Conceptual

- The measurement of aggregates presents serious problems despite several improvements in statistical techniques.

- These problems relate to the aggregation of microeconomic variables.

- If individual units are almost similar, aggregation does not present much difficulty. But if microeconomic variables relate to dissimilar individual units, their aggregation into one macroeconomic variable may be incorrect and hazardous.

- Thus, it is difficult to obtain reliable measures of 'averages' and 'aggregates' which form the subject matter of macroeconomics.

To conclude, macroeconomics enriches our knowledge of the functioning of an economy by studying the behaviour of national income, productivity, investment, savings and consumption. Further, it throws much light in solving the problems of redundancy, inflation, economic instability and economic growth. The concept of stock and flow are mainly used in the macroeconomics or in the theory of income, productivity and employment. Both the concepts of stock and flow variables are very significant in modern theories of income, interest rate, business cycles, etc.

1.3.7 Difference between Micro and Macroeconomics

Micro and Macroeconomics, the two approaches to economics, have 'individual' and 'group' characteristics and can thus highlight the significance of studying macroeconomics.

Microeconomics	Macroeconomics
1. The word 'micro' is derived from the Greek word *'mikros'* which means small.	1. The word 'macro' is derived from the Greek word *'makros'* which means large.
2. Microeconomics is the study of economic activities of individuals and small groups (homogenous) of individuals.	2. Macroeconomics is the study of aggregates and averages. It is the study of the economic system as a whole.
3. Microeconomics is an 'individualistic approach' to the study of economic theory.	3. Macroeconomics is an 'aggregative approach'.
4. 'Price mechanism' is the basis of microeconomics.	4. 'Income mechanism' is the basis of macroeconomics.
5. The main objectives of microeconomics are to maximise utility by consumers (demand side) and maximise profits by firms (on supply side).	5. The main objectives of macroeconomics are full employment, economic growth, price stability and favourable balance of payments.
6. Microeconomics is referred to as the study by 'slicing method' because it splits the economy into small, individual units and studies each unit in detail.	6. Macroeconomics is referred to as the study by 'lumping method' because it studies the economic behaviour in its totality. For study purpose it divides the economy into sectors (lumps).
7. It can be said that microeconomics is the study of an economy through a worm's eye-view.	7. Macroeconomics is the study of an economy through a bird's eye-view.

Microeconomics	Macroeconomics
8. The significance of the study of microeconomics is for resource utilisation, business decisions and for social welfare.	8. The importance of macroeconomics is for formulation of economic policies for the nation, for analysing trade cycles, etc.
9. Microeconomics is considered as a static analysis.	9. Macroeconomics is considered as dynamic analysis.
10. Prof. Marshall's magnum opus, "Principles of Economics" (1890) dealt in detail with microeconomics.	10. J. M. Keynes' celebrated work, "General Theory of Employment, Interest and Money" (1936) is an outstanding work of macroeconomics approach.

To conclude micro and macroeconomics are two clear, rigid and distinct approaches to the study of economics. However, in practice, the distinction is not a water-tight compartment, because what is 'individual' in one situation may be 'aggregate' in another situation. For example, study of national income is subject matter of macroeconomics, but if we are studying international income as a whole, then the study of national income of a country is a study in microeconomics.

Though the two approaches to economics – microeconomics and macroeconomics – differ, yet there is a good deal of interdependence between them. According to Prof. Samuelson, "there is really no opposition between micro and macroeconomics. Both are absolutely vital. You are less than half-educated if you understand one, while being ignorant of the other". Therefore, the two approaches are not in any way mutually exclusive and, as such, must be properly integrated to secure fruitful results.

Points to Remember

- The discipline of managerial economics deals with aspects of economics and tools of analysis, which are employed by business enterprises for decision-making.

- In management studies, the terms 'Business Economics' and 'Managerial Economics' are often synonyms. However, both the terms involve 'economics' as a basic discipline useful for certain functional areas of business management.

- Every economy faces following fundamental economic problems –

  (a) What to produce and in what quantities?

  (b) How to produce these goods?

  (c) For whom are the goods produced?

  (d) How efficiently are the resources being utilised?

  (e) Is the economy growing?

- Economic problems can be solved by – customs, central planning authority, price mechanism.

- The price mechanism works in a free market economy. It is the 'price' that determines what to produce, how much to produce, allocates the resources, and brings about equitable distribution of income.

- The modern economists have clearly divided the study of economics into Micro Economics and Macro Economics.

- Nature of Managerial Economics – (i) Micro-economic in character; (ii) Pragmatic in nature; (iii) Normative economics; (iv) Incorporates macro economic theory; (v) It is a science as well as an art.

- Scope and subject matter of Managerial Economics – (i) Demand analysis and forecasting; (ii) Supply analysis; (iii) Cost analysis; (iv) Pricing decisions; (v) Profit management; (vi) Capital management; (vii) Environmental issues.

- Managerial economics is a blend of positive (pure) with normative (applied) science. It is positive when it is confined to statements about cause and effect and to functional relations of economic variables. And, it is normative when it involves norms and standards, mixing them with the cause and effect analysis.

- A managerial economist is an economic adviser to a firm or businessman.

- A firm is an organisation that combines and organises the resources or factors of production with the aim of producing goods and/or services for sale.

- Microeconomics is the theory of the small, of the behaviour of the consumers, producers and markets.

- Macroeconomics deals with economic affairs in the large, it concerns with the overall dimensions of economic life. It looks at the total size, shape and functioning of the entire economic experience, rather than working of articulation or dimensions of the individual parts. It studies the character of the forest, independently of the trees which compose it.

Questions for Discussion

1.   Define managerial economics and bring out its characteristics.

2.   Bring out the important aspects covering the scope of managerial economics.

3.   Explain the nature and significance of managerial economics.

4.   How does the background of managerial economics assist in business decision-making?

5.   What are the responsibilities of a managerial economist?

6.   Describe the concept of microeconomics and macroeconomics.

Chapter 2...

Demand Forecasting

Contents ...

Objectives ...

➢ To understand the meaning, nature and scope of demand forecasting
➢ To study the usefulness of demand forecasting
➢ To learn about the different methods of Demand Forecasting and its importance
➢ To elaborate the guidelines for producing reliable demand forecast

2.1 Demand Forecasting

2.1.1 Introduction

Most business decisions are made in the face of risk or uncertainty, such as decision regarding how much of each product to produce, what price to charge, how much to spend on advertising, plan the growth of the firm, etc. All these decisions are based on forecasts of the level of future economic activity in general and demand for the firm's products in particular. The objective of economic forecasting is to reduce the risk or uncertainty that the firm faces in its short-term operational decision-making and in planning for its long-term growth.

2.1.2 Meaning of Demand Forecasting

The importance of demand or sales forecasting to business planning can hardly be over-emphasised. Good production and sales planning require forecasts of the business conditions and their relationship to demand. Any demand forecasting requires managers to predict the future which is unknown. In fact, it is to minimise the 'uncertainties' of the unknown future that these forecasts are needed.

A forecast is a prediction about a future event which is most likely to happen under a given set of conditions. In a world full of uncertainties, formation of some view about the future is most essential. *Predictions of future demand for a firm's product or products are known as demand forecasts*. Thus, demand forecast refers to estimation of the demand for the given commodity in the forecast period. For example, the good here is a Ford Car and the forecast period is the year 2009, then the forecasting problem is to estimate the demand for Ford cars in 2009. Actually, the most important factor which goes into making an effective manager is his sense of predicting future events that will affect the firm.

Demand forecasting is different from demand estimation in the sense that demand forecasting predicts about future trend of sales while the demand estimation tries to find out expected present sales level, given the present state of demand determinants. Forecasts can be both sales expressed in numbers or in monetary value in nature, and are used mostly for planning purposes.

- When prediction about future is based on the assumption that the firm does not change the course of its action, it is referred to as *passive forecasts*.
- When forecasting is done under the condition that future changes are likely to occur in the course of actions by the firm, it is referred to as *active forecasts*.
- For example, if any car company thinks of bringing an improvement in the quality of its cars and at the same time is committed to go in for a vigorous advertising campaign, there will be changes influencing the demand. To estimate the changes in variables, active demand forecasting is undertaken. Thus, active forecasts are more meaningful and realistic in assessing new policies in the market, as compared to passive forecasts.

Generally, business firms are interested in both passive and active forecasts. Often they predict sales after considering the changes in a host of policy variables, like prices of substitutes and complements, design, quality, advertisement expenditure, etc.

2.1.3 Purpose of Forecasting

A. Purpose of Short-term Forecasts

(i) **Product policy** is one such immediate purpose. A firm has to prepare a short-term plan for production which needs short-term forecasts so as to avoid either under-production or over-production.

(ii) For a realistic **price policy** the firm has to prepare a short-term demand forecasts.

(iii) **Cost-effectiveness** is an important consideration in management. This can be introduced with the help of demand forecasts.

(iv) **Securing short-term credit** on the basis of demand forecasts, the firm can tap various sources of credit in advance and thus save time and expenses which are likely to be wasted if the firm puts in efforts at the last minute when securing credit.

(v) **Distribution channels** can be arranged in anticipation of future demand if the forecasts of the demand are available.

B. Purpose of Long-term Forecasts

(i) **An expansion plan** is usually prepared for a long-term by a firm. Such a plan involves expansion of existing business/activity, diversification of production and training program for workers.

(ii) **Raising of capital for future expansion** is another important purpose. Long-term demand forecasts spell out the needs of capital and accordingly a plan of raising funds from various sources can be formulated.

(iii) **Long-term forecasts** can also assist the firm in *man-power planning*.

2.1.4 Nature and Scope of Demand Forecasting

It is possible to use a demand forecast in a number of ways. Hence, it is necessary to outline the nature and scope of demand forecasting. Following factors have to be considered to outline the scope of demand forecasting:

1. **Time – frame:** Every firm has to decide the period of time for which it needs to forecast. The method to be chosen and the accuracy of the method depend upon the time frame that the firm has chosen. Thus, the first step is to decide about the length of period for which the forecasting exercise is being taken up. The time – periods are usually divided into (a) short-term forecasts – a period up to 3 months; (b) medium-term forecasts – a period between 3 months and 1 year; (c) long-term forecasts – a period of more than 1 year.

   (a) **Short-term forecasts:** In case of short-term forecasting, factors considered are those which bring fluctuations in the demand pattern in the market, like weather conditions, change in tastes, fashions, etc. These factors influence the demand for consumer goods and thus indirectly influence the demand for machinery, raw material required to produce these consumer goods. In short, *seasonal factors* are main factors of short-term forecasting.

   (b) **Medium-term forecasts:** In case of medium-term forecasting, experience and sound judgement are more important than statistical forecasting. The medium-term forecasts can assist in the decision about timing of an activity, like advertising outlay. These forecasts contribute to revision of the decision based on long-term forecasts. The main feature of medium-term forecasts is the *trend analysis*. The trends assist in employee recruitment, training, etc.

(c) **Long-term forecasts:** In the long-run, the validity of the trend itself must be made sure of. If the trend is likely to change for the worse, this would adversely affect the firm's entire long-term strategy. For example, the long-term forecasts could suggest diversification policy for the firm. For this type of forecast there is great dependence on statistical techniques, though judgement in identifying variables still remains important since they are likely to influence future sales.

2. **Level of Forecasts:** Demand forecasts can be prepared on various levels:

   (a) **At Economy Level:** This forecasting is concerned with business conditions over the whole economy. These business conditions are measured with the help of various indices like those relating to national income, wholesale prices, etc. Thus, entrepreneurs can forecast the demand based upon the Gross National Product (GNP) and the indices of various variables available. The growth of the economy and its influence on the demand for all goods and services can be taken into account.

   (b) **At the Industry (or market) Level:** Forecasts regarding prospects of an industry and future demand for the product of an industry can be formulated on the basis of market surveys, past trends in demand and other statistical methods. Such forecasts can give indications to a firm regarding the direction in which the whole industry will be moving. For example, Voltas will like to know the way air-conditioner industry is likely to behave in future, so as to decide about the way this firm should plan for future. In relation to rest of the industry, every firm can compare its own position in relation to the position of the industry.

   (c) **At the Firm (or company) Level:** It is this level of forecast which occupies an important place in micro economic analysis. This type of forecast is at an individual firm's level. A big firm will forecast for its own product independent of the rest of the firms in the industry. Such forecasting shows whether or not the company is well placed to maintain or even improve its share in the market.

   (d) **Product-line forecasting:** This forecasting helps the firm to decide which of the product or products should have priority in the allocation of firm's limited resources. For example, Godrej may like to know whether it should produce more of storewell cupboards, locks, furniture, etc.

3. **For Established Products and for New Products:** For existing and established products, while forecasting demand, it is necessary to take into account knowledge of the current level of the demand for these products and present competition in this field. For the established products, past sale trends and competitive conditions are considered. The statistical methods of demand forecasting can be of great importance in case of established and existing products. This is not possible in respect of new products. Thus, for forecasting the demand for new products one has to use different methods.

4. **General and Specific Forecasts:** Many a times demand forecasts are prepared in general for all the products of a firm. However, a firm may need more detailed information regarding the quantum of demand for each individual product. This requires specific forecast. Details may change the overall picture based on general forecast.

5. **Classification of Products:** Economists broadly classify goods into capital goods, consumer durables and non-durable goods. While preparing demand forecasts it is essential to classify the products. For example, the demand for durable consumer goods can be postponed and generally the demand declines during depression. The demand for capital goods is a derived demand and thus faces severe fluctuations. The demand for consumer goods is related to the income of the community. Increase in income can result in higher demand for consumer goods. Thus, for each of these categories of goods there would be distinctive pattern of demand.

6. **Special Factors:** While forecasting, decision has to be made regarding the extent of sociological and psychological factors that influence the process of forecasting. For example, the nature of competition, the extent of uncertainty, the unforeseen risks, and possibilities of forecasts going wrong are some of the special factors to be looked into. Likewise there are product-wise differences in the combinations of such special factors entering into demand forecasts. For example, change in fashion is a special factor that enters into demand forecast for readymade garments and weather forecasts are significant to the producers of air coolers, rain coats, etc.

2.1.5 Steps involved in Forecasting

For an efficient demand forecast, following steps are involved:

1. **First Step: Identify the objective of forecast:** The purpose of the exercise may be estimation of one or more than one aspect – quantity and composition of demand, sales planning, price to be quoted, inventory control, etc. Thus, it is necessary to be clear about what does one want to get from the forecast.

2. **Second Step: Determining the nature of goods under consideration:** Different group of goods have their own distinctive demand patterns. Therefore, it is essential to classify them as capital goods, consumer durables and non-durables. This helps in identifying the approach of the forecasting exercise and in determining the variables to take into account in forecasting.

3. **Third Step: Selection of a proper forecasting method:** Selection of an appropriate method depends on the objective of forecasting, type of data available, period for which the forecast is to made, etc. For instance, if the data shows cyclical fluctuations then the use of linear trend will not be suitable.

4. **Fourth Step: Interpretation of results:** Forecasts alone do not have much meaning to management, interpretation is equally important. Many a times, the forecast results are to be well-supported by the background factors like government policy, general business environment, etc., which have not entered the exercise of forecasting.

To conclude, forecasts are to be revised frequently in the light of changing circumstances because forecasts are made on the assumption of continuation of past events.

2.1.6 Usefulness/Necessity of Demand Forecasting

Demand forecasts are attempted by several organisations and individuals. For instance, the industrial organisations undertake demand forecasting for their corresponding industrial products and firms in their corresponding brands. Worldwide forecasts are carried out by international organisations like United Nations Organisations, the World Bank etc.

Thus, it means that forecasting of demand by some technique or the other is highly essential. An entrepreneur can forecast on the bases of intuition or personal judgement. But, forecast based on personal judgement is a game of guesswork. In fact, the significance of the forecasting studies can hardly be exaggerated. These studies are needed to plan future production and thereby future needs for arranging various resources like manpower, raw materials and funds. And, unless the future demand is known well in advance there may not be enough time to plan and execute the production to meet that demand. Accurate demand forecasts are essential to avoid shortages (production short of demand) and excess of products (production more than demand) in the market. Both, overproduction or under-production influences the price structure of the various goods in the market.

There is no choice between forecasting and not forecasting. Because, not forecasting means that the firm assumes no change to take place in their product in this fast changing consumption habits of consumers. This is an unrealistic assumption on the part of the firm. Thus, the choice to make is in the various methods of demand forecasting rather than in the decision of whether to forecast or not to forecast.

A well-organised forecasting system may not be necessary as long as the concerned firms are small and their operations are simple. But as a business unit grows in size, in complexity and in diversity of its products and processes, forecasting becomes a specialised and a separate function of management.

Thus, we summarise the necessity of forecasting as follows:

1. **Achievement of Planned Objectives:** Every firm aims at certain pre-determined objectives. For attainment of these objectives, the firm needs a reasonably accurate forecast of future trends in the economy in general and of its sales income in particular.

2. **Preparing a Budget:** Every firm has to prepare a well conceived budget incorporating cost of production and expected earnings. The expectations of earnings must be backed by a forecast of annual sales and prices. Such a budget enables the firm to control its costs and to reduce the area of avoidable risks. Such a systematic exercise to guide the business is better than guesswork on the part of the entrepreneur.

3. **Stabilisation of Production and Employment:** Due to seasonal, cyclical and erratic changes in the economy, market demand fluctuates. However, the level of production cannot be changed every now and then. If an annual forecast of demand

is undertaken the firm can decide on the line of production planning for that coming year taking care of the seasonal variations. This policy would enable the firm to maintain a stable labour force. A stable labour force is essential as one cannot recruit or retrench work force at its will, with variations in market conditions.

4. **Future Expansion:** Every firm has to think in terms of its plans of expansion in future. It is a long-term plan that certainly is based on the demand forecast.

5. **Long-term Investment Programmes:** This plan of the firm of long-term investment is corollary to the earlier point (future expansion). Expansion plans for the future calls for long-term programme of investment and plan of future recruitment. Needless to say that investment plan is to be based on accurate demand forecasting.

6. **Sales Budgeting:** Demand forecasting is crucial for sales budgeting. It determines production and inventory plans, the level of costs and the level of employment. Sales budgets are also useful in computing standard costs, in establishing profit goals and in preparation of capital budgets, future cash flows and sources of funds. Sales forecasts and sales budget act as regulators of a firm's operations and serve to improve the quality of business decisions.

7. **Control of Inventories:** A satisfactory method of control of raw materials, semi-finished products, spare parts etc. must depend upon a satisfactory estimate of future requirements, their availability and their estimated prices.

Thus, forecasting can be of great help in introducing business discipline and scientific management.

2.1.7 Criteria for a Good Method of Demand Forecasting

There are various methods of demand forecasting. Out of these alternative methods available to a firm, it has to choose the best method. Which method would be the best? For answering the question we can outline the following criteria, which would serve as parameters for testing the various methods of demand forecasting:

1. **Plausibility:** The method of demand forecasting should be well known to the executives who are going to use it. At the same time, they should feel confident that the technique used by following any certain method will be helpful to them in formulating a particular demand forecast.

2. **Simplicity:** Various mathematical and economic models can be used with an advantage; however they are highly sophisticated and complex. Majority of these models thus, are not acceptable to small and medium-sized firms. Such models are more used by national and multi-national corporations because they can afford to have special cells for demand forecasting. Majority of the managements however require a method which is simple and easy to understand.

3. **Economical:** Techniques of demand-forecasting involve huge costs. These costs must be compared with the returns to be gained that is, to say a cost benefit analysis must be carried out. The method that yields high level of benefits but involves huge

costs may not be acceptable. In areas where accuracy is likely to bring in huge profits, the high costs of forecasting may prove to be worthwhile. Thus, economies suggest a balance of costs involved and benefits expected of the method of demand-forecasting.

4. **Accuracy:** Every firm expects its forecasting to be as accurate as possible. By accuracy, we mean closeness to reality. Some check of accuracy of past performance against the present happening and the forecast against future predictions is highly desirable. Accuracy can be increased by finding out deviations after every forecast. We must, however, remember the fact that precision would involve higher costs and would go against the criterion of economy.

5. **Availability:** The criterion of availability refers to the timely availability of the forecast as well as availability of adequate and up to date statistical data for the preparation of the forecast. To what extent is a forecast meaningful depends upon the statistical data used for the purpose of forecast. At the same time, if too much of data is collected and too much of time is spent in arriving at the forecasts, the forecasts are likely to be meaningless for decision-making. They would reach the management too late and the purpose will be defeated of forming demand on the basis of forecast.

6. **Durability:** The criterion of durability is important because a forecast prepared by incurring sizeable costs must last over a reasonable period of time. Forecasts which are based on stability of the underlying variables measured in the past and which are simple in nature are likely to be more durable.

7. **Flexibility:** A forecast should be flexible and not rigid because an element of uncertainty is always associated with business plans. A set of variables whose coefficients can be adjusted from time to time for meeting the changing conditions can prove to be a more practical way of imparting flexibility to a method of demand forecasting.

8. **Consistency:** Consistency implies that a firm's forecasts should be consistent with the forecasts at the level of the industry or on the national level. For example, forecast indicating buoyant demand for one's product would be inconsistent if the national level forecast is that of imminent depression and unemployment.

2.1.8 Determinants for Demand Forecast

(a) For Consumer Durables

The demand for consumer durables falls into two categories: replacement demand and new demand. The special peculiarities in forecasting for consumer durables are:

(i) **Changes in demographic factors:** Demand for consumer durables is closely related to the size and characteristics of population- growth rate, age and sex composition. For example, demand for toys is dependent on the birth rate in the near past. And, the number and size of households determines the demand for goods like refrigerator, television sets, etc.

(ii) **Limit of the market:** The potential market for additional units of the goods like cars, furniture becomes very limited and this demand is only replacement demand.

(iii) **Availability of the goods:** Larger the stock greater will be the amount of replacement, shorter the life of the good, earlier will be the replacement.

(iv) **Replacement and new demand:** Since replacement demand comes from those who already own the good while new demand results from the coming forward of new customers, each of these demands are determined by separate factors.

(v) **Consumers' level of income:** Larger is the possibility of increase in GNP or disposable personal income, greater will be the possibility of increase in demand. There is a close relationship between the discretionary income and demand for consumer durables. Discretionary income is defined as disposable personal income minus income tax plus temporary earnings.

(vi) **Tastes and preferences:** The knowledge of changes in consumer's tastes and preferences indicates about future trends in market demands.

(vii) **Consumer's purchasing power:** Higher the credits offered to the consumers, higher will be the demand for good. But, since he has to pay back the debt in future, it may lead to cut in the future discretionary power and reduce the demand. Hence, the forecaster tries to find out the status of consumer debt outstanding before estimating the demand for a durable consumer good.

The forecaster of consumer durables uses different techniques to determine his future level of sales. For finding out changes in consumer attitudes, credit outstanding, the forecaster has to resort to the survey of consumer plans. And, once future changes are known, then these can be fed into a regression model to get the level of future sales.

(b) For Non-durable Consumer goods

These are consumer goods which can be used only once, e.g., food, beverages, etc. Demand for such goods is influenced by factors like – purchasing power of the consumer, price of the commodity, population and its characteristics.

(i) **Disposable income (purchasing power):** Disposable income refers to personal income minus direct taxes. Economists are of the view that instead of purchasing power it is better to use discretionary income, particularly for demand for forecasts of luxuries.

(ii) **Price of the commodity:** Demand for a good depends upon its price in relation to the price of its substitutes and complements. For estimating and forecasting demand for non-durable consumer goods price elasticity and cross elasticity concepts can be used. Those non-durable consumer goods which can be stored and are independent of changes in fashion are more price elastic.

(iii) **Characteristics of population:** Demand for non-durable consumer goods are influenced by factors like total population, income groups, rural and urban ratios, level of education, etc. With the help of demographic variables, demand for each market segment can be estimated as distinct from total market demand.

(c) Capital Goods

Capital/Producer goods – factory buildings, machinery - are those goods which help in further production of goods. Capital goods have derived demand, which will depend upon the profitability, capacity utilisation, wage rates in the industry using the capital good. Further, demand for capital good is of two types – replacement demand and new demand. The forecaster can forecast the demand for any capital good in question by collecting data on factors like – the rate of obsolescence of capital good, the existing stock of capital good, availability of funds with the firm for capital goods, growth of industries using the capital goods, etc.

2.2 Methods of Demand Forecasting

The main challenge in the process of demand forecasting is to select an effective technique.

There is no full proof single method that enables organisations to anticipate risks and uncertainties of future. The method to be chosen, accuracy of the method depends upon the time frame that the firm has chosen. Generally, there are two approaches to demand forecasting.

The first approach involves collection of information regarding the buying patterns of consumers from people who are in contact with the consumers or through conducting surveys. The second method is to forecast demand by using historical and analysing it using various statistical techniques.

Thus, we can conclude that there are two techniques of demand forecasting for an organisation, those are survey method and statistical method. The survey method is generally used for forecasting demand for short-term decision-making, whereas statistical method is used to forecast demand for the long term organisation policies.

These two approaches are shown in Figure-2.1

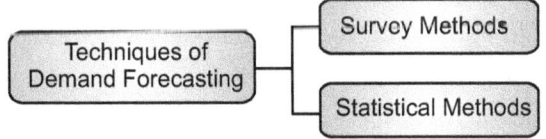

Fig. 2.1: Demand Forecasting Techniques

Let us discuss these techniques (as shown in Fig. 2.1).

2.2.1 Survey Techniques

Survey method is one of the most common methods to collect information in order to enable the firm to predict demand in the near future. This method encompasses the future buying plans of consumers and their likes and dislikes. In this method, an organisation conducts surveys with consumers to determine the demand for their existing and new products and services and this enables the firm to anticipate the demand for the existing products and the newer ones to be launched in the future. The survey method involves three exercises, which are shown in Figure 2.2

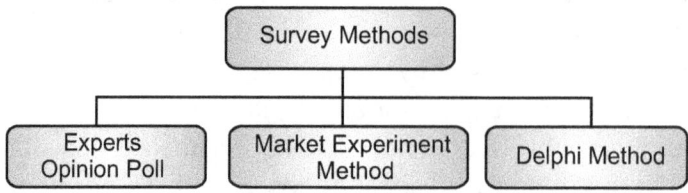

Fig. 2.2: Survey Methods

The exercises in the survey method (as shown in Fig. 2.2) are as follows:

1. Experts' Opinion Poll

The first step is that experts are requested to provide their opinion about how they perceive the product. It is most often found that sales representatives act as experts in an organisation. Since they spread across in different areas, regions, or cities and their main task is to communicate with the consumers, they can provide the latest and correct information.

They are well aware of the consumers' buying plans, their response to market change, and their perceptions for competing products in the same segment as the company concerned. They provide an estimate of the demand for the organisation's products based on the dealings with the consumers. This method is simple and does not involve much cost.

However, this approach has its own limitations, which are as follows:

(a) It provides estimates that are dependent on the marketing skills of experts and their experience. The experience and skill sets differ from individual to individual. Thus, making exact demand forecasts difficulties not possible.

(b) Opinions are based on the subjective judgment of the person, which may lead to over or under-estimation.

(c) It depends on data provided by sales representatives. At times, they may have inadequate information about the market which may result in erroneous conclusions.

(d) Ignores economic factors, such as change in Gross National Product, ease with which credit is available and the quantum of availability of credit, future prospects of the industry in which the company operates which may affect demand forecasting to a great extent.

2. Delphi Method

This method refers to a group decision-making technique of forecasting demand. In this method, questions are first asked individually to a group of experts to obtain their views on future demand for products. These questions are repeated until a consensus is obtained among the group.

In addition to this, each expert is provided information regarding the estimates made by other experts in the group in a way that the identity of the experts is kept confidential; so that he/she can revise his/her estimate with respect to others' estimates. This enables unbiased opinion and the forecasts made by the experts are cross checked.

Every expert is allowed to provide suggestions on others' estimates along with reasons for accepting/not accepting the others' opinions.

The main advantage of this method is that it is not time consuming and is also cost-effective as a number of experts are approached simultaneously and the organisation saves on other resources. However, this method may lead to subjective decision-making since personal experience and judgement is involved.

3. Market Experiment Method

It involves collecting necessary information regarding the current and future demand for a product from the market as a whole by carrying out experiments on consumers' behaviour patterns under actual market conditions. In this method, some areas of markets are selected which have similar features, such as population, income levels, cultural background, and tastes and habits of consumers.

The market experiments are carried out considering various situations like varying levels of prices and expenditure, so that the resultant changes in the demand can be recorded. These results help in forecasting future demand in a better way.

There are various limitations of this method, which are as follows:

(a) It is an expensive method; therefore, it may not be affordable by smaller organisations

(b) The results of experiments are affected due to various untimely social-economic conditions, such as strikes, political instability, natural calamities, etc

2.2.2 Statistical Methods

Statistical methods are complex set of methods to use for the purpose of demand forecasting. These methods are generally used for forecasting demand for the long-term requirements of the organisation. Demand forecasts under these methods are derived studying the past data of the organisation.

Past data can be obtained from various sources such as previous years' financial results and market survey reports of independent agencies. On the other hand, cross-sectional data is collected by conducting interviews with individuals who have been working with the organisation and performing market surveys. Statistical methods are cost-effective as compared to the survey methods and more reliable as the element of subjectivity involved is the least possible in these methods.

The different statistical methods are shown in Figure 2.3.

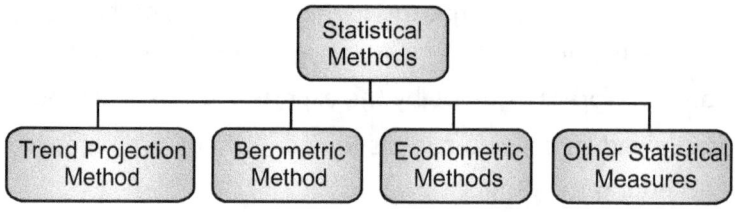

Fig. 2.3: Statistical Methods

The different statistical methods as shown in Figure-2.3 are as follows

1. Trends in Economic Data: Trend Projection Method

The trend projection method also called as the least square method is one of the most common methods of business forecasting. This method requires a large quantum of relevant and reliable data for forecasting demand. This method assumes that variables such as sales and demand that are responsible for past trends would remain the same in future that is, to say changes in economic conditions and other factors that affect the demand and sales are ignored.

As mentioned above sales forecasts are made through analysis of past data which is taken from previous year's books of accounts. In case of new organisations, sales data are taken from similar organisations operating in the same industry. This method uses sales data over a period of time (past data of a number of years) for forecasting the demand of a product.

Table 2.1 shows the time-series data of XYZ Organisation:

Time 2.1: Time Series Data on Sales of XYX Organisation

Year	Sales (in 1000 tonnes)
2006	20
2007	24
2008	22
2009	30
2010	36
2011	28
2012	40
2013	36
2014	42
2015	50

The trend projection method includes three more methods which are as follows:

(i) Graphical Method

The graphical method helps in forecasting the future sales of an organisation by plotting the relevant data on a graph and then analysing the graph. The sales data is plotted on a graph and a line is drawn on plotted points to study the pattern.

Let us learn this through a graph shown in Fig. 2.4.

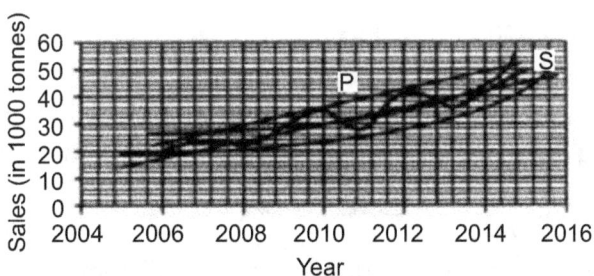

Fig. 2.4: An Example of Graphical Method

Fig 2.4 shows a curve which is plotted by taking into the account the sales data of XYZ Organisation (Table-2.1) from the year 2004 to 2016. Line P is drawn joining the mid-points of the curve and S is a straight line. These lines are extended to the right side to get the future sales for year 2016 which is approximately 47 tons. This method is very simple to implement and less expensive compared to the other methods; however, the projections made by this method may involve subjectivity on the part of the person making the forecast.

(ii) Fitting Trend Method

This implies a least square method in which a trend line (curve) is fitted to the time-series data of sales by using statistical techniques.

In this method, two types of trends are taken into account which is as follows:

(a) Linear Trend

It means a trend in which sales show a rising trend.

In a linear trend, the following straight line trend equation is fitted:

$$S = A + BT$$

Where,

$$S = \text{Annual sales}$$
$$T = \text{Time (in years)}$$

A and B are constant

B gives the measure of annual increase in sales

(b) Exponential Trend

An exponential trend is a trend in which sales increase over the past years at an increasing rate or constant rate.

The appropriate trend equation used is as follows:

$$Y = aT^b$$

Where,

$$Y = \text{Annual sales}$$
$$T = \text{Time in years}$$

a and b are constant

Using logarithm, the equation would be:

$$\text{Log } Y = \text{Log } a + b \text{ Log } T$$

The main advantage of this method is that it is simple to understand and implement. Moreover, the data required by this method is very limited (as only sales data is required). Owing to the above it is a less costly method However, this method also has some limitations which are as follows:

- It assumes that the past rate of changes in variables will remain same in future. In reality this is not true.
- This method fails to be applied for short-term forecasts and forecasts where the trend is cyclical with a lot of fluctuations.
- It fails to measure the relationship between dependent and independent variables.

(iii) Box-Jenkins Method

It refers to a method that is used only for forecasts for the short-term. This method forecasts demand on the basis of time-series data that does not show the long-term trend. It is used in those circumstances where the time series data shows periodical or seasonal variations with some degrees of regularity. For example, this method can be used for estimating the sales estimates of woollen clothes during the winter season.

2. Barometric Method

In barometric method, demand is estimated on the basis of past events or key variables that occur in the present. Another application of this method is to predict various economic indicators, such as saving, investment, and income. The Barometric method was introduced by Harvard Economic Service in 1920 and it was further revised by National Bureau of Economic Research (NBER) in 1930s.

This method enables one to determine the general trend of business activities. Let's assume that government allots land to XYZ society for constructing buildings. This implies that there would be a high demand for construction material like cement, bricks and steel.

The main advantage of this method is that it can be applied even without the availability of past data. However, this method cannot be applied in case of new products and in cases where there is no time lag between economic indicators and demand.

3. Econometric Methods

Econometric methods are a combination of statistical tools and economic theories of demand forecasting. The forecasts made with the help of this method are more reliable in comparison to the other methods. An econometric model consists of two types of methods which are regression method and simultaneous equations method.

These two types of methods are explained below:

(i) Regression Method

The regression method is referred to as the most popular method of demand forecasting. In this method, the demand function for a product is derived, where demand is the dependent variable and variables that determine the demand are independent variables.

If demand is affected by one variable only, then it is called single variable demand function. In this case, simple regression techniques are used. In a case where demand is affected by more than one variable, it is called a multi-variable demand function. Therefore, in such a case, multiple regressions are used.

The simple and multiple regression techniques are discussed as follows:

(a) Simple Regression

It refers to the study of relationship between two variables where one variable is independent and the other is dependent.

The equation to calculate simple regression is as follows:

$$Y = a + bx$$

Where,

$$Y = \text{Estimated value of Y for a given value of X}$$

$$b = \text{Amount of change in Y produced by a unit change in X}$$

$$a \text{ and } b = \text{Constants}$$

The equations to calculate a and b are as follows:

$$a = Y - bX$$

$$b = \frac{\Sigma x_i y_i}{\Sigma x_2}$$

$$\Sigma x_i y_i = \Sigma X_i Y_i - nXY$$

Now let us learn how to calculate simple regression with the help of an example. Suppose a researcher wants to study the relationship between the employee (sales group) satisfaction and sales of an organisation. For this purpose He/she has taken the feedback from the employees in the form of a questionnaire and has asked them to rate their satisfaction level on a 10-pointer scale where 10 is the highest and 1 is the lowest. The researcher has taken the sales data for every member of the sales team. He/she has taken the average of monthly sales for a year for a member.

The collected data is arranged in Table 2.2.

Table 2.2: Data to Calculate Simple Regression

Number of Observations	Employee Satisfaction (X_i)	Sales (in Lakhs), Y_i	X_i^2	X_iY_i
1	2	2	4	4
2	4	3	16	12
3	5	6	25	30
4	7	8	49	56
5	8	6	64	48
6	10	9	100	90
7	9	10	81	90
8	3	2	9	6
9	1	3	1	3
10	2	4	4	8
11	4	5	16	20
12	6	8	36	48
13	8	9	64	72
14	10	11	100	110
15	4	5	16	20
16	7	12	49	84
17	9	13	81	135
18	5	6	25	30
19	8	16	64	128
20	9	20	81	180
21	10	20	100	200
22	7	6	49	42
23	6	5	36	30
24	8	14	64	112
25	9	19	81	171
Total	161	224	1215	1729

The calculation of mean for employee satisfaction (X) and sales (Y) is as follows:

$$\text{Mean for X} = \frac{\Sigma X_i}{n}$$

$$\text{Mean for Y} = \frac{\Sigma Y_i}{n}$$

$$X = 6.44 \quad Y = 8.96$$

Following equation is used to calculate the value of b:

$$\Sigma x_i^2 = \Sigma X_i^2 - nX_2$$
$$\Sigma x_i y_i = \Sigma X_i Y_i - nXY$$

Calculation of the value of b for the above data is as follows:

$$\Sigma x_i^2 = \Sigma X_i^2 - nX_2$$
$$\Sigma x_i^2 = 1215 - 25 \times 6.44 \times 6.44$$
$$\Sigma x_i^2 = 178.16$$
$$\Sigma x_i y_i = \Sigma X_i Y_i - nXY$$
$$\Sigma x_i y_i = 1729 - 25 \times 6.44 \times 8.96$$
$$\Sigma x_i y_i = 286.44$$

$$b = \frac{\Sigma x_i y_i}{\Sigma x_i^2}$$

$$b = \frac{286.44}{178.16}$$

$$b = 1.61$$
$$a = Y - bX$$
$$a = 8.96 - 1.61 \times 6.44$$
$$a = -1.39$$
$$Y = a + bX$$
$$Y = -1.39 + 1.61X$$

The equation obtained above is the regression equation in which the researcher can substitute any value of X to find the corresponding value of Y.

For example, if the value of X is 9, then the value of Y would be calculated as follows:

$$Y = -1.39 + 1.61X$$
$$Y = -1.39 + 1.61(9)$$
$$Y = 13.1$$

With the help of above example, it can be inferred that if an employee is satisfied, then his/her output would increase.

(b) Multiple Regressions

This refers to study of the relationship between more than one independent and dependent variables.

Where there are two independent variables and one dependent variable, the following equation is used to calculate multiple regressions:

$$Y = a + b_1 X_1 + b_2 X_2$$

Where,

$$Y \text{ (Dependent variable)} = \text{Estimated value of Y for a given value of } X_1 \text{ and } X_1$$
$$X_1 \text{ and } X_2 = \text{Independent variables}$$
$$b_1 = \text{Amount of change in Y produced by a unit change in} X_1$$

b_2 = Amount of change in Y produced by a unit change in X_2

a, b_1 and b_2 = Constants

The equations used to calculate a and b values are as follows:

$$\Sigma Y_i = na + b_1 \Sigma X_i^1 + b_2 \Sigma X_i^2$$

$$\Sigma Y_i^1 Y_i = a \Sigma X_i^1 + b_1 \Sigma X_{1i}^2 + b_2 \Sigma X_i^2 X_i^2$$

$$\Sigma X_i^2 Y_i = a \Sigma X_i^2 + b_1 \Sigma X_i^1 X_i^2 + b_2 \Sigma X_{2i}^2$$

The number of equations depends on the number of independent variables that are being considered. If there are two independent variables, then there would be three equations and so on.

Now let us learn how to calculate multiple regression with the help of an example. Suppose the researcher wants to study the relationship between intermediate percentage, graduation percentage, and MAT percentile scored by a group of 25 students.

It is pertinent to note that intermediate percentage and graduation percentage are independent variables and MAT percentile is dependent variable. The researcher wants to find out whether the percentile in MAT scored by a student depends on the student's intermediate percentage and graduation percentage or not.

The collected data is shown in Table 2.3.

Table 2.3: Data to Calculate Multiple Regression

Number of observation	Intermediate percentage (X_i^1)	Graduation percentage (X_i^2)	MAT percentile (Y_i)
1	60	72	78
2	61	75	75
3	63	78	80
4	66	80	85
5	70	85	84
6	72	86	82
7	74	84	80
8	75	89	81
9	67	90	92
10	69	75	93
11	68	74	96
12	65	72	86
13	64	71	87
14	63	70	88
15	62	86	85
16	79	85	94

Number of observation	Intermediate percentage (X_i^1)	Graduation percentage (X_i^2)	MAT percentile (Y_i)
17	80	89	96
18	84	90	96
19	95	91	98
20	75	88	99
21	92	94	86
22	86	86	85
23	81	94	98
24	85	99	99
25	95	99	99
Total	$\Sigma X_i^1 = 1851$	$\Sigma X_i^2 = 2012$	$\Sigma Y_i = 2223$

The equations required to calculate multiple regression are as follows:

$$\Sigma Y_i = na + b_1\Sigma X_i^1 + b_2\Sigma X_i^2$$

$$\Sigma X_i^1 Y_i = a\Sigma_i^1 + b_1\Sigma X_{1i}^2 + b_2 X_i^1 X_i^2$$

$$\Sigma X_i^2 Y_i = a\Sigma X_i^2 + b_1\Sigma X_i^1 X_i^2 + b_2\Sigma X_{2i}^2$$

These equations are used to solve the multiple regression equation manually. However, you can also use SPSS (statistics software) to find out multiple regression.

If we use SPSS in the above example, we would get the output shown in Table 2.4.

Table 2.4: Summary of Variables used in Multiple Regression Analysis

Variables Entered/Removed			
Model	Variables Entered	Variables Removed	Method
1	Graduation, intermediate		Enter

a.   All requested variables entered.

Table 2.5: Summary of Regression Method

Model Summary		
R Square	Adjusted R Square	Standard Error of the Estimate
0.965	0.962	1.96938

a.   Predicators: (Constant), graduation, intermediate.

Table 2.5 shows the summary of the result obtained by using the regression model. In this table, R is the correlation coefficient of the independent and dependent variables, which is very high in our case. Standard error of estimate is quite low that is 1.97. It also indicates that the variation in the present data is less.

Table 2.6 shows the coefficients of regression model.

Table 2.6: Coefficients of Linear Regression Analysis

Coefficients*				
Unstandardised Coefficients		Standardized Coefficients	T	Sigma
B	Standard Error	Beta		
55.704	12.771		4.362	0.000
0.352	0.201	0.506	1.753	0.093
0.085	0.250	0.098	0.340	0.737
a. Dependent Variable: MAT				

Table 2.6 shows that the calculated t value is greater than the significance t value. Thus, a cause and effect relationship is shown by the coefficients between the independent and dependent variables.

Table 2.7 shows the AN OVA table for the two variables under study.

Table 2.7: Variation Analysis of Linear Regression

ANNOVA[b]		Sum of Squares	df	Mean Square	F	Sigma
Model						
1	Regression	2332.514	2	1166.257	300.702	0.000[a]
	Residual	85.326	22	3.3878		
	Total	2417.840	24			
a. Predictors: (Constant, graduation, intermediate).						
b. Dependent Variable: MAT.						

Table 2.7 shows the analysis of variation in the model. The regression row shows the variation that has occurred due to the regression model. However, the residual row shows the variation that occurred by chance and not due to a reason. In Table 2.7, the value of sum of squares for regression row is greater than the sum of squares for the residual row this shows that most of the variations are produced only due to the model.

The calculated **F value** is very large as compared to the significance value. We can thus say that the intermediate percentage and graduation percentage of a student have a strong effect on the MAT percentile scored by the student.

(ii) Simultaneous Equations

This involves solving several simultaneous equations.

Two types of variables are considered in this model, which are as under:

(a) Endogenous Variables

These variables refer to inputs that are determined within the model. They are controlled variables.

(b) Exogenous Variables

These refer to inputs that are determined outside the model. Examples of exogenous variables are time, government spending and weather conditions..

In order to develop a complete model, first and foremost endogenous and exogenous variables are determined. After that, necessary data related to both the variables is collected. Sometimes, the data is not available in required form, which requires us to present the data as required by the model. After developing the necessary data as per the requirements of the model, equations are derived. Lastly, the equations are solved for each endogenous variable in terms of exogenous variable. The solution is finally attained.

1. Other Statistical Measures

Apart from the above mentioned statistical methods, there are other methods that can be used for demand forecasting. These methods are very specific and used only in particular conditions for particular datasets. Therefore, their usage cannot be generalised for all types of data.

These measures are shown in Fig. 2.5.

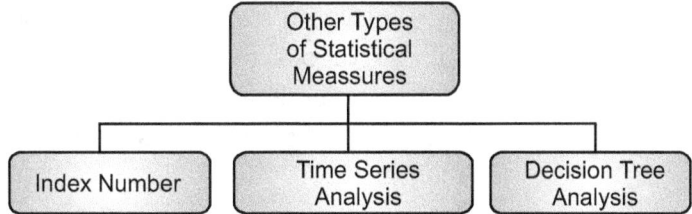

Fig. 2.5: Different Types of Statistical Measures

The different types of statistical methods (as shown in Figure 2.5) are discussed as follows:

(i) Index Number

This refers to the measures used to study the fluctuations in a variable or group of related variables in a particular period with reference to a base period. Index numbers are most commonly used in economics and financial research to study various factors, such as price and quantity of a product, inflation and other economic research.

There are mainly four types of index numbers, which are as follows:

- **(a) Simple index number:** This index number measures a relative change in a single variable with respect to the base year.
- **(b) Composite index number:** Composite index number measures a relative change in a group of related variables with respect to the base year.
- **(c) Price index number:** This index number shows a relative change in the price of a commodity in different time periods under consideration.
- **(d) Quantity index number:** This refers to the index number that measures a relative change in the physical quantity of goods produced, consumed or sold for a particular commodity in different time periods.

(ii) Time Series Analysis

Time series analysis is the analysis of a series of observations collected over a period of equally spaced time intervals. An example of time series is analysing the growth of a company from its incorporation to the current position. This analysis is applicable and useful in various fields such as public sector companies, economics and research related projects.

Time series analysis can be done in various aspects, which are as under:

(a) **Secular Trend:** This trend is denoted by T and is prevalent over a long period of time. Secular trend for a series of data can be in either direction, upward or downward. The upward trend shows the increase in a variable, for example, increase in prices of products; whereas, the downward trend shows the declining phases in a product's cycle, for example, decline in the sales for a particular product.

(b) **Short Time Oscillation:** This trend remains for a comparatively shorter period of time.

This trend can be classified into the following three types:

- **Seasonal trend:**

  The seasonal trend is denoted by S and occurs year after year for a particular time period (say a particular month(s)). The various reasons for such trends are weather conditions, festivals and other customs. Some examples of seasonal trend are the increase in the sale for sweaters in winters, increase in demand for sweets during various festivals.

- **Cyclical Trend:**

  Cyclical trends last for a longer period of time usually for more than a year and it is denoted by C. They are neither continuous nor seasonal in nature i.e. they do not reoccur periodically. An example of cyclical trend is a business cycle (boom and recession).

- **Irregular trend**

  As the name suggests irregular trends refer to trends that are unpredictable in their occurrence and it is denoted by I. Some examples of irregular trends are natural calamities like earthquakes, volcano eruptions, floods, etc.

(iii) Decision Tree Analysis

In the decision tree analysis, a tree-type structure is drawn which considers various solutions and their probabilities of occurrence to decide the best solution for a problem. In this analysis, we first find out different solutions/alternatives that can be used to solve a particular problem.

After that, we can find out the outcome of each option as to whether it is feasible or not. The options/decisions are depicted with a square node while the outcomes are demonstrated with a circle node. The decision tree is drawn from left to right.

The shape of the decision tree is shown in Figure 2.6

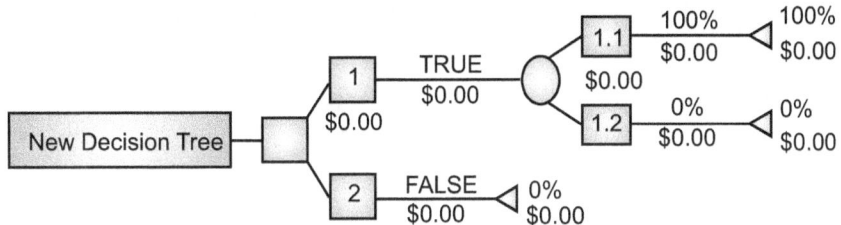

Fig. 2.6: Format of Decision Tree Analysis

Now let us understand the use of a decision tree with the help of an example. Suppose an organisation wants to choose a segment to increase the customer base.

This problem can be solved by using the decision tree shown in Fig. 2.7

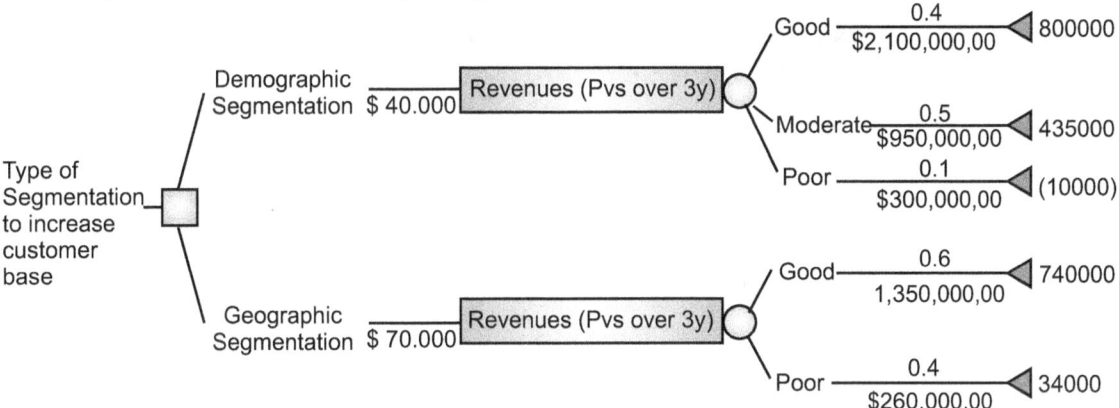

Fig. 2.7: Showing an Example of Decision Tree

In Fig. 2.7, the decision tree shows two types of segments, demographic segmentation and geographical segmentation. To analyse the outcome of the demographic segmentation, the company has to incur $40,000 (estimated cost). The outcome of the demographic segmentation can be good, moderate and poor with possibilities of 0.4, 0.5, and 0.1 respectively.

The estimated revenue projected for the three options (good, moderate, and poor) is as follows:

$$Good = \$\ 21500000$$

$$Moderate = \$\ 950000$$

$$Poor = S300000$$

Now, we calculate the outcomes of demographic segmentation in the following manner:

$$Good = 0.4*2100000 = 840000$$

$$Moderate = 0.5*950000 = 475000$$

$$Poor = 0.1*300000 = 30000$$

Similarly, in case of geographical segmentation, the cost incurred is $70000 (estimated cost). The outcome of the geographical segmentation can be either good or poor with probabilities of 0.6 and 0.4 respectively.

The estimated revenue projected for three years for the two options (good and poor) are as follows:

$$Good = \$\,1350000$$

$$Poor = \$\,260000$$

Now, we calculate the outcomes of geographical segmentation in the following manner:

$$Good = 0.6 \times 1350000 = \$\,810000$$

$$Poor = 0.4 \times 260000 = \$\,104000$$

Now, we would analyse the two outcomes for taking a decision to select one segment out of the two segments in the following manner:

For demographic segmentation:

$$Good = 840000 - 40000 = \$\,800000$$

$$Moderate = 475000 - 40000 = \$\,435000$$

$$Poor = 30000 - 40000 = \$\,(10000)$$

Similarly, for geographical segmentation:

$$Good = 810000 - 70000 = \$\,740000$$

$$Poor = 104000 - 70000 = \$\,340000$$

As we can see from the above calculation, if we select the demographic segmentation, then the maximum estimated profit that can be achieved is $800000. In demographic segmentation, there is a probability of incurring losses ($10,000), if the product is not successful in the market.

If we select geographical segmentation, then the maximum achievable profit is $ 740000. In geographical segmentation, we would earn less profit ($ 340000) if the product is not successful in the market. Therefore, it is better to use geographical segmentation for marketing the product, since there is no possibility of loss in either possibilities.

2.3 Reliability of Demand Forecasting

Understanding and predicting customer demand is of vital importance for the organisation in order to avoid stock-outs and maintain adequate inventory levels at all times. By nature, forecasts are never perfect; however, they are necessary to estimate the demand and prepare the organisation to respond to the demand. In order to maintain an optimum inventory level and an uninterrupted supply, accurate and reliable demand forecasts are imperative.

In order to succeed, it is necessary to make a reliable demand forecast for which a joint effort among the customers, suppliers, and internal company stakeholders is required. It must be continuously monitored and modified appropriately in order to align with both business strategy and customer preference. Demand forecast should be prominently displayed and discussed with appropriate levels in the organisation and the stakeholders and should not be sheltered or hidden from view.

There are three key steps to develop a reliable demand forecast:

1. **Understand — really understand — historic demand**

Historical demand patterns should not only be reviewed but a careful analysis must be done in order to identify drivers that influence the demand. For example, spikes in demand the result of one-time events such as a price adjustment, a successful marketing campaign, or the acquisition of several new customers. What are the factors that result in the occurrence of these events and under what circumstances might they be replicated?

2. **Monitor market trends**

Decisions should be taken on the basis of a thorough analysis of the market dynamics. This can be done through continuous communication with customers, bankers, and other individuals who are attuned to your marketplace.

The organisation must maintain a close contact with its customers, and obtain feedback at appropriate intervals of time. This habit, although time-consuming, has been the backbone of success in forecasting demand for most of the organisations.

3. **Identify and track key indicators**

What are the leading indicators of fluctuation in your customers' demand patterns? For example, if you are selling fishing poles, your key indicators of demand might include the obvious, such as water levels, fish population, and weather patterns across your sales regions. More importantly, however, you will want to consider demographics. Consider for a moment that as the baby-boomer generation transitions into retirement, it will have more time available for hobbies such as fishing, possibly increasing your sales. Maintaining a view of the changing demographics in your sales regions can create a good window into your future demand.

Points to Remember

- Predictions of future demand for a firm's product or products are known as demand forecasts.
- Steps involved in forecasting
    1. Identify the objective of forecast
    2. Determining the nature of goods under consideration
    3. Selection of a proper forecasting method
    4. Interpretation of results

- Necessity of Demand Forecasting

    1. Achievement of Planned Objectives

    2. Preparing a Budget

    3. Stabilisation of Production and Employment

    4. Future Expansion

    5. Long-term Investment Programmes

    6. Sales Budgeting

    7. Control of Inventories

- Criteria for a Good Method of Demand Forecasting

    1. Plausibility

    2. Simplicity

    3. Economical

    4. Accuracy

    5. Availability

    6. Durability

    7. Flexibility

    8. Consistency

- In survey method, an organisation conducts surveys with consumers to determine the demand for their existing and new products and services and this enables the firm to anticipate the demand for the existing products and the newer ones to be launched in the future.

- In Delphi method, questions are first asked individually to a group of experts to obtain their views on future demand for products. These questions are repeated until a consensus is obtained among the group.

- Market Experiment Method involves collecting necessary information regarding the current and future demand for a product from the market as a whole by carrying out experiments on consumers' behaviour patterns under actual market conditions.

- Demand forecasts under statistical methods are derived studying the past data of the organisation.

- Trend projection method uses sales data over a period of time (past data of a number of years) for forecasting the demand of a product.

- In barometric method, demand is estimated on the basis of past events or key variables that occur in the present.

- In regression method, the demand function for a product is derived, where demand is the dependent variable and variables that determine the demand are independent variables.

- Index Number refers to the measures used to study the fluctuations in a variable or group of related variables in a particular period with reference to a base period.

- Time series analysis is the analysis of a series of observations collected over a period of equally spaced time intervals.

Questions of Discussion

1. Discuss the different types of demand forecasting.
2. Mention the scope of demand forecasting.
3. Write a short note on regression analysis.

Chapter 3...

Production Function and Cost Function

Contents ...

Learning Objectives ...

➢   To understand the concept of short-run and long-run production function
➢   To elaborate the concept of short-run and long-run cost function
➢   To learn the relationship between production function and cost function

3.1 Production Function

3.1.1 Meaning

Identical to the demand theory that spins around the idea of the demand function, the theory of production rotates around the idea of the production function. A production function is an equation, table or graph presenting the highest amount of a commodity that a company can produce from a particular set of inputs throughout a period of time.

The idea of production function describes the ways in which the factors of production are joined by a company to produce different levels of output. More importantly, it shows the highest volume of physical output available from a particular set of inputs or the smallest set of inputs necessary to produce any given level of output.

The production function includes an engineering or technical relation, because the relation between inputs and outputs is a technical one. The production function is decided by a particular state of technology. When the technology expands the production function changes, because the new production function can get bigger output from the given inputs or smaller inputs which is sufficient to produce a given level of output. Further, the production function integrates the idea of efficiency. Thus, production function is not any relation between inputs and outputs, but a relation in which a particular set of inputs creates a maximum output. So, the production function includes all the technical methods of producing an output.

A method or process of production is a mixture of inputs needed for the production of output. A method of production is technically efficient to other ways if it uses one factor less and no more of the other factors as evaluated with another method.

Example: Technically Efficient Method of Production

Presume that commodity X is formed by two methods by using labour and capital.

Factor inputs	Method A	Method B
Labour	3	4
Capital	4	4

In the given example, method B is ineffective compared to method A because method B uses more of labour and the same quantity of capital as compared to method A. A profit maximising company will not be interested in inefficient methods of production. If method A uses less of one factor and more of the other factor as compared with any other method C, then method A and C are indirectly similar, For example, presume that a commodity is created by two methods.

Factor Inputs	Method A	Method C
Labour	3	2
Capital	4	5

In the given example, both methods A and C are technically efficient and are taken in the production function, which would be chosen depends on the prices of factors – The choice of any particular technique from a set of technically efficient techniques is an economic one, based on prices and not a technical one.

In a production function, the dependent variable is the output and the independent variables are the inputs. So, the production function can be stated as

$$Q = f (N, L, K, E, T)$$

Where, Q = Quantity Produced, N = Natural resources, L = Labour, K = Capital, E = Entrepreneur or organiser and T = Technology.

In a production function, only the inputs of labour and capital are considered independent variables. Usually, land is not included in the production function openly because of the implied assumption that land does not enforce any limitation on production. Still, labour and capital enter production explicitly. A simple condition of a production function is

$$Q = f(L, K)$$

Where Q, is the output, L and K are the quantities of labour and capital and f shows the functional relation between the inputs and output, the production function is based on an implied assumption that the technology is given. This is because an improvement in technical knowledge will lead to larger output from the use of same quantity of inputs.

3.1.2 Uses of Production Function

The production function can have various uses. It can be used to calculate the least-cost factor mixture for a given output or the highest output combination for a particular cost. Knowledge of production function is helpful in deciding the value of making use of a variable factor in the production process. Providing the marginal revenue productivity of a variable factor goes beyond its price, it will be profitable to increase its use. When the marginal revenue productivity of the factor becomes the same as its price then the additional employment of the factor is stopped. Since, the production function indicates the income to its scale thus it helps in the decision-making. If the proceeds to its scale are diminishing, then it is worthwhile to increase the production. The reverse is true if the returns to scale are increasing.

3.1.3 Types of Production Function

Production functions are of two different forms.
- The fixed proportion production function
- The variable proportion production function

These are explained as follows.

1. Fixed Proportion Production Function

A fixed proportion production function is one in which the technology needs a fixed combination of inputs, say capital and labour, to produce a particular level of output. There is a way in which the factors are combined to produce a particular level of output efficiently. In this type of production, there is no prospect of substitution between the factors of production.

The fixed proportion production function is shown by isoquants which are 'L' shaped or 'right angle' shaped. This is given in Fig. 3.1 below.

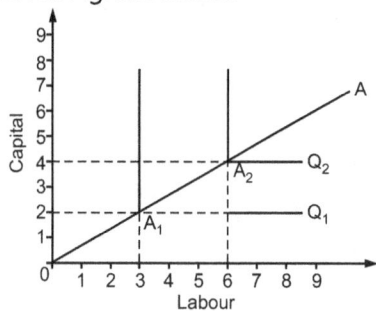

Fig. 3.1: Fixed Proportion Production Function

Presume that at point A, the output is one unit. The isoquant Q_1 passing through the point A_1 indicates that one unit of output is produced by using 2 units of capital and 3 units of labour. In other words, the capital-labour proportion is 2:3. In this case with 2 units of capital, any rise in labour further than 3 units will not increase output and, so, labour beyond 3 units is superfluous. Likewise, with 3 units of labour, any rise in capital beyond 2 units is superfluous. The twisted point indicates the most proficient mixture of factors. The capital labour ratio is maintained for any level of output. The output is doubled by doubling the quantity of inputs, that is, two units of output can be produced by 4 units of capital and 6 units of labour. Thus isoquant Q_2 moves through the point A_2. The line OA explains a production process, that is, a method of mixing inputs to get certain output, the slope of the line shows the capital-labour ratio.

The fixed proportion production function is featured by constant returns to scale, that is, a proportionate rise in inputs guides to a proportionate rise in outputs. These types of production functions give the basis for the input – output analysis in economics. So, this type of isoquant is also called input-output isoquant or "Leontief" isoquant after Leontief who invented the input-output analysis.

2. Variable Proportions Production Function

The variable proportion production function is the most well-known production function. Over here, a given level of output is produced by several alternative mixtures of factors of production, say capital and labour. It is understood that the factors are combined in endless number of ways. The common level of output got from the alternative combinations of capital and labour is given by an isoquant Q in Fig. 3.2 given below.

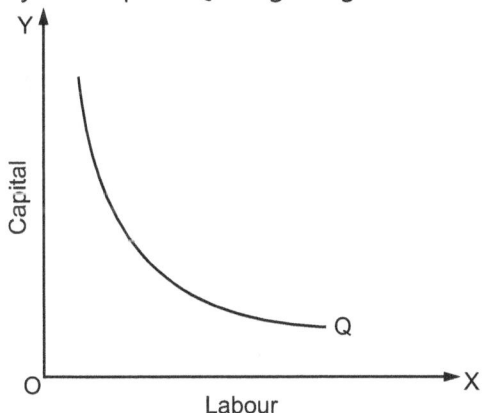

Fig. 3.2: Variable Proportions Production Function

The isoquant Q is the centre of efficient points of factor mixtures to create a given level of output. The isoquant is constant, even and convex to the origin. It assumes constant substitutability of capital and labour over a definite range, further than which factors cannot substitute each other.

Since the variable proportions production function is the most common given below is the detailed isoquant which is representing the variable proportions production function.

3.1.4 Short Run and Long Run Production Function

The discussion of production has paid no attention to the time required to build production facilities. It is important to consider the time factor in the aspects of production. Thus, in this section the behaviour of production is considered in the short run and long run.

The short run is a time in which the organisation can change variable factors such as supplies and labour after production but cannot change fixed factors such as capital. The long run is a time sufficiently long so that all factors together with capital can be altered.

The factors which increase in the short run are called variable factors, since they are easily changed in a short period of time. Hence, the level of production can be raised within the limits of obtainable plant capacity throughout the short run. So, the short run production function demonstrates that in the short run the output can be improved by changing the variable factors and keeping the fixed factors stable. In other words, in the short run the output is created with a particular scale of production, that is, with a given size of plant. The behaviour of production in the short-run where the output can be raised by increasing one variable factor keeping other factors fixed is called **law of variable proportions**.

The dimensions of plant are diverse in the long run and, therefore, the scale of production can be varied in the long run. The long-run analysis of the laws of production is referred to as **laws of returns to scale**.

3.1.5 Law of Variable Proportion

The Law of Variable Proportions appeared in economic theory as the Law of Diminishing returns. It is the theory of production when only one input is variable. Thus, we are in the short-run. The Law of Variable Proportion is one of the fundamental laws of economics. It has also been called as the Law of Diminishing Marginal Returns or Law of Diminishing Marginal Productivity.

Law of Eventually Diminishing Returns: The point worth noting is that the law does not state that each and every increase in the amount of variable factor employed in the production process will yield diminishing marginal returns.

It is possible that initial increase in the amount of variable factor employed in the production process may yield *increasing marginal returns*. However, in continuously increasing the amount of the variable factor employed, a point will be reached where the marginal increases in the total output will begin to decline or *marginal returns will begin declining*.

One Factor Fixed and Other Variable

Law of variable proportion shows the input-output relationship or production function with one factor variable while other factors of production are kept constant.

Suppose a farmer has 10 acres of land to cultivate. The land has some fixed investment, capital, such as tube well, farm machinery. The amount of land and capital is supposed as fixed factor of production. However, the farmer can vary the number of labour working on the farm. Hence, labour is the variable factor of production to bring about any change in the output.

Table 3.1: Shows the Law of Variable Proportion; in which one factor is variable (labour) and two factors (land and capital) are fixed

Number of workers	Total Product (TP) (Quintals)	Average Product (AP) (Quintals)	Marginal Product (MP) (Quintals)	
1	10	10	10	Stage
2	22	11	12	I
3	36	12	14	Increase
4	48	12	12	
5	55	11	7	Stage II
6	60	10	5	(Decrease)
7	63	09	3	
8	63	7.8	0	Zero
9	54	06	−9	Negative

Three Stages of Production: (Average & Marginal Relations):

Table 3.1 given above exhibits the typical relationship between the average and marginal product.

(i)   So long as the marginal product exceeds average product (MP > AP), see column of AP and MP (up to 3rd worker), average product will increase and *marginal product will be **higher** than the average product.*

(ii) *Marginal product **equals** average product* when average product is at its maximum (at 4th worker). MP = AP.

(iii) *Marginal product will be **less** than average product* when average product begins to decline (from 5th worker) that is, MP < AP.

(iv) Total Product is at its maximum when marginal product is zero.

Diagrammatic Illustration

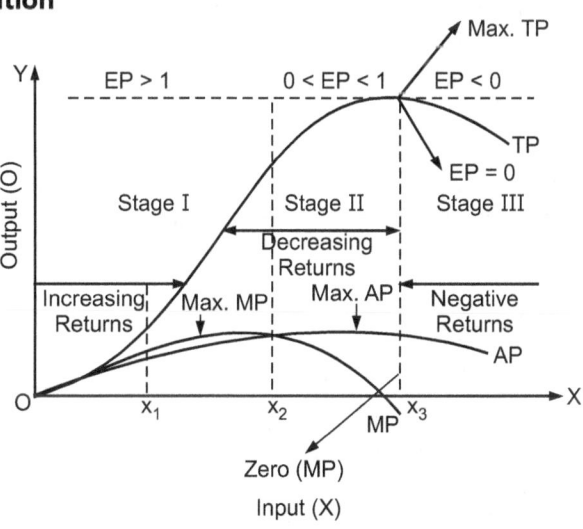

Fig. 3.3: Three Stages of Production

The total, marginal and average physical product (TPP, MPP, and APP) curves demonstrate the law of variable proportions.

The behaviour of TPP, MPP and APP during three stages of production:

Stage I

- From the origin to point X_2 it is the segment of Stage I.
- At point X_2 the marginal product of X equals its average product and average product is at its maximum.
- The production function is characterised by increasing marginal returns to the variable factor from the origin to point X_1 and then by diminishing marginal returns from X_1 to X_2.
- Stage I should not be identified only with increasing marginal returns as thereafter diminishing returns take place.

Stage II

- The second stage lies in the range from X_2 to X_3.
- Stage II begins where the AP of the variable factor is at its maximum and continues to the point at which TP is maximised and MP is zero.
- This stage is characterised by diminishing returns to the variable input over its entire range.
- Although TP is still increasing but increases at its diminishing rate.

Stage III

- Stage III is the segment beyond X_3, where TP curve starts declining.
- Here, MP of the variable factor is negative.

Which stage is Rational?

Only Stage II is a rational stage for the producer, which means relevant stage for a rational firm to operate. No firm will choose to operate either in stage I or stage III. In Stage I, it is profitable for the firm to keep on increasing the use of labour and in Stage III, MP is negative and hence not economic viable to use additional labour. Therefore, the firm has a strong incentive to expand through Stage I into Stage II.

A manager of any firm would consider Stage I and III as irrational because if it has to maximise profits then knowingly the firm will not apply the variable to the fixed factors in any combination which will yield a total product falling in either of these two stages. In stage I, the firm has scope of combining variable to the fixed factor and maximise its total product. While, in Stage III, the firm will not try to extend beyond the point of optimum utilisation of variable to the fixed factors.

Assumptions

The Law of Variable Proportion is based on following assumptions:

1. **State of technology to remain the same:** If technology changes, marginal and average product may rise instead of diminishing.
2. **Short-Run:** The law refers to the short-run time period in which at least one factor is fixed and others are variable. In the long-run all factors are variable and hence there is variation in the production function.

3. **Homogeneity in Inputs:** The variable inputs as applied by the economic unit are homogenous or identical in amount and quality.

4. **Divisibility:** It is possible to use various amounts of a variable factor on the fixed factors of production.

3.1.6 Law of Returns to Scale

Two features of production function which is important to understand are that *'the laws of returns' or returns to an input are not to be confused with 'returns to scale'*. Returns to scale refer to the behaviour of production or returns when all the factors of production are increased or decreased simultaneously in the same proportion. Thus, it refers to the behaviour of output in response to a change in the scale of production. Returns to an input describe what happens to output as only one input is varied, holding all others constant. Again, these returns may be increasing, diminishing or constant.

Thus, a closely related question in production economics is how a proportionate increase in all the input factors will affect total production. It is a question related to returns to scale and there are three possible situations in total production due to proportionate increase in all the input factors. Returns to scale may be constant, increasing or decreasing.

If we increase all factors, that is, scale in a given proportion and output increases in the same proportion, returns to scale are said to be constant. For example, if a simultaneous doubling or trebling of all inputs result in doubling or trebling of output, then returns to scale are constant. Fig. 3.4 (a).

If the increase in all factors leads to *more than* proportionate increase in output, returns to scale are said to be *increasing*. Fig. 3.4 (b).

If the increase in all factors leads to *less than* a proportionate increase in output, returns to scale are *decreasing*. Fig. 3.4 (c).

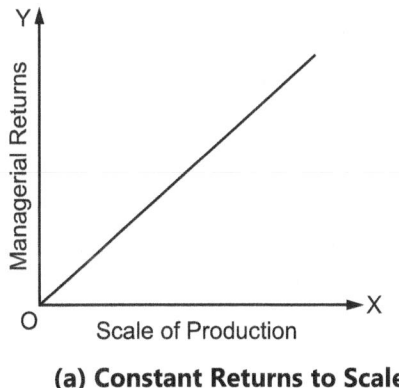

(a) Constant Returns to Scale

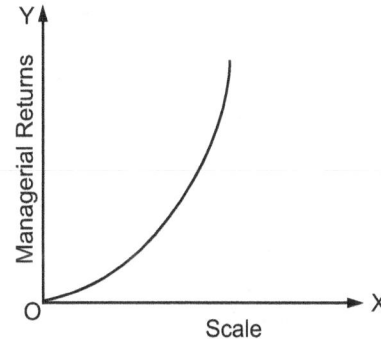

(b) Increasing Returns to Scale

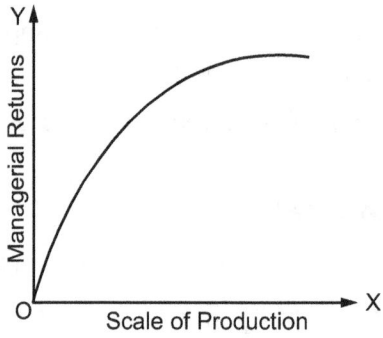

(c) Decreasing Returns to Scale

Fig. 3.4

Fig. 3.5 shows the most typical situation of a production function which increases first and then decreases. The increasing returns to scale are attributable to specialisation due to division of labour, efficient, large-scale machinery can be employed in the production process. However, beyond a point of production operation not only are further gains from specialisation limited, but also co-ordination problems may begin to increase costs to a great extent. Some economists are of the view that an entrepreneur is a fixed factor of production, while other inputs may be increased, he cannot be. On this view, diminishing returns beyond a point results because the variable quantities of all other inputs are combined with a fixed entrepreneur. Thus, when co-ordination costs offset additional benefits of specialisation, decreasing returns to scale begins.

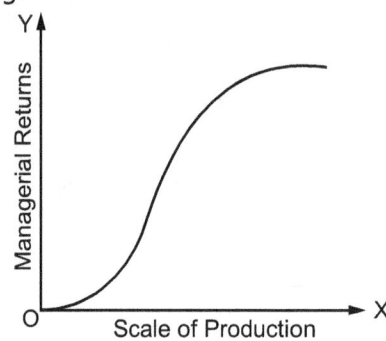

Fig. 3.5: Typical Production Function

Significance of Returns to Scale Concept

This concept has a great importance in the theory of production. If an industry is characterised by increasing returns to scale, the firm has a tendency to go for expansion and thus the industry will be dominated by large firms. Conversely, if the industry experiences decreasing returns to scale, the firm may have tendency to roll back on any further investments. In case of industries characterised by constant returns to scale, firms of all sizes would survive equally well.

Linear Homogenous Production Function

Linear homogenous production function implies that if all the factors of production are increased in some proportion, output also increases in the same proportion. Production function is homogenous of the first degree. It represents the case of *constant returns to scale.*

If there are two factors, A and B, then linear homogenous production function can be mathematically expressed as: **mO = f(mA, mB)**

Where   O = Total output/Production;

               m = Any real number

Thus, if A and B are increased by m-times, total production O also increases by m-times.

A well-behaved production function is the linear homogenous production function. The reason is that it can be easily handled and used in empirical studies. Further, an important property of this production function is constant returns to scale; hence it is easily used in calculations by computers and is extensively employed in linear programming and input-output analysis. Owing to the simplicity of this production function and its close approximation to reality it is widely used in model analysis regarding production, distribution and economic growth.

The expansion path of the linear homogenous production function, being of first degree, is always a straight line through the origin. This implies that with constant relative factor prices, proportions between the factors used for production will always be the same whatever is the amount of output to be produced. This relationship of inputs and output is quite simple and convenient for the entrepreneur because he has to find out just one optimum factor proportion and so long as relative factor prices remain constant, his decision regarding the use of factor proportions in the expansion of the production level remains the same and he takes no fresh decision.

The Cobb–Douglas Production Function

The Cobb-Douglas Production Function is a well-known production function. In its original form, it is applied to the whole of manufacturing in the U.S.A. In the post-war period, the Cobb-Douglas production function acquired great popularity among the economists.

In the Cobb-Douglas production function the output is the manufacturing production and the inputs are labour and capital.

This production function states that **labour contributes three-quarters** of increases in manufacturing production and the remaining **one-quarter by the capital.**

The production function is a linear and homogenous one. It implies that it refers to constant returns to scale.

Cobb-Douglas production function is

$$O = kL^a C^{(1-a)} \qquad \qquad \text{... (i)}$$

Where,   O = Output;

               L = Quantity of labour;

               C = Quantity of capital employed; *k* and *a* (a < 1) are positive constants.

The exponents a and $1 - a$ are the elasticities of production that is, a and $1 - a$ measure the percentage response of output to percentage changes in labour and capital respectively.

As mentioned above, the production function is linear and homogenous one and supposes that quantities of labour and capital are increased in equal proportions.

Let L become gL and C become gC (Suppose g is 1.10, there is an increase of 10 per cent in each factor of production. L = 0.75 (as it contributes three-quarters and C = 0.25 as it contributes one-quarter to increase in production). Then,

$$K\,(gL)^a\,(gC)^{1-a} = g^a g^{(1-a)} k\,L^a C^{(1-a)}$$
$$= gkL^a C^{(1-a)} \qquad\qquad\qquad \dots (ii)$$
$$= gO$$

The output increases in the same proportion or it is constant returns to scale.

Diagrammatic Illustration: Fig. 3.6.

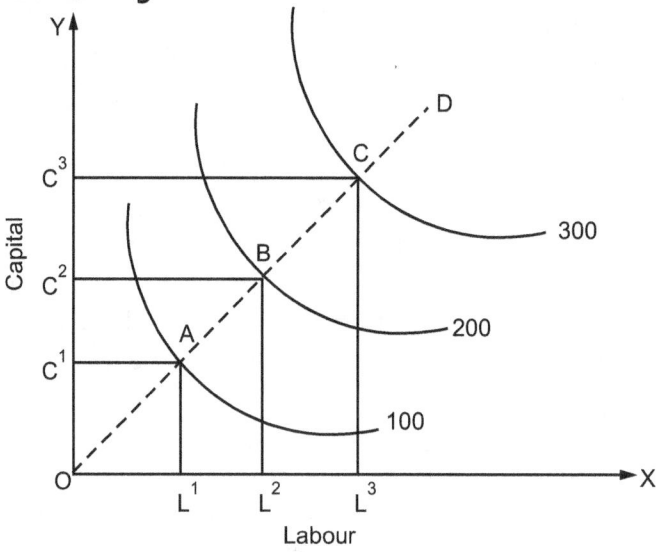

Fig. 3.6: Cobb-Douglas Production Function

- The OX-axis measures Labour input and the OY-axis measures Capital.
- OL^1 units of labour input combined with OC^1 units of capital are used for producing 100 units of output.
- Now, if the output were to be doubled to 200 units, the units of labour and capital is to be doubled, that is, OL^2 and OC^2 of labour and capital.
- It will be three times of labour and capital inputs for 300 units of output, that is, OL^3 and OC^3 of labour and capital respectively.
- Another method to illustrate is to take the expansion path, the scale line OD, connecting points A, B and C.
- It shows that the isoquants 100, 200 and 300 are equidistant. As such on the OD scale line OA = AB = BC, it shows linear homogenous production function. Because of this function, when labour and capital are increased in equal proportions, the output also increases in the same proportion.

Criticism

Many economists like **K.J. Arrow**, **H.B. Chenery**, **B.S. Minhas** and **Robert Solow** have criticised the Cobb-Douglas production function as

(a) The Cobb-Douglas production function is based on the unrealistic assumption of perfect competition in the factor market.

(b) The Cobb-Douglas shows constant returns to scale and in reality it is either the increasing or diminishing returns to scale that is observed in production.

(c) This production function takes into consideration only two inputs: labour and capital. It is therefore, not possible to generalise this function to more than two inputs.

(d) It takes into consideration the quantity of capital available for production. Full use of available capital can be made only in periods of full employment which is an unrealistic situation.

(e) It's another unrealistic assumption is that it is based on substitutability of factors and neglects the complementary factors.

(f) A major weakness of this production function is its aggregation problem. This problem arises when the function is applied to every firm in an industry and to the entire industry. In this situation there will be many production functions of low or high aggregation. Thus, the Cobb-Douglas production function does not measure what it aims at measuring.

(g) The practicability of the Cobb-Douglas function in the manufacturing industry is a doubtful proposition. It is not applicable to agriculture.

Despite its weaknesses, the Cobb-Douglas function has been used widely in empirical studies of manufacturing industries and in inter-industry comparisons.

3.1.7 Isoquant Curve: Equal Product Curves

Now, we discuss a more general case where the firm increases its output by using more of two inputs that are substitutes for each other, say, labour and capital. But, to understand a production function with two variable inputs, it is essential to first understand as to what is an isoquant? *An isoquant is also known as Iso-product curve, Equal product curve or a Production indifference curve.*

Table 3.2: Shows how different combinations of Labour and Capital Result in the same output

Units of Labour (L)	Quantity of Output (O)					
10	56	61	80	88	95	86
9	60	65	**85**	95	100	90
8	**55**	60	80	90	96	**85**
7	45	**50**	70	80	**85**	75
6	25	30	**50**	60	65	**55**
5	15	20	40	**50**	**55**	45
	1	2	3	4	5	6
	(Units of Capital K)					

Table 3.2 illustrates the case of two-variable inputs. If the firm wants to produce 85 units of output, it can do so by employing any of the combination of labour and capital respectively: either (9 units of labour and 3 units of capital), (8 units of labour and 6 units of capital), (7 units of labour and 5 units of capital). In graphical representation, the line joining these combinations of labour and capital is known as isoquant representing 85 units of output *(Op)*. If the output of the firm is to be 50 units, or 55 units, then the various combinations of labour and capital can be as seen in the table 3.2 above. Thus, the relationship between the two inputs: labour and capital: when shown graphically, results in an isoquant.

On graph a production function with two variable inputs, one can derive the isoquant tracing all the combinations of the two factors of production that yield the same output.

An isoquant is defined as the curve passing through the plotted points representing all the combinations of the two factors of production which will produce a given level of output.

For each level of output there will be a different isoquant. When the whole array of isoquants is represented on a graph, it is called an Isoquant Map, as seen in Fig. 3.7.

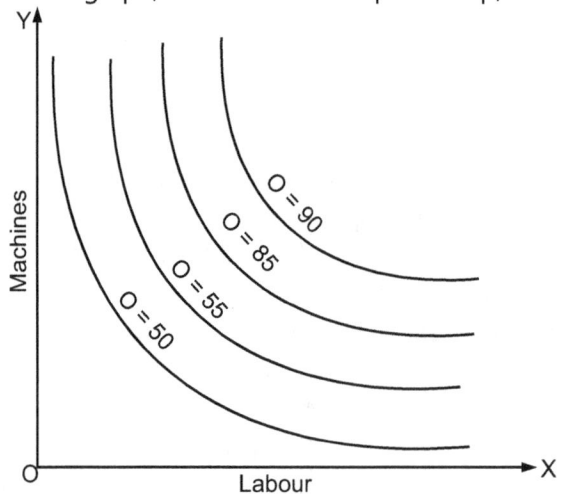

Fig. 3.7: Production with two variables [Inputs - Isoquants]

Substitutability of Inputs:

Isoquant diagram is based on an assumption that the inputs can be substituted for each other. Let us take a particular combination of X (labour) and Y (machinery) resulting in an output of 50 units. Referring to the table 3.2 by moving along the isoquant of 50 units output (7L and 2C), one finds other quantities of the inputs resulting in the same output. If the quantity of labour is reduced, say to 6 units and increasing the capital units from 2 to 3, in order to produce the same output, that is, 50 units of output.

MRTS

Technically, the slope of the isoquant is known as MRTS, that is, marginal rate of technical substitution or marginal rate of substitution in production. Thus, in terms of inputs of capital services K and labour L.

$$MRTS = dK/dL$$

Types of Isoquants

Isoquants may assume various shapes depending on the degree or elasticity of substitutability of inputs. Thus, the different shapes or types of isoquants are:

1. **Linear Isoquant:** Linear isoquant assumes *perfect substitutability between factors of production.* For example, a given output say 50 units can be produced by using only capital or only labour or by a number of combinations of labour and capital (1unit of labour and 5 units of capital, or 2 units of labour and 3 units of capital and so on)

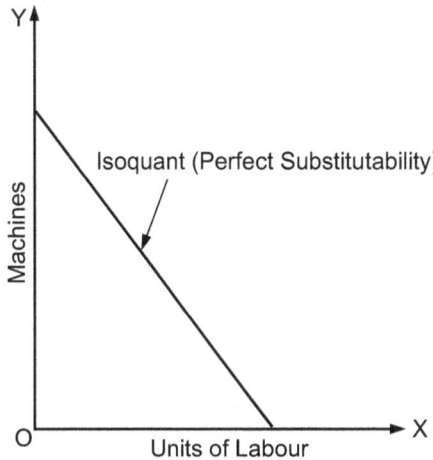

Fig. 3.8: Linear Isoquant

2. **Right-angle Isoquant (Input-output Isoquant):** When there is only one method of production for any commodity, its isoquants take the shape of right angle. Here there is complete non-substitutability between the inputs. In other words, if we assume strict complementary relationship, that is, *zero substitutability,* between the inputs, we get input-output isoquants. This type of isoquant is also known as the *'Leontief isoquant'.*

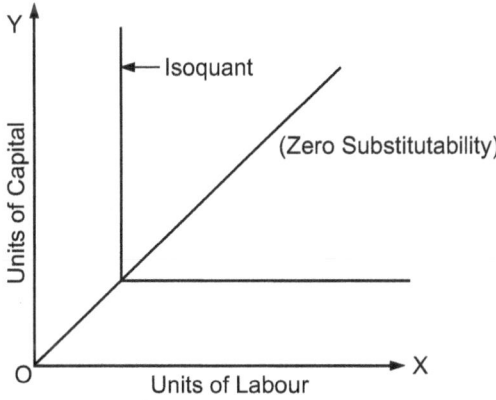

Fig. 3.9: Right angle Isoquant

3. **Kinked Isoquant:** This shape assumes *limited substitutability* of capital and labour. Since there are only a few processes available for producing any commodity (say, Q_1, Q_2, Q_3, Q_4), substitutability of factors is possible only at kinks. This form is called activity analysis isoquant or linear programming isoquant.

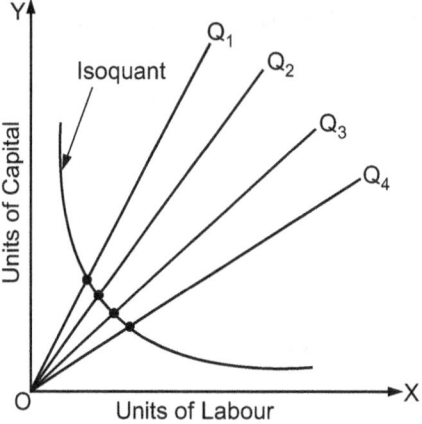

Fig. 3.10: Kinked Isoquant

4. **Smooth Convex Isoquant:** This shape assumes *continuous substitutability* of capital and labour only *over a certain range*, beyond which factors cannot be substituted for each other. Such an isoquant appears as a smooth curve convex to the origin.

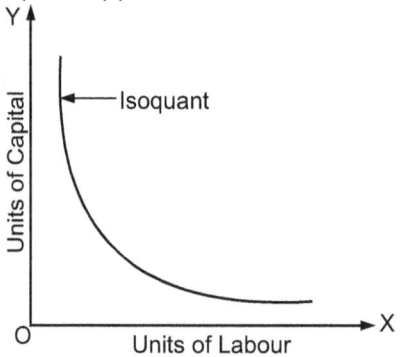

Fig. 3.11: Smooth Convex Isoquant

In all the above mentioned types of isoquants, it may be noted that the kinked isoquants are more realistic. Engineers, managers and production executives consider the production processes as discrete rather than continuous because capital equipments are available in a limited range.

Properties of Isoquants:

In our discussion we consider only the smooth convex isoquants, as they are easy to handle in practice. The smooth convex isoquant is assumed to have following properties:

1. **Downward-sloping:** An isoquant is downward-sloping to the right, that is, negatively inclined. It implies that if more of one factor is used, less of the other factor is needed for producing the *same* level of output.

2. **Isoquant to the right represents higher output:** Higher isoquant represents larger output. It implies that with the same amount of one input and the greater amount of the second input, it will result in larger output.

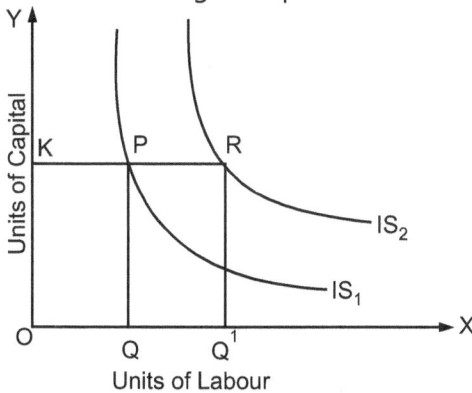

Fig. 3.12

3. **No two isoquants intersect each other:** Another important property of isoquants is that no two isoquants can intersect or touch each other. If two isoquants intersect each other, it will mean that there will be a common point on the two curves, for example, point B in Fig. 3.13. This intersection point would imply that the same amount of labour and capital can produce two levels of outputs, for instance, 50 and 60 units, as shown in Fig. 3.13, which is rationally a meaningless situation.

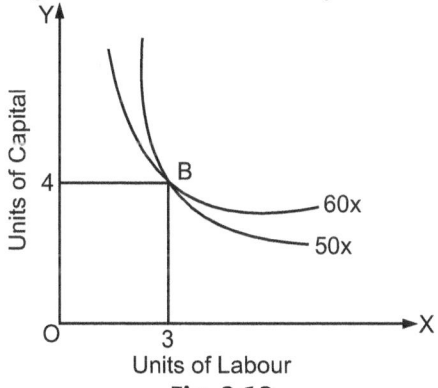

Fig. 3.13

4. **Isoquants are convex to the origin:** Like Indifference Curves; Isoquants are convex to the origin. This implies that the marginal significance of one factor in terms of another factor diminishes along an equal product curve. The convexity property of an isoquant can be proved. The slope of an isoquant at any point on the curve is the ratio dY/dX, that is, the units of Y required to substitute for each unit of X, so as to keep producing a given level of output. In Fig. 3.14 IS is the isoquant or equal product curve. OX axis represents factor X, and OY axis represents the factor Y. At point R, the producer combines OM of X and ON of Y factor, resulting in an output of say, 50 units. Now, to use one more unit of X (or MM_1 of X) and still be on the same

curve IS, the producer must give up NN_1 of Y factor. Thus, the marginal significance of MM_1 of X is NN_1 of Y and similarly the marginal significance of M_1M_2 of X is N_1N_2 of Y factor. The marginal significance of X in terms of Y has clearly fallen. The marginal significance of M_2M_3 of X is N_2N_3 of Y. Thus, to obtain every additional unit of X, lesser and lesser amounts of Y factor are given up so that the marginal significance of X in terms of Y diminishes along the isoquant and hence it takes the form of convex to the origin.

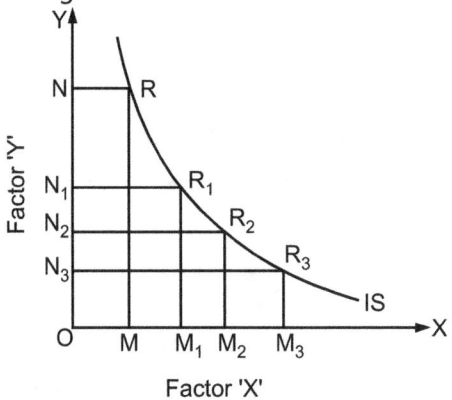

Fig. 3.14: Isoquants-convex to origin

Isoquant Map: For each level of output, there is a different isoquant. When the whole array of isoquants is represented on a graph, it is called an Isoquant Map or Equal-Product Map.

Fig. 3.15 shows how outputs vary as the combinations of the factor inputs are changed.

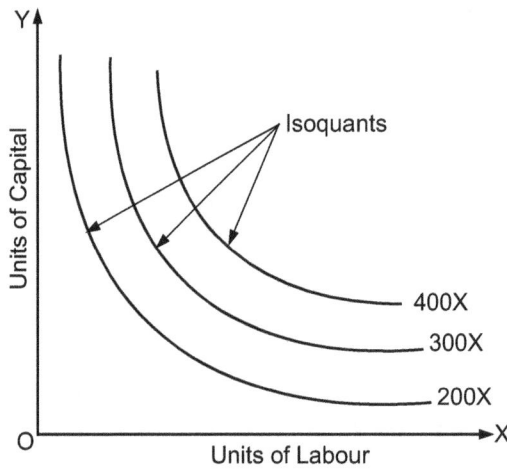

Fig. 3.15: Isoquant map

A higher isoquant represents a higher level of output. However, the distance between any two isoquants does not measure the absolute difference in volume of output that they represent.

Marginal Rate of Technical Substitution

Isoquants are negatively sloped in the economic relevant region. It means that if the firm wants to reduce the quantity of capital that it uses in production, it must increase the quantity of labour in order to remain on the same isoquant, that is, to produce the same output level.

Fig. 3.16 shows that the movement from point P to E on isoquant 10Q, the firm can give up 2.5K by adding 1L. Thus, the slope of isoquant 10Q between P and E is – 2.5K / 1L. Between points E and R, the slope of isoquant 10Q is -, and so on.

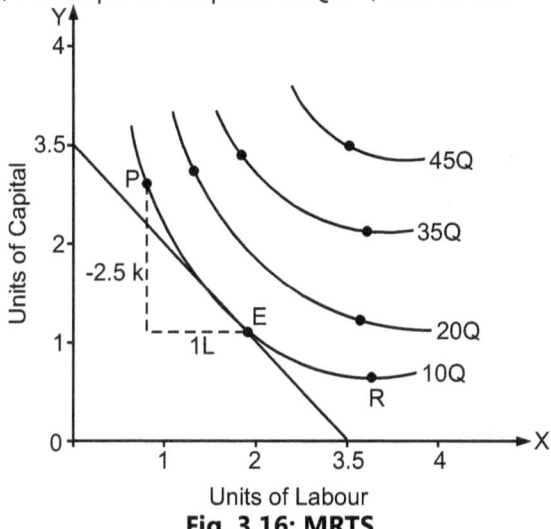

Fig. 3.16: MRTS

- MRTS is the *absolute value* of the slope of the isoquant, that is, by how much is the rate of technical substitution.
- For a movement down along an isoquant, the MRTS of labour for capital is given by - K / ΔL. We multiply K / ΔL by -1 to express MRTS as a positive number. Thus, the MRTS between points P to E on the isoquant for 10Q is 2.5
- The MRTS at any point on an isoquant is given by the absolute slope of the isoquant at that point. Thus, the MRTS at point E is 1.
- The MRTS of labour for capital is also equal to MP_L/MP_K.
- All points on an isoquant refer to the same output level. Thus, for a movement down a given isoquant, the gain in output resulting from the use of more labour must be equal to the loss in output resulting from the less capital use.
- The increase in the quantity of labour used (ΔL) multiplied the marginal product of labour (MP_L) must equal the reduction in the amount of capital used (-ΔK) multiplied the marginal product of capital (MP_K). Therefore,
$$(\Delta L)(MP_L) = (-\Delta K)(MP_K) \qquad \qquad ... \text{(i)}$$
- So that
$$MP_L/MP_K = (-\Delta K)/\Delta L = MRTS \qquad \qquad ... \text{(ii)}$$
- It means that MRTS = the absolute slope of the isoquant $((-\Delta K)/\Delta L)$ and to the ratio of the marginal productivities (MP_L/MP_K).

Economic Region of Production (The Ridge Line):

The isoquants have positively sloped portion, as shown in Fig. 3.17. The isoquants showing output of 50x and 100x. These positively sloped portions are irrelevant as the firm would not operate on the positively sloped portion. This is because the firm could produce the same level of output with less capital and less labour. Economic theory believes that the producer operates on the efficient ranges of output. These are the ranges over which the marginal products of inputs are diminishing but are positive. In economic theory only when the marginal products are negative the production function is considered as inefficient. It means that the firm should not use combinations of inputs with negative marginal products, no matter how cheap they are.

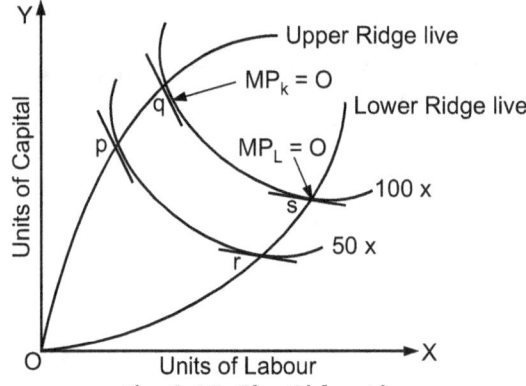

Fig. 3.17: The Ridge Line

The efficient range of output will be represented by the portion of an isoquant that has a negative slope, while the inefficient combination of inputs is represented by the positively sloped part of an isoquant.

Positive slope of an isoquant means that to maintain the same level of output, the firm must use more of both the inputs. In such a situation the marginal product of one of the input is negative (in other words, its additional use will lead to a fall in output), hence in order to maintain the same level of output, more of the other inputs that have positive marginal product will have to be used.

Ridge lines *separate the relevant (that is, negatively sloped) from the irrelevant (that is, positively sloped) portions of the isoquants.* In other words to separate inefficient ranges of output from the inefficient ranges, we need to draw lines between the negatively sloped and the positively sloped portions of the isoquants and such lines are referred to as the ridge lines.

A ridge line is the locus of points of isoquants where marginal product of input is zero. In Fig. 3.17, the upper ridge line joins all such points (for example, p, q, etc) where marginal product of capital (MP_k) is zero, while the lower ridge line joins points (for example, r, s, etc.) where marginal product of labour is zero (MP_L).

The production techniques are efficient technically inside the ridge lines. Outside the ridge lines, the marginal products of inputs are negative, that is, more of both inputs are needed to produce a given level of output. Naturally, no firm or any rational entrepreneur would like to operate in stage III of production, that is, outside the *ridge lines which set the economic region of production.*

Thus, we conclude that the negatively sloped portion of the isoquants within the ridge lines represents the relevant economic region of production. This refers to stage II of production for labour and capital where both MP_K and MP_L are positive but declining. Producers will never want to operate outside this region.

Isocost (or Budget) Line:

From Isoquants we can observe that any desired level of output can be normally produced by a number of varied combinations of inputs. But the task is to determine the specific combination of inputs that a *producer should select*. For this, the firm needs additional information to attain the highest possible level of output for a given level of cost or the lowest possible cost for producing any given level of output.

In determining the optimal combination of inputs, producers must take into account the relative prices of inputs so as to minimise the cost of producing a given level of output. In other words, inputs have market prices and if firms use more of the relatively cheaper input and less of the relatively costlier input, the cost of production can be minimised.

As mentioned above, inputs have market prices and an individual firm is only a price-taker, that is, prices of inputs for an individual firm are usually given. The choice with the firm is to buy as much of the inputs as it can by employing the resources available with it. The different possible combination of inputs which the firm can buy with the help of its resources, given input prices, is represented by an isocost line (like budget line in indifference curve analysis).

Illustration: Suppose that the firm desires to spend ₹ 5000 on a particular process which involves two factors: labour and capital. Let the price of labour be ₹ 100 per unit and per unit of capital as ₹ 200. With ₹ 5000 as the firm's resources, the firm can buy either 50 units of labour or 25 units of capital or any of such combination that would fully exhaust the firm's resources, that is, ₹ 5000. A straight line joining 25 units of capital with 50 units of labour will pass through all such combinations of capital and labour which the firm can buy with its outlay of ₹ 5000. Such a line is called *isocost line. An isocost line shows various combinations of the factor inputs that the firm can buy with a given outlay and factor prices.* This is shown in Fig. 3.18 L_0K_0. Every point on an isocost line costs the same to the firm (₹ 5000 in our illustration).

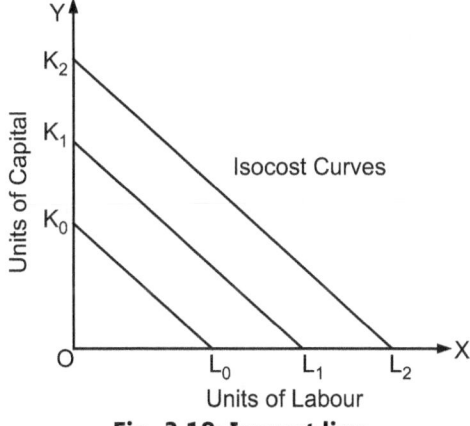

Fig. 3.18: Isocost line

The isocost or the budget line can be expressed symbolically as:

$$A = P_L L + P_K K$$

Where, A = total budget allocation for inputs labour (L) and capital (K)

P_L and P_K = Prices of labour and capital respectively

L and K = quantity of labour and capital respectively

The isocost curve or the budget line takes the form of a straight line as the prices of inputs are taken as constant. Slope of the budget line equals relative prices that can be shown by the following equation:

$$A = P_L L + P_K K \text{ or } K = A/ P_K - P_L / P_K . L$$

Thus, the slope of the budget line is: PL / P_K

The Optimal Combination of Inputs

The firm wishes to produce at the least possible cost or whatever expenditure the entrepreneur wishes to make, he desires the highest output with that outlay. To accomplish either of the two tasks, production must be organised in the most efficient manner, that is, the resources must be used in an optimal combination.

Optimal Input combination for Minimising Costs or Maximising Output:

The optimal combination of inputs required for a firm to minimise the cost of producing a given level of output or maximise the output for a given cost expenditure is given at the tangency point of an isoquant and an isocost. For example, Fig. 3.19 shows that the lowest cost of producing 10 units of output (that is, to reach isoquant 10Q) is given by point E, where isoquant 10Q is tangent to isocost line AB. The firm uses 5L (5 units of labour) at a cost of₹ 50 and 5K (5 units of capital) at a cost of ₹ 50 also, for a total cost of ₹ 100 (shown by isocost AB). The output of 10Q can also be regarded as the maximum output that can be produced with an expenditure of ₹ 100 (shown by isocost line AB).

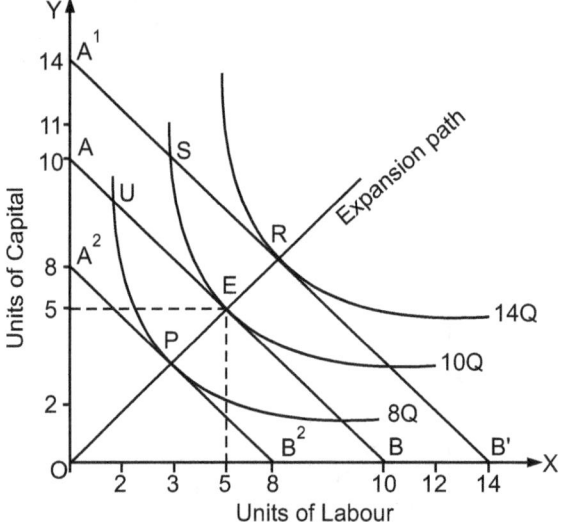

Fig. 3.19: Optimal combination of inputs

The firm could also produce 10Q at point S (with 3L and 11K) or at point T (12L and 2K) at a cost of ₹ 140 (isocost A^1B^1). But this is not the least-cost input combination required to produce 10Q. In fact, with this outlay of ₹ 140, the firm could reach isoquant 14Q at point R. Similarly, the firm could produce 8Q efficiently at point P on isocost A^2B^2 at a cost of ₹ 80 or inefficiently at point U and V on isocost AB at a cost of ₹ 100. Thus, proved that *the optimal input combination required to minimise the cost of producing a given level of output or the maximum output that the firm can produce at a given cost outlay is given at the tangency of an isocost and an isoquant.*

Joining the points of optimal input combination, that is, the points of tangency of isoquants and isocosts, gives us the **expansion path** of the firm. In Fig. 3.19, OPER is the expansion path for the firm.

- The expansion path shows the minimum cost of reaching isoquants, that is, producing 8Q, 10Q and 14Q are ₹ 80, ₹ 100 and ₹ 140, given by the points P, E, and R respectively.

- It also shows that with total costs of ₹ 80, Rs.100 and ₹ 140 (with iso-costs A^2B^2, AB and A^1B^1) the maximum outputs that the firm can produce are 8Q, 10Q and 14Q respectively.

- All expansion paths are straight lines through the origin, as seen in Fig. 3.19.

With optimal input combinations (that is, at the points of tangency of isoquants and isocost lines), the (absolute) slope of the isoquant or marginal rate of technical substitution (MRTS) of labour for capital is equal to the (absolute) slope of the isocost line or ratio of input prices.

that is,   MRTS =   ... (a)

w = Wage rate of labour;

r = rent price of capital.

Since the MRTS = MP_L / MP_K, the condition for the optimal combination of input can be rewritten as:

$$MP_L / MP_K = w / r$$ ... (b)

Alternatively, it can be

$$MP_L / w = MP_K / r$$ ... (c)

Equation (c) indicates that to minimise production costs (or to maximise output for a given cost expenditure), the extra output or marginal product per rupee spent on labour must be equal to the marginal product per rupee spent on capital. If $MP_L = 5$, $MP_K = 4$, and w = r, the firm would not be maximising output or minimising costs as it is getting more extra output for a rupee spent on labour than on capital.

To maximise output or minimise costs, the firm would have to hire more labour and rent less capital. When the firm does this the MP_L falls and the MP_K rises. The process would have to continue until condition (c) of equation holds.

The same general condition for the optimal input combination would have to hold regardless of the number of inputs and not only for labour and capital.

Profit Maximisation

A firm maximises its profits when revenue earned equates the costs that it has incurred. To be more specific, to maximise profits, a firm should employ each input until the marginal revenue product of the input equals the marginal resource cost of hiring the input.

With constant input prices (as an individual firm is a price-taker), the firm should hire each input until the marginal revenue product (MRP) of the input equals the input price (input cost).

With the firm having labour and capital, variable inputs, it has to hire labour and capital until the MRP of labour (MRP_L) equals wage rate (w) and until the MRP of capital (MRP_K) equals the rent price of capital (r). This statement can be symbolically written as:

$$MRP_L = w \ldots \text{(d)}$$
$$MRP_K = r \ldots \text{(e)}$$

If labour and capital are hired in a manner to satisfy the equation (d) and (e), it implies that condition (c) for optimal input combination will also be satisfied. To see this, the marginal revenue product (MRP) of an input equals the marginal product of the input (MP) multiplied by the marginal revenue (MR) generated from the sale of the output. Thus, equation (d) and (e) can be rewritten as:

$$(MP_L)(MR) = w \hspace{4cm} \ldots \text{(f)}$$
$$(MP_K)(MR) = r \hspace{4cm} \ldots \text{(g)}$$

Dividing the equation (f) by equation (g), we get

$$MP_L / MP_K = w / r \hspace{4cm} \ldots \text{(h)}$$

When cross-multiplying equation (h) we get the condition for optimal combination of inputs given by equation (c).

$$MP_L / w = MP_K / r \quad \ldots \text{(as seen in equation c)}$$

A point to be noted is that there is an optimal input combination for each level of output (points P, E and R in Fig. 3.19, but only at one of the outputs (where MRP of each input = input price) will the firm be able to maximise profits. In other words, *to maximise profits, the firm must produce the profit maximising level of output with the optimal input combination.*

3.2 Cost Function

3.2.1 Introduction

Cost function is a derived function. It is developed from the production function, which explains the efficient method of production at any particular time. The production function denotes the technical relationships between inputs and the level of output, therefore, cost differs with the changes in the level of output, nature of production function or factor prices – therefore, representatively, the cost function can be described as

$$C = f (X, T, P_f)$$

Where, C = Total cost, X = Output, T = Technology, P_f = Prices of factors.

Total cost is an increasing function of output, C = f (X), with other conditions remaining the same. The clause 'ceteris paribus' means 'all other factors which determine costs are constant'. If these factors change, they will have an effect on the cost. The technology is itself determined by the physical quantities of the factor inputs, the value of the factor inputs, the competence of the entrepreneur, both in organising the physical side of the production and in making the correct economic choice of methods. Thus, any change in these determinants moves the production function and thus shifts the cost curve. For instance, the opening of a method of organising production or the request of an educational programme to the, existing labour shifts the production function upwards and thus shifts the cost curve down. Likewise, the development of raw material, or the upgrading in the use of the same raw materials leads to a downward shift of the cost function.

As no output is achievable without an input, an increase in factor prices, ceteris paribus, leads to an increase in the cost. The factor prices depend on the demand and supply of factors in the economy.

Of all the determinants of cost, the cost-output relationship is regarded as the most significant one, therefore, in economic analysis the cost function is analysed with accordance to output. This is because the cost-output relationship is subject to quicker and more common changes.

3.2.2 Relation between Production and Cost Function

Production functions and cost functions are the keystones of business and managerial economics. A production function is a mathematical relationship that addresses the important features of the technology by ways of which an organisation changes resources such as land, labour and capital into goods or services such as steel or cement. It is the economist's refinement of the most important information enclosed in the engineer's blueprints. Mathematically, Y denotes the quantity of a simple output created by the quantities of inputs indicated $(x_1, ..., x_n)$. Then the production function $f(x_1, ..., x_n)$ explains how a particular output is created by endless combinations of inputs $(x_1, ..., x_n)$, provided by the technology in use. Several important traits of the structure of the technology are arrested by the shape of the production function. Relationships amongst the inputs include the level of substitutability or complements among pairs of inputs, as well as the ability to combine groups of inputs into a smaller list of input aggregates. Relationships between output and the inputs consist of economies of scale and the technical efficiency with which inputs are utilised to create a particular output.

Each of these features has suggestions for the shape of the cost function, which is familiarly related to the production function. A cost function is also a mathematical relationship, one that speaks about the expenses an organisation incurred on the quantity of output it produced and to the unit prices it paid. Mathematically, E denotes the expense that an organisation acquires in the production of output quantity Y when it gives unit prices $(p_1, ..., p_n)$ for the inputs it hires. Then the cost function $C(p_1, ..., p_n)$ explains the lowest expenditure needed to produce output quantity Y when input unit prices are $(p_1, ..., p_n)$, given) the technology in use and so $E \geq C(y, p_1, ..., p_n)$. A cost function is an increasing function of (y, p_1, ..., p_n), but the levels to which the least cost increases with an increase in the amount of output produced or in any input price depends on the attributes explaining the structure of production technology. For example, scale economies allow output to enlarge faster than input usage. In other words, proportionate increase in output is bigger than the proportionate increase in inputs. Such a condition is also indicated as elasticity of production in relation to inputs being bigger than one scale economics thus generates an inducement for large-scale production and by related reasoning scale diseconomies create a technological restriction to large-scale production. For another example, if a pair of inputs is a close replacement and the unit price of one of the inputs rises, the ensuing increase in cost is lesser than if, the two inputs were poor substitutes or complements. Lastly, if depletion in the organisation causes actual output to decrease short of highest possible output or if inputs are dislocated in glow of their respective unit prices, then actual cost goes beyond the minimum cost; both technical inefficiency and inefficiency in allocation are expensive.

As these examples suggest, under fairly common situations the shape of the cost function is a reflection of the shape of the production function – Thus, the cost function and the production function usually pay for equivalent information regarding the structure of production technology. This likeness of relationship between production functions and cost functions is known as 'duality' and it explains that one of the two functions has certain characteristics, if and only if, the other has certain features. Such a duality relationship has a number of important connotations. Since the production function and the cost function are based on various data, duality allows others to hire either function as the basis of an economic analysis of production, without fear of finding disagreeable inferences. The theoretical properties of connected output supply and input demand equations are inferred from either the theoretical properties of the production function or, more easily, for those of the dual cost function.

Empirical analysis aims at finding the nature of scale economies, the degree of input substitutability or complements, or the degree and nature of productive inefficiency can be organised using a production function or again more easily using a cost function.

If the time period under reflection is adequately short, then the assumption of a particular technology is valid. The long-term effects of technological progress or the edition of existing greater technology can be introduced into the analysis. Technical progress increases the maximum output that can be got from a given collection of inputs and so in the presence of unchanging unit prices of the inputs technical progress decreases the bare minimum cost that is incurred to produce a particular quantity of output. This phenomenon is just an extension to the time period of the duality relationship that links production functions and cost functions. Of particular empirical interest are the scale of technical progress and its cost-reducing effects and the possible labour-saving prejudice of technological progress and its employment consequences that are passed from the production function, to the cost function and then to the labour demand function.

3.2.3 Short-Run Cost Function

In the short-run the company cannot change overhead factors such as plant, equipment and scale of its organisation. In the short-run output is increased or decreased by changing the uneven inputs like labour, raw material, etc. Thus, the short-run costs of production are sectioned into fixed and variable costs. Alternatively, in the long-run all factors are adjusted, thus, in the long-run all costs are variable and none are fixed.

1. Total Cost: Fixed and Variable

The total cost (TC) of the company is a function of output (q), it increases with the increase in output and it differs thoroughly with the output. In symbols, it is written as

$$TC = f(q)$$

As the output is produced by fixed and variable factors, the total cost is divided into two parts: total fixed cost (TFC) and total variable cost (TVC),

$$TC = TFC + TVC$$

•   **Fixed Cost**

Fixed costs are those which are free from output. They are paid even if the company produces no output. They do not change even if the output changes. They stay fixed whether the output is big or small. Fixed costs are also called 'overhead costs', 'sunk costs' or 'supplementary costs'. They include payments such as rent, interest, insurance, depreciation charges, maintenance costs, property taxes, administrative expenses like manager's salary and so on in the short period, the total amount of these fixed costs does not increase or decrease when the volume of the companies output rises or falls (See Table 3.3).

•   **Variable Cost**

Variable costs are those which are acquired on the employment of variable factors of production. They differ with the level of output. They increase with the rise in output and decrease with the fall in output. By definition, variable costs stay zero when output is zero, they consist of payments for wages, raw materials, fuel, power, transport and the like. **Marshall** called these variable costs as "prime costs" of production.

The relation between total variable cost and output is not linear, that is, variable cost does not increase by the same quantity for every unit increase in output. This is indicated in the table given as follows.

Table 3.3: A Schedule of a Firm's Total Cost

Output (q)	Total Fixed Cost (TFC)	Total Variable Cost (TVC)	Total Cost (TC)
(1)	(2)	(3)	(4)
0	100	0	100
1	100	25	125
2	100	40	140
3	100	50	150
4	100	70	170

Output (q)	Total Fixed Cost (TFC)	Total Variable Cost (TVC)	Total Cost (TC)
(1)	(2)	(3)	(4)
5	100	100	200
6	100	145	145
7	100	205	305
8	100	285	385
9	100	385	485
10	100	515	615

Table 3.3 shows a basic cost plan which is presenting the relation between costs for each different levels of output. Here the following relations are observed as follows.

- The column (2) indicates that TFC stays fixed at all levels output.
- The column (3) indicates that TVC differs with the output and it is zero when the output is nothing. It is also observed from the column (3) that TVC does not change in the same amount. Originally, as the output increases, TVC increases at a declining rate, but after a point it rises at an increasing rate. This is because of the operation of the law of variable proportions.
- The column (4) indicates that total costs are the same as the fixed plus variable costs. TC differs with the change in output in the same ratio as the TVC.
- The above costs and output relations are also indicated in Fig 3.20. By marking the cost data of Table 3.3, graphically and combining the marked points by smooth curves, we can get total fixed total variable and total cost curves.

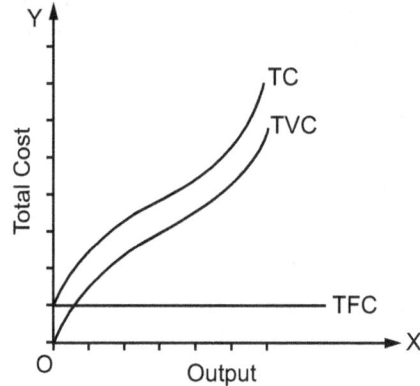

Fig. 3.20: Total Cost Curves

It is seen from Fig 3.20 that since total fixed cost remains stable, TFC curve is parallel to the X-axis. The TVC curve starts at zero and then increases slowly in the beginning and ultimately, becomes sharper as the output rises. The TC curve is found by adding up upright TFC and TVC curves. The shape of the TC curve is the same as that of TVC curve because the same vertical distance separates TC and TVC Curves.

2. Unit Costs

There are four different kinds of unit costs, namely, average total cost (or as generally called average cost), and average fixed cost, average variable cost and marginal cost.

- **Average Total Cost (ATC)**

One of the most significant cost concepts is average total cost. When contrasted with the price or average revenue it allows a business to determine whether or not it is making a profit. Average total cost is total cost separated by the number of units produced that is,

$$\text{Average Total Cost} = \frac{\text{Total Cost}}{\text{Quantity}} \text{ or ATC} = \frac{TC}{q}$$

As, the total cost is the sum of total fixed cost and total variable cost, the average total cost is also the sum of average fixed cost (AFC) and average variable cost (AVC). Therefore, Average Total Cost [ATC) = Average Fixed Cost (AFC) + Average Variable Cost (AVC).

- **Average Fixed Cost (AFC)**

By separating total fixed cost by output there is a result of average fixed cost.

$$\text{AFC} = \frac{TFC}{q}$$

As the same amount of fixed cost is divided evenly between the different units of output, AFC decreases constantly as output rises.

- **Average Variable Cost (AVC)**

Average variable cost is total variable cost separated by the output. Thus,

$$\text{AVC} = \frac{TVC}{q}$$

The average variable cost usually falls as the output rises from zero to the normal capacity level of output because of the process of rising returns. Further than the normal capacity output, any rise in output increases AVC quite harshly on account of the process of diminishing returns.

- **Marginal Cost (MC)**

Marginal cost is the additional cost of producing one extra unit of output. In economics the term 'marginal' applied to utility, cost, production, consumption or whatever means 'incremental' or 'extra'. Therefore, marginal cost is the total cost of n units of output minus the total cost of n − 1 units. In symbols

$$MC_n = TC_n - TC_{n-1}$$

As, fixed costs do not change with outputs, MC is autonomous of fixed cost, alternatively, variable costs differ with output in the short-run and therefore, MC is measured from the total variable cost. Thus, marginal cost is the addition to the total variable cost for producing an additional unit of output. In other words, marginal cost is equivalent to the change in TVC.

- **Computation of AC, AFC, AVC and MC**

The computation of AC, AFC, AVC and MC and their relationships are shown by a theoretical example and it is given in Table 3.4.

Table 3.4: A Schedule of Short-Run Costs

Quantity	Total Fixed Cost	Total Variable Cost	Total Cost	Marginal Cost	Average Total Cost	Average Fixed Cost	Average Variable Cost
Q	TFC	TVC	TC = TFC + TVC	MC	ATC = TC/q or ATC = AVC + AFC	AFC = TFC/q	AVC = TFC/q
(1)	(2)	(3)	(4)	(5)	(6)	(7)	(8)
0	100	0	100	–	–	–	–
1	100	25	125	25	125	100	25
2	100	40	140	15	70	50	20
3	100	50	150	10	50	33.3	16.7
4	100	70	170	20	42.5	25	17.5
5	100	100	200	30	40	20	20
6	100	145	145	45	40.8	16.6	24.2
7	100	205	305	60	43.6	14.3	29.3
8	100	285	385	80	48.1	12.5	35.6
9	100	385	485	100	53.9	11.1	42.8
10	100	515	615	130	61.5	10	51.5

Column (7) indicates that AFC falls endlessly as the output rises. It can be observed from column (8) that AVC falls at first, reaches a smallest amount and ultimately rises with the increase in output – From column (6) it is observed that ATC also decreases initially, reaches the least amount and then rises as output increases. It can be observed that ATC is the sum of AFC and AVC. Column (5) indicates that MC too performs in the same way as AVC and ATC.

- **Relationship between AC, AFC, AVC and MC Curves**

The relationship between AC, AFC, AVC and MC is described graphically by drawing individual cost curves in Fig. 3.21. The behaviour of cost curves is described below.

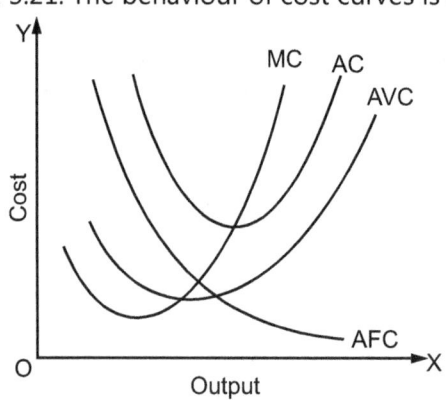

Fig. 3.21: Marginal and Average Cost Curves

As AFC falls gradually the output increases, the AFC curve also falls gradually from left to right. In mathematical terms, AFC curve moves toward both axes, that is, it gets very near to but never touches either axis. As the constant fixed cost is separated by different levels of output then the AFC curve becomes a rectangular hyperbola. This means that if AFC is multiplied at any point on the AFC curve with the corresponding quantity of output, there will always be the same total fixed cost. This feature of the AFC curve indicates that TFC is stable throughout.

The AVC curve decreases at the beginning, reaches a least amount and then rises as the output increases. It decreases slowly as the company's output goes up from zero to the normal capacity level – Once normal capacity output is reached AVC curve increases sharply with the rise in output. This is because of the fact that the use of more and more of the variable factors, say labour, leads to overloading and also to various problems of organisation. Additionally, as the fixed factors are used more severely, the machines break down almost regularly. All these lead to a quick increase in AVC.

If AFC and AVC curves are added together we get ATC curve or as generally called, average cost (AC) curve. At first as output increases ATC curve falls because of the prevalence of falling AFC curve. At high levels the output AVC curve rises rather sharply and therefore, ATC curve raises after a point, the constant fall in average fixed costs is too small to offset it. Thus AC curve is 'U' shaped.

MC curve is also 'U' shaped as in Fig. 3.21. Marginal cost curve decreases at the beginning, then reaches a smallest point and finally increases. The shape of the IVIC curve is determined by the law of variable proportions, that is, by the behaviour of the marginal product of the variable factor. MC curve joins AC and AVC curves at their lowest amount. This is because of an important relationship between marginal and average costs.

The relationship between AVC, ATC and MC can be described as follows:
- AVC, ATC and MC decline first, then reach a smallest amount and finally rise as output increases.
- The rate of change in MC is larger than that in AVC and so MC is lowest at an output lesser than the output at which AVC is lowest.
- The ATC decreases for a longer variety of output than the AVC and thus the minimum ATC is at a bigger output than the smallest AVC.
- VIC = AVC, when AVC is lowest.
- MC = ATC, when ATC is minimum.

3.2.4 Long-Run Cost Function

In the long-run a firm can bring about a change in its size and organisation structure in response to volatile demand conditions. In other words, as a part of long term strategy the firm can adjust its scale of operations or size of plant to produce any required output (usually a higher level) in the most efficient way. Thus, in the long run changes can be brought in the fixed factors of production. The management of the organisation can be restructured to run a firm of a different size. Capital can also be used in a different manner considering the most profitable alternatives. In short, all factors of production are variable in the long run and therefore the scale of operations can be altered altogether.

The length of time of the long-run depends on the industry in which the firm operates. In a few service industries, such as dry-cleaning, the period of the long-run may be maximum up to a few weeks or months. For capital intensive industries, such as electricity-generating plant, the construction of a new plant itself takes several years and therefore, long-run in that case may be many years. The length of time of the long-run thus depends upon the time required by the firm to make all inputs variable.

The long-run is often referred to as the planning sphere since the organisation can construct or reconstruct the plant in a way that reduces the expenditure of producing any estimated level of output. Once the plant has been constructed, the organisation plans for the operations in the short-run.

Long Run Average Cost Curve

In the long run, a firm has a choice among various alternatives to decide an appropriate plant size for its operations.

Corresponding to each scale or size of the plant chosen by the firm there will be an average cost curve. Hence, the long run represents a series of alternative short run average cost curves, associated with different plants, out of which the firm has to make a choice for its actual operation. The long run average cost curve is derived from aggregate of a number of short run average cost (SAC) curves. This is explained in Fig. 3.22.

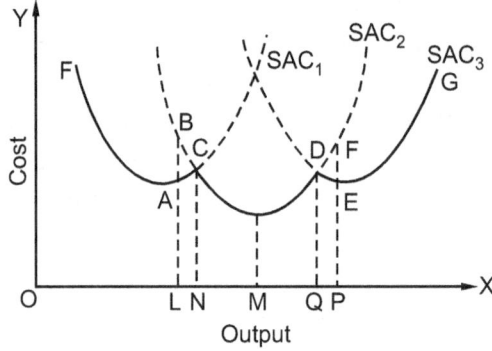

Fig 3.22: Long Run Average Cost Curve

The above figure is drawn on the assumption that there are three plants out of which the choice is to be made and they are depicted by the short run average cost curves SAC$_1$, SAC$_2$, SAC$_3$. A given plant is best suited for a particular level of output. It can be seen from Fig. 3.22 that output OL can be produced at a lower cost with the plant SAC$_1$, than with the plant SAC$_2$. The cost of producing OL output on plant SAC$_1$, is AL and it is less than the cost of producing the same output with plant SAC$_2$. The difference in cost is equal to AB, if the firm wants to produce ON output it can produce it either by plant SAC$_1$, or plant SAC$_2$. But it would be advantageous for the firm to use the plant SAC$_2$ for ON level of output because the larger output OM can be obtained at the lowest average cost from this plant. Thus, output larger than ON but less than OQ can be produced Lit a lower average cost with plant SAC$_2$.

For output larger than OQ, the firm will have to employ plant SAC$_3$. For instance, output OP can be produced at average cost of PE with plant SAC$_3$.

Thus it is clear from the above analysis that in the long-run the firm has a choice regarding the choice of plant it desires to set up and it will employ that plant which yields possible minimum average cost for producing a given output. Thus long-run average cost curve represents the lowest possible average cost that will be incurred for producing various levels of output. Assuming that there are only three plants as in Fig. 3.22, then LAC curve is the thick wave like portions of SAC curves, that is, FACDEG. The dotted portions of these SAC curves are of no importance to the firm in the long-run because the firm would prefer to change the size of the plant rather than operate on them.

If we make an assumption that the size of the plant can be varied by infinitely small gradations so that there are numerous SAC curves corresponding to infinite number of plants, the long run average cost curves will be smooth one as in Fig. 3.23. Since, we are assuming an infinite number of SAC curves, every point on the LAC curve will be a tangency point with some SAC curve. Thus, the LAC curve is the locus of the points of the lowest average cost of producing various levels of output.

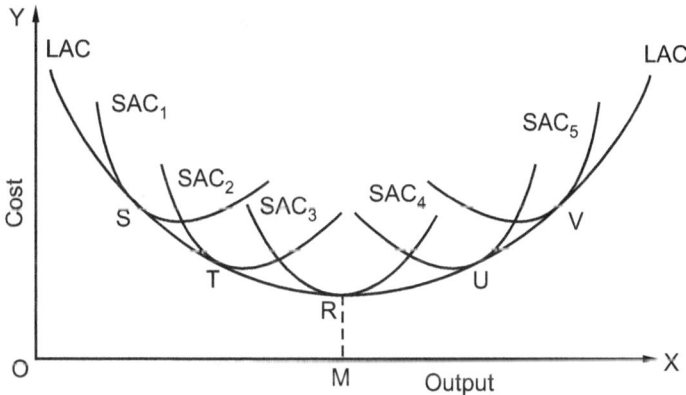

Fig. 3.23: Long sun smooth envelope curve

It should be noted that, with one exception, the LAC curve is not tangent to the minimum points of the short-run average cost curves. This exception occurs at the optimum level of output, In Fig. 3.23, this occurs at the output OM at which the lowest point of SAC$_3$ coincides with the minimum point on the LAC curve at point R. The plant SAC$_3$ which produces the optimum output OM at the minimum cost RM is the optimum plant. For outputs less than OM the lowest long run costs occur on the falling portions of SAC curves, In Fig. 3.23, LAC curve is tangent to failing portions of SAC$_1$ and SAC$_2$ at points S and T respectively, but points of S and T are not the minimum points of SAC$_1$ and SAC$_2$. On the other hand, for outputs greater than OM, the lowest long run average costs occur on the rising portions of short run average cost curves.

3.2.5 L-Shaped Long-Run Average Cost Curve: Modern Cost Theory

A significant development in cost theory is that the long-run average cost curve is L-shaped rather than U-shaped. The L-shape of the long-run average cost curve means that in the beginning when output is expanded due to the increase in plant size and associated variable factors, cost per unit falls rapidly due to economies of scale being achieved.

Even after a sufficiently large scale of output, the long-run average cost does not rise; it may either remain constant or it may fall slightly. At an exceptionally large scale of production, the managerial cost per unit of output may rise, but the technical or production economies more than not offset the managerial diseconomies so that the total long-run average cost does not rise or may even fall continuously, though at a very small rate. Thus the empirical evidence gathered by economists in recent years indicates that the long-run average cost curve is L-shaped.

Empirical evidence gathered by the economists indicates that initially the long-run average cost rapidly falls but after a point it either remains flat throughout or at its right-hand end it may even slope downward gently. For example, **Joel Dean** in his cost function studies finds that long-run average cost curve is L-shaped.

Likewise, in his empirical study of cost functions **J. Johnston** found strong evidence for L-shaped long-run average cost curve. Besides, using data of Indian industries **Vinod Gupta** who studied long-run average cost functions for 29 manufacturing Indian industries found that in 18 of them long-run cost was L-shaped and not U-shaped. L-shaped long-run average cost curve is illustrated in Fig.3.24.

The difference between L-shaped LAC of Fig. 3.24 and the U-shaped LAC is that there is no rising portion in the former. Indeed, as stated just above, the empirical evidence shows that LAC may even slope gently downward at its right hand end.

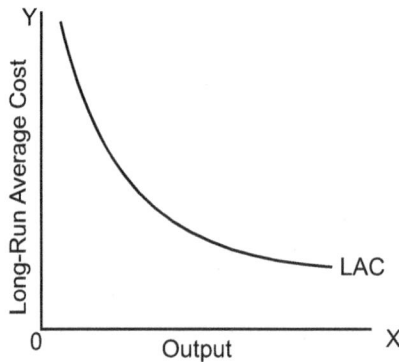

Fig. 3.24: L-shaped Long-Run Average Cost Curve

Thus, there is a visible contradiction between traditional economic theory according to which LAC is U-shaped and the results of empirical cost-function studies by the economists which find LAC to be L-shaped. There are two reasons responsible for the continuous occurrence of economies of scale which lead to fall in cost per unit of output.

Production or Technical Economies:

First, it is pertinent to note that there are substantial technical economies of scale enjoyed by a firm when it expands its scale of operations in the beginning. This leads to the steep fall in the long-run average cost with the initial increase in scale of production.

However, it has been observed that even after most of the economies of scale have been achieved by the firm and it reaches a minimum optimal scale, given the technology used in the industry, the unit cost of production may fall due to some technical economies which it can continue to enjoy even after the minimum optimal scale.

The new techniques of production are adopted for a large scale of production due to which the production cost per unit falls.

Even with the existing known techniques some economies can always be obtained due to the following:

(1) Decentralisation and improved skills and productivity of labour,

(2) Lower repair costs after a certain scale of production is achieved and

(3) Production by a firm of some of the materials and equipment it needs at a lower cost for its production process instead of buying them from other firms that is, in-house manufacture of raw materials and intermediate components at a lower cost of production .

Development of Appropriate Managerial Techniques:

In the traditional cost theory, the rising part of the LAC is explained by the challenges faced by the firm in management, supervision, co-ordination and control which leads to an increase in the unit cost of production after a certain scale of production is attained. With respect to this it has been noted that modern management science has developed appropriate organisational and managerial set-up for efficient working of the firm depending on each plant size.

For different scales of production and sizes of firms appropriate management techniques have evolved over a period of time and each management technique is applicable to a range of output. Only at a very large scale of production, the managerial costs may rise.

Any rise in managerial costs even after a very large scale of output may be offset by production economies that accrue to the firm. However, there is still a controversy as to whether the long-run average cost is really L-shaped when usual assumptions made in economic theory are considered.

A. Critical Evaluation

Now, the question is how can the L-Shaped long-run average cost curve be explained and how can the apparent contradiction between the traditional cost theory and empirical evidence be removed.

The following two explanations have been provided to remove the above said contradiction:

1. Technical Progress

One reason why modern empirical studies do not find U-shaped long-run average cost curve is that the traditional economic theory assumes that technology remains unchanged or there is no technological progress on the contrary, in the real world, technological progress does take place over time.

As a result of technological progress in the real world over a period of time, long-run average cost curve will shift downward. The empirical investigations of the economists which are based on times series data will not find the rising average cost considering the existence of technological progress achieved.

In case of unchanged technology, as it is one of the assumption in traditional cost theory, long-run average cost curve (LAC) is U-shaped, empirical studies was conducted on the basis of data belonging to different points of time (time series data) between which technological progress had already taken place or in case of inter-cross section studies conducted on both small and large firms using different technologies one would find the average cost falling. Owing to the technological improvement one cannot find the average cost rising in empirical cost function studies. This is illustrated in Fig. 3.25.

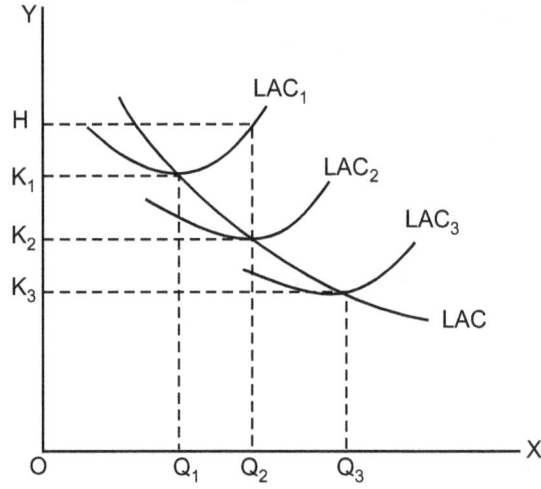

Fig. 3.25: Shifting down of LAC due to Technology Progress

Suppose in the initial phase the firm is producing OQ_1 output at cost OK_1 by operating on LAC_1. If the demand for the firm's product increases to OQ_2, then in the context of unchanged technology the firm will expand production along LAC_1 and will produce OQ_2 at cost OH. Now, if the technological progress has taken place and the firm installs a new plant whose long-run average cost is LAC_2, the firm will produce on the new curve LAC_2, the output OQ_2 at cost per unit which is less than both OK_1 and OH.

Likewise, when the firm at some later date has expanded output to OQ_3 in response to the progress increase in demand for its product, the technology might have advanced in the mean time so that the firm produces OQ_3 at OK_3 cost per unit which is less than OK_2.

By joining the minimum points of long-run average cost curves we get a curve LAC which gently slopes downward due to technological improvement that has taken place over a period time, whereas with unchanged technology long-run average cost curves LAC_1, LAC_2, and LAC_3 each with a different but unchanged technology is U-shaped. Empirical cost-function studies made by economists at different points of time would estimate OK_1, OK_2 and OK_3 unit costs at output OQ_1, OQ_2, and OQ_3 respectively and would therefore suggest that long-run average cost curve was like the thick curve LAC.

Therefore we can conclude that, with a given and unchanged technology long-run average cost curves are U-shaped while the empirical evidence would find L-shaped long-run average cost curve due to technological progress that takes place over time.

What the empirical evidence suggests is that technological progress may often be to such an extent that unit cost will reduce even in a situation where, with given technology, the problem of managing a bigger firm would increase unit costs.

2. Learning Curve Effect

Learning curve effect or learning by doing that is, to say gaining efficiency by performing the same function, is another factor which causes the long-run average cost to slope downward throughout. The greater the amount of work a person has done since the time he started doing a particular work, the greater the experience he attains over a given period of time and with the experience he learns to do things in a better way than before thus being able to perform the same work in a faster and efficient manner.

This tends to reduce the cost per unit since efficiency is gained in performing the work. It is well known that a firm learns to produce a commodity more efficiently as the aggregate amount of its production increases over time. A good deal of empirical evidence is available which helps to prove that firm's cost of production depends not only on the quantity of output of a commodity it produces each month or year but also on the aggregate amount of that commodity produced since the time it started its production of that commodity. The aggregate output by a firm to date determines the degree of learning the firm has acquired in the process and the efficiency gained by it in doing so.

Therefore, we can draw a learning curve which relates the average cost of production of a commodity to the aggregate amount of output produced to date of that commodity. This learning curve slopes downward indicating that as the aggregate amount of output produced of a commodity by a firm increases over time, cost per unit goes on declining.

It should be noted that with the increase in aggregate production of a commodity over time, learning gained by a firm is not only in respect of improving efficiency or gaining experience in physical operations in the production of a commodity but also in respect of improving the overall organisation of the plant.

Besides the factor of technological progress, learning effect provides us another reason as to why long-run average cost curves are L-shaped rather than being U-shaped. To quote Professors **Stonier** and **Hague**, "Even, with a given technology, a firm can Team' to produce at; a lower unit cost the longer the period of time that has elapsed since a previous observation and the greater the aggregate amount of that product that has consequently been made". It may be, therefore, that technological change is not the only reason why long-run cost curves are L-shaped rather than U- shaped.

Professor **G.A. Smith** who has examined empirical evidence in this connection has concluded that with a very large size of firm, labour costs, assembly costs and distribution costs increase to a higher level and therefore large-sized plants with increasing average cost are not set up in actual practice and therefore empirical evidence cannot assess the cost situation in them.

Therefore, according to Professor Smith, empirical evidence does not refute the U-shaped nature of long-run average cost curve. Walters after examining the empirical studies by Dean and Johnston reached the conclusion that, "there is no large body of data which convincingly contradicts the hypothesis of a U-shaped long-run average cost curve and the fruitful results which depend on it".

Points to Remember

- **The law of diminishing marginal utility** is one of the main laws of economics. This law says that as the amount of commodity consumed rises, the utility obtained from each successive unit decreases with the consumption of all other commodities remaining the same.

- An **indifference curve** is defined as the locus of points, each showing a different combination of two substitute goods, which give the same r level of satisfaction to the consumer.

- The **Marginal Rate of Substitution** is the rate at which one commodity can be substituted for another, the level of satisfaction remaining constant.

- A **production function** is an equation, table or graph presenting the highest amount of a commodity that a company can produce from a particular set of inputs throughout a period of time.

Questions for Discussion

1. Discuss the concept of short-run and long-run production function.
2. Elaborate the concept of short-run and long-run cost function.
3. Explain the relationship between production function and cost function.
4. Explain the basis of increasing returns to scale.
5. What do you mean by production function?
6. Why is average cost curve U-Shaped?

Chapter 4...

Pricing Policies

Contents ...

Learning Objectives ...

➢ To understand the concept, objectives and process of pricing.
➢ To learn about the different pricing policies.
➢ To know the usage of different pricing practices for business decisions.
➢ To explain what can be the basis of pricing and what methods exist.

4.1 Pricing

4.1.1 Introduction

In the real world firms have multiple objectives and profit-maximisation is one of these objectives. Hence, all firms determine selling price and quantity which equates marginal revenue with marginal cost. Price denotes two aspects – on one hand it is *revenue* to the seller and on the other it is the *perceived value* of the good or the service to the buyer. Thus, the basic question is what is the right price for a product? When identifying the use of different price strategies it is important to understand the situations when a firm would need to decide about the price of its product. It is not only the seller of a *new product* who has to decide on its price but also the sellers of *modified or improved* products would have to decide about the price, for example, new colour scheme in cars are available at higher price.

Further, to suit to the different *dimensions of the market structure* (degree of competition), consumer's buying capacity, etc. are to be understood before reviewing pricing strategy for a new market or a new market segment. Even the *objective of the firm* also plays an important role in pricing decisions. For instance, a firm aiming at increasing market share will have different price strategy than a firm aiming at profit maximisation. Even the change in the *cost of production* influences the pricing decision of a firm. *Elasticity of demand* of a product also has to be considered in determining price. A *change in government policy* regarding taxation, subsidies and administered prices would also lead to change in existing prices. Thus, it can be said that a change in any of the factors which affect the firm's product would require reviewing its price strategy.

4.1.2 Objectives of Pricing Policy

Pricing policy is a part of the general operational planning of the firm. However, one should identify the objectives to be achieved before determining the price of the product.

While determining the price, the firm may consider one or more of the following objectives –

1. **Profit maximisation:** This being the primary objective of running any kind of business, every firm aims at achieving a pricing policy for its products which earns the maximum revenue and thus maximum profits for the firm.

2. **Market share:** One of the ways of capturing markets and increasing market share is lowering the price of the product in relation to the competitors' product.

3. **Target return on investment:** The returns expected by a firm influence the pricing of a product to a great extent.

4. **Meet or prevent competition:** In order to cope up with the competition or prevent it completely, as the case may be, the firm may prefer lowering the prices of its product and try to match the pricing adopted by the competitors.

5. **Price stabilisation:** Another objective of pricing is to stabilise the product prices, that is, to ensure that there are no unnecessary fluctuations over a considerable period of time.

6. **Resource mobilisation:** The pricing policy should be such that sufficient resources are made available for the firm's expansion, developmental investment, etc. and other growth strategies.

7. **Survival and growth:** An important objective of pricing policy is survival in the industry and achieving the expected rate of growth.

8. **Prestige and goodwill:** Pricing also aims at maintaining the prestige of the firm and increasing the goodwill of the firm.

9. **Achieving product-quality leadership:** Some companies aim at establishing quality products to their customers at a premium price.

4.1.3 Factors affecting Pricing Decisions

The pricing decisions for a product are affected by internal and external factors. The factors can be described as follows –

A. Internal Factors

1. Cost

While fixing the prices of a product, the firm should consider the fixed and variable costs incurred by the firm. The price of the product should be such that the costs incurred by the firm are recovered at the same time a profit margin is earned.

2. The predetermined objectives

The predetermined objectives of the firm should be given due importance before fixing the prices of the product. For instance, if the primary objective of a firm is to increase return on investment, then it may charge a comparatively higher price (a higher profit margin will be added), and if the objective of the firm is to increase its market share, then it may charge a lower price.

3. Image of the firm

The price of the product may also be determined on the basis of the brand name created by the firm over a period of time. For instance, HUL and Procter & Gamble can demand a higher price for their brands, as consumers trust and recognise their brands easily.

4. Product life cycle

Every product has a certain life (from its introduction in the market to its final withdrawal from the market). The stage at which the product is in its product life cycle also affects the pricing of the same. For instance, during the introductory stage the firm may charge lower price to attract the customers and note their response, and during the growth stage, a firm may increase the price considering the response obtained earlier.

5. Credit period offered

The pricing of the product is largely affected by the credit period offered by the company. Longer the credit period, higher may be the price (since time value of money is involved), and shorter the credit period, lower may be the price of the product.

6. Promotional activity

The extent of promotional and marketing activity undertaken by the firm helps it determine the price. Usually firms that incur heavy advertising and sales promotion costs keep the pricing of their product high in order to recover the cost.

B. External Factors

1. Competition

One of the most important factors affecting the pricing decisions is the competition faced by the firm's product in the market. If there is a situation of cut-throat competition the pricing policy should be such that it matches the prices of competitor's goods, whereas if there is no competition at all or if there is negligible competition, the firm can set the prices of the products higher.

2. Consumers
The standard of living of the customers, purchasing power, the value of the product as perceived by the customers should be given due importance while fixing the prices of the products.

3. Government control
Government rules and regulations must be considered while fixing the prices since they have a direct impact on the price and thus the revenue of the firm. For certain products of national importance, government may announce administered prices, and thus the firm's pricing policy will be affected.

4. Economic conditions
The economic conditions prevailing in the market have to be given due consideration while fixing the prices. At the time of recession, there is less money at the consumers' disposal; thus, the firm will prefer lowering the prices to an extent that influence the customers to chose the firm's products.

5. Channel intermediaries
The profits of the channel intermediaries will influence the price of the product; the longer the chain of intermediaries, higher would be the prices of the goods.

6. Government policy
Pricing decisions are also affected by the price control policies of the government when it is thought proper to arrest the inflationary trend in prices of certain commodities in the nation's interest.

4.1.4 Process of Pricing
An organisation goes through the following steps in setting its pricing policy.

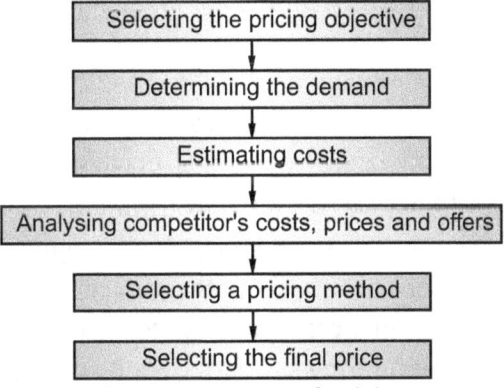

Fig. 4.1: Process of Pricing

1. Selecting the pricing objective: The first and foremost step is identifying pricing objectives. The company first decides where it wishes to position itself in the market. The five major objectives of pricing are – survival, maximum current profit, maximum market share, maximum market skimming, or product-quality leadership.

Companies usually pursue survival as their major objective if the industry in which they operate faces extreme competition or changing customer wants rapidly. As long as prices cover the variable costs and some fixed costs incurred by the company it stays in business.

However, survival is a short-run objective; in the long run, the firm must aim at adding maximum value through its products.

Many companies try to set a price that will maximise their current profits. The main task is to estimate the demand of the company's product and costs associated with it at various price levels and choose the price that produces maximum current profit, cash flow or rate of return on investment. This strategy assumes that the firm has knowledge of its demand and cost functions and will be able to make a best estimate of the same. However, in reality these are difficult to estimate.

The primary objective of some companies is to maximise their market share. They believe that a higher sales volume will lead to lower unit costs and thus a higher long-run profit. They set the lowest possible price, assuming the market is extremely price sensitive. The following conditions favour setting a low price of the products – the market is highly price sensitive, and a low price stimulates market growth rapidly. Production and distribution costs fall with accumulated production experience, that is, occurrence of learning curve over a period of time; a low price discourages actual and potential competition. Companies unveiling a new technology favour setting high prices to "skim" the market. Apple and Sony are a few frequent practitioners of market skimming pricing.

Whatever be the specific objective of the business, businesses that use price as a strategic tool will profit more than those who simply let costs or the market determine their pricing.

2. Determining the demand: After identifying objectives, the firm then needs to determine demand for its products. Each price alternative will have a different level of demand which will have a different impact on a company's marketing policies. In the normal case, demand and price are inversely related; the higher the price, the lower the demand and vice-versa. In the case of luxurious goods, the demand curve sometimes slopes upward. For example a perfume company raised the price of its product and sold more perfume bottles rather than less of them. Some consumers perceive that higher the price means better the product. However if the price is extremely high, the level of demand may fall.

Customers are most price-sensitive to products that have higher costs or are consumed frequently. They are less price-sensitive to low cost products or items they buy infrequently. Customers are less price-sensitive in a case where price is only a small part of the total cost of obtaining, operating and servicing the product over its expected period of use. A seller can charge a higher price than its competitors and still make more profits with more business flowing to it if the company can convince the customer that it offers the lowest total cost of ownership (TCO).

The process of estimating demand therefore leads to –

(i)   Estimating price sensitivity of market.

(ii) Estimating and analysing demand curve.

(iii) Determining price elasticity of demand.

3. Estimating costs: Demand of a product sets a ceiling (maximum level) on the price the company can charge for its product. Costs set the floor (minimum level). Every company aims to achieve a pricing policy that covers its cost of producing, distribution and selling the product, including a fair return for its effort and risk undertaken.

Costs can be classified into two types. Fixed costs (also known as overheads) are costs that do not vary with production or sales revenue; they are also called as period costs and are incurred irrespective of the level of production. Examples of fixed costs are rent, interest, salaries and so on. As the name suggests, variable costs vary directly with the level of production. However, these costs tend to be constant per unit produced. Average cost is the cost per unit which is calculated by dividing the total costs with the number of units produced.

To price intelligently, the management thus needs to know how its costs vary with different levels of production.

4. Analysing competitor's costs, prices and offers: Analysing competitor's costs, prices and offers is an important factor in setting prices since competitors' pricing policy has a direct impact on the firm's sales.

While demand sets a ceiling (maximum limit) and costs set a floor (minimum limit) to pricing, competitors' prices provide an in between point that is of extreme importance while deciding the pricing strategy of the firm. The price and quality of each competitor's product or service can be known by sending out comparison shoppers to price and compare the firm's products with that of competitors. Surveys can be conducted in order to know how consumers perceive the price and quality of each competitor's product or service. If the firm's product or service closely resembles that of a major competitor then price will have to be close to the competitor or the sales will be lost. If the firm's product or service is inferior, the firm will not be able to charge as much as the competitor. One should be aware that competitors might even change their prices in response to price of the firm that is the competitors will be tracking the firm's prices too.

5. Selecting a pricing method: The firm should choose the appropriate method on the basis of pricing objective out of various alternate methods available.

6. Selecting the final price: Pricing methods narrow the range from which the company must select its final price that is to say pricing methods enable a firm to eliminate a few prices from the cluster of alternatives available. In selecting the appropriate price, the company must consider additional factors, including psychological pricing, gain and risk pricing, the influence of other marketing-mix elements on price, company-pricing policies, and the impact of price on other parties. Overall consideration of all the factors affecting the product price must be done.

4.2 Pricing Policies

The main pricing policies can be classified into three broad groups –
1. Cost-oriented Pricing
2. Competition-oriented Pricing
3. Pricing based on Economic considerations
4. Special Considerations in Product Line Pricing
5. Other Pricing Strategies

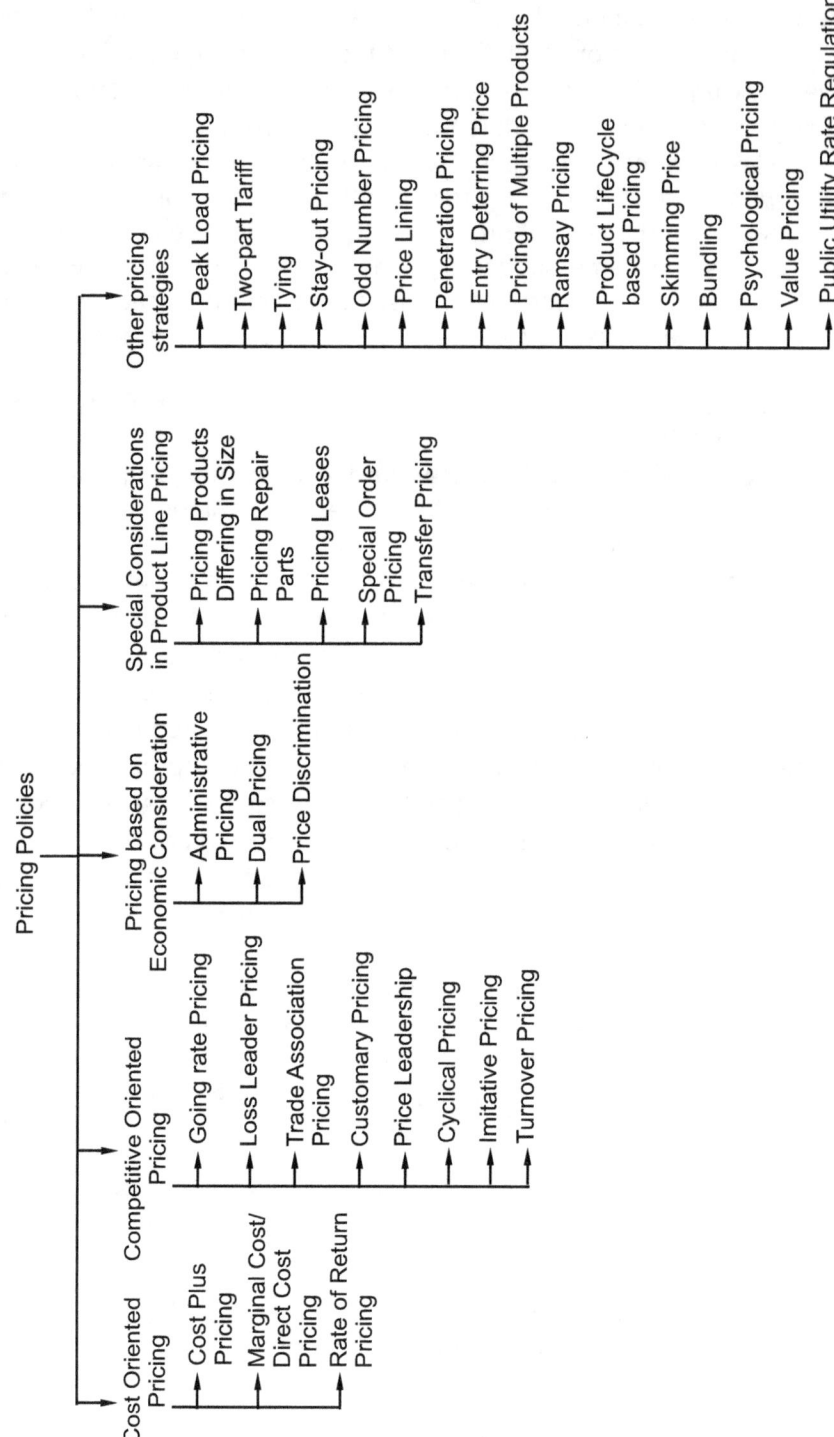

Fig. 4.2: Pricing Policies

4.2.1 Cost-Oriented Pricing

It includes the following:

1. Cost-Plus Pricing (or Mark-Up Pricing)

A firm has to earn some profits to survive in the long run, irrespective of the market structure or its objective; the natural basis of determination of price should be the cost of production with some percent margin. Hence the term *'cost plus pricing'*. Under this system, price of the product is the sum of cost plus a profit margin.

This is the most popular method of pricing in practice because – (i) it is simple to compute; (ii) it assures profits in business; (iii) it is an objective method, that is, more scientific method; (iv) it's popularity is due to the reason that it takes care of business uncertainties and ignorance.

In this method the price is determined by adding a fixed mark-up to the cost of acquiring or producing the product.

The question arises is which cost? Is it total cost including the fixed and variable cost or only the variable cost?

Hall and Hitch found that firms aim at long run profit maximisation and generally do not attempt to maximise short run profit by equating MR = MC principle. The firms simply calculate the variable cost of the product, add to it the allocated fixed cost, and then add a mark-up.

Illustration: If the direct or variable cost of the product is ₹ 100, its allocated overhead is ₹ 60 and the desired mark-up is 50 percent, the price of the product will be ₹ 100 + 60 + 0.5 × 160 = ₹ 240. Thus, calculation of a cost-plus price is done in two steps: (i) determination of relevant full-cost, and (ii) determination of what 'plus' the firm adopts.

Firms which aim to maximise profit would use *total cost of production as the basis of price.* For fixation of price per unit of output, average cost would be considered. Hence, cost plus pricing is also called Average Cost Pricing or Full Cost Pricing.

A firm, thus, will consider total cost per unit or average cost (Average Fixed Cost + Average Variable Cost) and determine a mark-up, depending upon various considerations, such as, target rate of return, degree of competition, price elasticity and availability of substitutes.

Price, thus, arrived would be: **Price = AC + u**

Here, u is the percentage of mark-up.

Illustration: Micro Tech Company has invested ₹ 10 crores in plant and machinery, with a capacity to produce 10,000 units of computers per month. Total Variable Cost (TVC) is estimated at ₹ 5 crores and the firm expects a return of 20 percent on total investment. What should be the price of computers if we assume that the firm can sell its entire output?

Basic Price = Total Cost = 10 + 5 = ₹ 15 crores.

Return Margin expected = 20% of 15 = ₹ 3 crores.

Total Revenue (TR) = 15 + 3 = ₹ 18 crores.

Price = 18,00,00,000 ÷ 10,000 Units = ₹ 18,000 per computer.

Limitations of cost-plus or full-cost pricing – (i) while fixing the mark-up, the firm considers its costs but not the market demand; (ii) this method cannot be applied to industries dealing with perishable goods; (iii) it does not consider adequately the competitive forces.

Advantages: This method is quite a popular method in small and retail businesses due to its benefits, such as (i) this method is easy and convenient for a firm to adopt, even in cases where the firm handles multiple products; (ii) cost-plus pricing reduces the cost of decision-making; (iii) cost-plus pricing is more popular and suitable in industries where price leadership prevails; (iv) the prices fixed in this manner are fair from the consumers point of view; (v) it fulfils the goal of profit maximisation.

2. Marginal Cost/Direct Cost Pricing

The marginal cost pricing implies that the price of the product is based on the *incremental* cost of production. The full-cost pricing is based on average cost; the incremental or marginal cost pricing is based on *variable cost only*. The difference between the full-cost and marginal cost pricing is *fixed cost only*.

The full-cost pricing is a long period phenomenon; the incremental-cost pricing is a short-period phenomenon.

The concept of marginal cost is known in economics but in practical business the 'marginal' is replaced by 'incremental' because in real life situations one does not generally find changes in variable costs with *one unit change* in output. Rather the firms try to analyse the increase in cost as result of some significant amount of change in output.

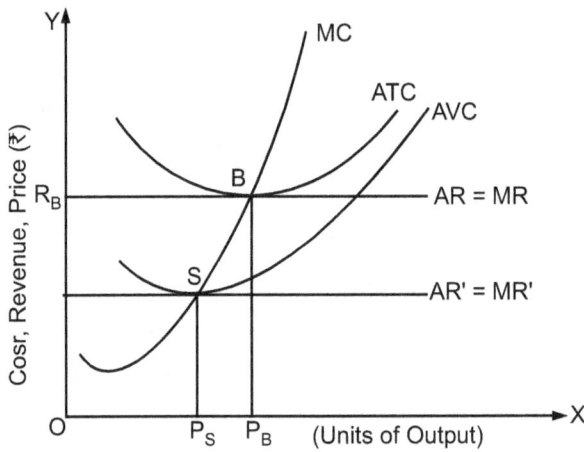

Fig. 4.3: Incremental Cost and Full Cost Pricing

In the *short run*, in a perfectly competitive market situation, a firm will 'shut down' only when the price is below the average variable cost, while in the long run the firm must cover its average cost (average cost = average variable + average fixed costs, which equals fully-distributed costs). Thus, in case of incremental cost coverage there is a guarantee that the firm does not 'shut down', but since it does not cover the fixed costs fully, it does not guarantee that the firm will operate at 'break-even' point.

In Fig. 4.3 point B is the break-even point, S is the 'shut-down' point. Their respective prices and quantities are shown by points R_B, R_S, P_B, P_S.

Merits of Marginal/Incremental/Direct Cost Pricing

(i) Marginal cost pricing is quite useful for pricing over the life cycle of the product;

(ii) Marginal cost pricing is satisfactory in case of multi-product, multi-process and multi-market firms, where full-cost pricing is quite absurd as different products, markets and processes do not have equal impact on costs;

(iii) Marginal cost pricing allows a firm to develop a far more aggressive pricing policy than does the cost plus pricing. An aggressive pricing policy should lead to higher sales and maybe reduced marginal costs with the help of increased marginal physical productivity and lower input prices.

Limitations

(i) The marginal cost pricing does not guarantee that the firms will operate at the break-even point;

(ii) At times those who manage the firm are unaware of the marginal cost pricing method;

(iii) In a period of recession, firms using marginal cost pricing may lower cost and prices to maintain their sales and may lead other firms to reduce prices resulting in cut-throat competition;

(iv) Marginal cost pricing helps in the short-run period and can be effectively applied on temporary basis and thus does not apply to a long period stable pricing policy.

The marginal cost pricing method is adopted by the firms when –

(i) It wants to introduce its products into new markets the firm must bother mostly about its variable costs;

(ii) The firm faces stiff competition in the market; here too the firm must take care of its variable costs; or

(iii) It has unutilised capacity. For example, if there is some unutilised capacity in a tourist vehicle, it is advisable to carry additional traffic even at reduced fare rather than letting the vacant capacity remain unutilised.

3. **Rate of Return (or Target) Pricing**

A refined version of cost-plus pricing is the Target Pricing. When, due to certain reasons, the firm has to revise its prices it needs to ensure that the prices so revised would allow it to maintain either –

(i)   A fixed percentage mark-up over cost;

(ii) Profit as a fixed percentage of total sales; or

(iii) A fixed return on existing investments.

Rate of return or Target Pricing is determined in the following five steps –

- The firm specifies an expected rate of return on investment (it is expressed as earnings divided by capital invested) – Step 1.

- To determine a 'normal rate' of output by the firm and then to estimate the 'full cost' on the basis of this normal rate of production. – Step 2.

- To estimate 'capital turnover' (which is expressed as invested capital divided by full cost) – Step 3.

- To multiply capital turnover ratio with the expected rate of return on investment (same as step 1) and this will give mark-up percentage – Step 4.

- Step 5 gives computation of rate of return pricing which is obtained by adding up the full-cost and mark-up, that is, P = Full Cost + Mark-Up.

- To sum up the above said steps in formulae form –

$$\text{Mark-up} = x = \frac{\text{Capital invested}}{\text{Full cost}} \times \frac{\text{Earnings}}{\text{Capital invested}} = \frac{\text{Earnings}}{\text{Full cost}}$$

The rate of return price changes when the cost changes. In the same way, if the demand conditions or competition for the product changes it leads to change in mark-up and leading to change in price.

This method of pricing has the same merits and shortcomings as cost-plus pricing. However, this method enjoys additional benefits like – (i) in case of rate of return pricing full cost is based on 'normal' output and cost, which is not so in the case of cost-plus pricing; (ii) in this pricing, mark-up is based on expected or planned rate of return on investment, whereas cost-plus pricing is based on an arbitrary mark-up.

4.2.2 Competition-Oriented Pricing

This category includes –

- Going-Rate Pricing
- Loss Leader Pricing
- Trade Association Pricing
- Customary Pricing

- Price Leadership
- Cyclical Pricing
- Imitative Pricing and Suggested Pricing
- Turnover Pricing

1. Going-Rate Pricing

A question is often asked as to why all the brands of packaged pasteurised milk packets, or packaged drinking water are priced the same? The answer is that all the players are using the going-rate pricing strategy. This strategy is adopted when most of the players do not indulge in separate pricing but prefer to follow the prevailing market price. The simplest form of going-rate pricing is where the firm simply examines the general pricing structure in the industry and fixes the price of its own product accordingly. Certain practical advantages of this price policy are that in situation where there are particular problems in measuring costs, this method proves to be logical and rational to adopt. Even in case of industries characterised by price-leadership adopt this pricing method as it saves the firm from the dangers of price-wars. Another advantage of this price policy is that the calculations in going-rate policy are less costly and troublesome for the business than the exact calculations of cost and demand of the product. The small or new firms may not be sure of shift in demand by charging a price different from the prevailing market price. Lastly, the products sold by the players are very close substitutes, hence their cross elasticity is very high.

The Brookings study reveals that the approach of going-rate pricing is followed even in some large U.S. firms, besides the medium and small ones. These firms follow a 'market-determined' price, which implies a price prevailing in the market due to market forces or set by a price leader. Going-rate price policy is witnessed in monopolistic and oligopoly markets where product differentiation is minimal or is only apparent, and consumer's switching cost is almost negligible. Such a policy is generally followed in case of products whose development has reached a stage of maturity. As a result, both producers and consumers have come to accept a stable price relationship, whereby prices are arrived at in relation to the price set by the competitors. Thus, the consumers ask for a good soap or shampoo instead of a particular brand.

2. Loss Leader Pricing

This approach is widely used in retailing business. It is a policy which aims at increasing profits. An interesting strategy adopted by the firms, which manufacture or sell multiple products, charge relatively low price on some popular product with the hope that the customers, who come to buy the popular product, will also buy some other products produced and sold by the firm. Such a product is the firm's loss leader. The loss leader does not mean that this product is necessarily sold at a loss. It only means that the actual price charged is lower than what could have been charged. The main idea of making a popular product a loss leader is that the profits thus sacrificed will be made good by profits on the other products.

The firms sometimes compel their buyers to buy some product/products along with the purchase of a popular product. The customer in turn sees the products forced on him as a loss hoping to make up the loss through profit on the popular product. For example, HP has resorted to such price practice as it charges low price for its entire range of printers but every printer has a specific cartridge and these are relatively high priced. Thus, the printer is the loss leader, whereas the cartridge compensates for the loss. An important point to be noted is that the term loss leader does not necessarily mean *loss on cost of production* of the good.

Bob R. Holdren conducted a study of the market behaviour of the grocery stores and found some features essentially to be present for a product to serve as a loss-leader, such as –

(i) Demand for commodity should not be elastic;

(ii) The buyers should have knowledge of prices of the same good in other selling units;

(iii) The quantity to be bought by the buyers should be large enough so as to feel the benefit of price reduction;

(iv) Goods should be more or less of the same quality as others are selling; neither should price reduction give an impression of quality reduction.

3. Trade Association Pricing

To avoid uncertainties of pricing decisions and the downward pressure on prices due to competition, firms come to the agreements – *express or implied* – to maintain prices at a similar level. Though *express* agreements are declared as illegal, the firms can easily and safely enter into an *implied or tacit* agreement. However, individual firms may find it worthwhile to break out of any such agreements and it leads to possible alternatives like –

(i) The price-cut may spark off a price war between the firms which continues till one or all firms give up the struggle; or

(ii) If the firm breaking out of the agreement is able to keep its rivals in the dark about the price-cut. In such a case, though rare, the firm can gain out of price-cut only when either the original buyers of this firm are unaware or are loyal to this firm. Generally, due to these possible outcomes, firms do not break out of the collusion, whether explicit or tacit.

4. Customary Pricing

In case of some commodities the prices get fixed because they have prevailed over a long period of time. Any change in costs for such products gets reflected in quality or quantity of the product rather than its price. For instance, the price of a cup of tea or coffee in the market is customarily fixed. The customary price may change only when there is significant change in the cost of production otherwise any small changes in cost of production will result in either quality change or smaller quantity per cup. If a new firm enters the market and has lower costs than the existing firms, still it may sell at customary price because any reduction in price by the new entrant firm will trigger off a price war. Any firm which plans to enter must consider the effect of the entry on price, even if the entry appears profitable. The entry of new firms will influence the total supply and demand for the already existing firms' output and the entrant firm may actually realise that the price cannot support his cost. Thus, if the new firm cannot set their price closer to customary price they cannot survive.

5. Price Leadership

In monopolistic or oligopolistic market structure, there is one or many big firms whose cost of production is low and they dominate the industry. In such a situation, the small firms are not likely to enter into a price war with these big firms. In such a case, these small firms may follow the price fixed by the leader. For example, Hindustan Lever may be accepted as a leader in the soap industry or Cadbury in the chocolate industry. Small firms may change the price only when there is a general change in the cost of production and the price leader has recognised and adjusted his price on that basis.

The price charged by the small firms need not be equal to the price charged by the price-leader. There might be some differences in their prices but it is for sure that any change in the price is always in the same direction for both the price-leader and the follower firms, generally in the same proportion too. As a result, both will have their own markets to cater, thus avoiding diversion of customers. It may be noted that during the period of rising prices it is easier to maintain price leadership pattern but during falling prices, the firms are generally attracted by the idea of getting others' customers by providing price concessions and it needs a great deal of statesmanship on the part of the price-leader to maintain his position.

6. Cyclical Pricing

The various methods of pricing employed are not only based on different market structures – perfect and imperfect competition but are also influenced by seasonal and cyclical fluctuations in economic activity. The seasonal factors operate on short-term basis – up to a year – and cyclical fluctuations influence economic activity for a long run – up to 3 or more years.

Businesses do not operate in isolation and firms need to take stock of economic conditions in formulating their policies. In fact firms cannot ignore the ups and downs in the economy in which they are operating. Thus, *when pricing by a firm is based on an assessment of general economic environment, it is known as cyclical pricing.* In a condition of depression in the market, the firm has to reduce the price to continue in the market and the reverse is that in the period of boom the firm will reap the benefits of rising prices in the market. The firm has to make these adjustments in prices even when the cost of production remains the same.

There are several methods which a firm can adapt in cyclical pricing. The firm may resort to changes in the structure of discounts and allowances as a part of cyclical pricing. It may fix a standard (or full) cost and adjust his mark-up according to changes in the market environment. There are many alternative policies for consideration while deciding upon cyclical price adjustments and the simplest option is no price change.

If a firm considers that the cyclical fluctuations in demand for the product is due to changes in incomes, profits which are beyond the control of the firm and are not closely related to price, the firm chooses to keep the price unchanged. Producers of industrial material and equipment have generally followed this policy.

Price leaders in oligopoly markets generally justify their price adjustments to changes in costs. However, big industries with large stocks of goods and material feel the impact of changing costs much less than the small firms with small inventory.

Firms in industries which are characterised by strong price leadership find that an appropriate policy would be to vary prices in conformity with *the prices of substitutes.*

A firm can decide to adjust and change its prices according to changes in general price index but it is not very scientific because the general price index also includes the price changes of goods which have no relation with the product of the firm.

Price adjustments may be done in a way that *market share* of the firm is stabilised.

Rigid pricing suggests that firms should follow a stable pricing policy irrespective of the phase of economic cycle because if consumers can postpone their purchase they would not be affected by a fall or rise in prices and the firm does not benefit by change in price of its product. Under flexible pricing firms keep their prices flexible to meet the challenges of change in demand. The argument for flexible pricing is that during recession prices should be reduced in view of the decreased paying capacity of consumers and can be raised during prosperity to take advantage of higher demand.

In short, whether the firms should continue with the same pricing, irrespective of the phase of cyclical fluctuation or should they adopt different strategies across the phases? Though there is no certain answer to such a critical question yet attempts are made to identify pricing strategies at each phase.

7. Imitative Pricing and Suggested Prices

This pricing approach is used in retail business. In oligopolistic market conditions, the firms imitate their price leader. But in non-oligopoly situations also, a firm considers it useful to imitate the prices set by other firms. This makes decision-making quite easy and the decision-maker does not have to undertake the demand and cost analysis.

Suggested prices (Retail Pricing) is one that the manufacturer or wholesaler has found feasible, given market conditions and suggests to the retailer to charge this price from the customers. The producer fixes a price for its product. The product then goes to the wholesaler, who is allowed some commission on the company price. Finally the retailer gets the product and charges a price that includes its own commission. It is the retail price that the consumer pays. For all goods manufactured by large organised firms, the retailer has an upper limit known as Maximum Retail Price (MRP), which consists of the retailer's commission; hence it has a limited choice to decide on the price.

Many managements of retail trade prefer to work on suggested prices as they do not have to undertake its own individual analysis of market and cost conditions. This approach limits the flexibility of retail trade to meet the local conditions but this approach is believed to protect the small retailers from unfair competition from the large ones. On the other hand, the manufacturers and wholesalers prefer to stick to suggested price as it can help in control and stability of prices.

8. Turnover Pricing

It is generally believed that the mark-up on high turnover products should be lower because (i) these items are purchased frequently by the consumers; (ii) these items require less selling effort per rupee of sales, thus saving selling time; (iii) these items occupy space for a shorter period.

However, the above arguments given to keep the mark-up on high turnover products low is not very true. The reason is that the turnover is measured from the point of view of a seller, while frequency of purchase from the consumer's point of view. For example, a commodity like electric bulbs may have high turnover, but not a high frequency of purchase. The logic can be understood in another way and that is lower price results in higher turnover and in fact turnover is only one factor in the pricing decisions.

4.2.3 Pricing based on other Economic Considerations

This category includes the following pricing methods –

*   Administered Pricing;
*   Dual Pricing;
*   Price Discrimination or Differential Pricing.

1. Administered Pricing

The prices which are statutorily fixed by the government after considering the cost and the stipulated profit per unit are referred to as *administered prices*. The objective of administered prices is to control prices of essential goods and inputs and to provide them at economic prices to weaker sections of consumers and producers. Prices of certain goods like steel, coal, fertiliser, etc. are statutorily fixed. Another example is the Public Distribution System (PDS), where fair price shops sell essential commodities to public at administered prices.

The drawback with administered prices is that it is unable to compensate for a rise in costs and very often the retention price allowed by the government is very low. Further, while fixing the retention price, the increase in overhead cost is not taken into account. It is found that the industries that are subject to administered prices turn into sick units as they are unable to generate adequate funds for maintenance, modernisation and expansion. Moreover, such industries are hardly attractive to fresh investments. The solution lies in the fact that there should be some built-in mechanism in the administered prices to take account of any cost escalation.

2. Dual Pricing

A market, where a commodity is covered at the same time under the administered price as well as market price, is said to have dual prices. A part of the firm's output is subjected to administered price, while the rest of its output is sold in the free market. For example, sugar in India has a dual market system.

Administered prices are fixed by the government considering the cost and a stipulated mark-up. Generally, the administered price is lower than the prevailing market price. In the dual market system, there are two separate demand and supply curves for the product; one related to the fixed price and the other related to the free market price. When taken together, the demand and supply curves would show a link. The volume of supply and demand and the average price in the market is determined by the relative shares of the firm's output falling in the categories of administered and free market prices.

As mentioned, example of dual price system in India has been sugar. A major part of production reaches the public through the public distribution system, that is, at administered price, while the rest is sold in the free market. The objective of dual pricing is that the essential goods should reach the weaker sections of producers and consumers at a reasonable price. The difference between the fixed price and market price can be taken as a gauge to measure the pressure of economically stronger and non-priority group of consumers and producers on the demand for the dual-priced products.

Under dual pricing system we can discuss the multiple fixed prices. Consumers may be grouped into different categories on the basis of priority and then different prices are fixed for each category, while the remaining output is sold in the free market price. For instance, in the case of steel the government may fix the following categories in the order of priority, such as defence, railways, construction, and the rest of the consumers. Such a pricing is known as "differential pricing".

However, there has been misuse in the use of dual pricing system. For example in case of chemical fertilisers, the small farmers, who do not personally use these fertilisers, buy them at the low price from the government and pass them to the rich farmers.

3. Price Discrimination

'Price discrimination' is the art of selling the same commodity produced under a single control to different buyers at different prices. Price discrimination is possible and profitable only under the following conditions –

(a) **Existence of two or more than two markets:** There must be at least two markets in which a monopolist can classify his customers and charge different prices for an identical product.

(b) **Existence of different elasticity of demand in different markets:** In different markets, the elasticity of demand for a monopolist's product must be different. With the different elasticity the monopolist will succeed in charging high price in the inelastic market and low price in the elastic market.

(c) **No possibility of resale:** It should neither be permissible nor possible to purchase commodity from a cheaper market and resell it in the costlier market.

If buyers themselves become sellers, it will prevent a discriminating monopoly firm from selling the commodity in the costlier or higher price market.

(d) **Full control over supply:** Existence of monopoly element is essential for the success of price discrimination. If there is keen competition among the sellers, the uniform price will prevail in the entire market.

Types of Price Discrimination or Differential Pricing

There are many bases on which the open price discrimination is practised. These are as follows –

• **Time Price Differentials:** Demand for a product or a service has time dimension. The demand may shift in fairly short-time intervals. For example, demand for telephone facilities is more in the day time rather than at night. On the other hand, for theatres it is evening time and night which is more significant than the morning show demand. A seller who wishes to capitalise on the fact that buyer's demand elasticity change over time, will quote different price for the same product or service at different points of time. The variations in buyer's demand elasticity may occur within a short period of (clock-time) 24 hours (for example, telephone services) or it may change over days and months (seasonal changes).

o **Clock-time price differentials**: When demand elasticity of buyers undergoes a change within 24-hour period, the seller can discriminate between the buyers demanding services at different point of time within the 24-hour period. This price is clock-time price differentials and the aim is to charge higher price for the product or service during the period of relatively inelastic demand and lower price during the period of relatively elastic demand; for instance, day and night rates of long-distance telephone calls.

o **Calendar-time price differentials**: When price differentials are not based on demand elasticity differences but simply on time differences like days, weeks, months, we call them calendar-time differentials. These differences are often found in recreational activities like swimming pool charges, resort charges on hill-stations, prices of coolers, fans, etc. differ on basis of off-season and on-season demands. The aim of this pricing is same as clock-hour differentials, that is, exploit the variation in demand elasticity over time.

- **Use-Price Differentials:** Price differentials can be based on the type of use of the product or service by the buyer. For example, auditorium charges can differ for school using it for their annual function, to a missionary office for charity, to a party for commercial purpose. Similarly, electricity can be used for residential or industrial purposes and hence the charges can be different. In case of use-price variations, the seller divides the market into different segments according to the demand elasticity based on buyer's use of the product or service, and then set the prices differently for different segments.

- **Quality-price differentials:** The quality becomes a significant determinant of demand elasticity if the product caters to that group of consumers who are concerned about its quality. To charge such a price, the seller has to create differences in quality to sell his product. Sellers use many devices to create quality differences; change in appearance of the product, change in its sale channel, etc. It is found that consumers generally judge quality by the price of the product.

- **Quantity differentials:** When the seller discriminates on the basis of the quantity, it is referred to as quantity differentials. These can be (i) Cumulative discounts – price concessions given by the seller on the total quantity bought by a particular buyer during a period of time, say a calendar year. Discounts are given in price to encourage bulk buying and encourage buyer loyalty. (ii) Quantity discounts – these are price concessions based on the size of the lot purchased at one time and delivered at one location. The size of the lot is measured in terms of either physical units (goods of homogenous nature as they can be counted in number or weight, for example, scooters, and steel rods) or monetary units (goods of heterogeneous nature furniture, scientific instruments). The main aim of quantity discounts is to encourage bigger orders which reduce his cost of selling, packaging, delivery, accounting, administration, etc. (iii) Functional/Distributors discount – functional or distributors' discounts are according to the trade status, that is, wholesaler, retailer, etc. It is to be noted that while deciding about the discount rate and discount structure, the seller cannot ignore the tradition in the industry and the position of competitors in this regard. If he ignores them he would be inviting a price war.

- **Geographic Price Differentials:** Price discrimination can also be practised by a seller on the basis of differences in buyer's location and hence known as geographic price differentials. A seller may quote one of the two types of prices (a) prices at the point of origin of the goods (F.O.B. - free on board price) or (b) prices at the point of their destination – "delivered price" which includes cost of shipping the goods to the buyer's location or to the nearest point of transportation. It is often believed that the delivered prices are discriminatory. The final criterion of discrimination "is not the form in which the price is quoted, but the comparison of realised receipts of the seller" from the two forms of prices.

- **F.O.B. Pricing:** When a seller charges a uniform price from all the buyers falling into a particular trade status and buying similar quantities of a particular quality of a good, we call it F.O.B. pricing. This pricing is practised under conditions like –

  (i)   It is only when transportation cost is relatively small compared to the value of goods;

  (ii)   Fixed cost or overheads must not be very high to force the sellers to go out searching for customers in distant markets;

  (iii) The firm should not be under pressure from rivals and for this it is essential that products must be differentiated;

  (iv)   The firm must have plants which are dispersed and in close proximity to the demand points, so that the situations of excess demand or excess supplies do not occur.

- **Uniform Delivered (or postage stamp) Pricing:** A seller follows postage-stamp pricing if he charges the same delivered price at all locations of the buyers. Postage-stamp prices may be quoted in two ways –

(i)   A uniform price is quoted for every destination after including an average expenditure for freight; or

(ii)   A uniform F.O.B. price is quoted and the buyers are authorised to deduct their freight cost from the bill. In both the situations, discrimination is involved as the buyer who is located in proximity to the seller pays less than the one who is located far away. In products which have a national market and whose cost of transportation is relatively very small compared to the value of the product, postage stamp pricing is common and effective. Such pricing is followed in goods like cloth, cosmetics, and soft drinks, electrical and electronic equipments.

- **Zone Pricing:** Many a time, a seller, instead of charging a uniform price throughout the country, divides the economy into zones and charges the same 'delivered' price within each zone but different prices in different zones. This is referred to as zone pricing. Within a zone there is a uniform price but between zones price differs to the extent it is sufficient to cover his average freight cost as a whole. There is no discrimination till the seller's price zones are the same as high freight-rate zones (because the difference in cost only reflects difference in cost of freight) and in such a case zone pricing is the same as F.O.B. pricing.

- **Freight Equalisation Pricing:** When a seller charges the buyer the freight cost which would have been incurred by the latter (buyer) had he bought from the nearest seller, it is known as freight-equalisation pricing. The seller sets 'delivered' prices identical to those of the rivals and in the process absorbs freight cost. Freight equalisation policy has been adopted when (i) there is excess capacity; (ii) there is highly competitive product market; (iii) industry requires high fixed costs.

- **Personal Price Differentials:** Sellers follow personal price differentials in three forms – (i) charging a price lower than that charged from the rest of the customers; (ii) charging the market price but no service charges; (iii) charging the market price but no credit, which does not carry any interest charges. Sellers give price discounts to certain buyers for certain reasons like loyalty of the buyer to the seller, high regularity and frequency in purchase or simply for personal relations.

- **Cash Discounts:** Many a time price differentials have nothing to do with the quantity, quality, location or time, but with the promptness of payment and such payment promptness are called cash discounts. A buyer who purchases on credit indicates his weak financial position and is therefore required to pay more to cover up the risk of default. Cash discounts provide a comfortable liquidity position and minimise bad credit risks.

- **National Areas Price Differentials:** National areas price differentials exist when domestic buyers have to pay more than foreign buyers for a particular quantity of specific quality of a good, and the domestic buyers are not in a position to import from the cheaper international market due to trade restrictions. The price charged by a seller in the domestic market differs from that charged in the foreign market. This difference is mainly due to the nature of competition in the foreign and domestic markets and the government rules provide certain benefits when operating in one kind of market rather than another.

- **International Price Discrimination and Dumping:** The international price is either higher than domestic price or lower than it, depending upon market forces. Thus, firms do not charge same price in the international market as in the domestic market as the market conditions are not the same. At the same time, companies may charge different prices in different nations using discriminatory pricing methods. The firm may segregate its market on the basis of that particular country's paying capacity and price elasticity of demand. One very common form of such pricing is called as dumping; a strategy adopted by a nation where the product is exported in bulk to a foreign country at a price with is either below the domestic market price, or below the marginal cost of production. **Dumping is often referred to a pricing which is below the fair value of the product.** Thus, it is a kind of predatory pricing which is aimed at gaining monopoly in a foreign country or dumping (disposing) of excess inventory to avoid reduction in home price and help in reduction in producers' income.

- **Retail Pricing:** The pricing practices followed in retail trade are –

  Mark-up pricing: Most retailers resort to mark-up pricing, that is, prices fixed include the total cost of procuring the product + a normal mark-up. This mark-up is more or less fixed and is influenced by the amount of turnover and the storage costs.

  What the traffic can bear: It means charging the customer as high a price as the customer is prepared to pay.

  Price adjustment according to terms of sale: Charging a higher price if the buyer is given certain facilities like home delivery, credit facility, etc. On the other hand, it will be lower than the mark-up pricing or 'what the traffic can bear' policy if the buyer provides certain advantages to the retailer, like advance payment, etc.

  However, in certain cases, the retailer has little control over price. These are –

  ➤ Sometimes retailer of a product faces a tough competition in the market and hence has to sell the product only at the 'going rate' in the market.

> ➤ Certain products that are socially essential or used by the masses, the government fixes the price statutorily of the product; for example, petroleum and petroleum products, sugar, etc.

> ➤ In case of popular products with brand names, the manufacturers specify the price at which the product is to be made available to the customers and such a price (exclusive of local taxes) is printed on the product. The retailer earns his commission and has no influence on the price of the product; for example, Bajaj scooters, VIP suitcases, Hawkins pressure cookers, etc.

4.2.4 Special Considerations in Product Line Pricing

1. Pricing Products Differing in Size

Products like shoes, clothes, containers, etc. differ in size and the producer has two options while pricing such products – either charge different prices depending on sizes or may charge same price for all sizes.

(a) **Pricing according to the size:** In products where size is the measure of the value of the product, then bigger the size, higher the value, higher the price. For example, cooler, television set, sophisticated machinery etc. However, each multi-product firm producing various sizes of a product should develop a systematic relationship between the size of the good and its price, so that when additional sizes are introduced the prices are automatically known to the buyers.

(b) **Pricing same for all sizes:** In a situation where cost does not increase significantly with size, the seller may sell all sizes (at least in a group of sizes) of the product at the same price. For example, shoes for kids in the age group 0-5 years can be grouped as one size and sold at the same price.

2. Pricing Repair Parts/Spare Parts

Durable goods need repairs or need spare parts and pricing of spare parts is quite a complex problem. It involves the following to be considered –

- Too high a price may shy away the buyer and he may not buy the equipment from that manufacturer.

- The original supplier has a monopoly over those buyers who are committed to buy the spare parts only from them.

- It is true that due to competition from ancillary industry, the original seller cannot keep the price of his spare parts very high.

While pricing the spare parts the manufacturers have to consider that –

(i) Cost-plus pricing policy is followed;

(ii) The sum of prices of all the parts taken together should not be more than the price of the equipment.

In case of repair parts no competition exists and it is possible and profitable for the producer to keep the price high.

3. Pricing Leases and Licenses

Pricing leases and licenses means deciding the lease rent to be charged on the basis of the capacity of each user, when equipment is given on lease. If the equipment has various uses then a high rent can be charged from those getting higher surplus. The minimum limit for lease can be calculated by considering production, selling and services cost of the equipment.

When licenses are granted or use of patents is permitted, royalty is levied on the user which is decided by considering – the expenses incurred on developing the patented products/process; the upper limit of the royalty is decided after taking into account the benefit of the product/process to the licensee; the lower limit is decided by the incremental cost of administering and operating the licensing arrangements.

4. Special Order Pricing

While pricing for special orders, that is, one which are not regular, like evening gowns to be made for elite class customers or for attending award functions by the celebrities certain questions are to be kept in mind – What is the highest price the buyer can pay? What is the lowest price that the seller can accept? If alternative uses of resources are available, then acceptance of the special order and the pricing must be based on the opportunity cost principle.

The general practice is that the special orders are priced by adding to normal full cost a pre-determined mark-up to get fair profits.

Many a time the seller uses refusal price, that is, a price so high as to discourage the placement of the order. The aim of such a price is to encourage customers to buy standard brands of the seller.

5. Transfer Pricing

Large multi-product, multi-process companies, to avoid managerial diseconomies of scale, divide the establishment into smaller units, such as departments and divisions, making each unit an independent profit centre. This division results in transfer of goods, services and money from one unit to another within the organisation. Thus, when a multi-product firm is engaged in production of such goods where one product is an intermediary for the other unit of the organisation, it is said to be vertically integrated. The firm now faces the problem of fixing the price of a product demanded for internal use. Since use of these intermediaries is a part of the total cost of product but involves no cash outflow rather it is only a transfer of accounts from one subsidiary to another, it is called *transfer pricing*.

If transfer prices understate or overstate values and costs, the divisional decisions would go counter to the company's corporate objectives. The manner in which the transfer price is fixed will influence the output decisions of each division and of the firm as a whole, and thereby the overall profits of the firm. Thus, one of the vital problems of a large firm while dealing with transfer pricing is, what should be the price which one division charges from the other division of the firm for the product sold to the latter?

Transfer pricing has gained significant importance with the growth of MNCs. Globally over 60% of transactions are between associated enterprises, that is, from parent company to subsidiary or from one subsidiary to another. The price of goods or services transacted between associated concerns would add to the cost of production of the final good; hence transfer pricing is often misused to evade taxes on net profit. Governments keep strict check on transfer pricing so that corporates may not evade tax payments.

The transfer price rules which the group management lays down must be such that they pursue the following goals simultaneously –

- Maximisation of group-profits; and

- Maximisation of profits at each profit-centre, treating each division as an autonomous unit.

Three important cases of transfer pricing are –

(i) **Transfer Pricing of a product with a Competitive External Market:** In case the transferred product can be purchased and sold in the competitive market, the appropriate *transfer price is the market price.* In such a situation, group profit maximisation requires that all divisions operate at their respective MR = MC points (equilibrium point).

(ii) **Transfer Pricing of a Product with no External Market:** In case of inter-divisional transfer, that is, in case the product of a division can be sold to another division of the firm, then the transfer pricing is at the level of the marginal cost of production to maximise group profits.

(iii) **Transfer Pricing of a Product with Imperfect External Market:** Group profits are maximised at a *price which equals the marginal cost of production of the transferred product.* Fig. 4.4 shows transfer pricing of a product with imperfect external market.

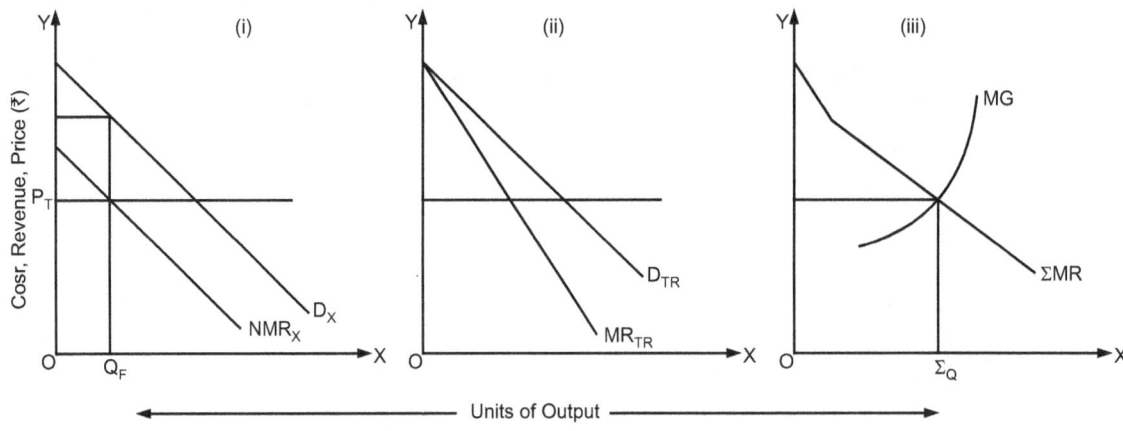

Fig. 4.4: Transfer Pricing with Imperfect External Market

In Fig. 4.4 D_X and NMR_X are the demand and the net marginal revenue (net of the cost of processing and distribution) curves of the transferee or final division.

D_{TR} and MR_{TR} are the corresponding demand and revenue of the transferring division. It can be seen that NMR_X starts at a lower point than D_X curve.

Fig. 4.4 (i) shows the demand and net marginal revenue curves, D_X and NMR_X, for the final division. In determining its profit maximising output, the transferring division will be instructed to regard NMR_X as its effective marginal revenue curve when selling to the final division.

Fig. 4.4 (ii) shows the demand curve for transferring division in its external market D_{TR} and the corresponding marginal revenue MR_{TR}.

Fig. 4.4 (iii) depicts the horizontal summation of the NMR_X and MR_{TR} curves as the combined marginal revenue curve ($\sum MR$). Fig. 4.4 (iii) shows how to obtain the profit-maximising level of output when charging discriminatory prices between different divisions.

This profit-maximising output level, of transferring division is the output level $\sum Q$, and its profit-maximising distribution of $\sum Q$ is where $\sum MR = NMR_X = MR_{TR}$, that is, at output levels at OQ_X and OQ_{TR}.

The price charges in the external market is OP_E. Price P_{TR} is the relevant transfer price.

The transferring firm sells OQ_X to the other division and OQ_{TR} in the external market.

4.2.5 Other Pricing Strategies

A variety of other pricing strategies that are adopted by firms depend on market conditions and the image of the firm.

1. Peak-Load Pricing

It refers to the charging of a higher price for a product or service during peak times than at off peak times. The demand for some services, such as electricity, is higher during some periods like in the summer season or in the evening than at other times such as during the day or in the winters. Electricity is also a non-storable service, that is, it must be generated when it is needed. To satisfy peak demand, electric power companies must bring into operation older and less efficient equipment and thus incur higher marginal costs and charge higher prices. Such price differences are not technically price discrimination as price differences would be based on cost differences. Even then sometimes they have been referred to as 'inter-temporal' price discrimination. Another example can be of airline services which provide various discounts on tickets purchased at different points of time. The weekend flights are of higher price than on the week days. Further, firms provide off-season discounts to encourage purchase of air-conditioners during winter and earn premium price during summer, which is the peak-load period.

Thus this is a kind of price discrimination in which consumers are segregated on the basis of time segments, different prices are charged for the same facility used at different points of time by the consumers. The time zone is divided into peak load; consumers using the product at this time pay higher price (mark-up price) and users at off peak period pay a lower price (say, incremental pricing).

2. Two-part Tariff

In oligopoly and in monopolistic market structure firms use this method of pricing to increase their profits. It refers to the pricing practice in which buyers pay an initial fee for the right to purchase a product or service and then pay usage fee or price for each unit of the product they purchase. For example, two-part tariff is observed in some amusement parks, where visitors pay entry fee and then to enjoy the various rides have to pay for the rides. Another example would be telephone companies charging a monthly fee plus a message-unit fee, golf and tennis clubs charging an annual membership fee plus a fee for each round or game played.

3. Tying

It refers to the requirement that a consumer who buys or leases a product also purchases another product needed in the use of the first. For example, when the Xerox Corporation was the only producer of photocopiers in the 1950s, it required companies leasing its machines to also purchase paper from Xerox. Sometimes tying of purchases is done to ensure that the correct supplies are used for the equipment to function properly and ensure the level of quality. It is used as a form of two-part tariff to earn higher profits. However, the courts often intervene to forbid restrictions on competition. For instance, McDonald's was forced to allow its franchises to purchase their materials and supplies from any McDonald's approved supplier rather than only from McDonald's. This increased competition, while still ensuring protection of the brand name.

4. Stay-Out Pricing

When a firm is uncertain about the price at which it will be able to sell its product, it starts with a very high price. If the firm is unable to sell at this high price then it lowers the price of its product and continues lowering till it's able to sell the targeted amount of the product. This approach ascertains the maximum possible price it can charge from its buyers.

5. Odd Number and Round Number Pricing

This is actually a method of price tagging and not a method of pricing. Here a firm fixes the price of its product in a manner which gives the impression of being low. For example, price of a product ₹ 49.90 rather than ₹ 50. It plays a psychological impact on consumers that the price is in 40s and not in 50s. This may have some impact on sales. Some firms like *Bata* have been following this price policy with some success and some firms round their prices to the next higher rupee to keep the accounts simple.

6. Price Lining

Price of one product in the total range of the products is fixed. In other words, price of the rest of the commodities is automatically determined by the relationship between the commodity whose price has been fixed and the rest of the commodities in the range. For instance, if a firm, producing shirts, fixes up the price for a particular size of shirts, then price for rest of the sizes is fixed at the same time, based on the differences in their sizes. The changes are also automatic when the price of one size of shirt changes.

7. Penetration Price

This policy aims to capture a large share of the market and thus the price charged is low price to stimulate demand for the product. When a firm plans to enter a new market which is dominated by existing players, its only option is to charge a low price, even lower than the ongoing price. This price is called *penetration price*. For example, in the soap market dominated by Hindustan Lever, Nirma entered with a success story with the help of this price strategy. The principle of marginal costing determines the penetration price. However, certain pre-conditions for this price strategy are –

(i) A highly price-sensitive market and market with high price elasticity;

(ii) Low price to discourage competition;

(iii) Benefits of economies of scale and the proportion of variable to fixed costs as low.

8. Entry Deterring Price

A barrier created by a large player to eliminate or reduce competition is to keep the price low, thus making the market unattractive for other players. A new entrant with high fixed cost will be deterred from entering the market at a price lower than the prevailing price. On the other hand, existing small players may not be able to survive at this price due to high average cost. This practice is also known as *limit pricing*. 'Limit pricing' is when a firm or firms may attempt to establish a price that reduces or eliminates the threat of entry of new firms into the industry. For limit pricing to be effective some sort of collusion is necessary among existing firms.

In case of entry deterring pricing the objective is to keep the market unattractive for new entrants. Success of this pricing strategy depends on the fact that the firm earns economies of scale and hence can afford to charge low price. Firms are attracted to an industry and increase the competition when the price is high. For example, in the Indian telecom market high tariffs have cost BSNL a significant portion of its market to its competitors like Airtel. If the tariff rates were low it would have acted as deterrent to new entrants in the industry, just like electricity rates charged by Public Sector Units which are subsidised and thus, prevent private players to enter the market.

9. Pricing of Multiple Products

Most modern firms produce a variety of products rather than a single product. Thus, in modern business, a firm is a multi-product producer. The firm's pricing of multiple products has to see into the interdependence of demands, plant capacity utilisation and optimal product pricing of joint products produced in fixed or in variable proportions. The multiplicity of products by a firm creates four kinds of relationships –

(a) **Demand relationships:** Due to cross elasticity, a price change in one product affects demand for the other, when the different products of the firm are either substitutes or complements of each other. The products sold by a firm may be interrelated as substitutes or complements. For example, A Star and Estilo produced by Maruti are substitutes, while the various other options, such as music system, power windows, etc, produced by Maruti are complementary to its automobiles. Thus, in pricing of interrelated goods (substitutes or complements), the firm needs to consider the effect of a change in the price of one product on the demand for the other. Because, a fall in the price of Estilo may reduce the demand for a substitute commodity A Star, sold by the same firm and may increase the demand for complementary products. For profit maximisation, thus, a firm needs to determine jointly and not independently the output levels and prices of the various products.

(b) Cost relationships: Costs are variable and fixed in nature. When multiple products are produced with the help of the same production facilities, some costs (variable) remain directly chargeable to each product. In other words, labour and raw material are directly chargeable. However, the other costs (fixed costs like rent, taxes, premium on insurance etc.) are common to all products.

(c) Production relationships: When multiple products result from a single production process, it is found that usually there is one primary (or main) product with one or more by-products, which may be produced in either fixed or variable proportions.

(d) Capacity relationships: When the firm has excess or idle capacity, the firm may use it to produce one or more additional products. As new products are added, that is the firm becomes multi-product, the fixed costs are shared on greater units and thus the firm enjoys greater efficiency with greater optimal output and price structure for all products.

The number of products of the firm in its product line classifies firms into single-product firms, and multi-product firms.

Multi-product firms can be of the following kinds –

(i) A joint product firm: It is a firm, which produces a main product and a by-product, which is saleable, for example in the field of agriculture, dairy as the by-product.

(ii) Related goods: A firm may extend its product line to several related products. In each of the product, there are large numbers of varieties, sizes, shades, etc. For example, a factory producing various kinds of hair colour – quality, colour and size of packs of ladies' and gents' hair colour. Since the product is raised from the same plant and uses same labour and raw material, there is a degree of interdependence between different product lines.

(iii) Products unrelated to each other: A firm may be engaged in a product line whose products are unrelated to each other. For example, Godrej producing steel cupboards, refrigerators, locks, soaps, shaving cream, etc. These products use different production facilities, raw materials and labour. The firms diversify in different unrelated product lines mainly to take advantage of their goodwill and to make use of their existing sales network.

Pricing in Multi-Plant and Multi-Product Firms

Multi-Plant Firm: Where a firm's output of the same product is produced on more than one site, the profit-maximising output rule states that marginal supply costs must be equal to marginal revenue. This rule remains unchanged. But in a multi-plant firm the marginal cost is the sum of the separate plants' marginal costs and production must be allocated between the plants so that the marginal supply cost at each plant is identical. Fig. 4.5 shows pricing in a multi-plant firm.

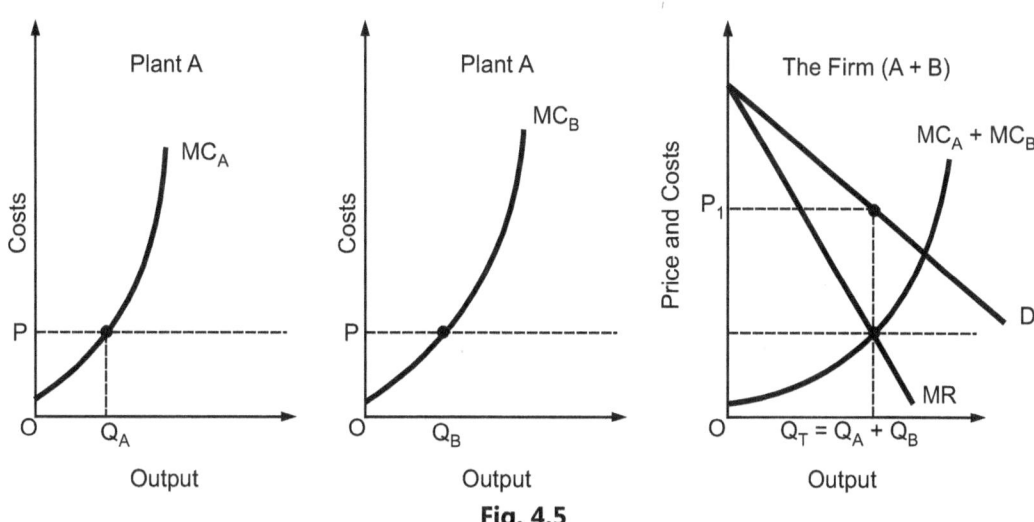

Fig. 4.5

10. Ramsay Pricing

According to Frank Ramsay, "price deviations from marginal cost should be inversely proportional to price elasticity of the product."

Economist Frank Ramsay presented a model for taxation which became very useful for pricing decisions of a multi-product firm. Ramsay suggested that the government should levy high tax on the goods which had low price elasticity; because a large increase in price would bring a small decrease in demand; and low tax on products which had high price elasticity (goods sensitive to change in price).

This method became popular among the multi-product firms. In economic theory a price above marginal cost will result in inefficiency of allocation of resources. But if a multi-product firm charges a price just equal to marginal cost for all its products then how would the firm recover the total cost? According to Ramsay pricing, the firm should fix the price close to marginal cost for the product which has demand of highly elastic nature and should charge substantial margin for the product having demand of low elasticity (as the demand may not contract with the rise in price). Thus, *price deviations from marginal cost should be inversely proportional to price elasticity of the product.*

11. Product Life Cycle-based Pricing

Every product passes through different phases or stages starting from introduction, to growth and maturity, leading to saturation and lastly reaches decline. Each stage is unique in itself. Under different stages a product faces different demand patterns and competition levels, hence it needs revising of price as it passes through different stages. Thus, an "intelligent" firm would devise different pricing for a product at different stages of its life cycle. Various examples can be cited of products or services in their introduction stage, such as first television with 3D facility and with a flat screen, first facility of internet banking, booking of tickets through internet, e-banking, etc. When these goods or services were introduced their prices were very high but in time the prices lowered to become affordable to many. On the other hand, black and white television went into its decline stage as there were no buyers for it.

The most popular pricing methods under this group are price skimming, product bundling and perceived value pricing. Fig. 4.6 depicts the various stages of the life cycle of a generic product, say TFT monitor or colour television.

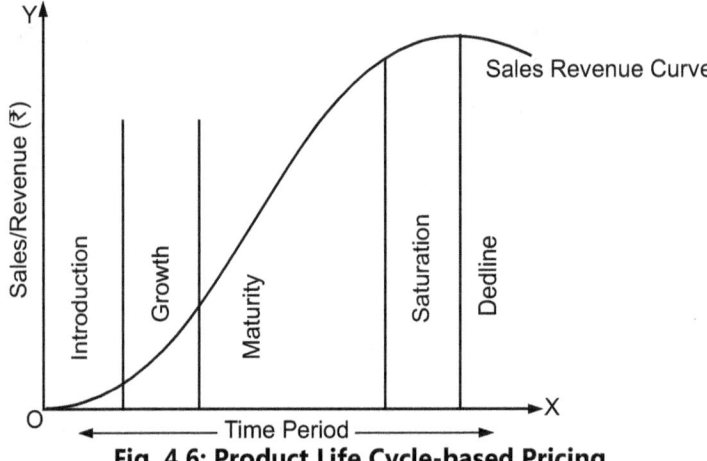

Fig. 4.6: Product Life Cycle-based Pricing

In the study of the life cycle of the product it can be said that in the *introduction stage* the market is small due to the novelty or newness of the product. The firm tries to popularise its product among the niche consumers and may charge a high price and skim the market by creating high value perception due to the novelty factor. In the *growth stage*, the product has created its own market and firms would charge lower price from rest of the consumers. In *maturity stage*, sellers try to attract consumers by sales propaganda, product bundling, cash back offers, etc. This is the stage when elite consumers desire for some innovative features in the existing products and for this progressive firms align their R & D strategy to remain in the market. With innovation the firm survives in this stage for a longer time than the firms which do not add any additional features in their product and they enter the decline stage.

12. Skimming Price

It is a discriminatory price policy as it aims at 'skimming the cream' by taking advantage of the target segment's willingness to pay a high price and earn super margins on sales. This price policy enhances the quality image, thus providing adjustments if the start price is high. Producers have knowledge that there is a segment of consumers who have deep pockets and who would like to be among the first few proud possessors of the latest product. The high price charged is to satisfy the snob appeal of the buyers and not for the intrinsic value of the product.

For such a price strategy certain pre-conditions are – (i) high price that keeps the competition out; (ii) unit costs relatively unaffected by small volume, high ratio of variable to fixed costs.

Price skimming strategy deals with a complete pricing package suitable for different life cycle stages of a product. That is, in the introduction stage it is high price and during maturity it is lower price. For example, one can experience the impact of this strategy whenever one buys the ticket of a movie on the first day-first show and those who wait for the rush to settle down pay almost half the price. Fig. 4.7 shows the behaviour of a price skimming firm.

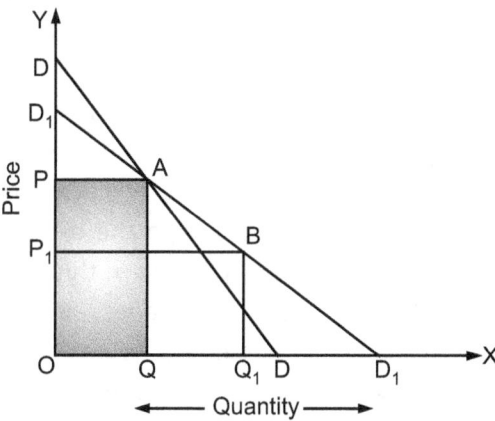

Fig. 4.7: Skimming Price

DD shows consumers who must watch the movie on the first day-first show at any price. These consumers have low price elasticity. The firm, here the owner of the theatre, charges OP price from these consumers. Since this number is not too large, therefore, the total demand at price OP is OQ. When the product reaches maturity, the firm reduces the price to OP_1 and the new demand curve is D_1D_1. The firm is able to serve a larger section of the consumers and also maximise its sales and revenue. Total sale of tickets would be equal to the OQ and OQ_1 and total revenue or TR is sum of areas OPAQ and OP_1BQ_1. It is a way of price discrimination of first degree.

13. Bundling or Product Packaging

It is a common form of tying in which the firm requires buyers buying or leasing one of its products or services to also buy or lease another product or service when customers have different tastes but the firm cannot price discriminate, as in tying. This strategy is often used as a double-edged weapon, for propagating a new product, as well as for selling a product in its stage of decline. By selling or leasing the product or service as a package or bundle rather than separately, the monopolist can increase its total profits. For example, The United Bank of India (UBI) has sought to bundle insurance with its tax-saving term deposit scheme.

In this case, it is UBI's 8 percent five-year tax-saving deposits. The bank's new initiative to mobilise deposits comes with free accident insurance for depositors who intend to make use of Section 80C of the Income Tax Act. The specified schemes, in addition to LIC and PPF, include certain term deposit products offered by banks. Another example can be given of offering silver, gold or platinum package by Dish TV. In every package along with the popular channels, depending on type of package, certain regional language channels are included and mentioned as free of cost.

14. Psychological Pricing or Perceived Value Pricing

"A product is as good as a consumer finds it" – this is the philosophy underlying this type of pricing. The price a buyer is willing to pay would reflect the value of that product to him/her. A segment of buyers believe that higher the price, better the quality and hence are willing to buy anything that is tagged at high price. That is why it is also referred to as *psychological pricing*. The sellers identify the perceived value of the good on the basis of their knowledge of market forces and charge a price corresponding with the perceived value. The sellers can take away consumer surplus to the extent of their understanding of the perceived value of the goods. An interesting aspect of this strategy is that sellers may try to influence perceived value through brand awareness and emphasis on quality. For example, Johnson & Johnson has a brand name and its quality in the range of products of new-born babies is well-known. As such the company can price it products using the perceived value of the consumers towards their product and take away consumer surplus by charging relatively higher price than other products in the same range.

Perceived value pricing is normally adopted during the growth and maturity stage so as to differentiate the product from that of competitors' and retain the quality conscious customers. For example, Titan watches, Philips products, Parker pens are some of the brands which have consistently resorted to psychological pricing by creating hype about high quality. This price is not at all governed by the cost of the production.

15. Value Pricing

"Under value pricing, sellers try to create a high value of the product and charge a low price".

In case of value pricing sellers try to create a high value of the product but keep the price low. The assumption is that the price charged should be lower than perceived value of product for the consumers. Thus in this method of pricing the seller allows some consumer surplus to the buyer. For example, Louis Philips brand of men's wear. They keep the price tag high to create brand perception and then allow heavy discounts to bring the price at a very low level. The buyer feels the satisfaction of buying a branded good at the price of local brands. Value pricing method is suitable for the maturity and saturation stage when demand can be maintained by keeping focus on higher quality and lower cost.

16. Public Utility Rate Regulation

Pricing in case of public utilities such as railways, electricity, etc. poses some difficulties like –

- These industries are "natural monopolies", that is their market size is so small in relation to the optimum capacity (with given technology) such that only one firm can be accommodated in the market, thus creating monopoly conditions and eliminating competition.
- In these industries production technology and distribution results in substantial economies of scale, so that large firms can produce at much lower costs than small firms.

While pricing public utilities there are three alternative pricing policies and these are – Monopoly Pricing; Full-Cost Pricing; and Marginal Cost Pricing.

Fig. 4.8 illustrates the three pricing policies. In this Fig. 4.8 it depicts a decreasing cost industry.

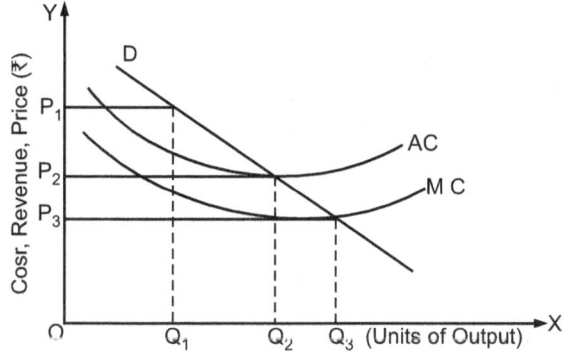

Fig. 4.8: Public Utility Pricing

The use of monopoly pricing shows that the product price would be OP_1 and output OQ_1. Naturally, it provides monopoly profits to the firm and would therefore be intolerable to the public.

If the public utility is following full-cost pricing, it would produce OQ_2 output and price its product at OP_2. This price provides a "fair return" on the investment in the utility. This pricing method is perhaps the most popular method in public utility pricing. But the economists have shown that welfare of the society cannot be maximised by using "full-cost" pricing as the value of the added services *exceeds* the marginal cost of the added output of these services. These economists, hence, favour the use of marginal cost for pricing public utilities.

Pricing on the basis of marginal cost, the suggested price would be OP_3. The welfare of the society is at its maximum in case of marginal cost pricing because at OP_3 the worth/value of the product to the marginal user (measured by price) equals the worth/value of the resources used up in the production of the marginal/last unit (measured by marginal cost).

It is to be pointed that in case of a firm having increasing cost the marginal cost pricing may result in a price which exceeds the total cost. In case of firm having decreasing cost, the price OP_3 would not cover total costs.

It is mentioned above that there are three pricing policies that can be followed in public utilities firms. If marginal cost pricing is followed, it suffers from certain limitations, such as –

(i) In case of the increasing cost industry such pricing policy fails to maximise social welfare;

(ii) If the industry is experiencing decreasing cost, marginal cost pricing cannot cover total cost and as a result has to depend on subsidy which invites political interference.

Due to inadequacy of the marginal cost pricing and the fact that most of the nationalised utilities maintain the rule that *revenues must cover costs*, the *full-cost pricing* is most popular in utility rate regulation.

Points to Remember

- *Price Discrimination* is the art of selling the same commodity produced under a single control to different buyers at different prices.
- *Customary Pricing*: In case of some commodities the prices get fixed because they have prevailed over a long period of time. Any change in costs for such products gets reflected in quality or quantity of the product rather than its price.
- When pricing by a firm is based on an assessment of general economic environment, it is known as cyclical pricing.
- The prices which are statutorily fixed by the government after considering the cost and the stipulated profit per unit are referred to as *administered prices*.
- A market where a commodity is covered at the same time under the administered price as well as market price is said to have dual prices.
- *Peak-Load Pricing***:** It refers to the charging of a higher price for a product or service during peak times than at off-peak times.
- *Two-part Tariff:* In oligopoly and in monopolistic market structure firms use this method of pricing to increase their profits. It refers to the pricing practice in which buyers pay an initial fee for the right to purchase a product or service and then pay usage fee or price for each unit of the product they purchase.
- *Penetration Price:* This policy aims to capture a large share of the market and thus the price charged is a low price to stimulate demand for the product.
- *Entry Deterring Price:* A barrier created by a large player to eliminate or reduce competition is to keep the price low, thus making the market unattractive for other players.

- *Ramsay Pricing:* According to Frank Ramsay, "price deviations from marginal cost should be inversely proportional to price elasticity of the product."

- Every product passes through different phases or stages starting from introduction, to growth and maturity, leading to saturation and lastly reaches decline. Each stage is unique in itself. Under different stages, a product faces different demand patterns and competition levels, hence it needs revising of price as it passes through different stages.

- It is a discriminatory price policy as it aims at 'skimming the cream' by taking advantage of the target segment's willingness to pay a high price and earn super margins on sales.

- The sellers identify the perceived value of the good on the basis of their knowledge of market forces and charge price corresponding with the perceived value. "A product is as good as a consumer finds it" – this is the philosophy underlying this type of pricing.

- Under value pricing, sellers try to create a high value of the product and charge a low price.

- Products like shoes, clothes, containers, etc. differ in size and the producer has two options while pricing such products – either charge different prices depending on sizes or charge same price for all sizes.

- The general practice is that the special orders are priced by adding to normal full cost a pre-determined mark-up to get fair profits.

- Use of the intermediaries is a part of total cost of product but involves no cash outflow; rather it is only a transfer of accounts from one subsidiary to another; hence it is called *transfer pricing*.

Questions for Discussion

1. "Pricing in practice is completely divorced from the theory of the firm." Explain with special reference to dual pricing.

2. Write short notes on (a) Product-line Pricing; (b) Limit Pricing; (c) Differential Pricing; (d) Cyclical Pricing.

3. What do you understand by 'transfer pricing'? How is it determined when for the intermediate product there is imperfectly competitive market?

4. Distinguish between skimming and penetrating pricing policies of a business firm. What are the reasons for firms to follow different pricing policies?

5. How are prices determined for services of public utilities?

6. What is peak-load pricing? Why is it popular in pricing the public utilities? List the main drawbacks of this pricing technique.

Chapter **5**...

National Income Determination and Changes in it

Contents ...

Learning Objectives ...

➤ To understand the meaning, importance and factors influencing national income
➤ To study the various concepts of national income
➤ To learn the state of under employment and full employment of national income
➤ To evaluate the effects of government expenditure and net export on national income equilibrium
➤ To explain the concept, process and limitations of Investment Multiplier

5.1 National Income

5.1.1 Introduction

The concept of national income occupies an important place in economic theory.

National income is the aggregate money value of all goods and services produced in a country during one year. The wear and tear of plant and machines, that is, depreciation is deducted.

National Income is distributed among the four factors of production – land, labour, capital and organisation – in the form of rent, wages, interest and profit.

Of all the concepts in macroeconomics, the single most important one is the gross domestic product (GDP), which measures the total value of goods and services produced in a country. The GDP and its various national accounts concepts are truly among the great inventions of the 20th century. The GDP gives an overall picture of the state of the economy just as a satellite in space can survey the weather across an entire continent.

5.1.2 Meaning and Definitions of National Income

The total income of nation is called 'national income'. There are three interpretations of the term national income, which can be understood from the three different types of definitions, given to us by Marshall, Pigou and Fisher.

1. Marshall's definition: Marshall's definition represents a *total value of production.*

"The labour and capital of a country, acting upon its natural resources, produce annually a certain net aggregate of commodities, material and immaterial, including services of all kinds. The word 'net' implies the depreciation of plant involved in production to arrive at net income (from gross to total income). The depreciation is to be deducted from the gross produce before the true or net income can be found. To this is added the income due to foreign investments. This is true net annual income (national revenue) or the national dividend."

2. Pigou's definition: Pigou's definition of national income represents a *receipt total.*

Pigou defines national income as, *"the national dividend is that part of the objective income of the community including income derived from abroad, which can be measured in money."*

Pigou's definition is more precise because only those goods and services are included in the national income whose value can be expressed in monetary terms.

3. **Irving Fisher's definition:** Fisher's definition represents an *expenditure total*.

Marshall's definition is from 'production end', Fisher's approach is 'consumption end'. Fisher defines it as, *"the national dividend (income) consists solely of services received by ultimate consumers, whether from their material or from their human environments. Thus, a piano or an overcoat made this year is not a part of this year's income, but an addition to capital. Only the services rendered to me during this year by these things are income."*

From the above definitions,

(i)   National income refers to the income of a country, say India;

(ii) National income includes all types of goods and services which have an exchange value, counting each one of them only once.

5.1.3 Features of National Income

To sum up, the features of national income –

1. The *aggregate economic performance* of a nation is measured by the national income data.
2. National income is the *flow of goods and services* which become available to a nation during a year.
3. In monetary terms, national income is the *aggregate money value* of all goods and services produced by a nation during one year.
4. National income is a *heterogeneous* whole. It is total variety of goods and services produced by an economy valued at its market price.
5. National income is always expressed with reference to *'time'*, say one year.
6. National income is a *flow concept* and not a stock.
7. National income is estimated in terms of *'gross' and 'net' values* of a product. When depreciation is deducted from the 'gross' values, we obtain 'net' values of a product.

5.1.4 Importance of National Income

National income is of vital **importance** for the economy of a country.

1. National income data shows the monetary measure of the volume of production in a year, that is, it shows aggregate production in the country.
2. National income is a sign of growing economic progress.
3. National income data gives an idea of the rate of national income growth in a country.
4. The data shows the comparative significance of the various sectors contributing in the national income, that is, which sector contributes the largest, is clear with the help of national income data.
5. We get an idea of standard of living of the country by comparing the national income of the country with other nation's national income figures.
6. The data is indispensable for the formulation of economic policy of government.

7. It throws light on the volume of consumption, saving and investment in the economy.

For all the above reasons we need to take utmost precaution while measuring national income of the country.

5.1.5 Factors Influencing National Income

There are a number of factors which determine the size of the national income in a country. Following are the three main factors –

(a) **Quantity and Quality of Factors of Production:** This is one of the most important factors that influence the national income of an economy. The quantity and quality of land, the climate, the rainfall, etc. determine the quantity and quality of agricultural output, and hence, the size of the national income. The quality of labour, depending upon education and training, influences the volume of industrial production. The quantity and quality of capital determines the total output. Similarly, the quantity and quality of organisational ability determines the size of the national income.

(b) **The State of Technology:** A country with a poor technical know-how cannot have a large-sized national income, as it will not be in a position to make the best possible use of its resources.

(c) **Political Stability:** This factor is an essential pre-requisite for maintaining production at the highest level. The economic development of several countries has been staggered in the past by political instability.

5.1.6 Concepts of National Income

The different concepts of national income are –

1. **Gross Domestic Product (GDP)/Gross National Product (GNP) (at Market Price)**

Gross Domestic Product at market price is the money value of all final goods and services produced during an accounting year within the domestic territory of a country.

Gross National Product at market price is a money value of all final goods and services produced by a country during an accounting year including net factor income from abroad.

GNP at market price (GNP$_{mp}$) can be obtained by adding –

(a) Private consumption expenditure (C)

(b) Gross domestic private investment (I)

(c) Government expenditure on goods and services (G)

(d) Net foreign investment (E)

(e) GNPmp = C

One of the main purposes of GDP is to measure the overall performance of an economy. If one were to ask an economic historian what happened during the Great Depression, the best short answer would be GDP fell down, the value of goods and services declined, caused unemployment, steep stock market decline, bank failures and so on.

Components of GDP

(a) **Consumption (C):** The first part of GDP is consumption or 'personal consumption expenditures'. This expenditure is divided into 3 categories – durable goods, such as automobiles, non-durable goods (food) and services (medical care).

(b) **Investment and Capital Formation (I):** Nations devote part of their output to production of capital durable goods that increase future production. Investment consists of the additions to the nation's capital stock of buildings, equipment, and inventories during a year. The national accounts include mainly tangible capital (buildings, bridges, etc.) and omit intangible capital (research and development). Thus, investments represent additions to the stock of durable capital goods that increase production possibilities in the future.

There is difference between 'gross' and 'net' investment. Gross investment includes all investment goods produced and it is adjusted for **depreciation,** which measures the amount of capital that has been used up in a year. The gross investment includes all machines, factories, etc. produced in a year even though some are produced to replace old capital goods that were destroyed or were thrown in the scrap heap.

To know about the increase in society's capital, gross investment is not a real measure as it includes a necessary allowance for depreciation and it is too large – too gross. To find the net increase in capital, subtract from gross investment depreciation or the amount of capital used up. To estimate capital formation we measure net investment, and net investment is always newly created capital. (Net investment = gross investment minus depreciation).

(c) **Government (G):** Government purchases both consumption type goods like uniforms for military and investment-type goods like building bridges, factories, etc. In measuring government's contribution to GDP, we simply add all these government purchases to the flow of consumption, investment expenditures.

(d) **Exclusion of Transfer Payments:** GDP includes only government purchases of goods and services; it excludes spending on transfer payments. Transfer payments are payments to meet important social purposes. Examples of transfer payments include unemployment insurance, old-age payments, etc. Government transfer payments are government payments to individuals that are not made in exchange for goods or services supplied, hence they are omitted from GDP. Thus, wages to a teacher received from government is for her services rendered and hence is a factor payment and will be included in GDP. But, if the teacher receives some welfare payment, such a payment is not in return for a service and is a transfer payment, hence to be excluded from GDP. Even government interest payments are considered transfers and hence omitted from GDP.

(e) **Net Exports:** The last component of GDP and an increasingly important one in recent years is **net exports**, the difference between exports and imports of goods and services.

Although GDP is the most widely used measure of national output, two other concepts are frequently cited and they are Gross National Product (GNP), Net Domestic Product (NDP).

What is the difference between GDP and GNP? GNP is the total output produced with labour or capital owned by Indian residents, while GDP is the output produced with labour and capital located inside India. For example, some of the India's GDP is produced in Honda plants that are owned by Japanese corporations. The profits from these plants are included in India's GDP but not in India's GNP because Honda is a Japanese company. In the same way, when an Indian economist flies to Japan to give a paid lecture, then payment for that lecture would be included in Japanese GDP and in Indian GNP.

To sum up, *NDP* equals the total final output produced within a nation during a year, where output includes *net* investment; NDP = GDP – Depreciation.

GDP is the total final output produced with inputs owned by the residents of a country during a year.

2. Net National Product (NNP)

In the production of GNP of a year, we use some capital. The capital goods like plant and machinery wear out or depreciate in value due to the efflux of time. The wear and tear or use up of capital or destruction of capital or depreciation in its value – all is termed as '*depreciation*'. Thus, *when depreciation charges are deducted from GNP we get NNP*. It is Net National Product or NNP at market price as it is the market value of all final goods and services after depreciation deductions.

$$NNP_{mp} = GNP_{mp} - D.$$

3. National Income at Factor Cost (NNP$_{FC}$)

It means sum of all incomes earned by factors of production for their contribution in production of net output. In fact, whenever we talk about National Income, it is National Income at Factor Cost.

National Income at Market Price *includes* indirect taxes and subsidies.

National Income at Factor Cost *excludes* indirect taxes and subsidies.

Illustration: A bottle of syrup is produced at the cost of ₹14 in a factory. When it is sold in the market, indirect taxes are added and the price now becomes ₹16 (₹14 + ₹2 of taxes) per bottle.

Thus, **NNP$_{FC}$ + Indirect taxes = NNP$_{mp}$.**

On the other hand, subsidy causes the price to be lower than the market price. The factors are paid ₹14 to produce a bottle of syrup. But, in the market it is sold at ₹12. Thus, ₹2 is the subsidy borne by the government.

Thus, **NNP$_{FC}$ – Subsidies = NNP$_{mp}$.**

National Income or **NNP$_{FC}$ is minus indirect taxes plus subsidies,**

that is, NNP$_{FC}$ = NNP$_{mp}$ – Indirect taxes

or NNP$_{FC}$ = NNP$_{mp}$ + Subsidies.

4. **Personal Income (P.I.)**

Personal Income is the sum of all incomes actually received by all individuals or households during a given year.

Thus, P.I. = National Income – Social Security contributions – Corporate Income taxes – Undistributed Corporate Profits + Transfer Payments.

5. **Disposable Personal Income (D.P.I.)**

From Personal Income when we deduct personal taxes like income tax and personal property taxes we obtain D.P.I.

Thus, **D.P.I. = Personal income – Personal taxes**

Fig. 5.1 shows the flow of economic activity from GDP to Disposable Income.

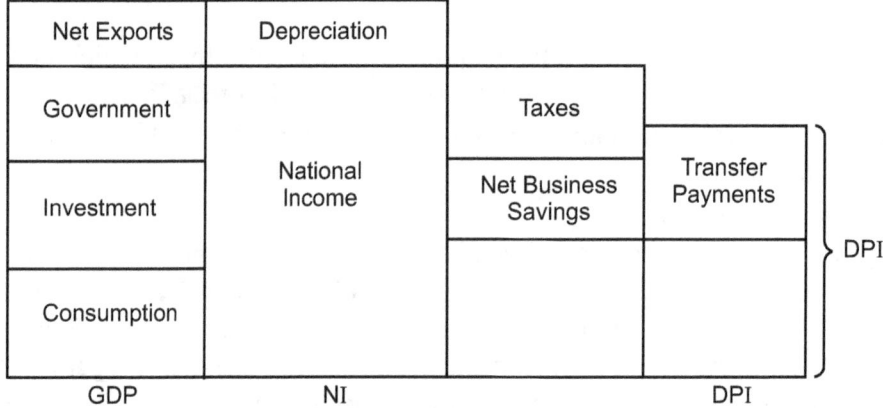

Fig. 5.1: The Flow of Economic Activity from GDP to Disposable Income

Fig. 5.1 shows that GDP = total gross income to all factors; N.I. = sum of factor incomes and is obtained by subtracting depreciation from GDP; and D.P.I. = the total incomes, including transfer payments but minus taxes, of the household sector.

5.1.7 Difficulties in Measurement of National Income

Derivation of national product and income accounts presents many serious difficulties for the national income statisticians. These difficulties and problems are mostly due to certain ambiguities which are inherent in the national income measurement. Some of these difficulties are discussed here that are 'statistical' and 'conceptual' in nature.

(1) **Inadequate Statistical Data:** The available statistics in developing countries are inadequate and also unreliable. For instance, statistics relating to agriculture in India are incomplete. Further, no reliable estimates of production costs in Indian agriculture are available. Neither statistics is available for small-scale and medium industrial units.

(2) **Lack of Occupational Specialisation:** In developing countries, there is little of occupational specialisation. Many persons take up more than one activity to earn their livelihood. This poses a problem of collecting information about their incomes.

For example, the small farmers not only do farming but also migrate to the industrial cities during the slack season to supplement their small earnings from agriculture.

(3) **Lack of Knowledge:** A number of small producers in developing countries are illiterate and ignorant. They are not in a position to keep any account of their productive activities. They are not able to give information about the value of their output. As a result, an element of guess work enters into the assessment of income in large sectors of an economy.

(4) **Goods and Services to be Included:** An economic good, which is the result of economic activity, may be either tangible goods such as chair, pen or in the form of intangible service such as doctor's or teacher's service. If we have to include every good or service which satisfies human want in 'economic' good, it would mean including the activity of washing one's own clothes. It is impossible to include the value of personal services rendered to oneself in the national product accounts. The services rendered to oneself do not pass through the market; hence in economics we consider them as non-economic activity.

A convenient way to separate an economic activity from its non-economic activity is to take the help of *market mechanism*. 'Economic' activities are those which result in the production of those goods and services that are sold in the market for 'a price'. However, this method is only for highly developed economies where almost every activity is assessed in money terms through the market transaction. If this approach is adopted for national income measurement, bulk of household activities performed by the housewives will be *excluded* from the national income accounting. For example, the value of the meals cooked and served by the housewife in the home kitchen is excluded from the national product and when the same meals cooked and served in the 'mess' is included in the national product.

Thus, there is a great difficulty in distinguishing between 'economic' and 'non-economic' activity.

(5) **Omitted Market Transactions:** In any economy a large number of transactions take place in the market. However, all the transactions cannot be included in the national product. The market transactions which are unrelated to economic activities are excluded from the national product. Such activities are discussed below –

(i) **Transfer Payments:** Factor payments are for some economic activity rendered by the factor. But, transfer payment represents merely a redistribution or transfer of income from person to person or from government to person, etc. Since a transfer payment does not represent payment made for the productive services rendered in the production of final goods and services, it is *not included* in the national product. For example, unemployment doles, old age insurance schemes, scholarships, prize money, etc.

(ii) **Capital Gains:** It means appreciation in the value of the capital assets resulting from increase in the market value of such assets. Such gains are important for asset holders but do not owe their origin to current economic activities, hence are excluded from the national product.

   (iii) Illegal Activities: Income earned through black market transactions, theft and smuggling activities is excluded from national income. The reason is that such activities are outlawed by the community and hence should be excluded from the national product which measures only the socially useful activities.

(6) Self-Consumption: The problem of imputing 'values' to the non-marketed goods and services presents a most serious problem in national product computation. The existence of a large non-monetised section in underdeveloped countries also poses problems in national income measurement. A substantial part of the agricultural output in these countries does not reach the market at all, that is, there is less marketable surplus as it is either used for self-consumption or it is exchanged for other goods and services.

When the economy is completely monetised, it will become possible to measure the non-monetised production. Imputing 'value' to the non-monetised goods and services is laced with many problems. For example, if as a benefit from a publishing house, a manager receives free books from the publisher; at what price is it to be valued in national product? Should it be valued at the price at which the publisher sells to his buyers or at the price that he charges the book vendors? In short, the goods and services for self-consumption or are not marketed makes the computing of national income erroneous.

(7) Government Activities: The difficulty arises with regard to the treatment of the government activities in national income accounting. Generally, the administrative functions of the government, for example, justice, administration, defense, should be treated as giving rise to final consumption of such services by the society. Thus, the contribution of 'common' government activities will be equated to the amount of wages paid by the government to judges, soldiers, etc. However, in case of capital formation, it is treated as equal to the capital formation by any other firm and enterprise.

(8) Activities of Foreign Firm: Next difficulty is related to the income arising out of activities of the foreign firm in a country. Should this income be part of the national income of the country owing the firm? International Monetary Fund (IMF) is of the opinion that production and income arising from an enterprise should be accounted to the territory in which production takes place. But the profits earned by foreign companies are ascribed to the parent country.

National income is looked upon as a measure and index of economic welfare of a country. A country with a higher per capita income is supposed to enjoy greater economic welfare or a higher standard of living. Hence, an error in the measurement of national income leads to a faulty picture of country's well-being. Thus, the statistical errors in the accounting of national income can be corrected by understanding the concepts of the various terms of national income.

5.2 Determination of Equilibrium Level of National Income

A study of determination of national income will be better understood with the help of simple mathematics. National income is the level at which aggregate demand equals aggregate supply.

A simple model of income determination is one in which we do not consider the impact of government expenditure and taxation and also exports and imports. The national income in that case is the sum of consumption demand (C) and investment demand (I), which can be shown as,

$$Y = C + I$$

Where, Y stands for the level of national income.

Suppose the consumption function is of the following form –

$$C = a + bY$$

a is the intercept term in the consumption function and therefore represents the autonomous consumption expenditure which does not vary with income, b is a constant which represents the marginal propensity to consume (mpc $\Delta C/\Delta Y$). Thus, total consumption demand is equal to the sum of autonomous consumption expenditure (a) and the induced consumption expenditure (bY).

Now suppose that investment demand equals I_a. This investment I_a is autonomous because this does not depend on income earned. From the above discussion, we get the following three equations for the determination of the equilibrium level of national income.

$$Y = C + I \qquad \qquad \text{... (i)}$$
$$C = a + bY \qquad \qquad \text{... (ii)}$$
$$I = I_a \qquad \qquad \text{... (iii)}$$

By substituting the values of C and I in equation (i), we get

$$Y = a + bY + Ia \qquad \qquad \text{... (iv)}$$
$$Y - bY = a + Ia$$
$$Y(1 - b) = a + Ia$$
$$Y = \frac{1}{1 - b}(a + I_a) \qquad \qquad \text{... (v)}$$

The equation (v) shows the equilibrium level of national income when aggregate demand is equal to aggregate supply. The equation (v) reveals that autonomous consumption and autonomous investment $(a + I_a)$ generates so much expenditure or aggregate demand which is equal to the income generated by the production of goods and services. From the equation (v) it also follows that the equilibrium level of national income can be known from multiplying the elements of autonomous expenditure (that is, a + I_a) by the term 1/1-b which is equal to the value of multiplier.

The multiplier is nothing but the increase in income that occurs when autonomous investment (or consumption) increases by ₹ 1, that is, multiplier is $\Delta Y/\Delta I$ and its value is equal to 1/1-b where b stands for marginal propensity to consume (MPC). Thus, multiplier ΔY/ΔI = 1/1-b. Further, it also follows that equilibrium level of income is higher, the greater the marginal propensity to consume (that is b) and autonomous investment (I).

Now, higher the marginal propensity to consume (b), greater will be the value of multiplier. For example, if marginal propensity to consume (b) is 0.8, investment multiplier is

$$ΔY/ΔI = 1/1 - 08 = 1/0.2 = 1 \times 10/2 = 5$$

If MPC or b = 0.75, multiplier is

$$= ΔY/ΔI = 1/1 - 0.75 = 1 - 0.25 = 100/25 = 4$$

We can find out the increase in income (ΔY) resulting from a certain increase in investment (ΔI) by using this multiplier relationship. Thus

$$ΔY/ΔI = 1/1 - b$$
$$ΔY = ΔI \, 1/1 - b$$

If marginal propensity to consume is equal to 0.8, with the increase in investment by ₹100 crores the increase in income will be –

$$ΔY/ΔI = 1/1 - b$$
$$ΔY = ΔI \times 1/1 - b = 100 \times 1/1 - 0.8$$
$$100 \times 1/0.2 = 100 \times 5 = 500 \text{ crores}$$

Illustrations of Equilibrium Level of Income with Numerical Examples

A few numerical examples will make it clear how the equilibrium level of national income is determined.

Problem 1

Suppose in an economy, autonomous investment (I) is ₹ 600 crores and the following consumption function is given –

$$C = 200 + 0.8Y$$

Given the above information, find out the equilibrium level of income.

Solution

The equilibrium level of income is –

$$Y = C + I$$
$$C = 200 + 0.8Y$$
$$I = 600$$

Substituting the values of C and I in the equation (i) we get –

$$Y = 200 + 0.8Y + 600$$
$$(Y - 0.8Y) = 200 + 600$$
$$Y (1 - 0.8) = 800$$
$$Y = 800/0.2 = 800/2/10 = ₹4000$$

Problem 2

Suppose the consumption function of an economy is C = 0.8 Y. Planned investment by entrepreneurs for a year is ₹ 500 crores. Find out what will be the equilibrium level of income.

Solution

$$Y = C + I$$
$$C = 0.8Y$$
$$I = ₹ 500 \text{ crores}$$

Substituting the values of C and I in (i) we have

$$Y = 0.8Y + 500$$
$$Y - 0.8Y = 500$$
$$Y(1 - 0.8) = 500$$
$$0.2 = 500$$
$$y = 500 \times 10/2 = ₹ 2500 \text{ crores}$$

Problem 3

Suppose the consumption of an economy is given by

$$C = 20 + 0.6Y$$

The following investment function is given –

$$I = 10 + 02\ Y$$

What will be the equilibrium level of national income?

Solution

Note that in this problem, investment varies with income. However, this will not change our method of determining equilibrium level of income.

$$Y = C + I$$
$$C = 20 + 0.6Y$$
$$I = 10 + 0.2Y$$

Substituting the values of C and I in (i) we have

$$Y = 20 + 0.6Y + 10 + 0.2Y$$
$$Y = 30 + 0.8Y$$
$$Y - 0.8Y = 30$$
$$Y(1 - 0.8Y) = 30$$
$$0.2Y = 30$$
$$Y = 30 \times 10/2 = 150$$

Thus, the equilibrium level of income is equal to 150.

How to Overcome Recession: Shifting Aggregate Expenditure Curve Upward

Now, an important question is what measures can be undertaken to overcome recession or involuntary unemployment which is caused as a result of deficiency of aggregate demand brought about by reduction in investment.

From the analysis done above it is clear that in order to bring about an increase in equilibrium level of national income, there needs to be an increase in any of the components of aggregate demand, namely, consumption demand (C), private investment demand (I), government expenditure (G), and net exports (NX). A reduction in personal taxes by the government can bring about an increase in national income by an upward shift in the consumption function. In 1964, the reduction in income tax by John Kennedy government in USA was quite successful in boosting consumption demand and thereby raising aggregate output.

As a result of an increase in aggregate output, more income and employment was generated. The rate of unemployment in USA decline rapidly and the American economy was lifted out of depression. In 2002 and again in early 2008, then President George W. Bush made a significant cut of 3.5 billion dollars in income tax to revive the American economy. He refunded good amount of income tax collected from the people in these years. As a result of cut in direct taxes, the disposable income of the people increases which tends to raise their demand for goods and services.

However, there is a limitation of bringing about a cut in direct taxes for raising aggregate demand because people would prefer to save a part of the incremental disposable income rather than spending it. This phenomenon occurred in the United States in the year 2008.

To boost aggregate demand, indirect taxes can also be reduced. An example of this is, in India in December 2008, in order to correct the sagging demand for industrial products under the fiscal stimulus package, 4 percent across the board cut in central excise duty was made. Reduction in indirect taxes too has a limitation because benefit of this reduction in excise duty may not be fully passed on to the consumers by reducing the prices of goods.

Secondly, an increase in the rate of private investment can bring about an increase in the equilibrium level of national income (GNP) and employment. Through an effective monetary policy businessmen can be encouraged to invest more by lowering the rate of interest and increasing the availability of credit in the economy. We know that lower the rate of interest, higher will be the level of private investment in the country.

Alternatively, the government may encourage private investment by reducing corporate tax rates so that post-tax rate of profit will be higher than before. The higher level of investment will shift the aggregate demand curve (C + I + G) upward and subsequently determine a higher level of national income and employment.

Thirdly, the recession can be overcome and national income (GNP) and employment can be increased by increasing the capital expenditure by the government (G). The main recommendation of Keynes was to increase expenditure on Public Works Programme to raise the level of national output and income to restore equilibrium at full-employment level.

Recently in 1993-94, President Clinton stepped up public expenditure on public works in the USA to overcome recession in the American economy and reduce unemployment.

Now in 2009 President Obama has planned to give a fiscal stimulus of over $800 billion the major part of which is the increase in government expenditure to raise aggregate demand to overcome recession in the American economy. In India also fiscal stimulus packages were announced in 2008-09 under which government expenditure, especially on infrastructure, was increased to revive the Indian economy from the slowdown.

Lastly, the expansion in positive net exports (NX) (that is exports > imports) will also cause an increase in equilibrium level of national income and employment. Exports can be promoted in various ways like announcing export subsidies or tax concession on profits earned through exports as well as making credit available at lower interest rate for purpose of exporting goods. Another common measure adopted by the government to promote exports is the depreciation of domestic currency. Depreciation makes the exports cheaper and imports costlier leading to an increase in net exports (NX_n).

However, when there is global recession, depreciation of its domestic currency by each country will offset the effect of others. It follows from above that an appropriate mix of fiscal and monetary policy measures are adopted to increase aggregate demand and thereby lift the economy out of the recession phase.

5.3 Underemployment and Full Employment of National Income

According to the classical economists, only at full employment level in an economy, it is possible to attain equilibrium level of income, that is, there is no involuntary unemployment in the economy. However, as per the Keynesian theory, equilibrium level can be achieved at –

(i)   Full employment level; or
(ii) Underemployment level, that is, less than full employment level; or
(ii) Over full employment level, that is, more than full employment level.

5.3.1 Full Employment Equilibrium

Full employment equilibrium refers to a situation where the aggregate demand is equal to the aggregate supply at full employment level.

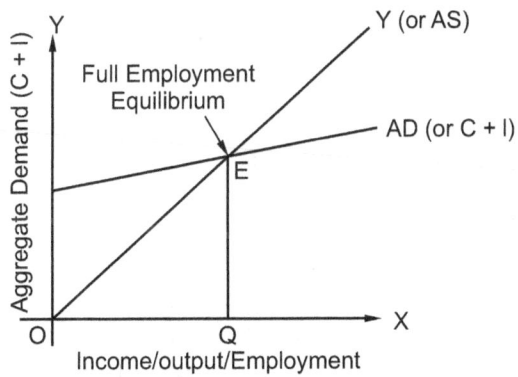

Fig. 5.2

1. In Fig. 5.2, E is the full employment equilibrium because aggregate demand 'EQ' is equal to full employment level of output 'OQ'.

2. At OQ level of output, all those who are willing to work at the prevailing wage rate, are able to find employment, that is, there is no involuntary unemployment.

In simple words, when equilibrium between AD and AS takes place at full employment of resources, it is called full employment equilibrium. At this point none of the resources remain unused and there is no involuntary unemployment.

At this level, aggregate demand is just enough to ensure full utilisation of all the available resources. It implies that at such a level aggregate demand is neither in excess of aggregate supply nor is it deficient but equal to supply at 'full employment level'. This is an ideal situation which every economy desires to achieve and strives to maintain at all times.

The situation of full employment equilibrium has been shown in Fig. 5.3. X-axis measures the level of output (or AS) whereas Y-axis measures aggregate demand [that is, consumption demand -I- investment demand). Level of output (AS) is expressed by 45° line whereas the line AD represents aggregate demand.

Both the lines intersect at point E which yields full employment equilibrium because at this point aggregate demand EM is equal to full employment level of output OM. (Remember, point E is equidistant from both the axes because E lies on 45° line.) Thus, economy is at full employment equilibrium at output level of OM since all those who are willing to work at the wage rate currently being offered have secured employment.

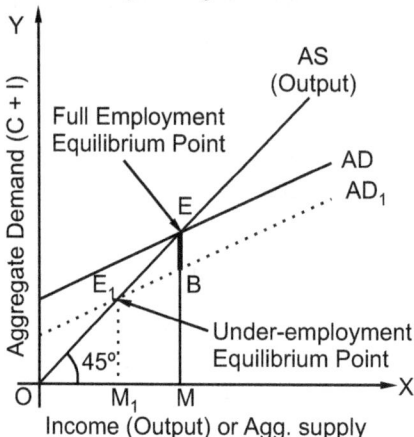

Fig. 5.3

5.3.2 Underemployment Equilibrium

Underemployment equilibrium refers to a situation where the aggregate demand is equal to the aggregate supply, all the resources are not fully employed. This equilibrium occurs prior to the full employment level. Thus, underemployment equilibrium means equality between 'aggregate demand and aggregate supply but at less than full employment'.

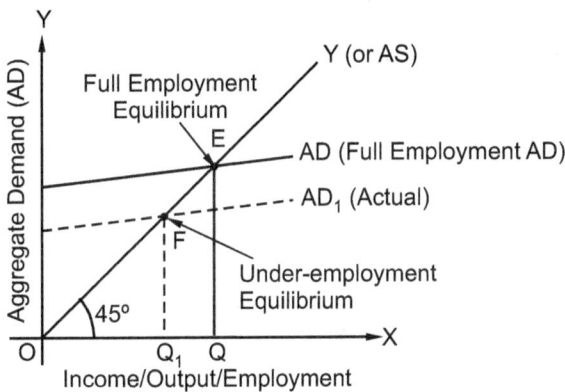

Fig. 5.4

1.   In Fig. 5.4, AD_1 = AS at point 'F which is lower than full employment level.

2.   As OQ_1 is less than OQ, point 'F' signifies the under employment equilibrium.

At this state of equilibrium level of aggregate demand is less than full employment level of output. In other words, in producing the outputs at underemployment equilibrium, all resources of the economy are not fully employed hence the demand is less.

This situation is not caused by low level of aggregate supply but is caused by deficiency of aggregate demand. As mentioned above the level of demand is less than full employment level of output; this situation is called deficient demand which pushes the economy into underemployment equilibrium. It leads to an increase in the gap between aggregate demand and 'aggregate supply at full employment', that is, it creates a deflationary situation.

The situation of underemployment equilibrium has been shown in Fig. 5.3 wherein full employment equilibrium is at point E but underemployment equilibrium occurs at point E_1 because AD, (actual) curve intersects the same AS curve at E_1 due to inadequacy of demand. OM_1 is the underemployment equilibrium level of income which is less than OM full employment equilibrium level of income. Underemployment equilibrium gives rise to deflationary gap, as mentioned above, which is represented by EB in the Fig. Since, AD falls short of AS at full employment by EB, therefore, additional investment expenditure equal to the level of EB (that is, deflationary gap) is required to reach full employment equilibrium.

5.3.3 Overfull Employment Equilibrium

It refers to a situation where aggregate demand is equal to aggregate supply beyond the full employment level. It occurs after the full employment level is attained by the economy.

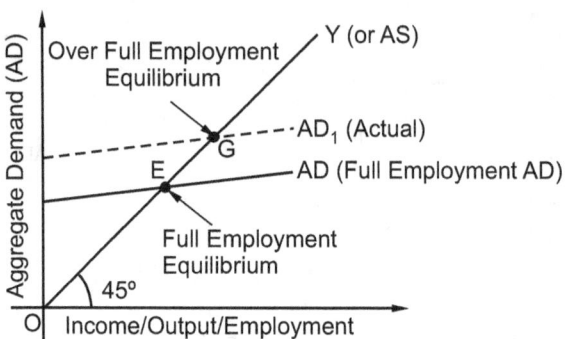

Fig. 5.5

1.   In Fig. 5.5, AD, = AS at point 'G' which is higher than the full employment level.

2.   As OQ, is more than OQ, point 'G' signifies the overfull employment equilibrium.

5.4 Effects of Government Expenditure and Net Export on the Equilibrium

5.4.1 Introduction

Effects of government expenditure and net export on the equilibrium in the economy can be explained with the help of various models, namely two-sector model, three-sector model and four-sector model of national income equilibrium.

5.4.2 Two-Sector Model

A two-sector model comprises of only domestic and business sectors.

Assumptions

The income determination in a closed economy is based on certain assumptions which are as follows –

1.   The economy consists of two sectors where only consumption and investment expenditures take place. This implies that the total output of the economy is the sum of consumption and investment expenditure.

2.   Investment relates to net investment, that is, after considering the effect of depreciation.

3.   It is a closed economy, that is, it does not have any business relations with the outside world.

4.   There are no corporate firms in the economy; thus, there are no corporate undistributed profits (retained earnings).

5.   There are no taxes in the economy which means that disposable personal income equals NNP.

6.   There are no transfer payments.

7. There is no government.

8. There is autonomous investment.

9. The economy is at less than full employment level of output.

10. The price level remains constant up to the level of full employment.

11. The money wage rate is constant.

12. There is stable consumption function.

13. The rate of interest is fixed.

14. The analysis relates to the short period.

Explanation

Aggregate demand can be obtained by the summation of consumption expenditure on newly produced consumer goods by households and on their services (C), and investment expenditure on newly produced capital goods and inventories by businessmen (I).

It is shown by the following equations

$$Y = C + I \qquad \qquad \text{... (1)}$$

Personal Income $\qquad Y_d = C + S \qquad \qquad \text{... (2)}$

But $\qquad \qquad Y = Y_d$

$$C + I = C + S$$

Or $\qquad \qquad I = S$

Where Y = national income, Y_d = disposable income, C = consumption, S = saving, and I = investment.

In the above equations, C + I relate to consumption and investment expenditures which represent aggregate demand of an economy. C is the consumption function which indicates the relationship between income and consumption expenditure.

The consumption function is shown by the slope of the C curve in Fig. 5.6 which is MPC (marginal propensity to consume). I is investment demand which is autonomous. When investment demands (I) is added to consumption function (C), the aggregate demand function becomes C + I.

C + S identity is related to the aggregate supply of an economy. That is why, consumer goods and services are produced from total consumption expenditure and aggregate savings are invested in the production of capital goods.

In an economy, the equilibrium level of national income is determined by the equality of aggregate demand and aggregate supply (C + I = C + S) or by the equality of saving and investment (S = I).

We explain these two approaches one by one with the help of Fig. 5.6 (A) and (B).

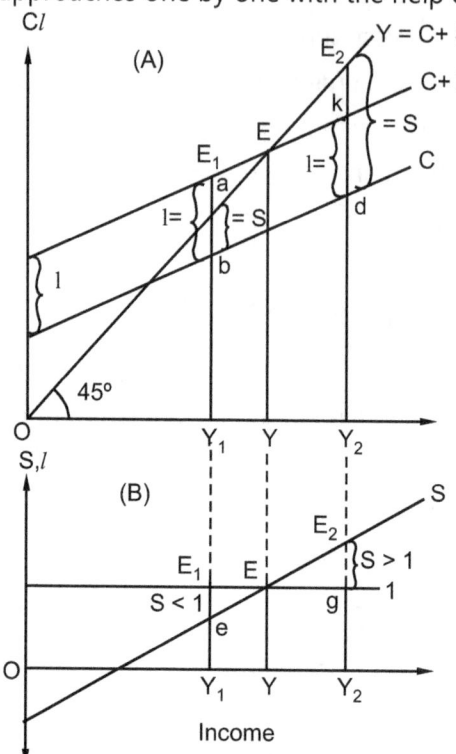

Fig. 5.6

Equality of Aggregate Demand and Aggregate Supply

The equilibrium level of national income is determined at a point where the aggregate demand function (curve) intersects the aggregate supply function. The aggregate demand function is represented by C + I in the figure. It is drawn by adding to the consumption function C the investment demand I.

The 45° line represents the aggregate supply function, $Y = C + S$. The aggregate demand function C + I intersects the aggregate supply function $Y = C + S$ at point E in Panel (A) of Figure 5.6 and the equilibrium level of income OY is determined.

Suppose there is disequilibrium in aggregate supply and aggregate demand of the economy. It can be in either case, aggregate supply exceeding aggregate demand or aggregate demand exceeding aggregate supply. How will the equilibrium level of income be restored in the two situations?

First, take the case when aggregate supply exceeds aggregate demand. This is shown by OY_2 level of income in Panel (A) of the figure. Here aggregate output or supply is Y_2E_2 and aggregate demand is Y_2k. The disposable income is OY_2 $(=Y_2E_2)$. At this income level OY_2, consumers will spend Y_2d on consumption goods and save dE_2.

But businessmen intend to make investment equal to dk in order to buy investment goods. Thus the aggregate demand for consumption goods and investment goods is $Y_2d +$ dk = Y_2k. But aggregate supply (or output) Y_2E_2 is greater than aggregate demand Y_2k by kE_2 (=$Y_2E_2 - Y_2k$).

Therefore, the surplus output of goods worth kE_2 is accumulated by businessmen in the form of unintended inventories. Since the inventory is unintended businessmen resort to reduction in production in order to avoid further accumulation. The consequence of reduction in production is reduction in output, income and employment levels and the equilibrium level of income will be restored at OY where the aggregate supply equals aggregate demand at point E.

The second situation of disequilibrium is where aggregate demand exceeds aggregate supply is shown by the income level of OY_1 in Panel (A) of the figure. Here the aggregate demand is Y_1E_1 and the aggregate output is Y_1a. The disposable income is OY_1 (=Y_1a).

At this income level, consumers spend Y_1b on consumption goods and save ba. But businessmen intend to invest bE, to buy investment goods. Thus the aggregate demand is $Y_1b + bE_1 = Y_1E_1$ which is greater than the aggregate supply of goods Y_1a by aE_1.

To meet this excess demand worth aE_1, businessmen will have to reduce inventories by this amount (that is selling from the inventory). In order to stop further reduction in their inventories and maintain their inventory levels, businessmen will increase production. Thus, as a result of the increase in production, output, income and employment levels will rise in the economy; subsequently the equilibrium level of income OY will be restored at point E.

Equality of Saving and Investment

The equilibrium level of income can also be presented as the equality of the saving and investment functions that exist in the economy. It is pertinent to note that intended (or planned) saving also equals intended (or planned) investment since the equilibrium level of income is determined when aggregate supply (C+S) equals aggregate demand (C + I) in the economy. This can be shown algebraically as follows –

$$C + S = C + I$$
$$S = I$$

The equilibrium level of income in terms of the equality of saving and investment is shown in Panel (B) of Figure 5.6, where I is the autonomous investment function and S is the saving function. The saving and investment functions intersect at point E which determines the equilibrium level of income OY.

If there is disequilibrium in the sense of inequality between saving and investment, the equilibrium position will be restored through the operation of market forces. Suppose the income level is OY_2 which is above the equilibrium income level OY.

At this income level OY_2, saving exceeds investment by gE_2. It means that people prefer consuming and spending less at this level and saving more portions of their incomes. Thus aggregate demand is less than aggregate supply which will lead to the accumulation of unintended inventories with the manufacturers. To stop the further accumulation of unintended inventories, manufacturers will reduce the level of production. Consequently, the output, income and employment will be reduced till the equilibrium level of income OY is reached at point E where S = I.

On the contrary, if the income level is less than the equilibrium level, investment exceeds saving. This is shown by OY_1 level of income when investment Y_1E_1 is greater than saving. The excess of intended investment over intended saving means that aggregate demand is greater than aggregate supply by eE_1.

Since aggregate output (or supply) is less than aggregate demand, manufacturers will sell out the inventories held by them. To stop further reduction in their inventories that is to maintain the inventory levels held by them, they will increase production. Consequently, output, income and employment will increase in the economy restoring the equilibrium level of income (OK) at point E.

The determination of equilibrium level of income simultaneously by the equality of aggregate demand and aggregate supply and of saving and investment is explained in Table I below.

Table 5.1

Panel (A)		Panel (B)
Y = C + I	at the equilibrium point E	and S = I
Y > C + I	to the right of E	and S > I
Y < C + I	to the left of E	and S < I

5.4.3 Three-Sector Model: Effects of Government Expenditure on the Equilibrium

A three-sector model of income determination consists of a two-sector model and the government sector in addition. The government increases aggregate demand by spending on goods and services, and by collecting taxes.

Government Expenditure

In order to explain government expenditure, given all the above assumptions except no existence of government sector in the two-sector model, income determination is as follows.

By adding government expenditure (G) to equation (1) of the two-sector model, Y – C + I, we get,

$$Y = C + I + G$$

Similarly, by adding government expenditure (G) to the saving and investment equation, when we have

$$Y = C + I + G$$
$$Y = C + S \; [S = Y - C]$$
$$I + G = S$$

Both are illustrated in Figs. 5.7 (A) and (B). In Panel (A), C + I + G is the new aggregate demand curve which intersects the aggregate supply curve 45° line at point E_1 where OY_1 is the equilibrium level of income. This income level is more than the income level OY without government expenditure.

Similarly, according to the concept of saving and investment, the new investment curve I+G intersects the saving curve S at point in Panel (B). Consequently, the income level OY_1 is obtained which is more than the income level OY without government expenditure.

It should be noted that by adding government expenditure to consumption and investment expenditure (C + I), the national income increases by YY_1 which is more than the government expenditure, $\Delta Y > G$ in Panel (A) of the figure. This is due to the multiplier effect which depends upon the value of MPC or MPS where MPC or MPS < 1.

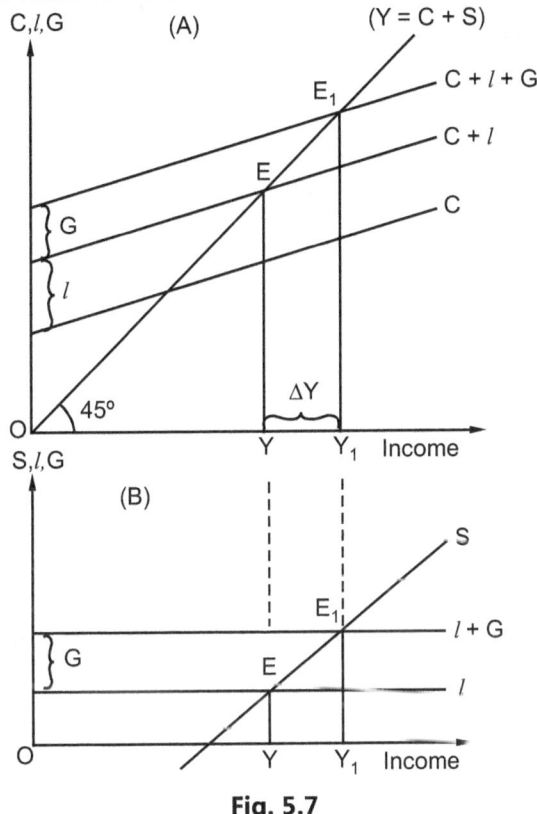

Fig. 5.7

Taxation

Now let us study the effects of various taxes on the level of national income. When the government imposes a tax, the amount of tax is reduced from the national income and what remains is the disposable income. Thus,

$$Y - T = Y_d$$

Where Y-national income, T=tax, and Y_d = disposable income. Now disposable income will be less than national income by the amount of tax, $Y_d < Y$. With the fall in disposable income, people will reduce expenditure on consumption. This will lead to reduction in national income, which will depend on the amount or rate of tax and the value of MPC.

Given all the above-mentioned assumptions in which government expenditure is constant, the effects of taxes on national income are illustrated in the following figures.

First, the effect of a lump-sum tax on income is shown in Fig. 5.8. The equilibrium level of income without a tax is at point E where the aggregate demand curve (C + I + G) intersects the aggregate supply curve 45° line and the income level OY is determined. By imposing a lump-sum tax, the consumption function is reduced by the amount of tax.

As a result, the aggregate demand curve C+ I + G shifts downwards to C_1 + I + G and intersects the aggregate supply curve 45° line at point E_1. This result in the reduction of income level from OY to OY_1 Thus with the imposition of a lump-sum tax, the national income is reduced by YY_1.

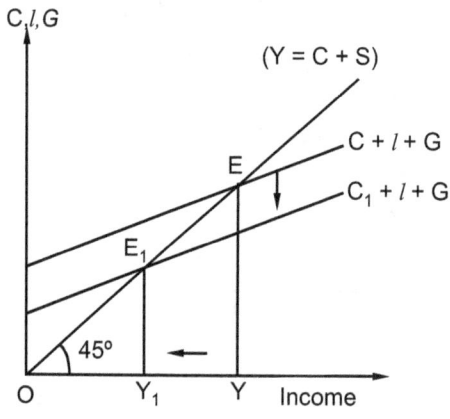

Fig. 5.8

Now we take a proportional tax which is imposed on income as a constant percentage. With the increase in the rate of tax, consumption and national income will decrease and vice versa. The effect of such a tax on income level is shown in Fig. 5.9.

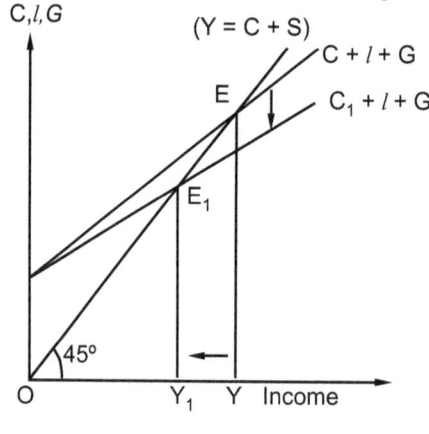

Fig. 5.9

The aggregate demand curve C+ I + G before the imposition of tax intersects the aggregate supply curve 45° line at point E and the income level OY is determined. After imposing the tax, the C+ I+ G curve shifts downward to C_1+ I + G due to a fall in consumption, and it intersects the 45° line at point E_1 consequently, the equilibrium level of national income is reduced by YY_1.

Effect on Saving and Investment

The effect of a tax on saving and investment also determines the equilibrium of national income as follows –

$$Y = C + I + G$$

And

$$Y = C + S + T$$

$$Y = C + I + G = C + S + T$$

Or

$$K = I + G = S + T$$

It is clear from the above equation that when planned investment (I) plus government expenditure on goods and services (G) equal planned saving (S) plus tax (T), the equilibrium of national income is established. I + G are inflows or injections in the national income and S + T are outflows or leakages. If they are equal to each other, the national income is in equilibrium.

This is shown in Fig. 5.10. Here, E is the equilibrium point before imposing the tax where S and I + G curve intersects and the income level OY is determined. With the imposition of a tax, the S curve shifts upward to the left as S + T and the new equilibrium is established at point E_1 with I + G and the national income falls from OK to OY_1.

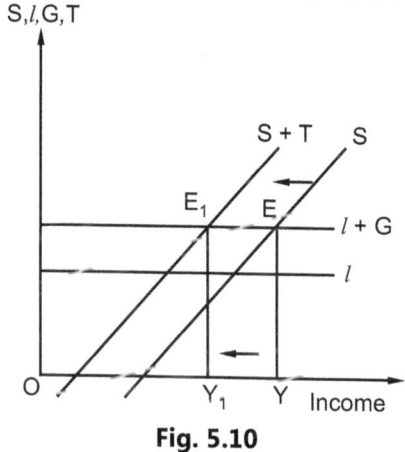

Fig. 5.10

5.4.4 Four-Sector Model: Effects of Government Expenditure and Net Export on the Equilibrium

We shall now study the determination of national income in an open economy that is an economy which has trade relations with other countries across the globe. For this, we relax the assumptions that there are no exports or imports and government expenditures. This means that we shall consider imports and exports and government expenditures and taxation in our analysis.

It may be noted that government expenditures behave similar to investment since they raise the demand for goods in the economy. They are injections in the national income. On the other hand, taxes are leakages in the national income similar to savings because they tend to reduce the demand for consumer goods by leaving less disposable income in the hands of consumers.

The impact of exports and imports is similar to that of the government expenditure. Exports are injections because they increase the demand for goods in the same economy. Imports, on the other hand, are leakages in the national income because they represent the supply of goods to the given economy.

Assumptions

The analysis of the determination of national income in an open economy is based on the following assumptions –

1. The domestic economy's international trade is small in relation to total world trade.
2. There is less than full employment in the economy.
3. The general price level is constant up to the full employment level.
4. Exchange rates are fixed.
5. There are no tariffs, trade and exchange restrictions.
6. Gross exports are determined by external factors.
7. Exports (A), investment (I) and government expenditure (G) are autonomous.
8. Consumption (C), imports (M), savings (S) and taxes (I) are each a fixed proportion of national income (Y) and their relationships with national income are linear.

Determination of Equilibrium Level of Income:

Considering the above assumptions equilibrium is said to exist in an open economy when its national expenditure (E) is equal to its national income (Y).

This can be represented by the following equation for the equilibrium level of income:

$$Y = E = C + I + G + (X - M)$$

But

$$Y = C + S + T$$

Therefore,

$$C + S + T = C + I + G + (X - M)$$

In the above analysis, C + S + T is gross national income (GNI) and C + I + G + (X – M) is gross national expenditure (GNE). Thus the equilibrium level of income in an economy is determined when aggregate supply, GNI = GNE, aggregate demand, or, C + S + T = C + I + G + (X – M).

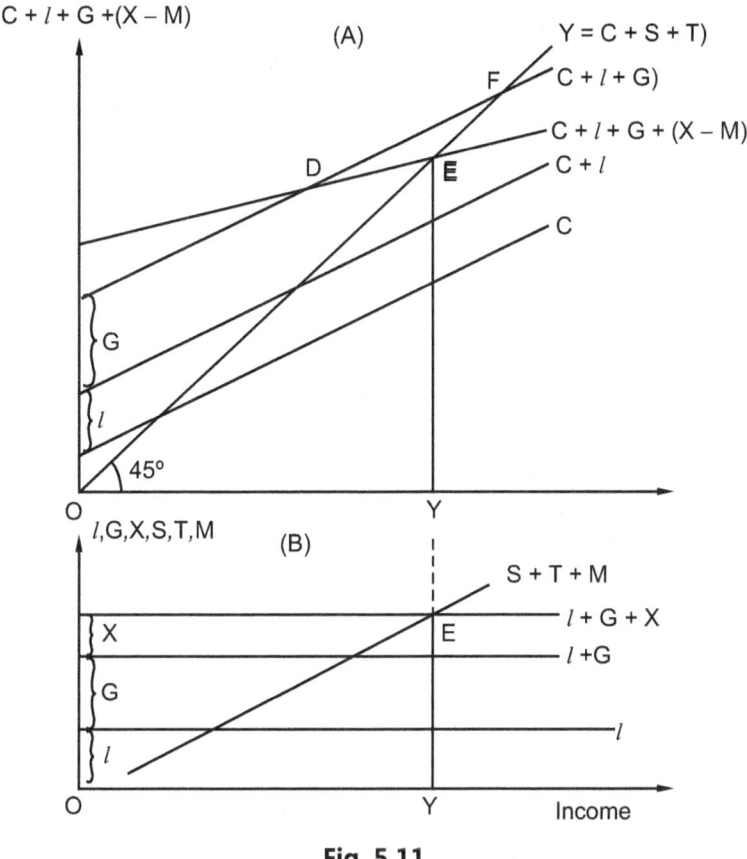

Fig. 5.11

This is shown in Figure 5.11 where C is the consumption function. On this curve, T autonomous investment is superimposed to form the C + I function, and autonomous government expenditure G is superimposed on C + I to form the C + I + G function. When net exports of X – M are superimposed on C + I + G, we get the aggregate demand function C + I + G + (X – M). The 45° line is the aggregate supply function which represents C + S + T.

It should be noted that so long as C + I + G + (X – M) > C + I + G, exports exceed imports and there is net addition to aggregate demand. At point D in Panel (A) of the figure, X – M = O. Beyond point D, C + I + G > C + I + G + (X – M) and imports exceed exports, and this gap continues to grow as income increases. This leads to net reduction in aggregate demand so that the aggregate demand function C + I + G + (X – M) lies below the domestic demand function C + I + G.

The equilibrium level of income in an open economy, OY is determined at point E where the aggregate demand function C + I + G + (X – M) intersects the aggregate supply function C + S + T.

The above analysis shows that in the absence of foreign trade, the equilibrium level of income would have been at a higher level, as determined by the equality of C + I + G = C + S + T at point F whereas with foreign trade it is at a lower point E.

An alternative method for determining the equilibrium level of income in an open economy in terms of saving and investment equality is as follows –

$$C + S + T = C + I + G + (X - M)$$
Or
$$S + T = I + G + (X - M)$$
Or
$$S + T + M = I + G + X$$

Where S + T + M refers to total income and I + G + X refers to total expenditure. When S + T + M is equal to I + G + X, the equilibrium level of income is determined. This is shown in Panel (B) of Fig. 5.10 where the S + T + M curve intersects the I + G + X curve at point E and the equilibrium level of income OY is determined.

5.5 Investment Multiplier

5.5.1 Introduction

The concept of Marginal Propensity to Consume (MPC) is closely connected to the concept of the *Multiplier*. It is considered as one of Keynes' path breaking contribution to economic analysis. The concept of multiplier was first developed by R. F. Khan in his article *"The Relation of Home Investment to Unemployment"* (1931). Khan's multiplier was the 'Employment Multiplier'. Keynes took the idea from R. F. Khan's employment multiplier and formulated the 'Investment Multiplier'.

Keynes considers his theory of multiplier as an integral part of his theory of employment.

The multiplier expresses the relationship between an initial increment in investment and the final increment in aggregate income. Thus, *the multiplier is the ratio of the change in income to the change in investment.*

The investment multiplier (K) has been defined as *"a ratio of increment in income (ΔY) to an increment in autonomous investment (ΔI)".*

It points to the fact that when there is an increment in investment, income will increase by an amount which is K times the increment of investment.

In the words of *Hansen*, Keynes' investment multiplier is the coefficient relating the increase of investment to an increase of income.

Thus,
$$K = \frac{\Delta Y}{\Delta I}$$

Alternatively,
$$\Delta Y = K \times \Delta I$$

Here, Y = income, I = investment; Δ = denotes change (increase or decrease);

K = the multiplier.

It shows as to how many times the effect of an initial change in investment is multiplied by causing changes in the aggregate income.

Whenever an investment is done in the economy, the effect is to increase aggregate income not only by the amount of the original investment, but by something much more than it. The reason is simple, the original investment increases income not only in the industries where the investment is made, but also in certain industries whose products are demanded by men employed in investment industries.

The size of the Marginal Propensity to Consume (MPC) decides the size of the multiplier, as the two are closely related to each other. Thus, "higher the marginal propensity to consume higher shall be the size of the multiplier and vice versa." In fact, the size of the multiplier can be derived from the MPC.

The multiplier is equal to the reciprocal of 1 minus the MPC.

Thus, $K = \dfrac{1}{1-m}$

Here, K = multiplier; m = marginal propensity to consume (MPC).

Hence, if the m (marginal propensity to consume) is known to us, K can be determined according to this formula.

5.5.2 Process of Income Multiplication

Suppose, the MPC is $\dfrac{1}{2}$, then $K = \dfrac{1}{1-1/2} = \dfrac{1}{1/2} = 2$.

The multiplier can be also derived from the Marginal Propensity to Save (MPS) and it is the reciprocal of MPS, therefore $K = \dfrac{1}{MPS}$ or $K = \dfrac{1}{S}$

Here, K = multiplier; MPS or S = marginal propensity to save.

> MPC + MPS is equal to 1

If the MPC is deducted from 1, we are left with the MPS. Hence, it is said that we can obtain K provided we know either the MPC or MPS.

Let us suppose that the MPC is $\dfrac{9}{10}$, by deducting $\dfrac{9}{10}$ from 1, we get $\dfrac{1}{10}$ which is the marginal propensity to save. The reciprocal of $\dfrac{1}{10}$ is 10 and this is the multiplier. Hence, *the multiplier is the reciprocal of the Marginal Propensity to Save (MPS) which is always equal to 1 minus the Marginal Propensity to Consume (MPC).*

MPC very rarely is zero. It means nothing is spent by the consumers out of the increased incomes. In other words, the whole increase of income is saved and the multiplier is 1. In such a case, if the new investment is ₹ 10 crores in public works and the MPC is zero; it means that the whole of ₹ 10 crores is saved, the multiplier is 1 and the aggregate income increases only by ₹ 10 crores.

The other limiting case is when MPC is 1. It implies that the consumers spend the whole of the increment of their incomes on consumption and *nothing in saved* (MPS = zero). This will result in an explosive situation, for example, investment of ₹ 10 crores in public works. The men who are employed will receive ₹ 10 crores and shall spend the whole of it on consumer goods. Other workers who receive increased incomes shall also spend them. In this way, ₹ 10 crores shall emerge and re-emerge and result in an infinite increase in income. Such a situation is rare but can be witnessed during hyper-inflation, as the multiplier will be *infinity*.

> **MPC = zero and MPC = 1, both the situations are rare**

The multiplier can never be 1 or infinity. It generally varies between 1 and infinity, that is, the multiplier is greater than zero but less than 1.

Table 5.2 gives values of the multiplier corresponding to certain values of the MPC.

Table 5.2: Derivation of the Multiplier

MPC $\left(\dfrac{\Delta C}{\Delta Y}\right)$	MPS $\left(\dfrac{\Delta S}{\Delta Y}\right)$ (or MPS = 1 – MPC)	K (Multiplier (Coefficient)
0	1	1
½	1/2	2
2/3	1/3	3
¾	1/4	4
4/5	1/5	5
8/9	1/9	9
9/10	1/10	10
1	0	α (Infinity)

5.5.3 Numerical Illustration

The actual process of multiple expansion of income brought about by increased expenditure on consumption goods as a result of new investment is shown below. Suppose that *n* investment of ₹ 10 crores is made in a public works project and the MPC is ½. It means that the multiplier is $2\left[K = \dfrac{1}{1-m}\right]\left[K = \dfrac{1}{1-1/2}\right]$. Hence, an investment of ₹ 10 crores will lead to an aggregate income of ₹ 20 crores. **Table 5.3** explains the working of the multiplier.

Table 5.3: Working of the Multiplier

(in ₹ crores)

Round	Increment in investment (ΔI)			Increment Income (ΔY)
1		10	=	10
½	×	10	=	5
$(1/2)^2$	×	10	=	2.50
$(1/2)^3$	×	10	=	1.25
$(1/2)^4$	×	10	=	0.62
	Total		=	**19.37**

In the *first round*, the income shall increase by ₹ 5 crores, MPC being ½, the first set of income recipients will spend only 50 percent of their income. In the *secondary round*, income shall increase by ₹ 2.50 crores (it is ½ of ₹ 5 crores). In the *third round*, income increases by ₹ 1.25 crores (it is 50 percent of 2.50 crores) and in the *fourth round*, income rises by 0.62 crores (it is ½ of 1.25 crores). Finally, the aggregate income will have increased to ₹ 20 crores (that is, 2 times of the original investment as K = 2). In the above arithmetical example, it is to be noted that the whole process of income propagation is spread over time. It implies that the income does not increase to ₹ 20 crores all at once and simultaneously. If each round takes 5 months and 4 rounds are involved, then it will take 20 months for an investment of ₹ 10 crores to increase income by ₹ 20 crores. However, Keynes has ignored the 'time lags' in this process of income propagation.

To conclude, *the size of the multiplier varies directly with the size of the MPC. Thus, if Marginal Propensity to Consume (MPC) is high, higher shall be the multiplier (K) and vice versa.*

5.5.4 Diagrammatic Illustration

The concept of multiplier can be illustrated graphically. Suppose that the MPC in a community is ½ or the MPS is ½ and the multiplier (K) is 2. Further, suppose that the community which is already investing a sum of ₹ 30 crores now decides to increase the investment by another ₹ 10 crores. Since the multiplier is 2, the income of the community shall increase by ₹ 20 crores as a result of additional investment of ₹ 10 crores.

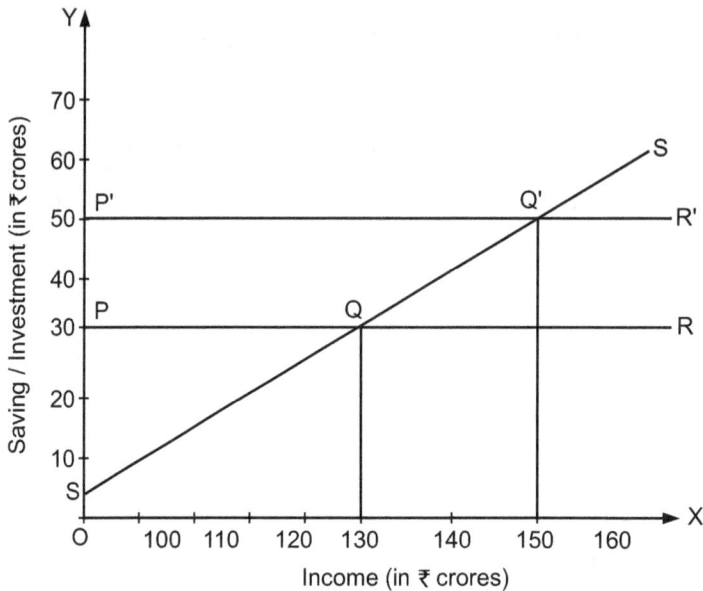

Fig. 5.12: Multiplier

In **Fig. 5.12**, PR represents the original investment of ₹30 crores. SS represents the saving curve. The additional investment of ₹ 10 crores is represented by P'R'. The distance between the two curves PR and P'R' is ₹ 10 crores. Q was the original point of equilibrium between saving and investment and the income of the community is ₹ 130 crores. With an additional investment of ₹ 10 crores, the new investment curve P'R' intersects the saving curve (S) at the new equilibrium point Q' and the income increases by 150 crores (K is 2, therefore from ₹ 130 crores to ₹ 150 crores). Thus, with an additional investment of ₹ 10 crores, the income has increased by ₹ 20 crores.

The theory of investment multiplier bears a significant amount of truth. It is true that an increase in investment has secondary consequences that result in an increase in income larger than the initial increase in investment. However, certain difficulties arise from the use of the multiplier concept. For example, in the above illustration it has been assumed that everyone had MPC ½ (50 percent). This is not very realistic assumption. Because, varying conditions are likely to produce varying MPC. In such conditions it is difficult to estimate the value of the multiplier. Thus, the theory of the multiplier is subject to certain limitations.

5.5.5 Limitations of the Multiplier

The multiplier is based on certain assumptions. Non-fulfilment of these assumptions will hamper the effective operation of the multiplier theory. Following are the limitations of the multiplier principle –

1. **No change in MPC:** To achieve the actual value of the multiplier, it is essential to assume no change in MPC during the working of the multiplier, as the multiplier depends on the MPC. It is assumed that the value of the multiplier will not change, when MPC undergoes a change.

2. **No time lags in the successive rounds of consumption:** To achieve the full value of the multiplier, it is assumed that there are no time intervals between the receipt of income and spending of it. It means that the consumers should immediately spend the income as soon as they receive it. This is not realistic, as in reality, there is always a time lag between the receipt of income and spending of that income, even if the time interval is of short period. It is obvious that longer the time interval between the receipt and the spending of the income, weaker will be the operation of the multiplier, that is, smaller will be its value.

3. **Existence of less than full employment:** The multiplier assumes that there is the existence of involuntary unemployment in the economy. Because, so long as there is involuntary unemployment, that is, less than full employment, in the economy, income, output and employment will continue to expand as a result of the operation of the multiplier. But, after the full employment stage, additional investment will only increase the prices (inflation) and not output, income and employment.

4. **No investment from induced consumption:** It is assumed that the accelerator principle does not operate and that the investment increases only by the original amount. If the accelerator is allowed to operate then the value of the multiplier would be far greater and would be achieved at an earlier stage in the process of income propagation.

5. **Maintenance of additional investment:** To achieve the full value of the multiplier, it is essential that the various increments are repeated at 'regular' intervals. In case of failure to do so, it will not be possible to raise the income to the multiplier, that is, multiplier effect will not be observed. And, any break in the continuity of investments would bring a fall-back in the national income to the original level. Thus, new investment is indispensable for the operation of the multiplier.

6. **Availability of consumer goods:** The success of the working of the multiplier depends upon the availability of consumer goods. If consumer goods are available in adequate quantity, the multiplier will continue to work and new income would increase. But, if consumer goods are not available then the income recipients will not be able to spend as much on consumption goods as they would desire.

7. **Net increase in investment in the economy:** It means that an act of investment in one sector should not be off-set by an act of disinvestment in some other sector of the economy. If it happens so, then there shall be no net increase in investment and it is possible that the operation of the multiplier will be obstructed as increase in investment in the public sector is neutralised by fall in private investment.

8. **Existence of a closed economy:** It is necessary to assume the existence of a closed economy in the country in question. Thus, the multiplier assumes that the country in question has no trade relations with the outside world. If the concerned country has trade relations with other countries, it is possible for the multiplier to be of lesser value. For example, if the concerned country enjoys an export surplus, there will be net addition to the income stream and the value of the multiplier would be greater

than its anticipated value. On the other hand, if the country is faced with import surplus, there will be a leakage from the income stream and the value of the multiplier may turn out to be lesser than its anticipated value.

To conclude, the multiplier principle will operate to the full extent only if these assumptions are actually realised in practice. Thus, these assumptions give rise to a lot of limitations of the multiplier principle.

5.5.6 Conditions for the Successful Operation of the Multiplier

Following are the conditions essential for the effective operation of the multiplier –

1. **Availability of excess capacity in consumer goods' industries:** For the complete operation of the multiplier, it is necessary that there exists excess and unutilised capacity in the consumer goods industries. The reason is that, in case excess capacity exists, an increase in investment would result in an increased demand for consumer goods. This increased demand would be met by using this unutilised or surplus capacity in the consumer goods industries. More workers would be employed in such industries and the multiplier would operate.

2. **Elastic supply of capital:** It would be activated when the multiplier theorem is working. An increase in investment would provide more employment to the workers. This is possible when there are no bottlenecks in the supply of capital, raw materials and other resources for the purpose of business expansion.

3. **Industrialised economy:** One of the conditions for the working of the multiplier is the existence of an industrialised economy in the country. In an agricultural economy, the multiplier does not operate fully. Existence of industrialised economy is essential as –

    • The demand for industrial consumer goods is higher in an industrialised than in an agricultural economy. Whether it is public or private investment, it results in a greater demand for industrial consumer goods in as industrialised economy rather than in an agricultural economy.

    • The agricultural output depends more on natural factors than on the industrial output. Adverse natural forces may actually reduce agricultural output despite increase in investment.

4. ***Absence of voluntary unemployment:*** An essential condition for the working of the multiplier is the existence of involuntary unemployment in the economy, that is, absence of any voluntary unemployment. Involuntary unemployment is when the workers cannot find jobs even though they are willing to accept the ruling wage-rate. Thus, an increase in private or public investment (by increasing the demand for consumer goods) would result in an increase in the level of income, output and employment. The multiplier will fail to operate, if involuntary unemployment does not exist. This is because the increase in investment after full employment stage will result in increasing only the price level (inflation) rather than the volume of employment.

5.5.7 Leakages in the Working of the Multiplier

It is clearly stated that the MPC is rarely 1 (that is, 100 percent). It means that the whole of the increment in income is not spent on consumption. If it were so, then full employment would be attained. But, as pointed out, the MPC is seldom 1. The reason is that there are several leakages from the income stream. If MPC is ½, then ½ of the new income leaks out of the income stream and only the remaining ½ is spent on consumption. These are as follows –

1. **Price rise:** Due to price inflation, a good amount of increased income may be spent on higher prices instead of encouraging consumption, income and employment.

2. **Repayment of debts:** A part of the new increment of income may be used by the income recipients to pay-off old debts and thus have no effect on consumption.

3. **Idle cash deposits:** A portion of the increased income may be saved and held back in the form of idle bank deposits which would not promote the consumption function.

4. **Savings:** This is an important leakage in the process of income propagation as it is well-known that MPC is rarely 1. In actual practice, people do not spend the entire increment in income on consumer goods and a part of it is saved. The 'saved' part of the increased income 'filters out' of the income stream, assuming that the savings are not converted into investments. This leakage in the form of savings limits the value of the multiplier. Thus, *higher the propensity to save lower shall be the value of the multiplier.*

5. **Purchase of old stocks and securities:** A portion of the new income may be used in the purchase of old stocks and securities from others who fail to spend the proceeds on consumption.

6. **Purchase of imported goods:** The part of the income that is spent on the purchase of imported goods does not add to domestic income and employment. Such a spending on imported goods will have no effect on the consumption of domestic goods and hence is certainly a 'leakage' from the domestic income stream.

7. **Taxes and savings:** Taxes and corporate savings determine the MPC of the people and have inevitable repercussions on the multiplier value. As taxes increase, they reduce the purchasing power of the people and hence it is a 'leakage' from the income stream. In the same way, undistributed profits of business corporates represent a leakage as they are not available (in the form of dividends) to the share-holders to be spent on consumer goods.

To the extent that these leakages from the income stream can be 'plugged', the initial increase in investment would have greater *multiplier effect* on the income propagation process.

Despite the above limitations, the multiplier is a very useful tool for economic analysis.

5.5.8 Reverse Working of the Multiplier

It is quite possible that the multiplier may work in the 'reverse' direction. Suppose that there is a net reduction in investment to the tune of ₹ 10 crores and with MPC being 0.5 the multiplier is 2 and hence the total fall in income would be ₹ 20 crores.

With reduction of ₹ 10 crores in the first round, men engaged in investment industries will reduce their consumption expenditure by 50 percent. Similarly, in each subsequent round, men will go on reducing their expenditure by 50 percent until the total income has decreased by ₹ 20 crores (as the multiplier is 2).

Thus, higher the value of the multiplier, greater shall be the reduction in the aggregate income.

A nation with higher MPC and lower MPS will suffer more from the reverse working of the multiplier. Higher MPC is better to a nation when the multiplier works in forward direction. A high multiplier would subject the economy to a more shocking decline of income whenever there is a fall in the aggregate investment. However, the picture is not so gloomy and pessimistic as *MPC is generally less than unity (that is 1) or MPC is not infinity.*

Hence, it can be said that just as consumers do not spend the entire increase in income on consumption, likewise they do not reduce the consumption expenditure by the full extent of the decrease in income. If the MPC was equal to 1, then the reverse working of the multiplier would result in complete collapse of the economy.

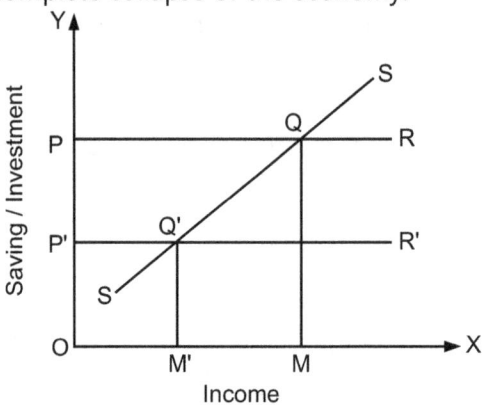

Fig. 5.13: Reverse Working of the Multiplier

In Fig. 5.13 SS is the MPS curve (1/2) multiplier is 2. The SS curve is intersected by the PR curve at point Q. The equilibrium level of income is OM at QM. The investment falls from OP to OP' (that is, by ₹ 10 crores). The income also declines from OM to OM' and a new equilibrium Q'M' is established. The fall in income MM' is double the fall in investment of PP'.

5.5.9 Significance of Keynes' Multiplier

The multiplier has become part and parcel of the Keynesian theory of employment. In fact, it is the 'centre-piece of the macroeconomic theory'. It is considered as an important theoretical concept as it focuses on *investment* as the major dynamic element in the economy.

(i)   It has highlighted the *importance of public investment*, particularly during depression and unemployment. A small increase in public investment leads to a large increase in income, output and employment.

(ii)   The multiplier principle helps the government *in formulating an appropriate employment policy* during depression.

(iii)   The concept of multiplier indicates that employment is directly created by investment and also shows that *income was generated throughout the economic system*, just like a stone thrown in water causes ripples in the water.

(iv)   The concept of multiplier *helps in analysing the course of the trade cycle* and also assists in devising an anti-cyclical policy to iron-out business fluctuations in the working of the economy.

(v)   The multiplier principle has revolutionised the modern economic theory and also *helped in policy-making at the state level.*

(vi)   The multiplier principle highlights the importance of *deficit-budgeting*. During depression, increased public expenditure takes place through public investment programmes by creating a budget deficit. This will help in increasing the income and employment.

5.5.10 Criticism of the Multiplier

Keynes' concept of the multiplier has been subjected to severe criticism.

(i)   Hazlitt refers to this concept as *"a strange concept about which some Keynesians make more fuss than anything else in the Keynesian system"*. He bluntly points out that there is *never any precise, pre-determined or mechanical relationship* between investment and income.

(ii)   The multiplier rests on an *assumption* which is *not at all realistic*, namely, that there is already *existing unemployment* in the economy. Critics point out and question as to why Keynes should assume mass unemployment as a 'general situation' and full employment as a 'special situation'.

(iii)   Another *unrealistic assumption* of Keynes' multiplier is that certain *part of the community's income is not spent and is 'hoarded'*. Keynes assumed that the unconsumed income is not invested. It is the propensity to consume that determines the multiplier and what is not spent on consumption is not spent on anything at all, that is, it is hoarded. This statement of the principle is in contradiction to what Keynes had said earlier that saving and investment were identical. According to Keynes what is saved must be invested so that savings and investments are equal. The acceptance of the multiplier concept gives rise to the problem of inequality between savings and investments. Thus, according to Hazlitt, Keynes' concept of the multiplier is not in conformity with the definition of savings and investment given in the 'The General Theory'.

(iv)   *Prof. D. H. Robertson, A. P. Lerner and R. M. Goodwin* points out that Keynes' multiplier does not take into account the effect of induced investment. It is a one-sided theory while dealing with the theory of income propagation, as the multiplier considers only the effects of increase in consumption consequent upon increase in income, but takes no note of the effects of increase in consumption on investment.

(v) Prof. Stigler has criticised the multiplier as the *fuzziest part of Keynes' theory.*

(vi) According to Prof. Hutt, Keynes has done great intellectual harm by putting forward the multiplier theory.

But despite these scathing criticisms, the multiplier principle has considerable practical applicability to macroeconomic problems.

Points to Remember

- National income is the aggregate money value of all goods and services produced in a country during one year. The wear and tear of plant and machines, that is, depreciation is deducted.

- Factors Influencing National Income

    1.   Quantity and Quality of Factors of Production

    2.   The State of Technology

    3.   Political Stability

- Gross Domestic Product at market price is the money value of all final goods and services produced during an accounting year within the domestic territory of a country.

- National Product or NNP at market price as it is the market value of all final goods and services after depreciation deductions.

- National Income at Market Price includes indirect taxes and subsidies.

- National Income at Factor Cost excludes indirect taxes and subsidies.

- Personal Income is the sum of all incomes actually received by all individuals or households during a given year.

- From Personal Income when we deduct personal taxes like income tax and personal property taxes we obtain Disposable Personal Income

- Full employment equilibrium refers to a situation where the aggregate demand is equal to the aggregate supply at full employment level.

- Underemployment equilibrium refers to a situation where the aggregate demand is equal to the aggregate supply all the resources are not fully employed.

- Overfull Employment Equilibrium refers to a situation where aggregate demand is equal to aggregate supply beyond the full employment level. It occurs after the full employment level is attained by the economy.

- The investment multiplier (K) has been defined as "a ratio of increment in income (ΔY) to an increment in autonomous investment (ΔI)".

Questions for Discussion

1. What is the meaning, importance and factors influencing national income?
2. Describe the various concepts of national income.
3. Elaborate the state of under employment and full employment of national income.
4. Evaluate the effects of government expenditure and net export on national income equilibrium.
5. Explain the concept, process and limitations of investment multiplier.

Chapter **6**...

Macroeconomic Problems and Macroeconomic Policies

Contents ...

Learning Objectives ...

➢ To study the causes and effects of inflation

➢ To understand the concept of stagflation

➢ To learn the causes, effects and measures to correct disequilibrium of Balance of Payment

➢ To learn the basic goals and instruments of macroeconomic policy

➢ To explain the monetary and fiscal policies to correct recession

➢ To elaborate the fiscal and monetary policies to control inflation

6.1 Inflation

6.1.1 Introduction

In the modern times, inflation is a global phenomenon. There is hardly any country in the capitalist world today which is not affected by inflation. Inflation is generally associated with rapidly rising prices of overall goods and services which cause a fall in the purchasing power of money. But, the term 'inflation' is a highly controversial term. Different economists have offered different definitions of inflation. The persistent inflation and the problems associated with it have claimed more attention of the economists than any other macroeconomic problem. This has led to a great increase in the literature on inflation.

6.1.2 Meaning of Inflation

Broadly speaking, inflation means a considerable and persistent rise in the general price level over a long period of time.

The term 'inflation' has widely attracted the attention of the economists all over the world, but despite this fact, there is no generally accepted definition of inflation. Some frequently quoted definitions of inflation are considered below.

According to Prof. Crowther, "Inflation is a state in which the value of money is falling, that is, prices are rising".

However, Crowther's definition is not complete. This definition has been criticised on the following grounds –

(a) Crowther terms every increase in the price level as inflation. This has harmful consequences on the economy. However, an increase in the price level during the depression period is not inflationary and has no adverse effects on the economy.

(b) Crowther's definition stresses more on the symptoms rather than the causes of inflation. It is observed that a rise in prices is the effect and not the cause of inflation.

Hence, this definition fails to explain the reason of rise in price from time to time.

Prof. Hawtrey defines inflation as the "issue of too much currency".

This definition too is unsatisfactory. It does not offer a clear criterion of the term "over-issue of currency".

1. According to Pigou, "Inflation exists when money income is expanding more than in proportion to the increase in earning activity".

2. In Prof. Kemmerer's words, inflation is defined as "too much currency in relation to the physical volume of business being done".

3. Prof. Coulbourn has also stressed on the same point as he says, "Inflation is too much money chasing too few goods".

4. Prof. Goldenweiser, "Inflation occurs when the volume of money actively bidding for goods and services increases faster than the available supply of goods".

In the above definitions, the general spirit is to define inflation as –

• A situation in which supply of money increases at a rate much faster than the supply of real output.

• The rise in the price level is caused by an increase in the supply of money.

• The increase in the supply of money is the cause and rise in the price level is the effect.

These definitions consider inflation as a purely monetary phenomenon.

The recent definitions of Cambridge economists, including Pigou and Keynes, have analysed inflation – a phenomenon of full employment.

According to Keynes, an inflationary rise in the price level cannot take place before the point of full employment. Keynes explains that every expansion of money supply does not result in a rising price level so long as there are unemployed resources in the economy.

It is only after the economy has attained full employment that the price level will increase. Thus, according to Keynes, the rise in the price level after the point of full employment is true inflation.

Any rise in the price level, before the point of full employment, can occur due to certain bottlenecks in the expansion of output in the economy. However, this is not true inflation and it can be referred to as semi-inflation, that is, inflation that is pre-full employment.

According to Hicks, "Our present troubles are not of a monetary character". Johnson defines inflation as "a sustained rise in prices".

Shapiro defines it as "a persistent and appreciable rise in the general level of prices".

According to Brooman, inflation "is a continuing increase in the general price level".

All these definitions clearly point out that the modern economists do not consider money supply alone as the cause of inflation.

From the various definitions, the meaning of the term inflation can be summarised as –

(a) Inflation is a phenomenon or rising prices. However, every rise in price is not inflationary.

(b) Inflation is a sustained rise in prices.

(c) Inflation is a general and dynamic phenomenon. It is general as it is not limited to only a particular sector of an economy. It is dynamic in nature and severity. Inflation occurs over a period of time.

(d) True inflation is witnessed only after reaching the full employment level.

(e) Inflation is characterised by an excess of demand or an increase in costs or the occurrence of both.

(f) Neo-Classicists define inflation as a monetary phenomenon. According to Friedman, "Inflation is always and everywhere a monetary phenomenon... and can be produced only by a more rapid increase in the quantity of money than output".

(g) Modern economists do not agree that money supply alone is the cause of inflation. Hicks say, "Our present troubles are not of a monetary character". Johnson defines inflation as a "sustained rise in prices."

(h) However, it is essential to understand that a sustained rise in prices may be of various magnitudes and accordingly, different names have been given to inflation based upon the rate of rise in prices, which are as follows –

  • Creeping inflation – price rise of less than 3 percent per annum;

  • Walking inflation – price rise between 3 to 7 percent per annum, but less than 10 percent;

  • Running inflation – price rise between 10 to 20 percent per annum;

  • Hyper-inflation – price rise from 20 to 100 percent per annum. It is runaway or galloping inflation.

6.1.3 Types of Inflation

On the basis of speed with which the price level rises in the economy, the classification of inflation is as follows.

1. **Creeping Inflation:** It is creeping inflation when the price rise is very slow like a creeper or a snail. The price level rises approximately by 2 percent annually. It is the mildest type of inflation and sometimes the government resorts to it to make the economy dynamic. This inflation works as a tonic for the developing economy. The slow rise in prices stimulates industry and trade. On account of its stimulating effect some economists welcome it for the economic development of a backward economy. There are some economists who support creeping inflation in the form of a slow and gradual rise in prices to keep the economy away from stagnation. Creeping inflation must be controlled effectively in time before it is too late because if proper control is not exercised over creeping inflation, it may assume alarming proportions with the lapse of time.

2. **Walking or Trotting Inflation:** Under walking inflation, the rate of increase of the price level acquires greater speed and rapidity. The price level rises at approximately 5 percent annually. Walking inflation, like creeping inflation, if not well handled can assume dangerous form of inflation.

3. **Running Inflation:** When the prices rise rapidly like the running of a horse at a rate of speed 10 to 20 percent annually, it is called as running inflation. In case, the government fails to curb running inflation in time, it may easily develop into galloping inflation.

4. **Galloping or Hyper-inflation:** When prices rise at double or triple digit rates from more than 20 to 100 percent annually or even more, it is hyper-inflation. This is the most dangerous type of inflation. Here the prices rise every minute and there is no upward limit to which the price level may rise in course of time. Prof. Keynes refers to this type of inflation as 'true inflation' and it occurs after the point of full employment has reached. There are two classic examples of galloping inflation in recent history – (a) The Great Inflation of Germany, after the First World War, and (b) The Great Chinese Inflation after the Second World War.

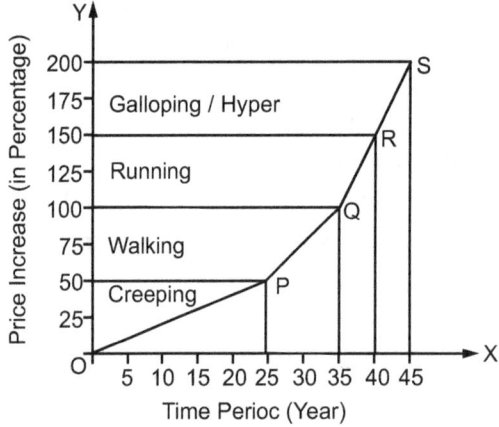

Fig. 6.1: Inflation based on Speed

In Fig. 6.1 the OX-axis measures the time period or the years, and the increase in price level (in percent) is shown on the OY-axis.

In the first period of 25 years, the prices of goods rise by 50 percent and the OP line represents creeping inflation. In the second period of 10 years, the prices have gone up by 50 percent. The PQ line represents the walking inflation. Running inflation is shown by the QR line. In the fourth period the price rises by 50 percent comprising three years in duration and it is shown by RS line. This is galloping or hyper-inflation. Thus, in a total period of 43 years, all the four types of inflation take place in succession and the price level rises by 200 percent during the entire period.

1. **Comprehensive and Sporadic Inflation:** It is comprehensive inflation when the prices of all commodities register a rise in the economy. Normally, when there is inflation, it is generally comprehensive inflation. If inflation is sector-specific it is sporadic inflation. The prices of only few commodities may rise upwards due to physical bottlenecks that impede any attempt to increase the production of goods. For instance, failure of rains may lead to failure of bumper crops and upward trend in the prices of food grains. Sporadic inflation can be dealt with effectively if the government resorts to price controls on the affected goods.

2. **Open and Repressed Inflation:** It is open inflation when the government takes no steps to check the rise in the price level. This inflation is allowed to continue unchecked without any attempts on the part of the government to correct it. Under open inflation, the market mechanism is allowed to work itself out fully without restrictions imposed by the government. The market mechanism can afford to pay a higher price for it; hence this mechanism distributes scarce factors among competing industries.

The hyper-inflation experienced by Germany after the First World War is an example of open inflation. Repressed inflation is when the government actively intervenes to check the rise in the price level. The government may resort to price controls and rationing of scarce commodities. The administration of controls on prices and rationing of scarce goods is an inseparable feature of repressed inflation. Hence the side effect of this type of inflation manifests itself in the form of profiteering, black-marketing, hoarding and corruption on a large scale. It distorts the production activity from essential to non-essential industries. The reason is that the prices of essential goods are statutorily fixed, while those of non-essential goods are left free and uncontrolled.

3. **Full and Partial Inflation:** This classification of inflation has been explained by Prof. Pigou. It is partial inflation when the price level rises slightly due to the expansion of money supply in the pre-full employment stage. This slight rise in price level and expansion in money supply goes to mobilise the idle resources in the economy. It results in more employment and output. However, increase in the money supply even after the point of full employment leads to a sharp uninterrupted rise in the price level with no increase in output and employment. Such a situation is a case of full inflation.

4. **Peacetime, Wartime and Post-war Inflation:** On basis of 'time' we have this classification of inflation. When the price level increases during peace time, it is peacetime

inflation. It is the result of increased government expenditure on developmental projects in the economy. In underdeveloped economies when such projects are undertaken, it results in inflation, referred to as peacetime inflation. During war time, the increase in the output of goods and services does not keep pace with the expansion of money supply. An inflationary gap inevitably emerges resulting in rising price level. This inflation arises during a period of war, hence wartime inflation. Post-war inflation generally takes place immediately after the end of hostilities and the suppressed demand springs up due to relaxation of price and physical controls by the government.

5. Currency Inflation and Credit Inflation: On the basis of 'factors' which cause inflation there can be currency, credit, profit-induced, deficit-induced, wage and scarcity-induced inflation. Inflation caused by excess supply of money in relation to the available output of goods and services is currency inflation. The excessive supply of money is faced with a limited supply of goods and services and results in inflationary rise in price level. When government encourages an expansion of credit without expanding the supply of money in circulation, it is known as credit inflation. The main objectives of credit inflation are –

(i) To mobilise financial resources for developmental plans;

(ii) To expand production;

(iii) To reduce the burden of indebtedness of the farmers.

6. Profit-induced and Deficit-induced Inflation: Sometimes the production costs start declining, and as a result the government resorts to artificial means to stop the trend of falling prices. In such a situation, the prices continue to stay at the old levels as the prices do not go up and are also not allowed to fall down. Prof. Keynes refers this inflation as profit-induced inflation. When the government's income does not match its increased expenditure consequent upon the outbreak of the war, it results in deficit-induced inflation. The government is not able to cover the deficit by resorting to new taxes and public borrowings. To finance the deficit the government resorts to printing new currency; this is deficit-induced inflation. To finance its developmental plans, government of underdeveloped economies resort to the printing press and it results in deficit-induced inflation.

7. Wage-induced Inflation: When the workers organise themselves into powerful trade unions and force the employers to increase their wages, this pushes up the production costs, increases the price level upward. This is wage-induced inflation.

8. Scarcity-induced Inflation: It is also known as production inflation. When the supply of money does not increase but the supply of goods decreases due to natural calamities, the prices move upward. It is inflation due to scarcity of commodities.

9. Mark-up Inflation: This type of inflation is due to the peculiar method of pricing of goods and services adopted by the huge business organisations operating in that country. The gigantic business organisations calculate their production costs first and then add to these costs a certain mark-up to yield the targeted rate of profit on their capital investment. The mark-up is on the high side and adds to inflationary pressure in U.S.A. The higher the demand, the greater is the size of the mark-up.

10. Ratchet Inflation: Under ratchet inflation, the prices in certain sectors are not allowed to fall, that is, are held in a fixed position, even when there are strong reasons for the prices to decline. Sometimes, it may happen so that the aggregate demand in the economy is not high but in certain sectors the aggregate demand is excessive and low in others. In sectors having high aggregate demand the prices would register a rise in prices and in other sectors the prices show a decline. But the prices are not allowed to fall in accordance with the low aggregate demand due to resistance from the industrialists and trade unions. Thus, the prices in the excess-demand sectors rise and are not allowed to fall in the deficit-demand sectors, consequently the net result is a rise in the general price level. This is known as 'ratchet inflation'.

11. Stagflation: Since the '60s a new type of inflation had come into vogue in the post-war period. This is stagflation. It is not inflation in the strict Keynesian sense as according to Keynes inflation is accompanied by overfull employment. The present day inflation is quite different from the traditional inflation. Today, 'stagflation' is a global phenomenon. It is inflation accompanied by stagnation on the development front – high prices and high unemployment go hand in hand. The whole western world particularly U.S.A., Britain, Italy and even developing countries like India have fallen prey to this most vicious type of inflation. Even the Keynesian measures to arrest inflation like budget surpluses, higher taxes and spending cuts have not been successful; in fact they have aggravated the problem of unemployment. Any measure undertaken to ease the situation of unemployment through increased capital investment adds to the inflation. Today, the world stands between the devil of inflation and the deep sea of unemployment.

12. Sectoral Inflation: When the rise in prices is not general but restricted to a particular sector of the economy, it is sectoral inflation. Sectoral inflation, if not taken care of, can spread to all the sectors of the economy. For example, during 1979-80 due to drought conditions agricultural prices shot up. But this sectoral (agricultural sector) inflation did not remain confined to the agricultural sector for long as the manufacturers had to push the prices higher due to higher cost of raw materials and increased wages.

13. Imported Inflation: Inflation which is caused in a country due to the operation of external inflationary pressures transmitted to the country concerned through foreign trade. For example, when a country depends heavily on imported goods and services, any inflationary pressure originating in foreign country is bound to have its repercussions on the domestic economy.

14. Demand-Pull Inflation: (Demand Inflation): Demand inflation is caused by an increase in the aggregate effective demand for goods and services in the economy. Demand inflation is a direct result of an excess of aggregate effective demand over the aggregate supply of goods and services.

The process starts this way – the increase in the supply of money leads to fall in the rate of interest and thus increases the demand for investment in the economy. With investment demand increases the demand for factors of production; in turn the factors of production receive money income for the services rendered by them. With increased money income, there is an inevitable rise in the expenditure for consumption goods. Thus, it is the increase in the demand for services of factors that lead to increase in their money incomes and it becomes natural on part of the factors of production to spend additional amounts on consumption goods.

Since the economy was operating already at full employment, hence an increase in investment expenditure results in inflation caused by increase in demand. The increased investment expenditure and consumption expenditure creates a situation of shortage of goods and services, increasing imports, rising wages, increasing employment, increasing profit margins, etc. These all are indicators of presence of demand inflation.

During a period of war, people generally keep postponing their purchases due to overall shortages of commodities in the economy. And, as soon as the war is over the longstanding demand for goods increases. Thus, this type of demand inflation generally arises in the post-war period. The demand inflation can be tackled by the government by curtailing unnecessary demand through the adoption of monetary and fiscal methods.

The Monetarists (Monetarism is a school of economic thought that emphasises the role of governments in controlling the amount of money in circulation) emphasise the role of money as the principal cause of demand-pull inflation. According to Friedman, "Inflation is always and everywhere a monetary phenomenon that arises from expansion in the quantity of money than the total output in the economy". Since the demand for money is fairly stable, excess demand for goods and services is mainly the outcome of increased money supply in the economy. Increased demand for goods, caused by increased money income raises the demand for labour. The workers demand higher wages, input costs and prices rise. Thus the money supply expansion works through output before inflation starts.

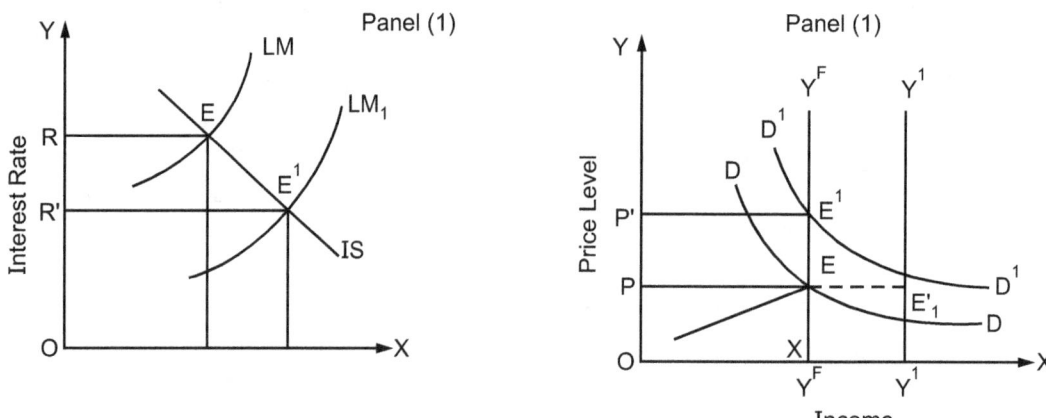

Fig. 6.2: Shows the Demand-pull Inflation

- Y^F is the full employment level of income which is depicted by price level P in Panel (2) and by intersection of IS and LM curves at E in Panel (1) at OR rate of interest.

- LM curve shifts to the right, that is, LM_1 with the increase in the quantity of money. LM_1 intersects IS curve at E^1 and the equilibrium level of income rises to Y^1 and this lowers the rate of interest to OR^1.

- The increase in demand is shown by a shift in aggregate demand curve from DD to D^1D^1 and the excess demand is to the extent of EE_1 ($= Y^FY^1$) in Panel (2).

- The vertical curve S is the fixed supply curve and the excess demand raises the price level to P^1.

- The rise in price level reduces the value of money, so that the LM_1 curve shifts to the left LM.

- Excess demand will not be eliminated until D^1D^1 curve cuts supply curve S at E^1. This will result in rising of price level to P^1 (Panel 2) and restoring original equilibrium position to E (Panel 1).

To sum up, demand-pull inflation is caused by increases in aggregate demand due to increased private and government spending, etc. Demand inflation encourages economic growth since the excess demand and favourable market conditions will stimulate investment and expansion.

15. **Cost Inflation (Supply Inflation):** It is also called as "supply shock inflation", and is caused by a drop in aggregate supply (potential output). This may be due to natural disasters, or increased prices of inputs. For example, a sudden decrease in the supply of oil, leading to increased oil prices, can cause cost-push inflation. Producers for whom oil is a part of their costs could then pass this on to consumers in the form of increased prices. Another example arises from unexpectedly high insured losses, either legitimate or fraudulent.

    Thus, cost inflation is generally caused by three factors – (a) an increase in wages; (b) an increase in the profit margins; and (c) imposition of heavy commodity taxes.

    (a)   These days labour is organised and using their collective strength they dictate their own terms to the employers. Powerful trade unions get the wages pushed up even without an equivalent increase in the productivity of the workers. This attempt on the part of the trade unions to push up the wages invariably causes cost inflation in the economy.

    (b)   Cost inflation is also caused when the industrialists push up their profit margins and then the prices cannot remain at their old levels. However, it is more the wage-push than the profit-push element that is significant in causing cost inflation. The reasons for it are that (i) profit constitutes a small part of the total price of the commodity. Thus, even if it is raised a little, it may not really bring a huge difference in the price of the commodity. (ii) The industrialists generally do not like to raise profit margin beyond a certain limit as they fear losing customers.

    Thus, the wage-push element is an important cause of cost-push inflation. It is more so because the industrialists should never be prepared to absorb the increase in wages by lowering down their own profit margins. Hence, any increase in the wages of the labour will lead to increase in price level and ultimately to cost inflation. When the cost inflation is due to wage-push factor, it has its effect gradually in all the sectors and does not remain confined to a particular sector or an industry. When cost inflation arises in one particular industry, it soon spreads to the other sectors of the economy because the various sectors are linked closely with each other. The output of one industry may serve as an input for another industry. Thus, cost inflation starting in one industry soon becomes an all-round phenomenon for the economy.

(c) The government may impose heavy taxes on different commodities. For example, it can be V.A.T. or now it is Local Body Taxes (LBT). In a seller's market the producers can easily shift the tax burden on to the shoulders of the consumers along with a margin of their own. This causes cost inflation in the economy.

Implications of Cost-Push Inflation are –

• It is associated with unemployment. Thus, some percent of unemployment is to be tolerated if inflation is to be controlled to an extent;

• But, if the government is committed to a policy of full employment then it has to tolerate wage increase and hence cost-push inflation;

• If the government attempts to increase aggregate demand during periods of the employment, it may lead to increase in wages instead of raising output and employment.

6.1.4 Causes of Inflation: Demand vs. Supply Factors

When there is a difference between the aggregate supply and the aggregate demand, there is a rise in prices. But, why is there a difference between the aggregate demand and aggregate supply? This can be explained with the help of causes of inflation which are as follows –

(A) Demand Factors/Increase in Demand

The phenomenon of excess demand for goods and services can arise in a number of situations, as believed by Keynes and other monetarists such as –

1. **Increase in Public Expenditure:** An increase in the public expenditure as a result of the outbreak of war or developmental planning invariably causes an increase in the demand for goods and services in the economy. This is an important reason that gives rise to the emergence of excess demand for goods and services in the country.

2. **Increase in Private Expenditure:** When optimism prevails in the business world, businessmen are eager to spend more money on capital goods and this in turn brings about an increase in the demand for consumer goods. This is because there is an increase in the income of the people who work in the capital goods industries. Therefore, they are in a position to spend more and thus there is an increase in the demand for all types of goods.

3. **Increase in Foreign Demand:** An increase in the foreign demand for the country's products (that is, export), reduces the stock of goods available for domestic consumption. It is obvious that when more commodities are exported to foreign nations fewer commodities are available for domestic consumption. This creates a situation of shortages and scarcity in the economy, giving rise to inflationary pressures.

4. **Reduction in Taxation:** Reduction in the taxes levied by the government causes excess demand in the economy. With reduction in taxes, it results in an increase of the purchasing power in the hands of the public, that is, increase in the disposable income in the hands of public. With this excess purchasing power, people buy more of goods and services for private consumption.

5. **Repayment of Internal Debts:** When the government repays past debts, more purchasing power is placed at the disposal of the people. They use it for buying goods and services for consumption purposes. This leads to an increase in the aggregate demand in the economy.

6. **Population Growth:** A rapidly growing population results in raising the level of aggregate effective demand for goods and services in a country. It acts as an inflationary force and consequently raising price levels.

7. **Existence of Black Money:** People spend such easy money extravagantly on luxurious items and this leads to rapidly rising prices.

8. **Deficit Financing:** When the government resorts to deficit financing by borrowing from the public and by printing new notes in huge quantity, it raises the aggregate demand in relation to the aggregate supply.

9. **Cheap Money Policy:** The bold policy of credit expansion leads to an increase in the supply of money which results in a rise in demand for goods and services.

10. **Rise in Consumer Spending:** When consumer spending increases, it increases the demand for goods and services. Increased consumer spending can be due to any reason, for instance, easy credit facility etc.

(B) Supply Factors/Decrease in Supply

The factors which lead to reduction in the supply of goods and services are as under.

1. **Natural Calamities:** Natural calamities such as floods, drought, earthquakes etc. adversely affect the supplies of agricultural products. These calamities cause shortage of food products, raw materials and thereby results in inflationary pressures.

2. **Scarcity of the Factors of Production:** At times the economy of a country may be faced with shortages of factors of production such as labour, capital equipment, raw materials etc. These shortages reduce the production of goods and services for consumption purposes. In fact, the shortage in the factors of production causes a serious obstacle to any effort to increase production in the country.

3. **Industrial Disputes:** Trade unions resort to strikes and if they happen to be unreasonably prolonged, they force the employers to declare lockouts. As a result, the supply of goods is reduced.

4. **Imbalanced Production:** If the emphasis is placed on the production of comfort and luxury goods and essential and consumer goods are neglected in the country, it creates shortage of goods in the market and causes inflation.

5. **Operation of the Law of Diminishing Returns:** When industries in the country use old and obsolete machines and outdated methods of production, the law of diminishing returns operates. This results in the rise of the cost per unit of production, raising the prices of products and causing inflation.

6. **Hoarding by Merchants:** When traders and merchants know that there is a short supply of any commodity, they will purchase and stock large quantities of these commodities. The stocks of essential goods often go underground during a period of inflation and rising prices, causing further scarcity of these goods in the market.

7. **Hoarding by Consumers:** It is not only the traders and merchants who resort to hoarding, but during inflation it is the individual consumers who also hoard essential goods to avoid payment of higher prices in the future. Thus, the consumers hoard essential commodities to ensure the uninterrupted supply of these commodities.

6.1.5 Impact of Inflation

An increase in the general level of prices implies a decrease in the purchasing power of the currency. That is, when the general level of prices rises, each monetary unit buys fewer goods and services. The effect of inflation is not distributed evenly in the economy, and as a consequence there are hidden costs to some and benefits to others from this decrease in the purchasing power of money. For example, with inflation, those segments in society which own physical assets, such as property, stock, etc. benefit from the price/value of their holdings going up, while those who seek to acquire them will need to pay more for them. Their ability to do so will depend on the degree to which their income is fixed. For example, increase in payments to workers and pensioners often lag behind inflation, and for some people income is fixed. Increase in the price level (inflation) erodes the real value of money (the functional currency) and other items with an underlying monetary nature.

A period of prolonged and continuous inflation results in the economic, social, political and moral disruption of the society. The effects of inflation can be discussed under various sub-headings, such as (A) Effects on production; (B) Effects on distribution; (C) Non-economic effects; and (D) Other consequences.

(A) Effects on Production: The effects of inflation on production are very important. As long as the economy has not reached full employment and inflation is proceeding at a mild rate, it may be helpful to an economy as the mild increase in prices acts as stimulant to the producers. An expansion of money supply in an underemployed economy will result in a gradual rise in the prices. The cost of production increases at a lower rate than the prices. This results in greater profit margins and optimistic conditions for entrepreneurs.

Investments rise, generating more income and employment till full employment is reached. But, after full employment, any expansion of money supply is very harmful for the economy. Thus, it is the hyper-inflation that disrupts the smooth functioning of the economy. The adverse effects of inflation on production are as follows –

(a) Runaway inflation results in a serious depreciation of the value of money and discourages savings, which in turn give a serious setback to capital accumulation.

(b) Inflation disrupts the smooth functioning of the price mechanism, thereby creating an all-round confusion in the economy.

(c) Due to reduced capital accumulation, the investment will suffer resulting in a low volume of production.

(d) The volume of production may also decline due to business uncertainty which may discourage entrepreneurs from taking business risks in production.

(e) It is not only the volume of production that suffers but the pattern of production may also undergo changes. Hyper-inflation may result in diversion of productive resources from the essential goods industries to the luxury goods industries. As a result, there is further shortage in supply of consumer goods for the common man.

(f) During hyper-inflation, it is a seller's market. This leads to serious deterioration in the quality of goods produced in the economy.

(g) Traders and consumers resort to hoarding of essential goods. Traders do so to earn higher profits or sell scarce goods in the black market. Consumers resort to hoarding of essential goods for fear of paying higher prices in the future.

(h) Hyper-inflation gives rise to speculative activities due to the uncertainty generated by persistent rise in price level.

(i) With the continuous rise in prices, the value of money falls. It drives out the foreign capital invested in the country.

(j) In due course of time, runaway inflation results in a flight of domestic currency due to the constant depreciation in the value of money.

To sum up, high or unpredictable inflation rates are regarded as harmful to an overall economy. They add inefficiencies in the market, and make it difficult for companies to make budgets or plan for the long-term. Inflation can act as a drag on productivity as companies are forced to shift resources away from products and services in order to focus on profit and losses from currency inflation. Uncertainty about the future purchasing power of money discourages investment and saving. Inflation can impose hidden tax increases, as inflated earnings push tax-payers into higher income tax rates unless the tax brackets are indexed to inflation.

(B) Effects on Distribution: Inflation has a deep impact on the distribution of income and wealth in the society. The flexible income groups, such as businessmen, merchants and traders are always the gainers in an inflationary period. On the other hand, the fixed income groups such as workers, salaried employees, teachers, pensioners, etc. are always the losers due to the inflationary rise in prices. Thus, inflation is unjust. It throws the economic burden on the weakest shoulders.

(a) **Debtors and Creditors:** During inflation, debtors are gainers, while the creditors are the losers. The reason is that, the debtors while repaying their debt return less purchasing power to the creditors than what they have actually borrowed and in this way the creditors receive less in real terms and are losers during the inflationary period.

(b) **Fixed-Income Group:** Persons who live on past savings, pensioners, interest and rent receivers suffer the most during an inflationary period as their incomes remain fixed while the prices rise sky-high.

(c) **Salary and Wage Earners:** They suffer during inflation as wages and salaries do not rise in the same proportion as the cost of living rises. If the salary earners and workers are well-organised into powerful trade unions, they may not suffer to a great extent during inflation. However, if they are unorganised, they are great sufferers as their wages and salaries may not increase in proportion to the cost of living.

(d) **Businessmen and Entrepreneurs:** Manufacturers, traders and merchants are gainers during inflation. They experience windfall gains as the prices of their stocks and inventories rise. They also benefit as the prices of their products rise, but the costs are quite 'sticky' and do not rise rapidly. In this way, inflation converts the entrepreneurs into 'profiteers'.

(e) **Investors:** Investors in shares (or equities) are gainers, while investors in fixed interest-yielding bonds and debentures do not benefit much. Income from bond and debentures remain fixed. The middle-class investors generally invest in bond and debentures and thereby stand to lose as they find their savings largely wiped out as a result of the depreciation in the value of money. On the other hand, the rich-class investors invest in equities and benefit during inflation.

(f) **Farmers:** During inflation, farmers are generally the gainers. The prices of the farm products increase more in proportion to the cost incurred by them. Moreover, farmers are generally debtors, thus they repay in terms of lesser purchasing power. However, small farmers do not really gain during inflation as they hardly have surplus to dispose off in the market.

To sum up, inflation redistributes income and wealth from those on fixed nominal incomes, such as some pensioners whose pensions are not indexed to the price level, towards those with variable incomes whose earnings may better keep pace with inflation. This redistribution of purchasing power will also occur between international trading partners. Where fixed exchange rates are imposed, higher inflation in one economy than another will cause the first economy's exports to become more expensive and affect the balance of trade. There can also be negative impacts to trade from an increased instability in currency exchange prices caused by unpredictable inflation.

(B) Non-Economic Effects

(a) Inflation is socially unjust and inequitable for the society as it favours the affluent class. This creates a sense of grievance among those who are adversely affected by inflation.

(b) Social conflict is seen in the society which can have serious political consequences by creating political instability.

(c) Inflation gives a serious blow to business ethics and morality.

(d) Attracted by quick profit, deterioration sets in the quality of products. Businessmen may also resort to adulteration and other anti-social tactics to boost up their profits.

(e) The general morality of the people in the country suffers, resulting in all-round corruption in the country.

(f) Inflation thus not only disturbs the smooth functioning of the economy but prepares the ground for social and political upheavals.

(C) Strengthening of Cost-Push Inflation

High inflation can prompt employees to demand rapid wage increases, to keep up with consumer prices. In the cost-push theory of inflation, rising wages in turn can help fuel inflation. In the case of collective bargaining, wage growth will be set as a function of inflationary expectations, which will be higher when inflation is high. This can cause a wage spiral. In a sense, inflation begets further inflationary expectations, which beget further inflation.

(D) Other Consequences

Inflation poses a serious danger to underdeveloped countries. The less developed countries require huge capital resources for their speedy economic development. However, during inflation, savings are discouraged and hence capital accumulation in the economy suffers. Inflation also discourages the inflow of foreign capital into the country. With reduced capital resources, an underdeveloped country finds it difficult to set up its progress towards economic development. Inflation encourages speculative activities in the economy.

6.1.6 Stagflation

The term stagflation was coined in the '70s when several developed countries received a supply shock in terms of rapid hike in oil prices. In 1973-75 in USA and in other developed countries inflation and unemployment were unusually high. Though the recovery from this situation began in 1975, the countries had to face another wave of stagflation during the period 1979-81.

Stagflation is a situation when a high rate of inflation occurs simultaneously with a high rate of unemployment, slow economic growth. It raises a great dilemma for economic policy as the actions designed to lower inflation may aggravate unemployment and vice-versa.

Stagflation is very costly and difficult to eradicate once it starts, in human terms and in budget deficits.

Causes of Stagflation

Two major reasons are generally cited by economists for the occurrence of stagflation.

1. Stagflation can occur when the productive capacity of an economy is reduced by an unfavourable supply shock, such as an increase in the price of oil for an oil-importing country. Such an unfavourable supply shock tends to raise prices and at the same time it slows down the economy by making production more costly and less profitable. As described by Milton Friedman, "too much money chasing too few goods".

2. Both stagnation and inflation can result from inappropriate macroeconomic policies. For instance, central banks can cause inflation by allowing excessive growth of money supply in the economy. The government can cause stagflation by excessive regulation of goods and labour markets.

Both these causes have been offered in the analyses of the global stagflation of the '70s. The stagflation began with a huge rise in oil prices and it continued as central banks used extensively monetary policy to counteract recession, which in turn led to runaway price and wage spiral – thus stagflation.

To conclude, the factors causing stagflation have been explained in terms of 'adverse supply shocks'. That is, shortages of aggregate supply caused due to cost-push factors (factors that lead to push the cost of production higher) results in leftward shift of the supply curve (reduction in supply). This leads to a rise in price level and reduction in output and employment, that is, inflation plus unemployment.

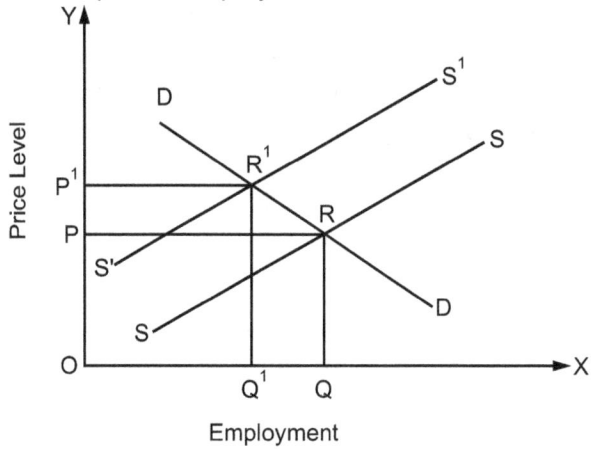

Fig. 6.3

In Fig. 6.3 OX-axis measures employment; OY-axis measures Price Level.

*   The aggregate demand curve DD intersects the aggregate supply curve at point R and that is the equilibrium of the economy.
*   At this equilibrium point the employment level is OQ and the price level is OP.
*   As the supply curve shifts upward (that is, left to the original) SS^1, the economy is at a new equilibrium at R^1.

- At the new equilibrium, employment declines to OQ^1 and the prices rise to OP^1.

Different economists have held different opinions for occurrence of stagflation in the economy.

The monetarists believe that the phenomenon of stagflation is a result of changes in inflationary expectations.

Supply-side economists are of the opinion that the actions taken by the government like higher tax rates, social security measures, minimum wage legislation, etc. increase cost of production and restrict aggregate supply of goods and services.

Measures to Control Stagflation

The different policy measures to control stagflation are as follows –

1. Management of Demand: Keynes and his supporters stressed on the management of aggregate demand to bring about short-run stability in the economy.

However, it has been experienced that management of demand through monetary and fiscal measures have been found ineffective in dealing with the problem of stagflation.

This is because the *expansionary* demand-managed measures increase both employment and prices, and with contractionary demand-managed measures reduce employment and prices at the same time.

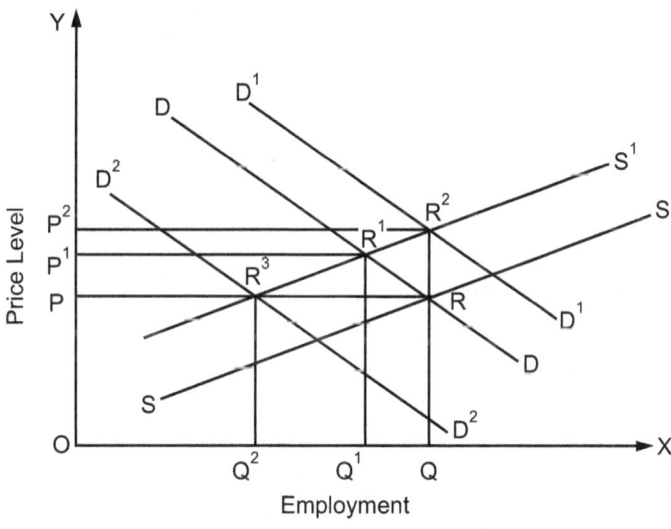

Fig. 6.4

- OX-axis measures employment level; OY-axis measures Price level.
- Point R is equilibrium where DD intersects SS, employment level is OQ and price level is OP.
- When aggregate supply curve shifts from SS to SS^1, equilibrium is R^1, employment falls to OQ^1 and price rise from OP to OP^1.
- To cure stagflation when *expansionary* demand-managed policy is adopted, aggregate demand increases from DD to DD^1.

- At new equilibrium point R^2, employment has increased from OQ^1 to the initial level OQ, but price level has further increased from OP^1 to OP^2.
- When contractionary demand-managed policy is adopted, aggregate demand will decline from DD to DD^2. At R^3, the price level has fallen to the initial level, that is, OP^1 to OP, but employment has fallen from OQ^1 to OQ.

Hence, demand-managed policy fails to control the problem of stagflation. In the short-run, expansionary monetary policy can increase employment at the cost of inflation. In the long run, this policy will lead to increase in both the price level and the unemployment rate.

2. **Management of Supply:** The supporters of *supply-side economics* prefer to solve the problem of stagflation through supply-management rather than demand-managed solutions. Importance is given to factors that influence the incentives to work, save and invest which determine the aggregate supply of output in the economy.

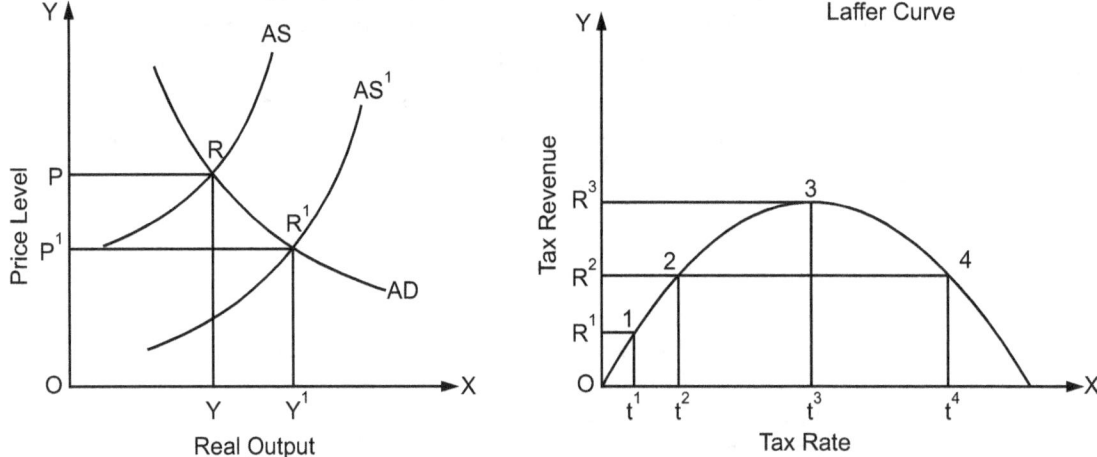

Fig. 6.5: (i) Management of Supply, (ii) Laffer curve

- A rightward shift of the aggregate supply curve from AS to AS^1 moves the equilibrium to R^1 where price level declines but aggregate output increases which will reduce unemployment.
- According to supply-side economists the stress should be on reduction in marginal tax rates which will encourage work effort, increase saving and investment and consequently promote economic growth and aggregate supply.
- Laffer curve shows relationship between tax rates and local tax revenue collected.
- At O the tax rate and the tax revenue are zero.
- Up to point 3, as the tax rate rises, the tax revenue also increases.
- If the tax rate increases beyond T^3, Laffer curve slopes downward showing that the tax revenue decreases. At this point the tax revenue is at its maximum, that is, R^3.
- Tax revenue falls to R^2 when tax rate is increased from T^3 to T^4.
- High tax rates serve as disincentive to work, save and invest and lead to decrease in income, output and employment.

- At 100 percent tax rate, there is no incentive to work, save and invest and the tax revenue will be reduced to zero.

The supply-side economists suggested that burden of government regulations such as minimum wage legislation, social security measure, etc., should be reduced along with the reduction in marginal tax rates.

1. **Income Policy:** Income policy can reduce not only the current rate of inflation but also the expected rate of inflation. Thus, the objective of this policy is to slow down or even stop a rise in the price level and the general level of money incomes. A proper income policy that is aimed at controlling inflation is to link the increase of money wages to the increase in productivity. However, the difficulty in this measure is strong opposition by worker's unions.

2. **Human Resource Policies:** This measure provides a long period cure on inflation and unemployment. Important measures under this policy are reducing frictions in the labour market, increasing labour mobility, upgrading skills and abilities and creating more jobs.

No single measure can be adopted to fight stagflation. It is only an integrated policy that can be adopted to attack the problem of stagflation.

6.2 Economic Growth

6.2.1 Introduction

Economic growth can be understood as the increase in the amount of the goods and services produced in an economy over a period of time. Conventionally, economic growth is measured as the percentage increase in real gross domestic product (real GDP). Calculating growth in real terms, that is, inflation adjusted terms enables one to net out the effect of inflation on the price of the goods and services produced in the economy.

A better way of measuring economic growth is calculating the real GDP per capita which is calculated by dividing the real GDP by the size of population.

6.2.2 Factors for Achieving Economic Growth

The following factors can prove to be an aid in achieving economic growth –

1. **Capital accumulation**

Purchase of capital equipment that is used for production of consumer goods is the key to economic growth. As a result of the investment consumer goods can be produced more efficiently.

2. **Technological progress**

Improvement in technology will enable the economy to make efficient use of the available resources, that is, more goods can be produced with the available resources. Consequently, this will lead to achieving a higher GDP.

3. **Improvement in quality of human resources**

Training the existing workforce can help attain better quality production and increased productivity. Hence, optimum utilisation of resources can be done.

4. **Research and development**

Continuous research to find alternative resources that can replace the current resources or finding new sources of the natural resources will add to the total output of the country.

6.2.3 Benefits of Economic Growth

1. **High standard of living**

With economic growth, people will have access to better goods and services. They will be able to afford a better and healthy standard of living as are a result of which the level of poverty will reduce.

2. **Improved public services**

Increase in levels of income leads to higher tax revenue for the government which in turn can be used for providing health services, education services and infrastructure facilities.

3. **Low level of unemployment**

An increase in economic growth leads to rise in demand for goods and services which in turn leads to increase in employment opportunities and opens up avenues in various fields. Thus, there will be a low level of unemployment in the country.

4. **Increased investment in 'green technologies'**

A country with a high level of economic growth can afford to invest in technologies which do not affect the environment in a harmful way as a result of their use. People will have cleaner air to breathe and a healthier environment to live in, leading to sustainable development.

6.2.4 Cost of Economic Growth

1. **Inflation**

One of the biggest risks of fast economic growth is inflation. If the aggregate supply of goods cannot match the aggregate demand in a country, it will result in a rise in the general price level of all goods and services.

2. **Opportunity cost**

Economic growth may be achieved because more investment is done in capital goods. This will be done at the cost of necessary consumer goods.

3. **Environmental problems**

Increased pace of economic growth can harm the environment leading to increased levels of noise and air pollution. The natural tree cover will be cut to create space to set up industries. The growth of industries will result in an increase in the output of substances which harm the surroundings.

6.3 Balance of Payments

6.3.1 Meaning and Definitions

*   According to **Charles P. Kinderberger,** *"Balance of Payments as systematic record of all economic transactions between the residents of the reporting country and the residents of foreign countries during a given period of time".*

- According to **Reserve Bank of India**, *"The balance of payments of a country is a systematic record of all economic transactions between the 'residents' of a country and the rest of the world. It presents a classified record of all receipts on account of goods exported, services rendered and capital received by 'residents' and payments made by them on account of goods imported and services received from the capital transferred to 'non-residents' or 'foreigners'"*.

  The above definition implies that –

  (i) The balance of payments of a country is a systematic record of all its economic transactions with the outside world in a given year.

  (ii) It can be said that it is a statistical record of the character and dimensions of the country's economic relationships with the rest of the world.

  In **B. J. Cohen's** words, *"Balance of payments shows the country's trading position, changes in its net position as foreign lender or borrower and changes in its official reserve holding"*.

  According to **Bo Södersten**, *"The balance of payments is merely a way of listing receipts and payments in international transactions for a country"*.

6.3.2 Features of Balance of Payments

The main features of balance of payments (BOP) can be listed as –

1. BOP is the method that countries use to monitor all international monetary transactions at a specified period of time. Usually, the BOP is calculated every quarter and every calendar year.

2. BOP statement is in the nature of a financial statement – it has double book-entry.

3. All trades conducted by both the private and public sectors are accounted for in the BOP to determine how much money is going in and out of a country.

4. If a country has received money, this is known as a credit, and if a country has paid or given money, the transaction is counted as a debit.

5. Theoretically, the BOP statement always balances in the accounting sense. That is, BOP should be zero, meaning that assets (credits) and liabilities (debits) should balance, but in practice this is a rare situation.

6. As such BOP statement can tell the observer whether the country has a deficit or surplus and from which part of the economy the discrepancies are seen.

6.3.3 Structure and Components of BOP Accounts

The balance of payments account of a country is constructed on the principle of double-entry bookkeeping. That is, each transaction is entered on the credit and debit side of the balance sheet. However, the difference between business accounting and balance of payments accounting is that in business accounting **debits** (–) are shown on the left side and **credits** (+) on the right side of the balance sheet. But, the practice in balance of payments accounting, the credits (+) is on the left side and debits (–) on the right side of the balance sheet.

A Credit Transaction is when a payment is received from a foreign country and Debit Transaction is when payment is done to a foreign country.

On the **credit transaction** side the main items are –

(a) Exports of goods and services;

(b) Unrequited (or transfer) receipts in the form of gifts, grants, etc. from foreigners;

(c) Borrowings from abroad;

(d) Investments by foreigners in the country;

(e) Official 'sale' of reserve assets including gold to foreign countries and international agencies.

On the **debit transaction** side the main items are – (these items include payments to be done to foreign country).

(a) Imports of goods and services;

(b) Unrequited (or transfer) payments to foreigners as gifts, grants, etc.;

(c) Lending to foreign countries;

(d) Investments by residents to foreign countries;

(e) Official 'purchase' of reserve assets or gold from foreign countries and international agencies.

In the balance of payments accounting –

(i)   The credit and debit items are arranged vertically, and

(ii)   Horizontally arranged are the different account heads of the balance of payments.

The Balance of Payments is classified into –

(a)   Balance of Payments on Current Account;

(b)   Balance of Payments on Capital Account;

(c)   The Official Settlements Account or the Official Reserve Assets Account.

The Structure of the Balance of Payments Account can be illustrated in the table below –

Table 6.1: The Structure of the Balance of Payments Account

Credits (Receipts)	**Debits (Payments)**
1. **Current Accounts** **Exports** (a) Goods (b) Services (c) Transfer payments	**Imports** (a) Goods (b) Services (c) Transfer payments
2. **Capital Account**	
3. **Official Settlement Account** (a) Borrowing from foreign countries (b) Direct investment by foreign nations (c) Increase in foreign official holdings	(a) Lending to foreign countries (b) Direct investments in nations (c) Increase in official reserve of gold and foreign currencies

(A) The Current Account of the Balance of Payments includes 3 items –

(i)   Visible trade relating to imports and exports (balance of trade);

(ii)   Invisible items, that is, receipts and payments for such services as shipping, banking, insurance, travel, etc.

(iii) Unilateral transfers such as gifts, donations, etc.

The current account shows whether the country has a favourable balance or deficit balance of payments in any given year.

In the current account (visible trade), merchandise exports and imports are the most important items.

Exports are shown as *positive items* and are calculated Free on Board (F.O.B.), that is, costs of transportation, insurance, etc., are excluded.

Imports are shown as a *negative item* and are calculated (C.I.F.), that is, costs, insurance and freights are included.

The difference between exports and imports of a country is its *balance of trade* (balance of visible trade/merchandise).

Thus, if money value of exports is greater than the money value of imports, the balance of trade is favourable. Alternatively, when imports exceed exports, the balance of visible trade is unfavourable.

The current account (invisible trade), includes the services, transfer payments or invisible items of the current account; however, reflects the true picture of the balance of payments account. The balance of invisible trade includes the balance of exports and imports of services and transfer payments.

The visible items and the invisible items determine the actual current account position.

Hence, if exports of goods and services exceed imports of goods and services, the balance of payments is favourable and alternatively it is unfavourable when imports of goods and services exceed the exports of goods and services.

In the current account, the exports of goods (visible items) and services (invisible items) and the receipts of transfer payments are entered as credits and they are 'receipts' from foreign nations. On the other side, the imports of goods and services and grant of transfer payments to foreign countries are debits as they give rise to 'payments' to foreign countries.

Hence, the net value (difference) of these visible and invisible trade balances is the balance of current account.

(B) The Capital Account

The capital account is where all international capital transfers are recorded. This refers to the acquisition or disposal of non-financial assets (such as a physical asset – land) and non-produced assets, which are needed for production but have not been produced, like a mine used for the extraction of diamonds.

The capital account of the country comprises of *its transactions in financial assets* in the form of –

(i)   Short-term and long-term lending and borrowings.

(ii)   Private and foreign investments.

Thus, the capital account shows international flow of loans and investments and represents a change in the country's foreign assets and liabilities.

   (i) **Short-term and Long-term Lending and Borrowings:** Long-term capital transactions implies international capital movements with maturity of one year or more and include direct investments like building of a plant in foreign country, portfolio investment (indirect investment) like the purchase of foreign bonds and stocks and international loans. Short-term lending and borrowing are international capital transactions for a period ranging between 3 months and less than one year.

   (ii) **Private and Government Investments:** These are two types of transactions in the capital account. Private transactions include all types of investment – direct, portfolio and short-term. Government transactions consist of loans to and from foreign official agencies.

In the capital account, the **credits** (or positive items), that give rise to 'receipts' from foreigners, are borrowings from foreign countries and direct investment by foreign countries result in **capital inflow**. On the other hand, lending to foreign countries and direct investments in foreign countries are capital outflow and represent debits (negative items). These capital outflows are **debit** as they are payments to foreigners.

The net value of the balance of short-term and long-term direct and portfolio investments is the balance of capital account.

Södersten and Reed have referred to the account as 'external wealth account'. This account shows the stocks of foreign assets held by the country (assets or positive items) and of domestic assets that are held by foreign investors (liabilities or negative items).

The *net value* of a nation's assets and liabilities shows the country's indebtedness. For example, if the country's assets are more than its liabilities, then the country is a *'net creditor'* and if its liabilities are more than its assets, the country is a *'net debtor'*. The sum of current account and capital account is referred to as the basic balance.

(C) The Official Settlements Account (or the official reserve assets accounts)

This account is a part of the *capital account.* In U.K. and U.S. balance of payments accounts show it as a separate account.

"The official settlements account measures the change in nation's liquidity and non-liquid liabilities to foreign official holders and the change in a nation's official reserve assets during the year. The official reserve assets of a country include its gold stock, holdings of its convertible foreign currencies and Special Drawing Rights (SDRs) and its net position in the IMF".

This account shows transactions in a country's net official reserve assets.

Errors and Omissions: This is a balancing item. It is carried out to balance the total credits and total debits of the three accounts. The balance of the credits and debits accounts must be equal in accordance with the principles of double entry bookkeeping. The balance of trade may be in disequilibrium in economic or accounting sense but the balance of payments of a country always balances in the accounting sense.

Current Account Balance - The Balancing Act

The current account should be balanced against the combined – Capital and Financial Accounts; however, this rarely happens. It is to be noted that with fluctuating exchange rates, the change in the value of money can add to BOP discrepancies.

If the current account is *surplus*, it means that,
- The country is acting as a net lender or investor in the rest of the world.
- The country has positive foreign investment.
- The country has savings more than it is investing domestically.
- The country is producing more than it is spending on goods and services, that is, have more income from this increased production.

If the current account is *deficit*, it means that,
- The country is a net foreign borrower.
- Domestic savings are less than domestic investment.
- The nation is spending more than its income/production.

There are three ways of measuring deficit or surplus in the balance of payments –
(i)   The basic balance comprises of current account balance of payments.
(ii) The net liquidity balance comprises of the basic balance and the short-term private non-liquid capital balance, allocation of SDRs and errors and omissions.
(iii) The third component of BOP is official settlement balance, which contains the total net liquid capital balance.

- If *total debits are greater than the total credits* in current and capital accounts, including errors and omissions, the net debit balance shows *deficit* in the balance of payments of a country. This deficit can be settled with an equal amount of net credit balance in the official settlements account.
- If *total credits are greater than the total debits* in current and capital accounts, including errors and omissions, then the net debit balance measures the *surplus* in the BOP of a country. This surplus can be settled with an equal amount of net debit balance in the official settlement account.

Table 6.2: The above balancing act

Trade balance ...	(i)	(i) and (ii) are **Autonomous items**
Transfer payments balance...	(ii)	
Thus, **Current Account Balance...**	(iii)	(iii) = (i + ii)
Long-term capital balance...	(iv)	
Thus, **Basic Balance**...	(v)	
Short-term private non-liquid capital balance...	(vi)	(v) = (iii + iv)
Allocation of SDRs...	(vii)	(vi), vii, viii are **Accommodating items**
Errors and omissions...	(viii)	
Net Liquidity Balance...	(ix)	
Short-term private liquid capital balance...	(x)	(ix = v = vii = viii)
Official Settlements Balance...	(xi)	(xi = ix + x).

- All transactions in the current and capital accounts are autonomous items as they are undertaken for profit motive and are independent of balance of payments considerations.
- Accommodating items are determined by the 'net' consequences of the autonomous items.

To conclude –

(a) The occurrence of disequilibrium in BOP – deficit or surplus – is mainly on the assumption that there is fixed exchange rate. But under freely floating exchange rates there can in principle be no deficit or surplus in BOP. This is because by appreciating (or depreciating) its currency the surplus (or deficit) can be corrected.

(b) Balance of payments always balances in an ex-post accounting sense. Balance of trade may be in disequilibrium but balance of payment has always to balance in book of accounts.

(c) Such a balance of payments can be in equilibrium only if there are no compensating transactions.

Liberalising the Accounts

- The rise of global financial transactions and trade in the late 20th century spurred BOP and macroeconomic liberalisation in many developing countries.
- With the advent of the emerging market economic boom – in which capital flows into these markets tripled from US $50 million to $150 million from the late '80s until the Asian crisis – developing nations were urged to keep restrictions on capital and financial account transactions to take advantage of these capital inflows.
- Many of the developing countries had restrictive macroeconomic policies, by which regulations prevented foreign ownership of financial and non-financial assets. The regulations also limited the transfer of funds abroad.
- With capital and financial account liberalisation, capital markets began to grow, not only creating a more transparent and sophisticated market for investors but also giving rise to foreign direct investment (FDI). These investments would bring a country greater exposure to new technologies and efficiency, eventually increasing the nation's overall GDP by allowing for greater volumes of production.
- Liberalisation can also facilitate less risk by allowing greater diversification in various markets.

6.3.4 Difference between Balance of Trade (BOT) and Balance of Payments (BOP)

Balance of Payments (BOP)	Balance of Trade (BOT)
1. BOP is a wider and more comprehensive concept and it includes all the entries that give rise to the inflow and outflow of foreign exchange.	1. BOT is a narrow concept and covers only the inflow and outflow caused by visible items or merchandise trade.

Balance of Payments (BOP)	Balance of Trade (BOT)
2. BOP, in addition to the values of visible exports and imports, includes various types of invisible items or non-commodity items which give rise to international receipts and payments.	2. BOT takes into account only visible exports and imports which are actually recorded at the ports.
3. BOP includes all the three components, for example, current account, capital account and official reserves account.	3. BOT is a part of BOP, as BOT represents only one component of BOP, that is, only merchandise trade.
4. BOP indicates real international monetary position of a country. Thus, it presents a much broader view of a nation's external transactions.	4. BOT is not comprehensive in nature and thus gives a partial view of the nation's external transactions.
5. BOP figures are available only at the year-end as they involve detailed calculations on the wide range of entries.	5. BOT figures are available more regularly as they are recorded at ports and the custom officials can certify their value and provide them on day-to-day basis.
6. BOP always balances in the accounting sense. If the debits are larger than credits, the country has to make accommodating inflows to balance the statement. BOP can be imbalanced in economic sense, but not in the accounting sense.	6. BOT can be in disequilibrium (deficit or surplus) in the accounting sense as in economic sense.

6.4 Disequilibrium in Balance of Payment

6.4.1 Introduction

The Balance of Payments of a country is said to be in equilibrium when the demand for foreign exchange is exactly equivalent to the supply of it. In other words, the Receipts ® equals Payments (P). Equilibrium in the BOP is a sign of the soundness of a country's economy.

Disequilibrium in the BOP is when either surplus or deficit is seen in it. There will be a deficit in BOPs when the demand for foreign exchange is more than its supply. And, there will be surplus when the supply of foreign exchange exceeds the demand for it.

6.4.2 Causes of Disequilibrium in Balance of Payment

The factors that cause disequilibrium in BOPs are numerous. The various causes may be broadly categorised into –

1. Economic Factors
2. Political Factors
3. Sociological Factors
4. Other Factors

(A) Economic Factors

There are a number of economic factors which may cause disequilibrium in the BOPs. Economic factors such as inflationary situation, development projects undertaken by the economy, change in national income lead to disequilibrium in BOPs. These factors are discussed as under –

1. Development Disequilibrium: Large scale developmental expenditure usually increases the purchasing power (that is national income) and the aggregate demand thereby leading to an increase in the prices. This also results in substantially larger imports. Development disequilibrium is common in the case of developing nations because the larger scale imports of capital goods needed for carrying out the various developmental programmes lead to deficit in their BOPs.

2. Cyclical Disequilibrium: One of the major reasons for the disequilibrium in BOPs is the occurrence of cyclical fluctuations. *Lawrence. W. Towle* points out that depression always brings about a drastic shrinkage in world trade. On the other hand prosperity stimulates the trade. For example a country enjoying a boom all by itself will ordinarily witness a more rapid growth in its imports than its exports, while the opposite will be true for the other countries. But production in the other countries will be activated as a result of the increased exports to the former country.

On the other hand, if the business partners of a country (for example USA) experiences depression, the business in the home (for example, India) is likely to be affected because there may be a fall in the goods demanded by those countries and hence the exports of the home country will suffer. Besides this there will also be a fall in the investment or intra – firm transfers.

3. Secular Disequilibrium: Sometimes BOP's disequilibrium is of secular nature, that is, it persists for long periods due to secular and long-run trends operating in the economy. For example in a developed country the disposable income is generally very high, hence the aggregate demand is high. At the same time, the cost of production is very high due to higher wages. As a result the prices are high. Thus, these 2 factors – high aggregate demand and higher domestic prices may result in higher imports than their exports.

In developing countries there is **persistent growth in the population.** This leads to high demand for goods and services and it results in higher imports. Further, **developing** countries have a **low capacity to save** due to low disposable income. At the same time they require a large amount of capital investment for the development process. Consequently, it leads to high import of capital machinery and other inputs.

4. Structural Disequilibrium: Disequilibrium in BOPs can be to structural changes. Such structural changes can be development of alternative sources of supply, development of better substitutes for exports, exhaustion of productive resources, changes in transport costs routes etc. For example, with increasing demonstration effect, the pattern of demand for goods is changing the consumption pattern of the western economies. This leads to decline in the demand for traditional exports.

5. Capital Movements: The capital movements occurring on a large scale can lead to imbalances in the BOP. A massive inflow of foreign capital into a country is followed by an unfavourable balance of payments. A large outflow of capital, on the other hand, is accompanied by a favourable balance of payments.

6. Inflationary Conditions: An inflationary rise in prices within the country may also produce imbalances in the BOP. The prices of export items may go up, causing a fall in the volume of exports from the country concerned. The inflationary spiral within the country may result in an increase in the volume of imports.

(B) Political Factors

Certain political factors could also cause BOP's disequilibrium. For instance –

(a) A country plagued with political instability results in disrupting the productivity within the country, causing a fall in the exports and increase in imports. Political instability cause large capital outflows and inadequacy of domestic investment and production.

(b) Payment of war reparations can also cause disequilibrium in the nations BOP.

(c) War with a neighbouring country or even elsewhere can have repercussion on the home country. It would lead to fall in demand for the home country's exports.

(d) Changes or closure of important trade route can have serious implications. Thus, factors like war or changes in world trade routes could also produce similar difficulties – disequilibrium in BOPs.

(C) Social Factors

Certain social factors influence BOPs. For example, changes in tastes, preferences and fashions, discovery of alternative sources of supply etc. may affect imports and exports and influence the BOPs. For example, the invention of synthetic rubber led to a serious decline in the export of natural rubber from countries like Malaysia, Burma etc. during and after the Second World War.

(D) Other Factors

Natural calamities such as chronic poor weather conditions influence BOPs.

For example,

(i) Developing countries that depend on exports of agricultural goods and natural calamities lead to substantial fall in exports, that is, rise in imports causing disequilibrium in BOPs.

(ii) Further major natural calamities like earthquake or cyclone, though brings in flow of aid in the short run, but leads to disequilibrium in BOP in the long run in terms of debt-servicing.

(iii) Natural calamities not only disrupt the agricultural production but also of industrial sector. The industrial sector depends for its raw materials on agricultural sector. When production falls, exports fall and imports decline.

6.4.3 Effects of Disequilibrium in Balance of Payment

Disequilibrium whether surplus or deficit in balance of payments position is considered as undesirable for a country. The implication of disequilibrium however depends on the location or source and the duration. Having said the above, following generalisations are possible –

(a) With respect to location or source, it can be said that a surplus in the combined current and capital accounts is considered desirable for a country.

On the other hand, a deficit in the combined current and capital account is considered as undesirable for the country.

(b) With respect to duration, if the disequilibrium whether surplus or deficit is temporary or short-term, then it is not of much concern for the country.

But, if the disequilibrium persists for a long term it is a matter of serious concern for the country and requires an immediate corrective policy action.

(c) A fundamental disequilibrium (in the form of deficit) is undesirable for the following reasons –

(i) A country where fixed exchange rate system is in followed it forces the country to go for devaluation of their home currency, while in a country where flexible exchange rate system is in existence it causes depreciation in the external value of the home currency.

(ii) Deficit would lead to an increase in external debt of the country and may lead the country into an external debt trap.

(iii) It leads to depletion in foreign exchange reserves of the country and makes the Balance of Payments position of country extremely vulnerable.

(iv) The country becomes dependent on the loans given by international organisations and foreign governments and raises a serious doubt about the maintenance of its external sovereignty in the international market.

(d) In practice it is observed that disequilibrium in the form of surplus is very rare while disequilibrium in the form of deficit is a common phenomenon. Thus the term disequilibrium is normally associated with deficit in Balance of Payments position of the country.

6.4.4 Methods to Correct Disequilibrium in BOPs

Disequilibrium can be in the form of surplus or deficit in BOPs. A country may not be bothered about a surplus in the BOPs, but every country strives to reduce and correct the deficit in BOPs.

The measures to correct the BOP's disequilibrium can be broadly put in two groups –

(i) Automatic Measures.

(ii) Deliberate Measures

(iii) Miscellaneous Measures.

(i) Automatic Measures

The automatic measures work well under the 'gold standard'. However, the BOP disequilibrium may be automatically disappearing when certain forces come into operation in the economy.

The theory of automatic correction is that if the market forces of demand and supply are allowed to have free play, then equilibrium can be restored automatically, in the course of time. Let us assume that there is 'deficit' in BOPs. In such a situation, the demand for foreign exchange exceeds its supply and results in increase in the exchange rate and fall in the external value of the domestic currency. This makes the exports of the country cheaper and imports expensive than before. Therefore, exports will increase and imports will fall owing to the fall in the value of the home currency and restore the BOP's equilibrium.

Under fixed exchange rate system, BOP disequilibrium may be corrected by adjustments in price, interest rate, income and capital flows.

(a) Price adjustments: Under **gold standard**, there is outflow of gold from a deficit country to the surplus country. This would cause a fall in the money supply in the deficit country and increase in the money supply in the surplus country. The prices will rise in the surplus country which will encourage the imports and discourage exports. On the other hand, there will be fall in prices in the country having deficit in BOP which will encourage exports and discourage imports. Thus, automatically it leads to restoration of BOP equilibrium in due course of time.

Under **paper currency** standard, similar changes will take place, that is, deficit or surplus in the BOP will cause fall or rise of the foreign exchange reserves and bring restoration in BOP equilibrium.

(b) Adjustments in rate of interest: A surplus or deficit in BOP also has its impact on the short-term interest rates. The monetary effect is in the sense that contraction or expansion of money supply resulting from the BOP deficit or surplus leads to a rise or fall in the rate of interest. The country facing deficit will encourage investors as the interest rate has risen and it makes them to withdraw their funds from abroad and invest in the home country. With BOP surplus in foreign country interest rate falls, foreigners will be encouraged to send money to the deficit country where interest rate has raised. These changes help to bring equilibrium in the BOP.

(c) Income adjustments: The Classical Economists did not consider the effect of income adjustments. However, J. M. Keynes demonstrated that under the fixed exchange rate system, changes in income will help restore BOP equilibrium automatically. For instance, a nation with persistent payments surplus will experience rising income causing increasing exports and in the deficit country it is the opposite.

(d) Capital flows: Changes in the interest rates, caused due to BOP disequilibrium will encourage capital flows between the deficit and surplus nations, bringing about restoration in the BOP equilibrium.

(ii) Deliberate Measures

Today, deliberate measures are widely employed. Deliberate measures refer to correction of disequilibrium by means of measures taken deliberately to bring restoration in BOP disequilibrium.

Deliberate measures are subdivided as follows –

(A) Monetary Measures

(B) Trade Measures and

(C) Miscellaneous Measures

(A) Monetary Measures: They are as follows –

  (i) Money Contraction (or Expansion): Monetary contraction or expansion, that is, supply of money, influence the level of aggregate domestic demand, domestic price level and the demand for imports and exports and can correct the disequilibrium in the balance of payments. For instance, the government of the country may resort to currency contraction to remove the disequilibrium in the BOP. Money contractions would reduce domestic prices, giving the much needed incentive to exports. Balance of payments deficit thus would require contraction of money supply. Hence, the fall in imports and rise in exports would help correct the disequilibrium.

  (ii) Devaluation: Devaluation implies reduction of the official rate at which the domestic currency is exchanged for another currency. It is a deliberate reduction in the external value of the currency of the country. It stimulates exports and discourages imports to correct the disequilibrium. Devaluation makes export of goods cheaper and imports dearer. Devaluation is also referred to as "expenditure switching" measure as it encourages switching of expenditure between foreign and domestic goods.

  (iii) Exchange Control: It is one of the popular methods to influence the balance of payments position of a country. Under this method, the government or the central bank assumes complete control over the foreign exchange reserves and earnings of the country.

Under exchange control system, the exporters have to surrender their earnings of foreign exchange to the government in exchange for domestic currency. By virtue of its control over the use of foreign exchange, the government can control imports. The government allocates foreign exchange to importers to enable them to make payments for imported goods. Importers have to obtain the needed foreign currency from the government. In this way, the government comes to have a full control over foreign exchange. This method is used to reduce the volume of imports as all non-essential imports or altogether stopped by the government by denying foreign exchange to importers. Many developing countries like India, Kenya, Sudan, Nigeria and others have been restricting imports by not releasing foreign exchange for non-essential goods.

(B) Trade Measures

Trade measures include –

(1) Export promotion and

(2) Measures to reduce imports.

1. Export promotion – To reduce/remove deficit in the BOP, it is essential to maximise the country's exports. Exports may be encouraged by reducing or abolishing export duties, providing export subsidy, encouraging export production and exports by giving monetary, fiscal, physical and institutional incentives and facilities.

(a) The government should either reduce or altogether abolish the export duties so that the exports become lucrative in foreign countries.

(b) The government should give subsidies to the export industries within the country. This would allow these industries to reduce their cost of production and have a competitive edge in the international market.

2. Reduction in imports – It is equally essential to cut down imports to correct deficit in the BOP of the country. Imports can be controlled by imposing or enhancing import duties, restricting imports through import quotas, licensing and even prohibiting altogether the imports of certain inessential items.

(a) **Imposition of new import duties and increase the existing import duties** would make the imported goods more expensive within the country and thus, reduce the demand for imported goods in due course of time.

(b) The country may adopt import quota system to cut down on the imports.

These are of many kinds, as discussed below –

(i) **Licence Quota System:** Under this system, the importers have to secure import licences from the government, which is granted by the government only after seeing the overall position of the country.

(ii) **Unilateral Quota System:** Under this system, the country imposes two types of restrictions on its imports. **Global Quota System** (the government fixes in advance the global quota for every imported item and hence, the country cannot import more than the fixed global quota). **Allocated Quota System** (under this system, the government not only fixes the global quota of the commodity concerned, but also decides in advance how much of the commodity is to be imported from individual countries).

(iii) **Bilateral Quota System:** According to this system, the government fixes the maximum quota of a commodity which is to be imported from abroad. Up to this extent of this quota, the commodity is imported at concessional import duty. Beyond the quota, a penal rate of import duty is charged.

(iv) **Import Prohibition:** An extreme measure that can be undertaken by the government is altogether prohibition of import of certain goods which are considered to be non-essential from the nation's point of view. Developing countries resort to import prohibitions of consumer luxury goods used by the affluent sections of the community.

(C) Miscellaneous Measures

A number of other measures can also help to make the Balance of Payment position more favourable. These measures aim at encouraging inflow of foreign currency on current account.

(i) **Development of tourism to attract foreign tourists:** Government encourages foreign tourists to visit the country in increasing numbers by offering them various facilities and concessional travel. This helps to increase exchange earnings of the country and helps to reduce the deficit in the BOP.

(ii) **Providing incentives to enhance remittances:** Large inflows take place on account of the remittances sent by Indians working abroad.

(iii) **Encouraging foreign investment in the home country:** Government induces foreigners to make investment in the country by offering them all kinds of incentives and concessions. This provides the government with extra foreign exchange and helps to correct the deficit in BOP. However, care should be taken that foreign investments have no adverse effect on the domestic industries.

(iv) **Foreign loans:** By securing loans from foreign banks or foreign government, equilibrium can be restored in BOP facing deficit. As the repayment of loans is spread over a longer period, it helps the government to remove the deficit in the BOP.

Flow-Chart illustrating Measures to Correct BOP Disequilibrium
Automatic Measures and Deliberate Measures

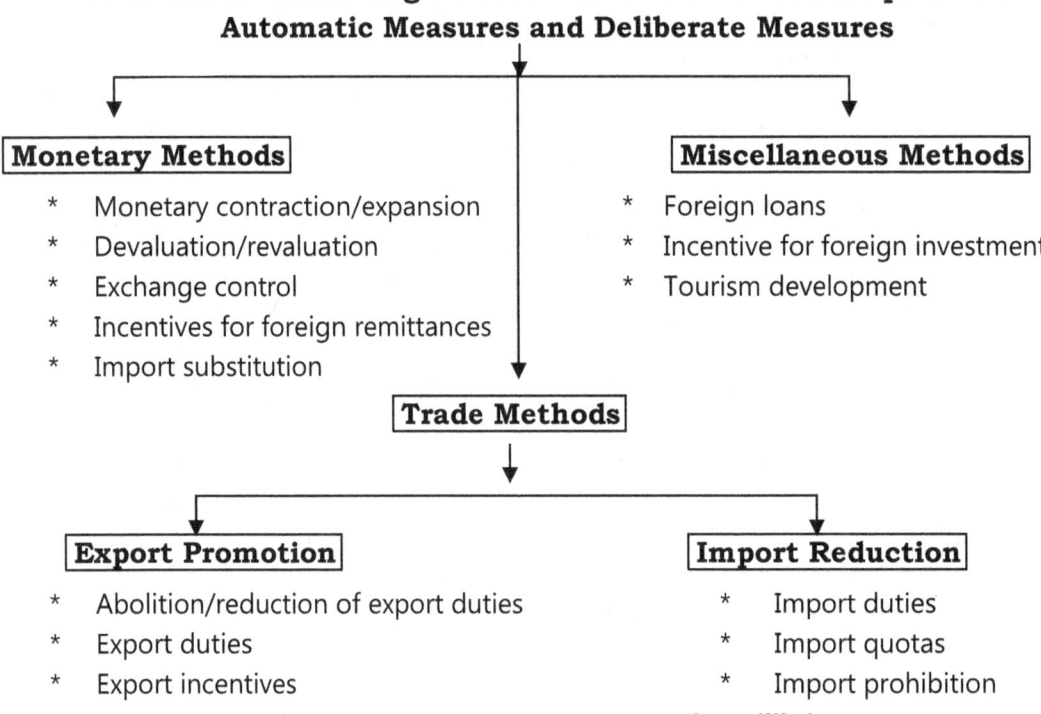

Fig. 6.6: Measures to correct BOP Disequilibrium

6.5 Macroeconomic Policy

6.5.1 Introduction

Macroeconomic policy consists of a set of rules and regulations framed by the government to control and simulate aggregate indicators of an economy. A few aggregate indicators are national income, money supply in the economy, inflation, unemployment rate, growth rate, interest rate etc. To sum up, policies framed to meet the macro goals of the country are called macroeconomic policies.

Fiscal policy, where the government makes changes in government spending or tax structure to stimulate growth in the country and monetary policy, which deals with changes in money supply or changes with the parameters that affect the supply of money in the economy are the two main regulatory policies. Other macroeconomic policies include contract laws, debt management policy, income policy etc.

6.5.2 Goals of Macroeconomic Policy

The macroeconomic policy aims to achieve the following objectives –

(i) Full employment

Performance of any government is judged in terms of the level of employment in the country and the stability of prices in the country. The above two may be called as the key indicators of overall health of any economy. In other words, the main aim of modern governments is to reduce both unemployment levels in the economy and control inflation rates.

Unemployment refers to a condition of involuntary idleness of labour force and other productive resources of the economy. Unemployment (of labour) is closely and directly related to the economy's aggregate output in a particular period. Higher the unemployment level in the country greater will be the difference between actual aggregate output during a period (or GNP/CDP) and potential output with the available resources. Considering the above one of the most important objectives of macroeconomic policy is to ensure full employment.

The objective of full employment became a priority of the policymakers in the era of Great Depression when unemployment rate in all the countries except the then socialist country, the USSR, were rising continuously. A free enterprise capitalist economy always exhibits full employment levels.

However, Keynes said that the goal of full employment, though a desirable one, is impossible to achieve. Thus full employment does not imply that nobody is unemployed at all. Even if 4-5% of the total population remain unemployed, the economy is said to be fully employed. Full employment, though theoretically possible, is difficult to achieve in a market-driven economy. Considering this, full employment objective is often referred to as 'high employment' objective. This goal is desirable indeed, but 'how high' should the employment level be? One of the authors takes a view that "The goal for high employment should therefore be not to seek an unemployment level of zero, but rather a level of above zero consistent with full employment at which the demand for labour equals the supply of labour. This level is called the natural rate of unemployment."

(ii) Price stability

The emphasis has now shifted from attaining full employment to achieving and maintaining price stability. Price stability does not mean an unchanged price level over a period of time. It is not necessary that price increase is unwelcome, particularly if the increase is restricted within a reasonable limit. In other words, price fluctuations of a larger degree beyond reasonable limits are always unwelcome.

However, it is difficult to define the permissible or reasonable limit of prise rise. But sustained increase in price level as well as a steep fall in the price level produces destabilising effects on the overall prices in the economy. Therefore, one of the objectives of macroeconomic policy is to attain and maintain a relative stability in price level. This goal not only prevents economic fluctuations but also helps in achieving a steady growth of an economy.

(iii) Economic growth

Economic growth in a market-driven economy is never steady as market-driven economies experience ups and downs in their performance levels. This objective became a priority in the period after World War II (1939-45). Many economists call such ups and downs in the economic performance as trade/business cycles. In the short run such cycles exhibit depression or prosperity (boom) phases.

One of the benchmarks to measure the performance of an economy is the rate at which the output increases over a period of time. The three major sources of economic growth are – (i) growth of the labour force, (ii) capital formation, and (iii) technological development. A country seeks to achieve higher economic growth over a longer period of time so that the standard of living or the quality of life of people, on an average, improves. While talking about higher economic growth, general, social and environmental factors are taken into account so that the needs of people of both present generations and future generations can be met that is ensuring satisfying today's needs not at the cost of future generations.

The goal of higher economic growth is often hampered by short-run fluctuations in aggregate output. In other words, one finds a conflict between the objectives of achieving long-term economic growth and price stability. In view of this conflict in the objectives, it is said that macroeconomic policy should promote economic growth with reasonable economic price stability.

(iv) Balance of Payment equilibrium and exchange rate stability

The major point of distinction between an international transaction and a domestic transaction is the exchange of foreign currency. As a long-term policy, all countries aim at balanced flow of goods, services and assets into and out of the country. Balancing the flow of goods and services leads to the stability of total international monetary reserves.

If a country's exports exceed imports, surplus or accumulation of reserves, like gold and foreign currency is experienced since more money is flowing in the economy. When the country loses reserves, that is, when its imports exceed far beyond its exports, it experiences balance of payments deficit. However, depletion of reserves reflects an unhealthy performance of an economy and thus poses various macroeconomic challenges in front of the country. This is the reason for which every country aims at building a substantial volume of foreign exchange reserves by concentrating on their exports.

The accumulation of foreign exchange reserves is largely dependent on the rate at which one currency is exchanged for another currency to carry out international transactions of imports and exports. The ideal situation is that foreign exchange rate should be stable as far as possible which is called an external stability in price.

External instability in prices hampers the smooth flow of goods and services across the borders to other nations. It also erodes the confidence of the world in the currency.

Due to the growing interconnectedness and interdependence between different nations in the globalised world, the task of maintaining external price stability objective has become more problematic.

(v) Social objectives

The list of objectives that have been referred here is an inclusive (illustrative) list.

Another objective of macroeconomic policy is to attain social welfare in the economy in the form of just and equitable income distribution. In a capitalist market-based society some people get more than others, that is, a few people earn the major chunk of revenue. In order to ensure social justice in the form of fair income distribution, policymakers use macroeconomic policy instruments.

Another social objective in our list is the goal of economic freedom. This implies the right of taking economic decisions by any individual (whether rich or poor, high caste or low caste would not matter).

6.5.3 Instruments of Macroeconomic Policy

Macroeconomic policy instruments include monetary policy, fiscal policy, and income policy in a narrow sense. But, in a broader sense, these instruments also include policies relating to labour, tariff, agriculture, anti-monopoly and policies on other relevant factors that influence the macroeconomic goals of an economy. Confining our attention to a restricted few policies and attributes, we intend to consider two types of policy instruments. The two "giants of the industry" are monetary (credit) policy and fiscal (budgetary) policy. These two policies aim at altering the aggregate demand so as to bring about a change in aggregate output (GNP/GDP) and prices, wages and interest rates, etc. throughout the economy.

Monetary policy attempts to stabilise aggregate demand in the economy by influencing the money supply in the economy, that is, the rate of interest, in an economy.

Monetary policy may be defined as a policy framed by the Central Bank to control the supply of money in the economy in order to achieve the macroeconomic goals.

Fiscal policy, on the other hand, aims at influencing aggregate demand by altering tax structure and expenditure of the government. The fiscal policy was first given importance in the '30s by J. M. Keynes who discredited the monetary policy as a means of attaining some of the macroeconomic goals – such as the goal of full employment.

There are several rounds of ups and downs in the effectiveness of both these policy instruments consequent upon criticisms and counter-criticisms in their theoretical foundations.

It is observed that as there are conflicts among different macroeconomic goals, policymakers are in a dilemma that neither of the policies alone can achieve desired goals. Additional policy measures like income policy, price control etc. are needed in order to ensure overall growth and achievement of macroeconomic policy objectives. Further, since the objectives represent economic, social and political value judgements they do not normally enter the mainstream economic analysis always. Ultimately, the result is that policymakers and bureaucrats are blamed as trouble-shooters.

6.6 Monetary Policy

6.6.1 Introduction

In recent years, the significance of monetary policy as an integral part of general economic policy has increased tremendously. In the narrow sense, non-monetary measures that influence the monetary situation have no place in this definition and monetary policy is understood to cover the measures undertaken by the government and the banking authorities to manage the money and credit supplies and regulations with reference to interest rates.

In a broad sense, monetary policy includes the monetary and non-monetary measures like wages and price controls, budgetary operations, etc. which influence the monetary situation in the economy.

6.6.2 Meaning

Monetary policy is the process by which monetary authority of a country; generally a Central Bank controls the supply of money in the economy by exercising its control over interest rates to maintain price stability and achieve high economic growth.

Monetary policy, as an instrument, is used to correct inflationary or deflationary situations in the economy. It is formulated by the government in consultation with the Central Bank.

There are many objectives that can be achieved through monetary policy. The objectives are generally chosen by the monetary authority on the basis of priorities dictated by the economic situations in the country.

In India, the central monetary authority is the Reserve Bank of India (RBI).

6.6.3 Objectives of the Monetary Policy

There are mainly five major objectives of monetary policy –

1. **Price Stability:** Price stabilisation has been suggested as a viable objective of monetary policy for an economy suffering from violent price fluctuations. Prof. Gustav and Cassels and Keynes suggested price stabilisation as a desirable objective of monetary policy.

    Price stability implies promoting economic development with considerable emphasis on price stability. The policy should facilitate the environment which is favourable for developmental projects to run swiftly while maintaining reasonable price stability.

    There are *evil consequences* of price instability –

    (i)   Violent price fluctuations create serious instability for the economy;

    (ii) Inflation is socially unjust as it redistributes income and wealth in favour of the rich people;

    (iii) Deflation causes depression in the economy.

However, certain advantages are there when price stabilisation is the objective of monetary policy.

Advantages

(i)   It will render the economy free of all cyclical fluctuations which causes harm to the economy;

(ii) It helps to promote business activity in the economy, as frequent price fluctuations can hamper the progress of business activity;

(iii) It facilitates performance of money functions, that is, money can perform its two important functions smoothly (money as store of value and money as a standard of deferred payments);

(iv) A policy of price stabilisation promotes the economic welfare of all the citizens in an equal measure;

(v)   It ensures equitable distribution of national income and wealth among the various sections of the community.

2. **Neutrality of Money:** According to economists like Hayek and Robertson, the monetary policy should aim at complete neutrality of money with relation to the economy. According to them monetary changes are the root causes of all economic fluctuations. These changes cause changes in prices, output and employment. Hence, they believe that if the changes in the money supply are eliminated, there will be perfect stability in the economic system. According to these economists money is only a technical device and plays a passive role in the functioning of the nation's economy. Money should be neutral and not cause any changes in prices or other economic entities. Thus, money has only a strictly neutral role to play in the economy.

3. **Exchange Stabilisation:** According to some economists, the main objective of monetary policy should be to maintain stability in the external equilibrium of the country, that is, maintain stability in exchange rates. It should be the constant endeavour of the monetary authority to adjust minor changes in the exchange rates with the internal price level. But it should not allow major fluctuations in the exchange rates which create a number of difficulties for the government.

    However, this objective is suitable to the country – (i) whose foreign trade is quite sizeable; (ii) a country which is dependent on foreign capital for its economic development.

    It is an important objective for monetary policy as wide fluctuations in exchanges create uncertainty in the minds of foreign capitalists who would not like to risk their funds in a country having exchange instability.

Advantages of Exchange Stability

(i)   Violent fluctuations in the exchange rates lead to speculations in exchange markets that further cause fluctuations in foreign exchanges;

(ii) Frequent fluctuations lead to loss of confidence and flight of foreign capital from the country;

(iii) The instability in exchange rates lead to instability in the internal price level;

(iv) Fluctuations in exchange rates cause a serious setback to the flow of trade between the countries concerned;

(v) Frequent fluctuations disrupt the economic relations and later the political relations of the country with other countries.

4. **Full Employment:** Lord Keynes was in favour of adopting full employment as the main objective of monetary policy by the government of a country. It ensures the maximum utilisation of productive resources in the economy. Other objectives such as price stabilisation, neutrality of money etc., however desirable, cannot promote full employment of productive resources in the economy.

Monetary policy as an instrument of full employment should aim at securing an increase both in consumption and investment expenditures to deal with the problem of mass unemployment.

To stimulate private investment, cheap money policy (lower interest rate loans) must be followed which would be effective stimulant to investments. It is believed that other objectives of exchange stabilisation and price stabilisation are automatically involved when the monetary authority adopts full employment as its objective.

Advantages of Full Employment Policy

(i) In the context of present-day situation it is an ideal objective of monetary policy when millions of people in the world are jobless;

(ii) It is a humanitarian policy as it tries to solve a human problem of unemployment and underemployment;

(iii) This policy promotes maximum social welfare of the community by providing jobs to millions;

(iv) This policy deserves support as it can eliminate cyclical fluctuations if well implemented.

5. **Economic Growth:** In recent years, economists hold an opinion that monetary policy should be an instrument for accelerating the process of economic growth in a country. They believe that (a) full employment is not possible without stepping up the rate of economic growth; (b) increasing economic growth is essential so that people may enjoy better standards of living; (c) an ever-increasing rate of economic growth is the condition essential for the survival of developing countries. Thus, in recent years 'growth' as an objective of monetary policy has acquired considerable significance.

The objective of economic growth is gaining popularity both in developed as well as in developing countries.

Economic growth is the continual increase in the real national income of a country spread over a period of time. In this process, money has a very important role to play as a mobilising agent, that is, to mobilise the idle physical and manpower resources with necessary monetary resources.

6.6.4 Criticisms Levelled against Each of the Objectives

1. **Price Stabilisation Policy**
   (i)   The concept of price stabilisation is rather vague as it does not clearly state as to which price level is to be stabilised in the economy – wholesale, retail, consumer or producer prices.
   (ii)   Price stabilisation policy deals with only symptoms, not the cause. Even if price stabilisation is adopted there is no guarantee for stabilisation of business activity as the causes of instability may be elsewhere.
   (iii) Price mechanism plays a crucial role in market economy of allocating the resources among the competing industries. A policy of price stabilisation will render the price mechanism obsolete and unnecessary.
   (iv)   With prices being stabilised there shall be no incentive left to the business community to increase production as there is no change in the profit margin.
   (v)   The policy of price stabilisation works harshly on the fixed-income groups, hence it is unjust and inequitable for certain groups of society.
   (vi)   Price stability is not a desirable objective for the monetary policy before the economy reaches full employment.

2. **Neutrality of Money**
   (i)   This concept is based on wrong assumptions as there is no direct and proportional relationship between the supply of money and the price level.
   (ii)   Neutral money may not assure a stable price level even if supply of money is kept constant at a particular level.
   (iii) A policy of neutral money is self-contradictory in character. The role assigned to the monetary authority (to keep constant supply of money) conflicts with the philosophy of *laissez-faire*.
   (iv)   This concept fails to explain the advent of depression.
   (v)   The policy of neutral money is unrealistic as in actual practice supply of money cannot be kept constant permanently at a particular level.
   (vi)   The basis of the policy is unrealistic as it has assigned passive role to money, as in present-day money plays a very active role and hence money cannot be neutral in its role.

3. **The Exchange Stabilisation**
   (i)   It is argued that fluctuations in exchange rate need not hamper the trading activities as their risk is covered to the forward exchange market.
   (ii)   When the objective of the monetary policy is not to allow fluctuations in exchange rates, any inflationary or deflationary movements originating abroad are bound to influence the internal stability of the country in question.

4. **Full Employment**
   (i)   The concept of full employment is ambiguous as different economists have interpreted this concept differently.

(ii) Full employment does not imply absence of complete unemployment as frictional and seasonal unemployment can coexist with full employment in the economy. Thus, the extent of unemployment is largely a matter of opinion.

5. **Economic Growth**

Prof. Howard Ellis strongly opposes the 'growth' objective of monetary policy in developing countries as these countries are highly susceptible to inflationary pressures.

6.6.5 Tools of Monetary Policy

The tools of monetary policy are the instruments which are used by the policy makers in order to attain some predetermined set of objectives. There are two types of instruments adopted by the monetary policy which are as follows –

(A) Quantitative Instruments or General Tools

They are also called as the general tools of monetary policy or credit control. These tools deal with the quantity or volume of the money in the economy. They are designed to regulate or control the total volume of bank credit available in the economy at any given point of time. The general tools of credit control comprise of following instruments namely –

1. Bank Rate Policy (BRP)

The Bank Rate Policy (BRP) is a very important technique used by the policy makers in order to influence the volume or the quantity of the credit available in a country. The bank rate refers to rate at which the Central Bank (that is RBI) rediscounts bills or provides advance to commercial banks against certain approved securities. It is "the standard rate at which the bank is prepared to buy or rediscount bills of exchange or other commercial paper eligible for purchase under the RBI Act". The bank rate affects the actual availability of the credit in the economy and the cost at which it is available. Any change in the bank rate necessarily brings out a resultant change in the cost of credit available to commercial banks in the country. If RBI increases the bank rate then it can reduce the volume of commercial banks borrowing from the RBI leading to a decrease in the supply of money in the economy since borrowing then becomes a costly affair. On the other hand, if RBI reduces the bank rate, borrowing for commercial banks will be easy and cheaper, subsequently leading to a boost in the credit creation. Thus any change in the bank rate is normally associated with the resulting changes in the credit availabillty in the lending rate and in the market rate of interest. However, the efficiency of the bank rate as a tool of monetary policy depends on a number of factors like existing banking network, interest elasticity of investment demand, size and strength of the money market, international flow of funds, etc.

2. Open Market Operation (OMO)

The purchase and/or sale of short-term and long-term securities by the RBI in the open market are termed as open market operations. This is a very effective and popular instrument of the monetary policy in the country. The following are the main objectives of OMO – to wipe out shortage of money in the money market, to influence the term and structure of the interest rate and to stabilise the market for government securities, etc. The working of OMO can be understood as follows – If the RBI sells securities in an open market, commercial banks and private individuals buy it. As a result of this the existing money supply in the economy gets transferred from commercial banks to the RBI. Contrary to this when the RBI buys the securities from commercial banks in the open market, commercial banks sell it and the money supply in the country's network increases. Using OMO transactions, the actual stock of money in the economy is controlled. Normally during the inflation period the aim is to reduce the purchasing power in the hands of people. RBI sells securities and curbs the excess money from the economy and during the recession or depression phase RBI buys securities and makes more money available in the economy through the banking system.

There are certain limitations that affect OMO namely – underdeveloped securities market, excess reserves with commercial banks, indebtedness of commercial banks, etc.

3. Variation in the Reserve Ratios (VRR)

The commercial banks have to keep a certain proportion of their total assets in the form of cash reserves with themselves and certain portion with RBI. Cash reserves to be kept with RBI are for maintaining liquidity and controlling credit in an economy. The proportions are named as Cash Reserve Ratio (CRR) and a Statutory Liquidity Ratio (SLR). The CRR refers to a certain percentage of commercial bank's net demand and time liabilities which they have to maintain with RBI and SLR refers to a certain percent of reserves to be maintained in the form of gold or foreign securities. In India, in the current scenario, the CRR by law remains in between 3-15 percent while the SLR remains in between 25-40 percent of bank reserves. Any change in the VRR (that is CRR + SLR) brings out a direct change in reserve positions of the commercial banks. Thus, by varying VRR commercial banks lending capacity will be directly affected. Changes in the VRR helps in bringing changes in the cash reserves available with the commercial banks and thus it can affect the banks credit creation multiplier. RBI increases VRR during the inflation in order to curb the excess money from the economy and to reduce the purchasing power and credit creation. But during the recession or depression it lowers the VRR thereby making more cash reserves available in the economy for credit expansion.

(B) Qualitative Instruments or Selective Tools

They are also known as the selective tools of monetary policy. Qualitative tools are not directed towards the quality of credit or the use of the credit. They are used for discriminating between uses of credit in the different sectors in the economy. There can be discrimination in various ways like discrimination favouring export over import or essential over non-essential credit supply. This method has direct influence over the lender and borrower of the credit. The selective tools of credit control comprise of the following instruments namely –

1. Fixing Margin Requirements

The margin refers to the "proportion of the loan amount which is not financed by the bank". In other words, it is that part of a loan which a borrower has to raise himself in order to get finance for his required purpose. A change in a margin means a change in the loan size. This method is used to directly influence the credit supply for the needy sector and discourage it for other non-necessary sectors. This can be achieved by increasing margin for the non-necessary sectors and by reducing it for other needy sectors. For example, if RBI feels that more credit supply should be allocated to agriculture sector it being a needy sector or a vital sector for the economy, then it will reduce the margin of the loans and even 85-90 percent loan of the total investment can be given.

2. **Consumer Credit Regulation**

    Similar to margin on loans, there is down payment in hire-purchase and instalment sale of consumer goods. Under these methods the down payment, instalment amount, loan duration, etc. is fixed in advance. Changes in the above can help in checking the credit use and inflation in a country.

3. **Publicity**

    Through it, Central Bank (RBI) publishes various reports periodically, stating what is good and what is bad in the system. This information can help commercial banks in channelising the direct credit supply in the desired sectors. Through its weekly and monthly bulletins, RBI makes the information available to the public and banks can use it for attaining goals of monetary policy.

4. **Credit Rationing**

    Central Bank fixes the limit of credit amount to be granted. Credit is rationed by limiting the amount available for each commercial bank that can be lent. The upper limit of credit can be fixed and banks are told to stick to this limit. This can help in lowering banks' credit exposure to unwanted sectors (other than the needy sectors).

5. **Moral Suasion**

    It implies to pressure exerted by the RBI on the commercial banks without any strict action for compliance of the rules. It is a suggestion given to the banks. This technique helps in restraining credit during inflationary periods. Commercial banks are informed about the expectations of the Central Bank through the monetary policy. Under moral suasion Central Banks can resort to various measures like issue of directives, guidelines and suggestions for commercial banks regarding reducing credit supply for speculative purposes.

6. **Control through Directives**

    Under this method the Central Bank issues directives on a periodical basis to the commercial banks. These directives guide commercial banks in framing their lending policy to various sectors. Through a directive the Central Bank can influence credit structures of the commercial banks, that is, supply of credit to certain limit for a specific purpose. The main theme of the directives to commercial banks is not lending loans to speculative sector such as securities, etc. beyond a certain limit.

7. **Direct Action**

    Under this method RBI can directly take an action against a bank. If certain banks are not adhering to the RBI's directives in spite of repeated notices, as a consequence RBI may refuse to rediscount their bills and securities. Secondly, RBI may refuse to supply credit to those banks whose borrowings are in excess to their capital, that is, those who haven't adhered to the limits set by RBI. Central bank can penalise a bank by changing some rates specific to the bank. At last it can even put a ban on a particular bank if it does not follow its directives and works against the objectives set by the monetary policy.

The success of the above tools is limited by the availability of alternative sources of credit in economy, working of the Non-Banking Financial Institutions (NBFIs), profit motive of commercial banks and undemocratic nature off these tools. A right mix of both the general and selective tools of monetary policy can help attain the desired results.

6.6.6 Role of Monetary Policy in Developing Economy

Following points are to be kept in mind by monetary authority in a developing country when deciding its policy –

1. The monetary authority should try to bring about an increase in bank deposits by encouraging the development of banking habits among the people.
2. The monetary authority should take effective steps to extend the sphere of the monetised sector which would make the monetary policy a more effective instrument of control in the economy.
3. It should extend banking facilities to those areas in the country which are either unbanked or under banked, that is, set up financial institutions in under banked areas and allow finances to flow into the priority industries for development of the economy.
4. The monetary authority should take effective steps to bring about an integrated interest rate structure in the economy as there are various types of interest rates present in the money market and they do not bear any definite relationship with the bank rate of the country.
5. It should take effective measures to establish close co-operation amongst the various constituent units of the money market.
6. The monetary policy should encourage the level of investment by making available savings mobilised by banks for purposes of investment and productions.

6.6.7 RBI's Objectives of Monetary Policy in India (As per Chakravarty Committee 1985)

The macroeconomic goals of monetary policy are –

1. **Price Stability:** It implies promoting economic development with emphasis on price stability.
2. **Controlled Expansion of Bank Credit:** One of the important functions of RBI is the controlled expansion of bank credit and money supply with special attention to seasonal requirement for credit without affecting the output.
3. **Promotion of Fixed Investment:** The aim is to increase the productivity of investment by restraining non-essential fixed investment.
4. **Restriction of Inventories:** Overfilling of stocks and products becoming outdated due to excess of stock often results is sickness of the unit. To avoid this monetary authority carries out this essential function of restricting the inventories. The main aim of this policy is to avoid over-stocking and idle money in the organisation (for example 'Just in Time' inventory system).

5. **Promotion of Exports and Food Procurement Operations:** Monetary policy pays special attention to encourage and increase exports and facilitate the trade. It is an independent objective of monetary policy.

6. **Equitable Distribution of Credit:** The policy of RBI aims at equitable distribution to all sectors of the economy and to all social and economic classes of people.

7. **Distribution of Credit:** Monetary authority has control over the decisions regarding the allocation of credit to priority sector and small borrowers. This policy decides over the specified percentage of credit that would be allocated to priority sector and small borrowers.

8. **Reducing Rigidity:** RBI tries to bring about flexibilities in its operations which provide a considerable autonomy. It encourages more competitive environment and diversification. RBI's control in financial system is to only maintain the discipline and prudence in operations of the financial system.

9. **To Promote Efficiency:** The central bank tries to increase efficiency in the financial system and tries to incorporate structural changes such as deregulating interest rates, ease operational constraints in the credit delivery system, to introduce new money market instruments, etc.

6.6.8 Expansionary Monetary Policy to Cure Recession or Depression

When the economy is faced with recession or involuntary cyclical unemployment, which is a result of the fall in aggregate demand in the economy, the central bank intervenes to cure such a situation. Central bank takes steps to increase the supply in the economy thereby increasing the purchasing power in the hands of people and/or lower the rate of interest with a view to increase the aggregate demand which will help in stimulating the economy.

The following three monetary policy measures are adopted as a part of an expansionary monetary policy to cure the economy from recession and to establish the equilibrium of national income at full employment level of output –

1. The central bank undertakes open market operations (OMO) and buys certain approved securities in the open market from the commercial banks. Buying of securities by the central bank, from the public, chiefly from commercial banks will lead to the increase in the credit availability with the banks or amount of currency with the general public.

With greater reserves available in hand, commercial banks can issue more credit to the investors and businessmen for undertaking more investment, that is, their lending power increases. An increase in the private investment will cause aggregate demand curve to shift upward. Thus, buying of securities will have an expansionary effect in the economy.

2. As a measure of curing recession, the central bank may lower the bank rate or what is also called discount rate, which is the rate of interest charged by the central bank of a country on its loans to commercial banks. At a lower bank rate, the commercial banks will be encouraged to borrow more from the central bank leading to an increase in the credit available at the lower rate of interest to businessmen and investors.

This will not only make credit comparatively cheaper but also increase the availability of credit in the economy. The expansion in credit or money supply will increase the investment demand which will lead to increase in aggregate output and income.

3.   Thirdly, the central bank may reduce the Cash Reserve Ratio (CRR) to be kept by the commercial banks thereby leading to a larger amount of funds available with the commercial banks for lending loans to businessmen and investors.

 As a result of this, credit expands and investment increases in the economy which has an expansionary effect on output and employment.

In April 1996, when Reserve Bank lowered the CRR from 14 percent to 13 percent, it was estimated that this would release funds equal to ₹5,000 crores for the banks and thereby would significantly increase their lending capacity.

Similar to the Cash Reserve Ratio (CRR) in India there is another monetary instrument, namely, Statutory Liquidity Ratio (SLR) used by the Reserve Bank to change the lending capacity and therefore credit availability in the economy.

According to Statutory Liquidity Ratio banks have to keep a certain minimum proportion of their demand and time liabilities in the form of some specified liquid assets such as government securities.

To increase the lendable resources of the banks, Reserve Bank can lower this Statutory Liquidity Ratio (SLR) thereby leaving more money in the hands of the commercial banks.

It may be noted that the use of all the above tools of monetary policy leads to an increase in reserves or liquid resources with the banks leading to an increase in the supply of money in the economy. Thus, appropriate monetary policy at times of recession or depression can increase the availability of credit in the economy and also lower the cost at which credit is available.

6.6.9 Tight Monetary Policy to Control Inflation

When aggregate demand in the country rises speedily due to large consumption and investment expenditure or, more importantly, due to the large increase in government expenditure relative to its revenue resulting in huge budget deficits, a demand-pull inflation occurs in the economy.

Besides, when there is too much creation of money for a specific purpose, it generates inflationary pressures in the economy. To check the demand-pull inflation, India and several other countries have adopted contractionary monetary policy which is popularly called tight monetary policy in the recent years. Tight or restrictive money policy is one which reduces the availability of credit and also raises its cost.

The following monetary measures which constitute tight money policy are generally adopted to control inflation –

1.   Increase in Bank Discount Rates: To arrest inflation, the Central Bank increases the rediscount rates. This action leads to an increase in the cost of borrowing funds for business and consumer spending, thus discouraging excessive activity based on borrowed funds.

When the rediscount rates rise, bank rates rise. Bank rates are interest rates charged by the commercial banks. An increase in bank rates tends to discourage borrowings by businessmen and consumers from banks resulting in a fall in the intensity of inflationary pressures in the economy.

However, this measure suffers from the following limitations.

(a) If the bank rates do not rise with the rise in rediscount rates, there may be no decline in the business and consumer borrowing. In this way, the inflationary pressures will continue.

(b) For the rediscount rates to be an effective anti-inflationary instrument, the commercial banks should have no easy access to additional reserves. For example, the commercial banks which are in possession of large amounts of short-term government securities can increase their reserves by selling these securities to the Central Bank or converting mature securities into cash, rather than approaching the Central Bank.

(c) Rise in rediscount rates will fail to check inflation if non-bank holders, like insurance companies of government securities were to convert their holdings into cash. This would increase the velocity of money due to increased cash balances. There is a general tendency on part of the holders of fixed income-yielding assets, to cash when prices are rising and value of money is falling.

2.   Selling of Government Securities: To check inflationary boom, government resorts to sale the government securities in the open market through the Central Bank. When public purchases them and pays for these securities, the banks' reserves with the Central Bank are reduced and they adopt a 'dear' and 'restrictionist' credit policy in relation to business requirements. With restricted and tight money conditions in the market, further growth of inflationary boom is curtailed.

Following are the limitations when operating this instrument.

(a) This instrument may be ineffective if the commercial banks are able to increase their reserves by selling their stocks of government securities to the Central Bank.

(b) The non-bank holders of government securities too, in the absence of other buyers, sell them to the Central Bank and deposit the proceeds with commercial banks. This would increase the reserves of the commercial banks and make ineffective the sale of the government securities by the Central Bank.

(c) The impact of gold may also reverse the anti-inflationary effect of this instrument.

(d) This instrument may be off-set by increased borrowings from or increased sales of treasury bills to the Central Bank by the commercial banks.

3.   Increased Cash Reserve Requirements: An increase in reserve requirements of the member banks also serves as an anti-inflationary instrument during inflation. It curtails the ability of the banking system in credit expansion. For example, if the Central Bank increases the legal reserve requirements from 10 percent to 15 percent of the demand deposits, the member banks will be obliged to keep larger reserves with the Central Bank and to that extent their ability to create credit will be curtailed.

This instrument suffers from the following limitations.

(a) If the commercial banks happen to have large surplus reserves, then even the raising of reserve requirements may not succeed in curbing credit creation.

(b) The ability of commercial banks to increase or replenish their cash reserves by selling government securities may lead to higher reserve requirements and make this instrument ineffective.

(c) A large inflow of gold due to the existence of export surplus will also increase the member banks' reserves and make the policy of higher reserve requirements ineffective.

4. Consumer Credit: This instrument focuses on curbing excessive spending by consumers during inflation. In advanced countries, and now even in developing economies, instalment purchasing plays an important role in consumer spending. Most of the durable consumer goods such as refrigerators, washing machines, etc. are purchased by the consumers on instalment credit. However, during inflation to reduce consumer spending on consumer durable goods, firstly down payment is increased and secondly the length of repayment period is reduced.

5. Higher Margin Requirements: Every commercial bank, before granting a loan to a businessman against collateral security keeps a certain specified margin, say 30 percent or 40 percent. For example, if the value of the security offered to the bank is ₹1,000 and the bank keeps a margin of 30 percent, then it will advance not more than ₹700 to the businessman. This margin is a cover against a fall in the value of the security. Thus, when at the instructions of the Central Bank, the member bank raises the margin it discourages excessive credit. In other words, higher the margin requirement, lower the amount of the loan that the borrower can obtain from the bank. In this way the banks check undue monetary expansion.

Monetary Policy: Keynesian View

Expansionary Monetary Policy	**Tight Monetary Policy**
Problem: Recession and Unemployment.	**Problem:** Inflation.
Measures	**Measures**
1. Central Bank buys securities through open market operations.	1. Central Bank sells securities through open market operations.
2. It reduces Cash Reserve Ratio (CRR). 3. It lowers bank rate. ↓ Money supply increases ↓ Interest rate falls ↓ Investment increases ↓ Aggregate demand increases ↓ Aggregate output increases by a multiple of the increase in investment	2. It raises Cash Reserve Ratio (CRR). 3. It raises bank rate. 4. It raises maximum margin against holding of stocks of goods. Money supply decreases ↓ Interest rate rises ↓ Investment expenditure declines ↓ Aggregate demand declines ↓ Price levels falls

6.7 Fiscal Policy

6.7.1 Introduction

In economics and political science, fiscal policy is the use of government revenue collection (taxation) and expenditure (spending) to influence the economy. The two main instruments of fiscal policy are changes in the level and composition of taxation and government spending in various sectors. These changes can influence the macroeconomic variables in an economy, such as the aggregate demand and the level of economic activity; the distribution of income; the pattern of resource allocation within the government sector and the private sector.

6.7.2 Meaning and Definition of Fiscal Policy

Fiscal policy may be defined *"as that part of governmental economic policy which deals with taxation, expenditure, borrowing and the management of public debt in an economy".*

The modern concept of fiscal policy states fiscal policy as *"a technique to attain and maintain full employment by manipulating public expenditure as well as revenue in such a way so as to keep equilibrium between effective demand and supply of goods and services as needed at that time".*

Fiscal policy refers to the budgetary policy and is an indispensable instrument of modern public finance.

Primarily, fiscal policy concerns itself with the flow of funds in the economy. For example, *taxation* diverts funds from the private sector to the government sector. *Public expenditure* diverts funds from government sector back to the economy. *Management of public debts* include floating of government loans, payment of interest etc.

Thus, fiscal policy exerts a very powerful influence on the working of the national economy.

6.7.3 Instruments of Fiscal Policy

The instruments of fiscal policy include the following –

1. **Nation's Budget:** The budget of a nation is a useful instrument to improve the operation of an economic system or mitigate the cyclical fluctuations. For example,
    *   *Deficit budget* (spending of government > revenue to the government) leads to expansion of aggregate demand.
    *   The policy of *surplus budget* is followed to control inflationary situations in the economy.
    *   *Balanced budget* leads to increase in net national income.
2. **Taxation:** This is a powerful instrument in the hands of the government to bring about changes in disposable incomes, consumption and investment. Taxation has a great impact upon the general level of economic activity.
3. **Public Expenditure:** This instrument of fiscal policy influences income, output and employment in the same manner as an increase or decrease in investment. Public expenditure has a more direct effect upon the level of economic activity.

4. **Public Borrowing:** It attempts to influence the level of aggregate spending through changes in the liquid asset position. During the last few decades this instrument has emerged as a powerful tool of fiscal policy.

6.7.4 Objectives of Fiscal Policy in a Developing Country like India

1. **To Promote and Accelerate Capital Formation in the Public and Private Sectors:** This can be done by (a) expanding investment in public and private enterprises; and (b) by directing the flow of resources to more socially desirable investment.

2. **To Mobilise Real and Financial Resources for the Public Sector without Hampering the Expansion of Resources for the Private Sector:** This is done by (a) taxation; (b) public borrowings; (c) deficit financing; and (d) stimulating private savings.

3. **To Remove Unemployment:** In developing countries the problem of unemployment is slightly different from that in a developed nation. Besides, cyclical and disguised unemployment, the developing country has to deal with underemployment too. To deal with disguised unemployment and underemployment, a policy of increased capital formation and planned economic development can be adopted. As regards fiscal measures to fight cyclical unemployment, it should not step up deficit-induced expenditure but diversify and modernise the economy that will be able to withstand the economic fluctuations.

4. **To Promote and Maintain Economic Stability:** Economic instability in developing countries is mainly due to instability in other countries. The fluctuations are more in prices than in output. Export earnings are particularly subject to fluctuations and foreign exchange resources are unstable and unreliable. The instability can be corrected by using particular taxes and long-term fluctuations can be checked by economic development.

5. **To redistribute the National Income:** Inequalities in incomes and wealth can be reduced by (a) progressive taxation of income and wealth; (b) suitable public expenditure programmes for poorer sections of the society.

6. **To promote and maintain Price Stability:** An anti-inflationary fiscal policy has an important role in a developing economy. It involves reduction in public expenditure, increase in taxation and public borrowings.

6.7.5 Fiscal Policy to Cure Recession

As we know, the recession in an economy occurs when aggregate demand decreases due to a fall in private investment, that is, when there is a shortage of funds in the economy. Private investment may fall when businessmen become highly pessimistic about making profits in future, resulting in decline in marginal efficiency of investment.

As a result of fall in private expenditure, aggregate demand curve shifts down creating a deflationary or recessionary gap in the economy. Fiscal policy aims at reducing this gap by increasing government expenditure, or reducing taxes.

Thus there are two fiscal methods to get the economy out of recession –

(a) Increase in government expenditure

(b) Reduction of taxes

These methods are discussed as follows –

(a) Increase in Government Expenditure to Cure Recession

The increase in Government expenditure in the form of starting public works, such as building roads, dams, ports, telecommunication links, irrigation works, electrification of new areas etc. is an important tool.

For undertaking these works, Government buys various types of goods and materials and employs workers for the projects. The effect of this is the increase in expenditure thereby leading to an increase in incomes of those who sell materials and supply labour for these projects.

The output of these public works also goes up simultaneously with the increase in incomes. Not only that, Keynes showed that increase in Government expenditure also has an indirect effect in the form of the working of a multiplier. The spending of those who get more income increases leading to an increase in demand of consumer goods depending on their marginal propensity to consume.

During the period of recession there exists excess capacity in the consumer goods industries. The increase in demand for them brings about expansion in their output which further generates employment and incomes for the unemployed workers. The increased incomes are spent and re-spent and the process of multiplier goes on working till it exhausts itself.

A question often asked is how large should be the increase in expenditure so that equilibrium is established at full employment or potential level of output. The answer solely depends on the magnitude of GNP gap caused by deflationary gap on the one hand and the size of multiplier on the other. It may be however be noted that the size of the multiplier depends on the marginal propensity to consume.

Financing Increase in Government Expenditures and Budget Deficit

An important question is how to finance the increase in government expenditure which is undertaken to cure the economy of recession. The increase in government expenditure must not be financed by raising taxes because an increase in the rates of taxes would reduce the disposable incomes in the hands of people thereby reducing the demand for goods. As a matter of fact, rise in taxes would offset the expansionary effect of rise in government spending. Therefore, proper discretionary fiscal policy at times of recession is to have the budget deficit if expansionary effect is to be listed.

Borrowing

A way to finance capital expenditure budget deficit is to borrow from the public by selling interest-bearing bonds to them for a longer duration. However, there is a problem in adopting borrowing as a method of financing budget deficit which is as follows – when the government borrows from the public in the money market, it will be competing with businessmen who also borrow for private investment.

The government borrowing will raise the demand for loanable funds which will drive up the rate of interest in the economy if it is not administered appropriately by the central bank. We know that the rise in rate of interest will reduce some private investment expenditure and interest-sensitive consumer spending for durable goods as funds will become expensive.

Creation of New Money

The more effective way of financing budget deficit is the creation of new money (additional currency) in the country. By creating new money to finance the deficit, reducing the private investment can be avoided and full expansionary effect of rise in government expenditure can be realised. Creation of new money for financing budget deficit or what is called monetisation of budget deficit has a greater expansionary effect than that of borrowing by issue of bonds by the government.

(b) Reduction in Taxes to Overcome Recession

Alternative measure to overcome recession and to achieve an expansion in output and employment levels is reduction of taxes. The reduction in taxes increases the disposable income in the hands of the people and causes the increase in spending levels by the people.

If tax reduction of ₹200 crores is made by the Finance Minister, it will lead to ₹150 crores in consumption, assuming marginal propensity to consume is 0.75 or 3/4. Thus reduction in taxes will cause an upward shift in the consumption function. If along with the reduction in taxes, the government expenditure is kept unchanged, aggregate demand curve C + I + G will shift upward due to rise in consumption function curve.

This will have an expansionary effect and the economy will be lifted out of recession leading to an increase in the national income and employment level. It is pertinent to note that reduction in taxes, with government expenditure remaining constant, will also result in budget deficit which will have to be financed either by borrowing or creation of new money.

It is worth noting that reduction in taxes has an indirect effect on expansion and output by causing a rise in consumption function. But, like the increase in government expenditure, the increase in consumption achieved through reduction in taxes will have a multiplier effect on increasing income, output and employment. The value of tax multiplier, as it is called, is given by

$$\Delta T \times MPC/1 - MPC \text{ or } \Delta C \times MPC/1 - MPC$$

6.7.6 Fiscal Policy to Control Inflation

The major anti-inflationary fiscal measures are –

1. Taxation: During inflation it is essential to reduce the size of disposable income in the hands of the general public as the supply of goods and services are less in comparison to the demand for them. Thus, it is necessary to take away the excess purchasing power from the public in the form of taxes. For this the existing rates of taxes should be steeply increased and new taxes should be imposed on goods and services. Perhaps, the best anti-inflation tax is the personal income tax with steep rates and high surcharges. This would definitely reduce the disposable income in the hands of the public and check inflationary pressures.

Thus, (i) direct and indirect taxes should be raised to the maximum limits to reduce the disposable incomes; (ii) tariffs or custom duties should be reduced to increase imports and thus increase the supply of goods in the country; (iii) the tariffs on necessities of life and other items in short supply should be reduced to increase the supply of goods and services and check inflation.

However, a word of caution is that while increasing taxes it should not be to the extent that money incomes are highly deflated and provoke depression in the economy.

2. Government Spending: During inflation effective demand increases. The increased private spending puts pressure on limited supply of goods and services available in the market. Thus, it becomes essential, on the part of the government to reduce its expenditure to the minimum and avoid greater pressure on limited supply of goods and services.

However, there are limitations in reducing government spending.

(a) In the war period, it is not easy for the government to bring down its expenditure.

(b) Heavy reduction in government expenditure may help to arrest inflation, but it may land the economy into recession in the long run.

(c) This policy may also clash with the long-term public investment programme.

3. Public Borrowing: The objective of public borrowing is to take away from the public excess purchasing power which can be utilised by the people to exert pressure on limited supplies of goods and services.

Public borrowing can be compulsory or voluntary. When a certain percentage of the wages or salaries are compulsory deducted in exchange for savings bonds, it is compulsory public borrowing. With this the purchasing power of the public is blocked for a definite period and reduces pressure on the limited amount of goods and services. Generally, public borrowing is voluntary.

(a) It involves the use of compulsion which is generally not readily acceptable to the public;

(b) It results in discontent when applied to people who are not in a position to contribute easily.

4.   Debt Management: The existing public debt should be managed in such a manner that it reduces the existing money supply and prevents further credit expansion. The government functions as an instrument of anti-inflation. For the government to conduct debt management, it is required to repay the bank held assets out of the budgetary surplus. The reason is that when the government securities held by the commercial banks are retired by the government out of budgetary surplus, then it would check the power of the banks to encash their securities and add to their reserves for credit expansion.

However, this instrument would be ineffective if the non-bank investors were unwilling to give up spendable money in exchange for government bonds. Secondly, the non-bank investors may use for purchasing the government securities, idle and surplus funds which would not have been spent at all. This action on part of non-bank investors would also make the weapon ineffective.

5.   Over-valuation: When the domestic currency in relation to foreign currencies is over-valued, it would serve as an anti-inflationary method – (i) It would discourage exports and thus make available the goods and services in the country; (ii) At the same time it would also encourage imports and again add to the limited supply of goods and services.

The limitation confronted is that when the other countries suffer from inflation, then the country concerned will have to overvalue its currency considerably to neutralise the inflationary effect of the rising cost of imports.

6.   Fixed Exchange Rates: Under fixed exchange rate currency regime, a country's currency is tied in value to another single currency or to a basket of other currencies. A fixed exchange rate is usually used to stabilise the value of a currency, in relation to the currency it is pegged to.

6.7.7 Monetary Policy vs. Fiscal Policy

- Monetary policy can have little control in depression, when there are certain non-monetary factors are in action. Here, it is the fiscal policy that proves more effective in controlling non-monetary factors. Hence, the monetary policy often proves ineffective in generating recovery from depression and fiscal policy can deal with the problems of deflation and unemployment.
- In *inflationary* situation, monetary policy is more effective than fiscal policy because monetary policy can control rising prices and speculative activities by regulating undue credit expansion and deficit financing in the economy.
- Monetary policy in a developing country helps to mobilise real resources, that is, money is only a mobilising agent. It cannot substitute for real resources, and it is the supply of real resources which determine the rate of economic growth in a country.
- Further, monetary policy in a developing nation is bound to result in inflationary pressures and rise in prices and price stability is of crucial significance in the country.

- However, the advantage of monetary policy over fiscal policy can be judged by the facts that it involves minimum direct government interference in the economy; whereas fiscal policy results in too much state intervention.
- Monetary policy is free from political strings whereas fiscal policy has all political strings attached to it.
- Monetary policy is generally objective, impersonal and non-discriminatory in nature. On the other hand fiscal policy is discriminatory in nature with regard to industries, sections of the community.
- Monetary policy is flexible in nature, whereas fiscal policy is rigid.

Monetary policy and fiscal policy, alone, cannot promote stability in the economy. The best solution is to combine and coordinate these policies together to eliminate economic fluctuations from the economy.

Points to Remember

- Inflation is a state in which the value of money is falling, that is, prices are rising.
- It is creeping inflation when the price rise is very slow like a creeper or a snail.
- Under walking inflation, the rate of increase of the price level acquires greater speed and rapidity.
- When the prices rise rapidly like the running of a horse at a rate of speed 10 to 20 percent annually, it is called as running inflation.
- When prices rise at double or triple digit rates from more than 20 to 100 percent annually or even more, it is hyper-inflation.
- It is comprehensive inflation when the prices of all commodities register a rise in the economy. If inflation is sector-specific it is sporadic inflation.
- It is open inflation when the government takes no steps to check the rise in the price level. Repressed inflation is when the government actively intervenes to check the rise in the price level.
- It is partial inflation when the price level rises slightly due to the expansion of money supply in the pre-full employment stage. Increase in the money supply even after the point of full employment leads to a sharp uninterrupted rise in the price level with no increase in output and employment. Such a situation is a case of full inflation.
- When the price level increases during peace time, it is peacetime inflation. During war time, the increase in the output of goods and services does not keep pace with the expansion of money supply. An inflationary gap inevitably emerges resulting in rising price level. This inflation arises during a period of war, hence wartime inflation. Post-war inflation generally takes place immediately after the end of hostilities and the suppressed demand springs up due to relaxation of price and physical controls by the government.

- Inflation caused by excess supply of money in relation to the available output of goods and services is currency inflation. When government encourages an expansion of credit without expanding the supply of money in circulation, it is known as credit inflation.

- Economic growth can be understood as the increase in the amount of the goods and services produced in an economy over a period of time.

- Balance of Payments as systematic record of all economic transactions between the residents of the reporting country and the residents of foreign countries during a given period of time

- Macroeconomic policy consists of a set of rules and regulations framed by the government to control and simulate aggregate indicators of an economy.

- Monetary policy is the process by which monetary authority of a country; generally a Central Bank controls the supply of money in the economy by exercising its control over interest rates to maintain price stability and achieve high economic growth.

- Fiscal policy may be defined "as that part of governmental economic policy which deals with taxation, expenditure, borrowing and the management of public debt in an economy".

Questions for Discussion

1. Discuss the causes and effects of inflation.
2. What do you understand by the term stagflation?
3. Describe the causes, effects and measures to correct disequilibrium of Balance of Payment.
4. What are the basic goals and instruments of macroeconomic policy?
5. Explain the monetary and fiscal policies to correct recession.
6. Elaborate the fiscal and monetary policies to control inflation.